THE ROAD FROM TENANCINGO

D1617522

R. BRUCE LOGAN

Black Rose Writing | Texas

The author grants the final approval for this literary material.

First printing

This is a work of fiction. Names, characters, businesses, places, events, and incidents are either the products of the author's imagination or used in a fictitious manner. Any resemblance to actual persons, living or dead, or actual events is purely coincidental.

ISBN: 978-1-68433-564-0
PUBLISHED BY BLACK ROSE WRITING
www.blackrosewriting.com

Printed in the United States of America
Suggested Retail Price (SRP) $19.95

The Road from Tenancingo is printed in Garamond

*As a planet-friendly publisher, Black Rose Writing does its best to eliminate unnecessary waste to reduce paper usage and energy costs, while never compromising the reading experience. As a result, the final word count vs. page count may not meet common expectations.

For Elaine, Cindy, Randy, Eliza, and Quyen

Key Characters:

Carried Forward from earlier books

Lien

Pete Trutch

Catherine Trutch

Paul Pham

Nakry

Boupha (Quyen)

The Montero Family

Juanita – trafficking victim

Pablo – father

Sofia – mother

Carlos – younger brother

The Rojas Family

Geraldo – trafficker/pimp

Martina – older sister

Miguel – younger brother

Enrique – father

Rosa – mother

Abuelo – grandfather

Others in Mexico

Rosita – *puta*, Puebla

Iz – *puta*, Puebla

Rafael – pimp, Puebla

Scarface – pimp, Tijuana

Bishop Diego, bishop OAX

Padre Sebastian – priest

Sister Antonina – nun

Alexandra Gomez –TBAA

Others in California

Don McBride USBP *

Maria Gutierrez –TBAA**

Andrew Zorbis –SKIUS***

Roger Upton – SKIUS

Frank – pimp, San Diego

Arnie – pimp, San Diego

Tillie – prostitute, San Diego

Roberto de Jesus – Student

*USBP – US Border patrol

**TBAA – Trans-Border Anti-Trafficking Alliance

***SKIUS –Saving Kids in the US

THE
ROAD FROM
TENANCINGO

Prologue

December, 2018
San Diego

As Roberto de Jesus drove east on Kerns Street, he lowered the windshield visor of the old pickup truck against the rising sun. This did little to screen out the brightness. He shaded his eyes with the palm of his hand.

Awash in gratitude, he welcomed this brilliant new day. He had much to be grateful for: a student visa to study at the San Diego Pima Medical Institute in Chula Vista; room and board in nearby Otay Mesa from his Uncle Ramon, while he pursued his associate degree in veterinary technology; and, most profoundly, his girlfriend Lucia. Soon, he hoped, he'd have a job as a veterinary assistant and begin the application process for a green card, a pathway to citizenship. Then he and Lucia would make a life together in Southern California. He thought of little else these days, as he neared the end of his second year of studies.

The spongy old truck rose briefly as it bounced over a bump in the asphalt and sunlight blinded Roberto. When he could see again, two pedestrians appeared right in front of him, just feet from the front bumper. *Madre de dios!* He slammed on the brakes and the truck screeched to a stop. The two, a man and a woman, both young, ran off the roadway. The woman, wide-eyed, glanced over her shoulder and stared into Roberto's eyes just before they ducked between two buildings on the other side of the street.

Roberto took a deep breath and watched them disappear up a small lane, their hands clenched together as the man tugged the woman along. Both wore clean but rumpled clothing. *Mojados. Illegales,* he realized, obviously running away from the border only 250 meters south, parallel to Kerns Street. What was it about her eyes? That intensity. Was she trying to send a message?

He made a turn into the parking lot of Importaciones de Jesus, the import-export warehouse owned by his Uncle Ramon, where Roberto worked Saturday mornings driving a forklift. Strictly speaking, he wasn't supposed to be working off-campus while in the US on an F-1 visa. But, *Oye!* He wasn't on the payroll, just helping his uncle on Saturdays in partial payment for his room and board. That should be okay with the *migras,* no?

Roberto parked and strode toward the employee entrance at the side of the concrete warehouse. The strip of scrubby, vacant land between the warehouse and the next building was strewn with rubbish, food wrappers, and empty cans. Uncle Ramon prided himself on keeping his home and business shipshape and tidy, so Roberto stopped to clean up the mess. He had worked halfway along the strip, stuffing trash into a plastic bag, when he stopped dead. A baby rattlesnake wriggled in front of him. He made a wide detour around the snake, looking for others. And rather than retrace his steps near the snake when he finished picking up, he went around to the back parking lot to enter through one of the loading doors.

That was when he saw it. Next to the edge of the paved rear parking lot, he spotted a hole in the ground, two feet in diameter, definitely no rodent tunnel. Inside the crude opening, a ladder. Roberto glanced up at the inner border fence along La Media Road, just 10 yards away. He looked back at Kerns Street. Had the couple come from here?

If so, what was the young woman silently trying to tell him? Did she need help?

Chapter One

September, 2018
Tenancingo, Tlaxcala, Mexico

Juanita Montero stood at the window and stared out at the surrounding rooftops. The houses on this street were excessively showy in a tasteless way — gaudy. Painted in bright garish colors like tangerine, Kelly green, and candy apple red, most stood three or four stories tall, with steeply pitched roofs. Some resembled tiered wedding cakes with cupolas and ostentatious floor-to-ceiling windows, many screened with barbed wire. The three windows in her fourth-floor turret were covered with heavy cyclone fencing and the surrounding metal roof was so sharply angled she had little chance of escape. She'd spent 14 hours in this room for each of the past three days, allowed to leave it only when Geraldo or his younger brother Miguel unlocked her door and led her downstairs to where the rest of the family gathered for meals or discussions, mostly about her.

From her vantage point, she could see several similar enclaves of huge, pretentious houses similar to the Rojas'. In the Nahua language, they were known as *calcuilchil,* or "houses of ass." Although if you asked a villager who lived in these houses, he would likely say, "El doctore," or "Un abogado muy importante. "

Also in view, along the muddy, potholed streets, were many more traditional village houses, modest constructions of stucco and adobe. In the town's main square, a few blocks away, the twin steeples of the colonial-style Catholic church dominated the skyline. Juanita stared wistfully at it. Then she crossed herself and swiped at a tear before it could roll down her cheek.

On the unpaved street below a silver Lexus LS glided to a stop over a mud puddle in front of the house. The Rojas family had three cars. Geraldo drove the Lexus, his older sister, Martina, had a Mercedes SUV, and the father, Enrique, proudly cruised his Jaguar through the streets. A chill ran down Juanita's spine as she watched Geraldo, clad in designer jeans and a tie-dyed T-shirt, stride across the street and bump fists with several other *chulos* before joining them at a wrought-iron table in front of a yellow stucco building. When the barmaid replaced a half-empty pitcher of beer and several bowls of chips and salsa, the group of men clinked their glasses, slapping backs and laughing obscenely.

Juanita's dark eyes clouded as she watched him. Four days ago she had been in love with him, but the last several days had changed everything.

She had met Geraldo only seven weeks earlier, on the third day of her first year at Universidad de Guanajuato, where she had landed a scholarship to study Architectural Art and Design.

Jubilant, celebrating her dream come true, she had stood atop the long green sandstone stairway that ascended from the narrow street of Lascuráin de Retana to the plaza in front of the towering white neoclassical building that housed the classrooms and auditoriums. She gazed out at the brilliant cityscape of Guanajuato and thought about the winding road that had taken her from her dusty village in the state of Oaxaca, far to the south — the endless hours of extracurricular study, the private English tutors, the recommendations from her teachers and village *lideres*. Her parents, honest and hard-working farmers, had gone hat-in-hand to officials, academics, legislators, and even a state Supreme Court justice to plead for their letters of recommendation. This day was the payoff for all those efforts.

Destiny beckoned as she stood with the warm breeze rustling her long skirt. The crepe de chine fabric fit snugly around her hips but fell modestly below the crisp white peasant blouse she had chosen. Its short ruffled sleeves, gathered shoulders, and wide boat neck exposed much of her shoulders and just a bit of décolletage. The vivid, colorful embroidery around the yoke looked almost glossy on this golden September morning. Her dark hair, gathered to one side and secured near her right ear with an elastic band, draped becomingly over her shoulder and fell across her chest in a luxuriant cascade of waves.

'Disculpe señorita, you are so beautiful the way the sun catches your hair and your eyes. Do you mind if I take your photo for the yearbook?"

Juanita turned toward a handsome, smiling man in tapered Levi's and a black silk shirt. His teeth gleamed, his eyes danced.

"Well, I suppose it would be okay," she said shyly.

Still smiling, he extended his right hand. "I am Geraldo Rojas." A pencil-thin moustache decorated his upper lip. "Here, let me turn you slightly to get the best light onto your lovely face." He placed his hands on her shoulders and deftly rotated her.

His warm, firm hands on her bare shoulders produced an unfamiliar stirring deep within her. She sucked in her breath, a hiccup almost, and then tried to disguise her reaction by clearing her throat. "Excuse me," she said, as Geraldo stood back and withdrew his smartphone from a hip pocket.

He took a series of photos, adjusting her stance and suggesting different facial expressions as he did so.

Completely new to posing for pictures, but taken with his suave manner, she soon fell into a comfortable rhythm with grace and poise. They concluded the shoot and walked to a nearby cantina where they enjoyed café con leche and a small platter of churros, conversing lightly about Juanita's home and family and her aspirations at Universidad.

Geraldo was in his last year in the Division of Engineering and expected to pursue a master's degree in information technology. He came from the small town of Tenancingo, two hours southeast of Mexico City, where his family worked in the entertainment business.

"You mean like television and movies?"

"Umm, no. More like promoting nightlife entertainment. You know, like clubs and places to dance and stuff."

"How could there be an opportunity for those things in a small town like Tenancingo?"

He laughed. "Very good question, Juanita. Actually, my family has interests in entertainment promotion all over Mexico and in El Norte, as well."

"Wow, in the United States?"

"Yes."

"I've never been to the US. Have you?"

"All over. New York, Chicago, Atlanta, Los Angeles, Las Vegas. I go up there during breaks from university to help look after my family's business interests."

A waitress appeared and offered more coffee. While pouring she caught Juanita's eye and slanted her head slightly toward Geraldo. Juanita noted an almost imperceptible movement of the waitress's eyes, like the flicker of a candle. But she took no meaning from it.

"Your family must be important people in the town of Tenancingo," she said to Geraldo.

"Actually, Tenancingo is a center for many families that are in this business. It's like a big network. It's probably safe to say that everyone in the town is dependent in some way on this type of business for their livelihood."

"Do you enjoy going to the US?"

"Sure. There's lots of money to be made there. And the cities I visit are very modern, clean, and exciting. Hey, would you like to come over to my apartment and see some of the other pictures I've taken for the yearbook?"

"Thank you, but I shouldn't."

He shrugged and raised his hands to shoulder height, palms outward. "Hey, I really respect you. I wouldn't try anything. Honest. Besides, one of my roommates will be there. So you won't be alone with me. You can trust me, Juanita. I just want to get to know you better. I promise."

Her eyes revealed her lingering caution, but impulsively she said, "Okay. But I can only stay for 15 minutes. I have a meeting in the library this afternoon."

Twenty minutes later they sat before a laptop, elbows touching, looking at digital photos of campus events and people. Juanita felt his body heat and again experienced a strange but pleasant warmth. Geraldo's roommate was napping in another room, so they were in fact alone.

"Hey, do you want to go dancing later?"

Juanita's perfectly sculpted eyebrows came together as she turned to look into his dazzling eyes. "I told you already, I have a meeting in the library. I think it will last until seven or so."

"I meant later tonight. I know a dance club on Plaza de la Paz in the centro historico. It has good music, good drinks, good coffee, and nice people. A lot of students go there. I could meet you there at about 8:30 or pick you up at your room. We can go over in my car."

"You have a car?"

"Yes. Well, it's mostly for business."

"Is this club part of your family's business?"

"This one's strictly a local place. I think it's owned by a retired professor from the Universidad."

Five hours later, Juanita and Geraldo sat at a glass-topped table at the edge of the dance floor in El Beso Secreto. Recessed LED lights in the high ceiling softly illuminated the polished wood dance floor. Locals in colorful, casual attire sat at round tables around the perimeter, while others danced rhythmically to a *guaguanco,* a sub-genre of the Cuban rumba. Animated chatter and the tinkle of ice in glassware accented the lively music played by a seven-piece brass and string combo on the raised dais at one end of the room. Set into an alcove with an arched ceiling, the dais area created the illusion of old-Mexico architecture in a modern building. The male members of the combo wore black suits, black shirts, and white ties, while the female vocalist wore an above-the-knees dress, black, with a rose pattern.

Having just worked up a light sweat during a salsa number, Geraldo and Juanita sat out the next dance. Juanita gazed around the large room and then into Geraldo's eyes. "I love this place. Thanks for bringing me here. This must be the only smoke-free place in Guanajuato."

"You'd be surprised. It's a progressive city. We have a lot of social consciousness here."

Juanita was impressed. Anyone who would use an expression like "social consciousness" had to be a caring person. She studied his face over the rim of her glass — an alcohol-free Margarita. Even in this dim light, his eyes danced and his teeth gleamed when he smiled. Yes, a kind person.

The guaguanco ended and the combo began the slow tempo of an old-fashioned waltz. Geraldo took Juanita's hand and led her onto the floor. With one hand around her waist, he drew her close just as the band struck up *Come Away with Me* in three-quarter time. The lovely, light voice of the vocalist washed across the room like foam on lapping waves. Juanita felt the heat from Geraldo's body, closely pressed to hers, and a corresponding stirring between her thighs. Embarrassed, she pushed herself slightly back from him. But Geraldo leaned forward and gently nibbled between her neck and shoulder. And then they kissed.

Over the next month, they saw each other on campus each day and dated several times during the evenings. They indulged in no heavy physical intimacy, just dancing and light kissing. Then one afternoon Geraldo took her gently by the hand as they sat having tea. "I'd like you to come to Tenancingo with me the weekend after next. It's time you meet my family."

Now, just five days after "meeting the family," she stood at the window of the Rojas' house in Tenancingo and stared at Geraldo drinking beer with his buddies — pimps and whoremasters, all of them. Overwhelmed with revulsion, she swallowed the sour juices rising in her throat and fell onto the bed sobbing.

Chapter Two

September, 2018
Seattle

Lien had imagined that driving a modern vehicle over well-maintained city streets would be a piece of cake, as her grandmother Quy liked to say. At 21, she had already survived unspeakable depravities as a child sex slave in Cambodia; she had fought and defeated the resultant PTSD; and as a member of a team who rescued trafficked children in Singapore, China, and Vietnam, she had been in highly dangerous situations. But today she would take her practical examination for a driver's license, her first ever, in Washington State.

Three months earlier, she had traveled from her home in Hoi An, Vietnam, to enroll in the University of Washington's School of Social Work. And since then, she had spent two weeks practicing for the road test under the tutelage of her 73-year-old grandfather, Peter Trutch.

If she could get this test over with, she could concentrate on her studies — a BA in Social Welfare, and, eventually, an MSW. Both Pete and Catherine, Lien's step-grandmother, had been worried that the culture shock of moving from a Vietnamese village to Seattle would overwhelm her, but so far the only thing that had flummoxed her was this road test. To use another of her Grandmother Quy's quotes, she was as nervous as a street dog in Hanoi.

Now with *Ong* Pete strapped into the front passenger seat, Lien checked the rearview mirror and both side-mounted mirrors. She turned and looked over both shoulders then put the Jeep Grand Cherokee into reverse and slowly backed out of the driveway of the Victorian house on Prospect Avenue. She took a deep breath and glanced sideways at her grandfather. His face looked calm and placid, despite how he busily pulled and twisted the fingers of his hands, clasped in his lap. Lien said nothing. People constantly commented on her poise and self-confidence. She would drive them to the DOL office in West Seattle, and she would pass the test.

As soon as the vehicle cleared the driveway and started moving forward, Pete's hands stopped twitching.

Lien tried to calm the anxiety in her voice as she asked, "Do I take the test in this car? Or do the license people have one I use?"

"I'm pretty sure you use this one. It wouldn't be fair if they used another car. This is the one you've been practicing in."

"Last night, I had this stupid dream. I had to take the test in a Vietnamese army jeep. I didn't know how to shift the gears."

"But that was just a dream."

"I know. But this is a government test, right? In Vietnam, the government often throws curls at you."

Trutch smiled. "You mean *curves*. Don't worry. This should be straightforward."

Forty-five minutes later, Lien and Trutch sat in uncomfortable plastic chairs in the waiting room of the examining facility. Eight others waited with them, some of them even more fidgety than Lien. One girl, about 16, sat across the room and turned the pages of the state driver's manual with trembling hands while blowing pink bubbles from a wad of gum.

Lien started when an imperious male voice called, "Ms. Nguyen Lien." He pronounced her patronymic *Nooyen*.

She rose. "Here, sir."

The man, bald and bespectacled, was about five foot six. He reminded Lien of Mr. Peepers, the shy science teacher and main character of a 1950s sitcom she had seen on ME TV shortly after arriving in the US.

***

Trutch also noted with amusement the examiner's resemblance to Mr. Peepers. But his chest swelled with pride as he watched his granddaughter stride across the parking lot, leading the mousy little man to the Jeep Cherokee.

She had come so far in the eight short years since he had first become aware of her existence.

He remembered with vivid clarity the morning he had opened the mailbox to find a strange letter written by an Australian graduate student working in Vietnam as a social worker. The contents triggered long-suppressed memories of his experiences in Vietnam as a combat officer, and of his brief liaison with a beautiful Vietnamese woman. Nearly four decades later, the letter informed him that he had both a son and a granddaughter in Vietnam, and that the granddaughter was missing, believed to be a victim of sex trafficking.

With his wife Catherine's guarded support, he went to Vietnam and Cambodia. Against the odds, and with careful planning, research, and help from an anti-trafficking NGO and an FBI agent stationed at the US Embassy in Phnom Penh, they had successfully rescued Lien.

From that moment on, his marriage, his life, and Lien's life had all changed dramatically. After a quarter century as a hard-as-nails army officer, Trutch had discovered his soft side — and he liked himself better for it.

He and Catherine had grown closer, and together they crusaded against child trafficking. Trutch's subsequent book, a novel, based on fact and his own experience, became a well-subscribed thriller. Throughout Lien's years in rehab in Vietnam, followed by education and work for the anti-trafficking agency Green Gecko, she, Catherine, and Trutch had become a close-knit family unit.

Now, 30 minutes after she'd slid behind the driver's wheel, her demeanor radiating poise and grace, the red Cherokee pulled back into the parking lot. Lien stepped from the car. She looked toward Trutch and thrust both arms into the air, waving V for victory with the fingers on both hands.

***

In contrast to her earlier exhilaration, Lien was pensive and silent as she drove north along the Alaska Way Viaduct. Several minutes passed before she spoke. "Paul Pham has been in touch with me since I've been here in Seattle. But I've been so busy with the driver license and registering at UW that I recessed any thoughts of him."

"Repressed," Trutch said. "But that's great he called. He's a good guy."

"Yes, *repressed*. I've been too busy concentrating to think about him until now."

"So, he's back in San Diego?"

"He left Hoi An a year before I did. So I haven't seen him in over a year. But he's my friend and now I'm thinking about him."

She'd been emotionally conflicted about Paul for three years, since they'd first met in Hoi An. A Buddhist monk then, he had seemed safe, and she hadn't been interested in a relationship with any man. Her experience in the Svay Pak brothel had left her convinced that no man would ever want her, or that she would ever want a man.

Little by little, Paul's obvious attraction to her, coupled with his comedic antics, had endeared him to her. They became close friends. He wanted more, but she remained cautious.

"Why did he leave Hoi An?" Trutch asked. "He had the best beachside bistro in the city."

"He wanted to get home to finish his degree at San Diego State. When he left for his gig as a monk in Vietnam, he'd already finished three years. He'll have his BA in Social Work soon."

In the silence that followed, as they rolled off the viaduct at Western Avenue and drove toward Queen Anne Hill, Paul's handsome face filled Lien's mind. He had asked her to come to San Diego for a visit. She had demurred, saying she needed to focus on her first quarter at UW. He countered with the suggestion that she come down over the five-day Thanksgiving break. And if things went well, she could come back during the two-week Christmas recess at both universities.

Still, she vacillated. He was sincere, funny, and cute, and she knew that her grandfather hoped they would become close. But was she ready for, or even capable of, a meaningful relationship? What if he pressed her for sex? Three years of rehab and another five of counseling and cognitive behavioral therapy had helped her to manage the PTSD that had consumed her. But so far, they hadn't even kissed — hadn't even held hands. Deep in her soul, she longed for love, but could she handle it?

Three nights earlier he had called again. "You loved your work for Green Gecko. Maybe you're interested in seeing a foundation that locates and rescues missing kids here. They're called Saving Kids in the US. SKIUS for short. They have a good track record of using technology to find missing kids in Southern California. I've started my Social Work practicum with another agency that networks with them."

"I don't know, Paul. Like I said, this will be my first quarter. I think I need to get my foot — I mean *feet* — on the ground."

"Are you kidding? You're one of the brightest people I know. You're passionate about doing whatever you can to rescue trafficked girls. Learning about this organization will massage your raison d'etre … uh that means your principal passion. Your reason for being."

"Trafficked?" The involuntary cringe gripped her.

"Yes. Some of the kids they find are … or at least are at risk of being … trafficked."

She had to admit that this NGO did arouse her curiosity. How did they operate? Could they be any more effective than Green Gecko? She hadn't known that trafficking was a problem in the US. But maybe this would be a good way to renew her friendship with Paul while deflecting any romantic involvement.

∗∗∗

The bell rang signalling the end of the period. Lien closed her notebook and organized her textbooks and backpack. She left the classroom without speaking to anyone, still somewhat awed at her first day of classes at UW. She hurried down the stairs amid the brief arias of multilingual conversations and the crush of backpack-laden students going to and fro, up and down. She exited through the double glass doors with a stream of others, onto the sidewalk toward the nearest crosswalk, determined to get onto the main campus and find a bench where she could mull over her thoughts about her very first class, She crossed at Forty-first Street and climbed a short flight of concrete steps to the leafy 641-acre campus. A mix of neo-gothic and modernist buildings, many ivy-clad, marched through the grounds along sightlines that showcased Mount Rainier to the southeast and Seattle's urban skyline to the southwest.

She had just seated herself on a wooden bench beneath the spreading red and yellow leaves of a bigleaf maple, when someone addressed her.

"Hello. Are you new on campus?"

She looked up into the lean face and almond-shaped eyes of another Asian woman, a beautiful smile defining her lips and teeth. "Yes. My first day. I've just been to my first class."

The other woman pointed across the street at the two-story brick, strictly utilitarian, building that housed the School of Social Work. "And you just came from Social Welfare 101 with Professor Barnaby. I noticed you in class. I think you must be Lien. I knew you were coming to UW, but I didn't expect to see you in my class on the first day."

Lien peered closely at the woman. She wore faded jeans, a nondescript green and grey blouse and white sneakers. Her jet-black hair was pulled into a tight bun at the back of her head. Gold earrings resembling a woman wearing an *ao dai* dangled from both lobes. Lien had a fleeting sensation of *déjà vu*. "Boupha?" she asked tentatively. "Are you Boupha?"

"I am Quyen. But eight or nine years ago I was known as Boupha in a place in Cambodia known as Svay Pak. And you were Lotus."

"Oh my god." Lien's hand shot to her mouth as long-suppressed memories surfaced. "I still suffer from that. But yes, I was in Svay Pak. My real name is Lien. But, what …? Why are you here? How did you know I was coming?"

"I'm also studying social work. But come. Let's go have a coffee and talk about it." Quyen offered her hand and helped Lien lift herself from the bench. "There's a really cool coffee shop just off campus in an alley between 15th and University Way. I'll take you there. My treat."

"I don't know. I feel like … I've just been struck by lightning. Look at the way I'm trembling. And we're eight years and eight thousand miles from Svay Pak."

"When's your next class?"

"Not until one."

"Come. Let me take you to Café Allegro. We can get 'caught up,' as the Americans say."

Quyen led them 200 yards into an unremarkable alley where they entered the ground floor of a three-story brick building, through what must have once been a rear loading door. It was now a glazed French door beneath a weather-beaten wooden sign, bearing a stylistic image of a coffee cup, steam drifting above it. The name of the shop followed by its address— 4214½ — hung from a shingle at the bottom of the sign. A bell over the doorway jingled as they entered the bohemian atmosphere of Seattle's first espresso bar, dating back to the 70s.

They wended their way through a closely packed logjam of ancient tables and chairs. Boupha said, "The front of this building, on University Way, was a funeral home in the 60s and this space back here was the embalming room. Sort of eerie isn't it?"

"Yeah, weird," Lien said, still in shock over suddenly meeting someone from the brothel.

They found a glass-topped table for four occupied by two bearded young men who invited them to share the spot. As they sat, Quyen went on, "A guy named Dave Olson was the first owner. He went on to be a big shot with Starbucks."

A waiter in a white shirt and a green apron approached. He took their order for two lattes.

Lien, gazed around at the eclectic art on the walls. "How did you get here to Seattle? I mean, like, how did you escape the ..." She lowered her voice to a whisper, "and end up in America?"

Quyen glanced at the two men then said *sotto voce*, "The night you disappeared, we were raided by the police. They took seven of us down to the station and interviewed us for hours. Then the next day a lady took us to a shelter called Phnom Penh Women's Shelter, PPWS. That's a place for rehab of trafficking victims. I was there for ..."

Lien interrupted and said in Vietnamese, "Let's switch to Vietnamese." With an eye movement she indicated the two men who had stopped talking to listen to their conversation. They both pretended to be interested in their phones, but their eyes kept rising to watch the women. One of them peered over the top of his half-glasses about every ten seconds.

"Did my friend Diamond get taken there too? To the PPWS I mean."

"Yes. All seven of us did. You were the only one missing. I stayed for two years and several other of the girls too. But your friend Diamond left after only about eight months."

"Yes," Lien said. Now that she had adjusted to the shock of seeing Quyen she was enjoying the steaming hot latte she'd been served. "It's really sad. I heard she went back to being a prostitute."

"I think she got addicted to yama in the brothel. We all did a bit. She even found a way to get some of it in the shelter, but it wasn't enough. I've actually been here for two years already. This is my third year at U dub. There was an American FBI man, Brad Cassidy, stationed in Phnom Penh, who had something to do with the raid on the brothel. I think he persuaded the Cambodian police to do it. After they rescued us, he'd come to the shelter to look in on us once a week. He just wanted to make sure we were all doing okay."

"I think my grandfather, Pete Trutch, may have met him when he was in PP looking for me. I've heard him mention the name Cassidy."

"Mr. Cassidy and your grandfather kept in touch. That's how I knew you were coming here. Mr. Cassidy told me. So, it was your American grandfather who came looking for you?"

"Yes. He found and rescued me from Poipet, on the Thai border. They were going to sell me across the border to a Thai pimp." Lien looked toward the two bearded men. Now that she and Quyen had switched to Vietnamese, the two guys had lost interest and were engaged in their own animated discussion. "I live with my grandfather and step-grandmother, Catherine, on Queen Anne Hill. But you still haven't told me how you got to America."

"The short story is that Mr. Cassidy sponsored me to come here on a student visa. He helped me get into the U and find housing with a local Vietnamese family who live in Ballard."

"So, he lives in Seattle too?"

"No. He's in Washington, DC, now, but he still checks on me."

"I know that some of the people who trafficked us are in prison, but I don't know what ever happened to Nakry, the horrible madame. Do you?"

"Believe it or not, Nakry's here in the US."

"WHAT?" asked Lien in English.

"She was freed the morning after the raid. Lack of evidence. That's what usually happens in Cambodia. But I guess one of her American clients had some pull. He helped her get refugee status here. I've heard from Mr. Cassidy that she is in Everett, Washington. Twenty miles from where we sit."

Lien sat numb at the news that, Nakry, that monster, was here, close by, in America.

Chapter Three

September, 2018
Tenancingo, Mexico

Juanita sat stiffly on a hard, straight-backed chair in the Rojas' family kitchen, several feet back from the large wooden table around which frequent family councils were conducted. Geraldo and his father Enrique both sat on the opposite side of the table, their elbows leaning on the wooden surface. Enrique drank from a bottle of Dos Equis. Geraldo's sister Martina and his mother, Rosa, perched at opposite ends of the table. Martina stared intensely at Juanita. The *abuelo*, the patriarch of the household, stood by the stove silently presiding over the session, his droopy grey moustache vibrating slightly each time he exhaled. The only family member missing was Miguel, Geraldo's younger brother.

Geraldo had insisted that Juanita wear bright red lip gloss for this gathering of the clan. The lipstick was smeared and askew, her mascara smudged, her wide eyes teary. Her usually luxuriant hair hung in unkempt strings. But a constellation of light freckles across the bridge of her nose made her unusually beautiful. She sat with her head up and her back straight, her hands pressed together in her lap.

"It's easy, Juanita," Geraldo said. "We just want you to help out in the family business for a while. You'll be a great asset to us. If you really love me as much as you say, you'll do this for us — all of us, including yourself. And you'll make tons of money for yourself. Do this for one year and you'll easily pay for four years at el Universidad. We'll help you to become a famous architect someday."

Four days earlier, only 24 hours after Juanita and Geraldo had arrived in Tenancingo, Martina had taken Juanita into the courtyard garden. Amid the blooming flowers and birdsong, she'd bluntly told her, "You are to go to work for our family entertaining men."

"*Como?* What do you mean? I don't sing or act. And I didn't come here to work. I have to get back to Guanajuato the day after tomorrow."

"You're not going to go back to Guanajuato for a while. You'll work for us by sleeping with men." Martina paused for effect.

"What are you saying? There's no way. That's not why I'm here. Geraldo loves me. He wanted me to meet his family." Then, as an afterthought, "You're crazy."

"Listen to me, Juanita. I'll tell you the facts of life. This family, and many of the families in this town, are in the business of shipping women to cities all over Mexico and the US to entertain men by sleeping with them. You'll be one of hundreds … thousands even … who do this for us."

"Shut up. Just shut up. I am not a *puta*. Geraldo and I will get married. I will be an architect. Where is Geraldo? I'm going to him now."

"I'm here, Juanita," Geraldo said, not unkindly, as he stepped through a masonry archway from another part of the garden. "It's true. We'd like you to go to work for us. Just for a while. Maybe a year. Then we can get married."

It took Juanita another day to fully grasp the fact that she had been duped. That Geraldo was not what he had seemed. That she was a prisoner in this house. For three days they left her locked in her room for hours on end, then moved her into the kitchen where each of the family members took a turn at brainwashing her about what would soon come. Her principal indoctrinators were Geraldo and Martina, who employed the good guy/bad guy tactic.

Now, in the kitchen, Geraldo said, "My family wants to help you and me be successful, Juanita. What are your concerns?"

Juanita stood abruptly. "You know damned well what my concerns are. I won't be a *puta* for you, your family, or anyone else. You betrayed me, Geraldo. *Bastardo!*" She stepped forward as though she was going to lunge across the table at him. Then, thinking better of it, she stopped. Her hands formed fists at her side. She stared hard at him, her dark eyebrows lowered and knit together.

"Now just calm down, darling." Geraldo carefully modulated his voice to project warmth. "Why don't I bring you a cup of tea?" He gave her a buttery smile.

Enrique spoke for the first time, his voice gruff and wheezy. "Sit down Geraldo. She doesn't need tea. It is a done deal, *muchacha*. No sense arguing about it." He studied his expensively manicured fingernails for a moment. "You're in our house. You will do as we please. Your training starts tonight. An important man in this town will come here to sleep with you tonight. Martina will tell you what you must do to please him."

Juanita, still on her feet, sprang forward, reached across the table, and made to grab him by the shirtfront. "No way, *bastardo*. *Ustedes son todos bastardos.*"

She missed. Enrique had simply slid his chair back a few inches so that he was out of reach. He licked a bit of foam off his salt and pepper moustache, then brushed it with his hand. It resembled a worn toothbrush.

Martina rose, came up behind Juanita, and pinioned her arms to her sides. She shuffled Juanita back to the hard chair and forced her to sit again. Then she stepped around to the side and slapped Juanita hard across the face. "Don't you try that bullshit again. You sit there and collect yourself for a minute. Then I'm taking you back upstairs to get you ready for your client."

Juanita's eyes flashed. She felt a warm numbness where she had been smacked on the cheek. She tried to rise again but Martina shoved her back down and held her by the shoulders. "I told you to fucking collect yourself."

Geraldo also jumped to his feet. He stood in front of Juanita. "It'll be all right Juanita. I'll help Martina take you upstairs. But first I want you to drink this." He held out a glass half full of amber liquid. "It's just tea. It will calm you."

Juanita shook her head. "No. No. No. Let me go."

The abuelo, Geraldo's grandfather, still standing silently by the stove, looked on with approval and amusement as the scene unfolded.

Martina pinched Juanita's nostrils closed and forced her mouth open, then tipped her head backwards. Geraldo poured the contents of the cup into her gaping mouth where it rolled into her throat.

Juanita gagged and tried to cough up the fluid but most of it found its way down. Her world swirled and a subtle warmth washed through her. Minutes later she felt a sense of well-being. She didn't feel drunk, or that she would pass out, only serene and at peace. Geraldo's arm around her shoulders reassured her as he and Martina led her up the stairs.

"I will not shleep with anyone but you," Juanita slurred through her fuzziness. "You can tell your … family that. You tell them that I will not … you tell them to go fug themselves." She managed a giggle at her own brazenness. "You firsht," she spat at Martina, as the grip tightened on her arm.

***

When Juanita awoke the next morning, her throat felt raw and her breathing was labored. Her body screamed for her to go back to sleep but part of her mind searched for meaning as to where she was, what she was doing, and what had happened. She struggled to stay awake and make sense of the fuzzy images that were teasing the back of her mind.

There had been a man. Was it Geraldo? It didn't seem like it. She didn't feel the glow that she had a few days ago, the one time she had slept with him.

Who then?

At some level, she comprehended that a strange man had come into her room, stayed for hours, and dominated the night. Juanita felt a twinge of pain in her genitals. Had she been raped by the stranger? She tried to picture him, but her clouded mind failed to conjure up a likeness.

Bits and pieces of her distorted memory revealed themselves singly and in bursts, like the snapping of popcorn. Martina had called the man something when he came into the room. Was it *Magistrado?* Was he a judge? Now she recalled a faint smell — foul, like tobacco and tequila. At the same moment she remembered that something bristly had repeatedly raked her breast. A moustache? She cautiously pulled down the sheet and examined her breasts. She recoiled in horror and quickly drew the sheet back up. Both nipples were blemished with ugly brown amoeba-shaped hickeys.

"You did fine."

Juanita jumped at the sound of Martina's voice. She sat smugly across the room, legs crossed at the knees, smoking a cigarette.

"*El juez* was pleased. His only complaint was that you didn't throw it back enthusiastically enough. But he still paid the full freight. Welcome aboard. You're now an apprentice whore in our stable."

Juanita shrieked, "Geraldo!" Then rolled over to charge out of the bed, her eyes clearly communicating the intent to rush at Martina. But they had restrained her, shackled one leg to the bedpost.

"You bitch," she screamed. "*Tue eres una pinche pendeja.*" Then she yelled "Geraldo!" again. "Let me loose, Martina." She writhed on the bed, twisting this way and that, pulling her immobilized leg, bellowing the whole time. She became aware of blood between her thighs, now cold and congealed. Her exertions caused her to again notice the soreness inside her.

Juanita now lowered her voice and levelled it at Martina, "I've been damaged. I hurt inside. I may be torn. Please, free me and get me a doctor."

"You don't need a doctor. The bleeding was slight and it has stopped. I'm going to free your leg now. But you'll stay in this room until Miguel comes to fetch you for breakfast. Get yourself cleaned up."

***

Geraldo wasn't present for breakfast. Nor were his parents, Rosa and Enrique. Only the abuelo, Martina, and Miguel, the younger brother. They sat around three sides of the table and watched Juanita, who sat at the fourth side, her eyes glued to the door on the other side of the room.

She wouldn't give any of them the satisfaction of making eye contact, and she ignored the disgusting plate of *frijoles y tortillas* as it cooled before her. "I want out of here. What have you people done with my phone?" She kept her voice cool but controlled. She knew a more malevolent tone would not bear any fruit in this situation, nor would an obsequious one. Best to play the middle ground, neither sucking up nor being forceful.

"You'll have no need of your phone for next little while," said Martina. "We're keeping you here for another two weeks or so. Next week is Carnaval in Tenancingo. There'll be much food, drink, and music. It's when the men, the *chulos* and *Padrotes* of the town, show off their girls and their cars by parading in the streets."

"I don't care about that." Juanita's voice rose slightly. "I want out of here. I'm going back to Guanajuato. One way or another, I'm getting out of this disgusting house and away from your evil family. You can all go to hell."

"Ah, but you have an important role to play next week, *mi hermosa, mi cariño*," she said sweetly. "Geraldo will showcase you and a couple of his other girls by driving you on Calle Principal in his Lexus with the top down. That will bring much business to our house in the evening. There will be music and dancing and lots of beer. It will be like a fiesta. And you will be a star performer. You're going to get your brains fucked out."

If Martina's vulgarity was intended to provoke an emotional outburst, it did not. Juanita glared at Martina without responding. She was trapped but determined not to show either weakness or useless bravado. Panic pooled in her stomach at the thought of being forced to service men, but she wouldn't let it show. She may be from a simple village but she wasn't a simple-minded 17-year-old girl. Her intelligence and self-assurance had earned her a spot at a prestigious university.

The abuelo spoke for the first time, his voice rasping like an out-of-tune saxophone. "You work for us now *muchacha*. You're not going anywhere until we decide it's time to put you into the pipeline for other cities."

The door on the far side of the kitchen opened and Geraldo swaggered in, wearing a huge smile intended for Juanita.

She refused to look at him or acknowledge him.

"Good morning, my sweet." He walked toward her, bent down and kissed her cheek.

Juanita jerked her head away and broke the contact. "Don't touch me."

Chapter Four

September, 2017
Seattle

In her bedroom in the Trutch house on Prospect Street, Lien lay flat on her back, eyes closed. The shock of learning that trafficking and slavery also existed in America had catapulted her back into those horrendous days of depravity in Svay Pak, Cambodia. There she had learned that the facts of life went way beyond what Grandmother Quy had told her about how babies were made. And she couldn't believe that the despicable Nakry now lived in the US. As madame of the brothel that had held Lien prisoner, Nakry had often brandished an electric cattle prod, which she used on any captive who failed to adequately service the predators who visited the brothel. In that gritty brothel, Lien had lost her virginity and her innocence.

Unable to bear these thoughts, she opened her eyes, gripped by intense anger. Her room in Seattle swung back into focus. She was safe. No one would harm her in this house. But, not for the first time, she hungered for revenge against those who had cruelly robbed her of a normal and loving life.

In Buddhism, the dharma and the eight-fold path prohibited not only the actions she envisioned, but the very thought of them. The Buddhist training and practice of her upbringing demanded ethical conduct and mental discipline. She was supposed to have trained her mind to see good in every situation.

How could she come to terms with these competing impulses? Her burning desire to visit revenge upon anyone engaged in trafficking raged furiously, while at the same moment her spiritual side sought to let go and live in the moment. She felt like prey, with two snarling animals ripping her flesh apart.

Lien forced herself to focus on her surroundings. Catherine had gone to great lengths to ensure her comfort with tastefully framed Vietnamese art and simple furnishings — a writing table, two upholstered chairs, and a dresser. The uncluttered, contemporary lines were in contradiction to the neo-Victorian style of the rest of the house, but designed to offer Lien comfort in the familiar.

Soft, evening light came through the sheer white curtains of the second-floor bedroom and wrapped her in warmth, and an opportunity to quiet her mind. She closed her eyes again and breathed deeply, long mindful inhalations through her nose and exhalations through her mouth, counting the breaths, calming. She attained the familiar deep state of relaxation while still being mindful. She continued to breathe … in … out … in … out.

She fell into a deep sleep but awakened with a start at 2:30 when a dream about trafficking in North America morphed into a crystal-clear, wakeful decision.

***

The next morning, Lien reached Paul on his cell phone as he was driving to class at SDSU, just before she left for her first class at UW. He pulled over to talk. If he would take her to the rescue organization he had mentioned, so she could learn more about how to help those who had been trafficked, she told him, she would travel to San Diego over the five-day Thanksgiving break in late November.

"Of course," he said. "Leave the details to me."

When they finished their brief conversation, she ate breakfast, applied light makeup, and headed out the door for campus. She needed to talk to Quyen.

Catching her as the two of them entered Professor Barnaby's lecture room, Lien said, "Let's go to Café Allegro again after class. I have important thoughts to share with you."

***

The same waiter, his green apron soiled, served them their lattes with a smile.

When he left, Lien told Quyen about her agonizing dream of Nakry and shared with her the conflicted feelings of wanting both revenge and peace. "But I really feel like I need to see her," Lien said. "Do you know where exactly in Everett she is?"

Quyen shook her head. "But Mr. Cassidy told me her last name is Kheang. Let's Google her." She entered "Nakry Kheang Everett Washington" into her Samsung Galaxy. Seconds later a list of irrelevant word groups, all embedded in longer, nonsensical sentences, appeared on the screen: "naked in Everett," "naked mole rat," "nakusp weather," "kheana barbeau," "kheau meat." Quyen opened the only listing that appeared promising: "Khmer American Friendship Club of Puget Sound."

"Bingo. It looks like she works in a dry cleaners." Nakry's name appeared halfway down a table of club member names. The second and third columns after her name, where contact information should have appeared, were empty. But the fourth column showed a place of work: Ruby Dry Cleaners, Wetmore Avenue, Everett.

"Oh Troi oi, I can't believe it's that easy. My heart is racing. I'm suddenly shaking."

The two women searched each other's eyes. Lien looked down at the screen again. The name was still there, *Nakry Kheang,* defiant, haunting. She took a sip of her latte and looked back at Quyen. "I want to go there. I can use my grandfather's car. Let's go to Everett and confront her. We should think about it for a few weeks and develop a plan of what we will say to her."

"But what will we do? What is the purpose of seeing her?"

"I want her to know that she didn't break us. I want her to know that eight years later we have our self-esteem, that we are strong, in college, that we will succeed in life despite what she did to us. I want her to know she can run, but she can't hide."

Chapter Five

August, 2018 (six weeks earlier)
San Agustín Etla, Oaxaca

On the outskirts of San Augustine Etla, two kilometers down a dirt road from where Calle Zaragoza meets the two-lane highway to San Juan Bautisa Guelache, a modest four-room house of stucco and terra cotta tile — typical of many farm houses in the *valles centrales* north of Oaxaca City — roosted on the corner of a two-hectare plot of barely-tamed farmland. Behind the house, on a patch of rocky ground, surrounded by a low wall of boulders, sparse clumps of grass competed with the stones. This was Pablo's goat pen. In the shed nestled in the corner of the enclosure, he had just slaughtered one of his male kids.

Juanita entered the shed. "Papa, I have the letter," she said breathlessly. "Carlos just picked it up in town."

Pablo looked up briefly, as he continued his task of cutting the intestine into lengths suitable for sausage casings. "You mean from El Universidad del Guanajuato?"

"*Sí, Papa*. It says I have been accepted and I can start next month. I'm so excited I'm trembling."

"This calls for a celebration." Pablo laid down the knife. "I just have to wash out these pieces of gut and turn them inside out before they start to digest themselves from the inside. Go tell your mother while I finish up here. She's over there, trying to get her maize to grow by adding goat droppings to the earth. Hah. Poop to grow the food that will make the tortillas that we will eat. They say we're at the top of the food chain, yet we eat food that grows from caca."

It had been three months since Pablo and Sofia Montero had driven from their tiny and marginally productive farmstead, in an ancient four-cylinder Toyota

Hilux pickup, to persuade influencers in their town and neighboring ones and at the state capital in Oaxaca, that their daughter was worthy of a scholarship at the university. Their village priest, a learned man with a good connection to the archbishop in the Archdiocese of Antequera in Oaxaca de Juarez, had set up a series of appointments for them. He had advised them what documents they should carry — transcripts, report cards, essays Juanita had written, birth records, the title to their meager plot of land — and how to behave during their various audiences. "Wear the clothes you would wear to mass on Sundays, clean and in good repair. Wear closed-toed shoes and socks, if you have any. Try to be humble, yet confident at the same time. Remember you are trying to sell your daughter's abilities, just as you try to sell your corn and goat meat at the market. You are meeting with these people on your agenda, so you must control each interview while at the same time letting the other person think he is in control. Here is a list of questions you may be asked. Prepare answers to them in advance, but make it sound like you are responding at that moment."

Pablo stammered only once during the course of nine meetings. When asked by a judge why he should put his signature to a paper recommending a young woman he had never known or met, Pablo hesitated, disarmed and silent for the moment. Then all he could manage to sputter was, "Señor, ah ... well...". But Sofia salvaged the interview by interrupting, "*Magistrado,* your signature would be a small investment in the future of a bright girl. This venture will pay great dividends to our state and country when Juanita is a talented architect." They got the letter.

Pablo finished rinsing out the sections of intestine. One by one, he rolled back the ends with his calloused fingers and turned them inside out. Using the side of a chef's knife, he scraped them until the inner lining of each casing was clean and uniformly pink. Then he rubbed them with coarse salt before immersing them in a bucket of salted water.

He was washing his hands from a wooden bucket in front of the shed when Juanita and Sofia approached from the field of corn just outside the stone wall. Sofia said, "I'm going to send Carlos to the *parroquia* to fetch Padre Sebastian and we'll invite our friends and neighbors to a celebration party tonight. We can roast some of the goat you just slaughtered and serve mescal and homemade cerveza."

***

The party turned into a potluck with many of the *vaqueros, paisanos,* and their *mujeres* from the neighboring farms and ranches contributing food and drink. The long trestle table, borrowed from the parish hall, and positioned on the barren ground beneath a mesquite tree, groaned under the weight of local specialties; tamales Oaxaquenos, chapulines, pan de yema, mole verde, tortillas de maize and a sweet corn pudding, all blessed by the padre, of course. Rich scents of chilies, garlic, and barbecued meat drifted about the gathering, whetting appetites.

The mood was jovial, the conversations lively, and the congratulatory speeches to Juanita sincere but fractured. The neighboring farmers and ranchers, most of whom could barely read, were in wonderment that Juanita would soon be leaving for university in Guanajuato. Few of them had ever been farther from home than to Oaxaca de Juarez. A leathery-skinned *caballero* in a stained Stetson, his belly taxing his shirt buttons, whistled for attention through chipped teeth. "*Hombres, mujeres,* our beautiful Juanita is going to the north to understand about the ways of the world," he shouted with a gravelly voice. "She will learn many things and have many rich and handsome men chasing her. She can take her pick. Eat your hearts out young studs."

A ripple of ribald laughter burst from among the half-drunken men.

A well-fed woman in her forties, wearing a soiled housedress shouted, "Pick a good one, Juanita. Not like any of these *pendejos.*"

A chorus of laughter erupted from the women.

Then a nattily dressed older gentleman spoke up. "Our Zapotec ancestors, here in what is now *el estado libre y soberano de Oaxaca,* believed that north was the direction of death. Bad things happened to all who traveled there. They would die at the hands of banditos, robbers, ogres, and monsters. But now we know that the world isn't flat and if one can avoid the narcos and the ejército, it isn't an evil place. Guanajuato state has great ranchos and haciendas. Vicente Fox, our former president and a fine gentleman, hails from there. The city of Guanajuato and its neighbor, San Miguel de Allende, are seats of culture and important monuments to Mexico's history. It was in these cities that the seeds of revolution were sown and the rise of modern Mexico commenced. Juanita will learn much while she is there. Her horizons will be broadened and she will experience the richness of the world beyond the valleys and mountains of Oaxaca. But Juanita, once you understand the ways of the world, please return to us and help to build a stronger state here."

The applause was polite but one man said, "Guillermo is waving his high school diploma at us again."

Padre Sebastian made an eloquent speech touting the value of higher education in serving God, but pointedly warned Juanita of the temptations she would confront on the university campus. He ended by making the sign of the cross and uttering a blessing: "God is the source of all wisdom and knowledge. Let us ask him to bless Juanita and all those who seek to learn, as well as their teachers."

A smattering of voices muttered, "Lord, hear our prayer."

Two hours into the party, Juanita's 15-year-old brother, Carlos, tapped a spoon on the side of a beer bottle to get everyone's attention. *"Damas y caballeros,"* he said, "We're here to honor my sister and her *magnífico* achievement. She will be the first of our family to go to university. I am so proud to be her brother. Now, let's have music. And I even have permission from my parents to drink a little cerveza tonight." He held up the beer bottle to a round of appreciative laughter.

An assortment of musical instruments materialized, including the strings and brass found in every indigenous village. A joyous sequence of *música ranchera* ensued and the crowd's energy rippled far into the night.

Chapter Six

October, 2018
Tenancingo, Mexico

The room was awash with the warm, amber light of autumn. At first Juanta thought she was home in her bed where the Oaxacan morning sunlight filled the bedroom she shared with Carlos. But reality struck as soon as she heard the first rumble of an automobile on the street below her room. No. It wasn't *her* room. It was a prison.

The door opened inwardly and Geraldo entered. "Get up and get dressed, my sweet. After breakfast, I'm taking you for a walk through the town. You haven't been outside in six days. The fresh air will do you good and I need you at your best for Carnaval tomorrow."

Juanita scowled at him. "Then get out of here while I dress."

Martina and Rosa were at the breakfast table. They ate heartily and noisily while Juanita pushed the rice and beans around her plate with a fork.

"So, Juanita," said Martina. "This is your debut on the streets of Tenancingo. Geraldo is going to parade you around to show off his fresh meat."

Juanita frowned at her plate and remained silent. She resented the suggestion that she was just a piece of flesh, but part of her perked up at the thought of getting outside. Maybe the key to her escape lay somewhere outside in the streets of this town. Surely there were good people who could help her. A priest, a nun, a *policía* perhaps.

Geraldo shot his sister an evil eye, then said to Juanita, gently, "Eat up and let's go."

Tightly gripping her hand, Geraldo led Juanita out the front door and down a narrow lane that fronted the ostentatious house. Apart from the several gaudy mansions owned by the sex slavers, it was a gritty street of broken asphalt, potholes, mud, and the typical detritus of a third-world town. The sidewalk was intermittently cracked, fractured, and in places non-existent.

They turned to the right on Calle 16 Septiembre, a slight improvement if only because it had character: a cobblestone street lined with buildings whose colored facades — painted or stained ochre, faded orange, deep maroon, or light blue — came right up to the sidewalk, which was wide and in good shape. The buildings, mostly two stories tall, were a mix of commercial establishments and storefronts with apartments on the second floor. Most ground floor windows wore wrought-iron grills, strictly utilitarian but twisted into curlicues to give them a slightly ornamental appearance.

They dodged around a rusty gas pump that sat squarely on the sidewalk in front of one building, maroon up to waist level and whitewashed above. Red letters stenciled onto the whitewash above the pump read: *Espendio Autorizado PEMEX*. She had learned in grade 11 history that the state-owned Petróleos Mexicanos had become a proud symbol of Mexico's sovereignty when, in 1938, President Cardenas sided with oil workers striking against foreign-owned petroleum interests for better pay and social services. His government nationalized the oil giants owned by American and Dutch companies, creating a state monopoly. Over 80 years, it had become a modern and dominant player in the Mexican economy. She wondered why so prestigious a firm still had such a modest facility. It seemed out of place. But she supposed it fit. Except for the splashy mansions and the pimp's expensive cars, the town did seem to be a backwater.

A mixed bag of high-end cars and rattletraps wended their way down the street. A faded red VW Beetle stood out to Juanita, not unlike the ancient model driven by Padre Sebastian, except this one had grey-painted fenders and a homemade wooden luggage rack on the roof. The occasional purple and white local bus rattled up the street, windows full of curious faces staring at Geraldo and Juanita. On the opposite side of the street, a quintessential small-town Mexican *hombre* — short, squat, Levis, and a droopy mustache and sweat-stained Stetson — led a donkey laden with bundles.

Under a sign reading El Infierno, Bar, Grill y Cantina, Geraldo ducked into a doorway, dragging Juanita.

It took a moment for Juanita's eyes to adjust from the bright sunlight outside to the gloom in the bar. A stomach-high counter with four stools gradually emerged on her right, with two of the stools occupied. A huge mural hung over the liquor bottles behind the bar — a blond topless mermaid sitting on a white sand beach, drinking from a bottle of Victoria beer. Her exaggerated breasts had upturned brown nipples.

Geraldo greeted the two men seated at the bar with fist banging and backslapping.

Both a little drunk, they giggled like children as they looked Juanita over. "Hey Geraldo. This is your new *chica? Muy agradable, cabrón.*"

Juanita looked away from the men and tried to pull her hand free from Geraldo's grip.

"Hey, sweetheart. That was a compliment." He held her hand more tightly, coaxing her past the oglers into the main part of the cantina.

The room was narrow with a row of tables down each side of a center aisle. The pitted and stained concrete walls were sparsely decorated with dusty mirrors, one cracked. Metal sconces, bereft of either candles or light bulbs, hung pathetically on the dingy walls. The only other customers, a black man in a Nike sweatshirt and his Mexican girl friend, painted up like a hooker, occupied a dusty table. The woman wore a white blouse, the top two buttons open, revealing her ample cleavage.

A syrupy-voiced waitress approached them, her black hair tied back in a ponytail. When she smiled at Geraldo she displayed a mouth full of crooked teeth. "*Buenas dias, Geraldo.* And who's this beautiful thing?"

"This is Juanita, from Oaxaca. Some day she and I will be married."

Juanita looked hopefully at the waitress, hoping the woman might help her in some way.

But the waitress merely rolled her eyes and winked at Geraldo as if to say, *oh sure — she's just another of your toys.*

Geraldo ordered a beer for himself and a cup of tea for Juanita. When two other men entered the cantina, he shouted, "Hey cabrónes, come and meet my girl."

They sauntered up to the table, looking every inch like *los repugnante machisimos,* cheap shirts unbuttoned to their navels, one with a badly shaped goatee, the other a ragged mustache covering his teeth. "Hey Geraldo, where will you market this one?"

They high-fived.

Juanita didn't mask her disgust, eyebrows lowered, corners of her mouth downturned.

One of the men pinched her chin. "Hey, she's a saucy little bitch."

She struck his hand sharply with a fist, forcing his arm away from her face.

"She's got spunk. She'll be a wildcat in the sack."

"Don't either of you *pendejos* get any ideas," Geraldo said. "This one's too high class for the likes of you."

Juanita didn't like this scene at all. Six men in the bar, five of them making lewd remarks about her, and only one woman, probably a hooker. She looked hopefully toward the open front door, and then quickly toward the back of the room, where she saw another door, padlocked. She spotted the WC on a side wall near the rear and said, "Geraldo, I need to pee."

"Of course my sweet. The toilet is just there." He gestured with his thumb.

There was no window in the tiny, smelly facility. Without lowering her jeans, she sat on the stained toilet seat and sighed, close to tears. Again. Her parents must be worried about her. She had called them four times during her first two weeks in Guanajuato. Her last call was two nights before leaving for Tenancingo, but she had neglected to tell them about having met a man or about traveling with him to meet his family. Surely they would wonder why they hadn't heard from her in a week. Would they try to find her? How would they know where she was? She had told no one at the university about going to Tenancingo, not even the nice *abuela* who owned the rooming house where she had been living. Now the tears came. She missed her family, even that little pain in the ass, Carlos.

***

The town was acrid with the smell of sulphur and alive with the sound of blanks being fired into the air as the afternoon parade got underway on the first day of Carnaval. Initially a celebration to commemorate the Tlaxaca region's indigenous peoples overcoming the trials and tribulations of colonialism, over the years it had debauched into an orgy of alcohol and sex. The parade featured garishly decorated floats, straying mariachi bands, costumed and masked marchers and dancers, many of whom were falling-down drunk. The highlight for many spectators, and indeed participants, was the fleet of luxury vehicles driven by extravagantly dressed men showcasing their clutches of prostitutes-in-training. This was seen as a marketing opportunity by the pimps and a window-shopping moment by the *cabrónes* from out of town.

Juanita sat scowling in the front seat of Geraldo's Lexus as he piloted it, top down, through the throngs, wearing an air of arrogance. Martina had forced her into a bra designed to accentuate her breasts by pushing them upward and out and then, with Rosa's help, squeezed her into a tight blouse with a plummeting neckline. She burned with humiliation and embarrassment. But the crowning insult had come when Geraldo and his sister pushed her into the front passenger seat wearing only a pair of bikini panties on her bottom, a move designed to discourage her from the temptation of leaping from the vehicle. It was largely unnecessary. She had no place to run.

Geraldo reached across and stroked her crotch through the thin fabric of the panties. "Smile for the people, my sweet. This is an investment in our future."

From the back seat, she heard the two veteran members of his coterie giggle. One leaned forward and said, "*Sí.* Smile little lamb. Your life will be better if you learn to relax and enjoy it."

Geraldo had dressed for success in a cherry-red, waist-length jacket with black and white zebra-striped lapels and cuffs and a matching cherry-red broad-rimmed Stetson. Beneath the jacket he wore a white turtleneck. For neckwear he sported an oversized gold crucifix encrusted with diamonds on a chain of emeralds.

He took both hands off the wheel and, steering with his knees, raised his arms in a Nixonian Vee to the crowd, gold rings glittering on six of his fingers. "The parade is almost over, Juanita. Afterwards, we'll have dinner. Then we'll walk about the town and mingle for a couple hours. We'll go to the square by the church where the trees are trimmed into the shapes of animals and blooming flowers. This is the most fun night of the year in Tenancingo."

Chapter Seven

October, 2018
Everett, Washington

Ruby Dry Cleaners, a one-story, modern building, took up half a block in a neighborhood of bleak two- and three-story retail and office buildings in downtown Everett. "Nervous?" asked Lien as she parked the Jeep Cherokee in a stall near the front door.

"A little," said Quyen. "It's been eight years, but all I can see in my mind's eye is the monster that Nakry was in Svay Pak. I can't picture what she might look like now, but I guess we'll know soon enough."

Lien took a deep breath. An involuntary flash of images and feelings exploded through her: an electric cattle prod touching the insides of her thighs; the body of a dead thirteen-year-old being carried away in a rice sack; the painful thrust of Colonel Khlot at the moment she lost her virginity; the leg irons; the beating around her head and shoulders. She shook off the flashback and said, "Let's get on with it."

The customer service area was busy. Three clerks, all Asian women, helped customers dropping off and picking up clothing. A fourth employee turned from a rack of hangers, approached the counter and asked Lien and Quyen how she could help them.

"Does someone named Nakry Kheang work here?" asked Quyen.

The clerk cocked her had slightly and said, "She's the owner," in a tone of voice that suggested that surely anyone who patronizes this place would know that. "She's out visiting her other stores now, but I've just heard from her and she's about five minutes away. I'll give you each an application to fill out and she'll have a look at them when she's back."

"Sure," Lien said, quickly grasping that this was a good entrée.

The clerk produced two short, one-page forms from under the counter. "Just have a seat over there." She indicated a comfortable seating area with three chairs around a coffee table strewn with reading material.

It took only a few minutes to provide the scant data required by the application forms. Both Lien and Quyen were feigning interest in the magazine assortment when the door opened and an Asian woman in a smartly tailored suit entered and strode confidently across the lobby. Her hair fell loosely to her shoulders, the color of brushed steel. She wore ruby-red lip gloss and blue eye liner and shadow. Lien and Quyen watched as she walked behind the counter and partway down the racks of clothing before disappearing through an office door.

Lien met Quyen's eyes, questioning. Was that her? Could that be Nakry?

Five minutes later, the office door opened and the woman leaned out and said, "Lien, Quyen, please come in."

The office occupied a corner of the building with floor to ceiling windows, and views in two directions — Puget Sound and Whidbey Island to the west and downtown Everett to the south. The two remaining walls contained low bookcases and Dali prints: *Young Woman at Window* and *The Persistence of Memory*. From behind a large teak desk, the woman beckoned Lien and Quyen to sit in two occasional chairs facing her.

She oozed sophistication and money. Dispensing with small talk, she made no eye contact but was otherwise all business, studying the two applications as she spoke. "We're always hiring in this little chain of dry cleaners. Most of our employees are students who come and go, so there's turnover. I see both of you have finished high school and are now attending U-Dub. That's good. I can probably use you in our Lynwood or Edmonds store if your class hours permit you to work about 16 hours a week. The wage is ten dollars an hour, fifteen-minute break every three hours and a 50 percent discount on your own cleaning. If you work evenings, we pay your carfare home."

Lien let a couple of moments pass. "I'm surprised you don't recognize us, Nakry."

The woman blinked and lifted her gaze to stare directly at Lien, eyes wide, brows raised. Her mouth formed a tiny "O" as she let an involuntary chirp escape. She shifted her gaze from Lien to Quyen, then back again. No one spoke.

Lien felt those eyes bore into her as though seeking out her soul, and shifted uncomfortably in her chair. A ship's long resonant whistle sounded from somewhere along the waterfront.

Nakry finally spoke, her voice soft and tremulous, devoid of its earlier authority. "Lotus?"

Another moment passed before Lien said, "That was the name you and your customers called me."

"And I was Boupha," Quyen said.

Another awkward silence ensued, punctuated only by three short blasts from the ship's whistle. Through the window behind Nakry, a container ship eased away from its berth under reverse propulsion.

Nakry abruptly stood and came out from behind her desk. She moved to where Lien sat and gripped Lien's elbow, urging her to her feet. Then, to Lien's utter amazement, Nakry embraced her in a long, warm cheek-to-cheek hug. "I am so sorry. I'm so sorry for everything I did to you." She released Lien and wiped tears from her eyes as she stepped to where Quyen now stood and gave her a lingering hug, as well.

She stood back, alternating her gaze between them. "I'm so happy to see the two of you." Her voice still trembled and her hands shook slightly. "I'm glad to see you both apparently doing well. I know you can't believe what you're hearing. You're probably having a hard time believing it's really me. But it is. I am Nakry, your wicked madame in Svay Pak."

Lien didn't know whether to be angry, offended, or empathetic. Adrenaline and dopamine coursed through her system in equal measure. She tried to calm herself by taking deep breaths. Quyen looked equally rattled.

"I'd like the chance to tell you my story. Then maybe you can believe that I've changed. I'm a very different person than when you knew me in Svay Pak. Will you come with me to my house for tea and a talk? It's only a few blocks from here, on Alverson Boulevard, near American Legion Park."

The two-story red brick colonial had a white colonnaded portico across the front. Large chimneys flanked each end and a row of white-trimmed dormers accented the front slope of the thick, cedar-shingled roof. Set well back from the street on a carpet of lawn, the building boasted a commanding view of Puget Sound.

The three women sat in a lush parlor before a crackling fire. A young Asian male served tea and moon cake. He gave the fire a poke and left the room.

"I came to the US under a K-1 Fiancé Visa to marry one of my clients from the … uh … the brothel in Svay Pak. I was desperate to get out of Cambodia. I had no idea what to expect when I landed in Seattle, but to make a long story short, the marriage was a nightmare. Frederick turned out to be a horrible ogre. I should have known this, given how we met, but again I was desperate. Turns out he was a pimp and a promoter of prostitution in Seattle.

"He made me go to work in a dry-cleaners in Ballard, actually a front for prostitution specializing in Asian girls, many of them trafficked. He forced me to service patrons in one of seven tiny rooms in the rear of the cleaning plant. I lived in the plant with a number of other girls, just as you did. Over the span of two years, I learned first-hand what horrors I had forced on the slaves working for me in Svay Pak. Like you two, I was beaten, raped, and tortured regularly. I got to know several of the trafficked women and became familiar with their stories of suffering and degradation under barbaric, inhuman conditions, similar to those I had inflicted on others. At my lowest point, I came to feel that what was happening to me was karma, what I had coming because of what I had put other women through. A prison term in a Cambodian jail would have been easier than the hell I suffered, but I would not have learned first-hand the suffering that I had caused young girls. I thought of suicide almost every day. One woman I befriended did commit suicide — right on the floor of the plant. And I thought, "That lucky girl. She's been released from hell.""

Nakry took a sip of her tea and swiped at her face. Both Lien and Quyen were crying as well.

"I lived that life of misery for nearly two years. Eventually, I knew I would survive. I was about ten years older than most of the others and had a lot more experience in life. I became like a big sister to many of them. They looked to me for courage. But it broke my heart when I couldn't deliver. I couldn't help them. I could only listen. I resolved that if and when I broke out of that life, I would do everything in my power to help trafficking victims. For that reason, many of the women who work in my cleaning plants are former victims. By giving them a life with some dignity, I hope I am atoning for what I did in Svay Pak." She sniffed and reached for a tissue.

Lien asked, "How did you break free of the slavery?"

"Frederick was killed in a motorcycle accident on the Alaska Way Viaduct five years ago. I was still legally married to him, although we had never lived as man and wife. With his life insurance, I started my business and I've used it as a vehicle to help trafficking victims."

Lien had listened to Nakry's story with an ache in her heart. It was all too familiar. "We came to your shop today with hate in our souls. We wanted to tell you how much we hated you for the suffering we went through. But you have suffered too. It's time for our hating to stop."

Lien then confided that she too was involved in anti-trafficking. She described her experience rescuing girls from Singapore and China and she told Nakry that she planned to dedicate her life to anti-trafficking when she finished her degree.

Nakry said, "If I can ever help in anyway, let me know. I mean that sincerely."

Chapter Eight

October, 2018
Tenancingo, Mexico

The municipality of Tenancingo is controlled by vicious criminal gangs, many of them affiliated with Mexico's major drug cartels. These gangs remain one of the Mexican authorities' biggest headaches. Now, with the evening of the first day of Carnaval in full swing, the anarchy had worsened. Even with the presence of three heavily armed Mexican Army Humvees occupying the plaza of La Parroquia de San Miguel Arcangel and several more army vehicles, bristling with soldiers and guns, patrolling the streets, the pimps, punks, and thugs ran amok. Crowds of merrymakers, mostly well infused with firewater, all wearing garish masks and towering headdresses, surged through the cobblestone streets howling, shrieking, and laughing riotously. Firecrackers, cherry bombs, and roman candles burst explosively, while anonymous party-goers broke windows or shattered glass bottles against buildings. The local policía, wearing their slovenly khaki uniforms, stood around, useless but amused, on street corners here and there.

Second Sergeant Jose Castro-Padilla stood next to the gunner manning the .50 caliber machine gun on the M-1025 Humvee parked at the east side of the church plaza. He commanded three of the high-mobility vehicles and their four-man crews; the other two were dispersed and parked at different points around the church plaza. A consummate professional, he looked every bit the part with his crisp military demeanor and freshly laundered fatigue uniform, adorned with the coveted chevrons of his rank. He took a long, last drag of his cigarette and flicked it toward the waves of revellers around the vehicle, producing a shower of red sparks as it scudded into the pavement. He knew full well that the crowd would soon be out of control and a disaster of some making was inevitable. He wished he had more soldiers and equipment to put this rabble down and send them to bed. The army should have equipped these Humvees with water cannons. But part of him wanted to be partying with them, joining in the fun, drinking free-flowing booze, and sampling some of the young flesh slinking through the streets.

Castro-Padilla glanced at the digital readout on his watch: 23:30. Another four hours and these dipshits would tire and head for home to fall drunkenly into bed.

He caught sight of Geraldo Rojas, well known to the sergeant, leading a *chica* diagonally across the street fronting on the church plaza. This one raised his ire. This *pendejo* and his family ranked among the major players in the criminal gangs of Tenancingo. Scum. They lined the pockets of the local *policía* — even some of his *ejército* superiors — so they were hard to touch. Just look at the *hijo de puta,* too vainglorious to wear a headdress like the rest of these overindulgent pricks. One day. One day, Geraldo, I'll get you. And when I do, you'd better hope your soul goes to heaven because your ass will be mine.

Sergeant Castro-Padilla looked more closely at the girl being tugged along by Geraldo. She looked vaguely familiar, although he hadn't seen her in Tenancingo. About 18 he reckoned, with a quality of youth and innocence. Nothing like the more seasoned *putas* slithering through the crowd. Her wide eyes suggested fright, but the set of her jaw signalled a determination to resist. Probably a newly seduced country girl in "basic training," unknowingly destined for the snake pits of Mexico DF, Juarez, or Tijuana. He wondered if she'd be forced to do an apprenticeship in nearby Puebla before they transported her to the big cities and eventually into *El Norte.* From there, she'd be unlikely to ever return to her home village.

Three years earlier, he had been consumed by deep melancholy when his own younger sister had disappeared. She had been a nursing student in Puebla when suddenly her calls had stopped. After a week, he took a short leave from the army and traveled to her campus to investigate. When he finally convinced the local *policía* to obtain approval from a judge and was shown into her room, he found her closet and her dresser drawers full. A few blouses and some lingerie lay in a hamper in the bathroom. The refrigerator contained a half-liter of milk, beginning to sour, and a chunk of mouldy cheese. No sign of a struggle. A used condom floated languidly in the toilet bowl. The conclusion: she had been raped or seduced, and then taken away, likely trafficked. No one had heard from her since.

His radio headset crackled with static as a distant voice used his call sign. He quashed an impulse to jump from his vehicle and dash into the street to rescue the strange *muchacha*. Instead, he spoke into the voice-activated microphone boom, "This is saber two-five, over."

His company commander issued a frag order, and he changed frequencies, broke squelch, and spoke into his microphone again: "Saber elements, this is saber two-five. Fire up your vehicles and assemble at my location. We're moving out."

Two other voices crackled back at him in rapid succession. "This is saber two-seven, wilco." "This is saber two-six, roger. What's up?"

"We've been ordered to interdict some mischief makers fifteen kilometers to the north."

The three vehicles formed up, nudged their way through the crowded streets and then left Tenancingo and raced up Highway 121 in a column formation. Soon they were doing a hundred kilometers per hour. Sergeant Castro-Padilla was in his element. Always exhilarated at this speed and impressed with his own importance and the power at his command, the adrenaline rush made his heart pump fiercely. He let one hand drop to his hardening *verga*. What could be more exciting and satisfying while one still had his pants on?

As the convoy neared the town of Teolocholco, a computerized voice on his GPS told him to leave the highway, and foray into the rugged terrain of the plateau. A glance at the map plotter confirmed this, and Castro-Padilla spoke into his mic. "Saber elements, turn right to zero-nine-zero degrees gyro. Deploy into a V formation. I'll take the point."

The three Humvees slowed to 20 kilometers, swung off the road, formed an inverted vee and headed east toward the Sierra Madre Oriental.

Moving cautiously through the brushy ravines and over the low ridges, they leapfrogged so that one vehicle could provide overwatch for the other two as they advanced. For 30 minutes they vaulted forward in this fashion, engines roaring and exhaust systems belching.

Sergeant Castro-Padilla spotted the brilliant but wobbly white light of what had to be an oxyacetylene cutting torch about a kilometer ahead. He keyed his microphone, "Fan out in a line formation. Slow to five kilometers per hour and advance cautiously on that light, but do not engage. I say again, do not fire upon them. Looks like we've found the problem. Thugs stealing gasoline from the pipeline."

During Carnaval, with the military and law enforcement preoccupied with their feeble attempts at crowd control and crime prevention, criminal elements liked to augment their cash flow by puncturing Pemex's nearby pipelines. They could siphon off thousands of gallons of gasoline to sell in the region's thriving black markets. His job now was to chase them off with a show of force. But not to kill or capture them. After all, his own superior officers, certain government officials, and probably a handful of Pemex executives themselves received graft to turn their backs on the cartel lackeys participating in this practice. Forcing them to break off, however, made for good press.

The light from the torch went out.

"We've been detected. Increase your speed to ten k and continue to advance on the place where the light was. Again, do not fire. Do not fire. Acknowledge."

It took only seconds for this disciplined approach to collapse. They had advanced to about 200 meters of the pipeline breach when one of the perps opened up on the vehicles with an HK-33 assault rifle, shattering the windshield and wounding the driver and one other occupant of saber two-seven. The Humvee scudded to a stop.

Corporal Jiminez, manning the .50 caliber on saber two-six, immediately cut loose with a long staccato burst of tracers that found their mark.

"Cease fire. Cease fire, you idiots," shouted Castro-Padilla through the radio.

But the damage was done. When the two remaining vehicles arrived at the scene and the soldiers dismounted, they found a tanker truck riddled with bullet holes. Miraculously it had not burst into flames, likely caught before they could fill the vehicle.

Castro-Padilla swept the beam of his powerful tac light around the scene. He shuddered when it shone on two bodies, badly chewed up by the rain of heavy bullets. This would definitely not play well with his superiors.

With his toe he rolled one of the bodies onto its back and shone his light onto the face. "*Ay, Christo,*" he muttered. He was in deep *mierda*.

***

At 08:00 the following morning, Second Sergeant Jose Castro-Padilla pressed the doorbell at the ornate entryway to the Rojas *palacio*. Unshaven, he looked ragged. He'd been up all night undergoing first an inquisition, and then a rigorous ass chewing from both his company and battalion commanders.

As the door opened a crack, he summoned as much dignity as he could muster, his back straight, his head high and his chin jutting out. "I'm here to see Señor and Señora Rojas," he bellowed. "Official government business."

The crack opened to about a foot, and the face of a weathered peasant woman, the *ama de casa*, appeared in the dimly lit foyer. *"Un moment, señor."* She left him standing at the doorway and disappeared.

Five minutes passed. He felt neither remorse nor anxiety about what he would tell the Rojas. He had been through hell from his superiors for the past six hours. Now he would derive some small pleasure from delivering the news to these criminals. He didn't mind the wait. He would revel in the moment.

Enrique Rojas appeared, wearing an open-collared white shirt, pressed and starched blue jeans, and expensive sandals, every inch the gentleman trafficker. "What is it, Sergeant? This had better be important."

"It is both important and urgent," Sergeant Castro-Padilla said, matching the arrogant tone. "I need to speak with both you and the señora. May I come in?"

"Follow me." He turned and led Castro-Padilla to the kitchen where Rosa and the abuelo were seated at the table, coffee mugs before them.

No one invited the sergeant to sit. Standing erect, he asked, "Do you know where your younger son, Miguel, is?"

"What do you want with him? He's probably still in bed upstairs. Just as his brother and sister are. It is Carnaval and they were out late last night."

"I'm afraid you won't find him in bed, señor." He paused for effect. "It is my duty to inform you he was killed at one o'clock this morning near the town of Teolocholco." The slightest hint of a smirk appeared at the corners of his mouth.

A breathy sob escaped Rosa and her hand shot up to cover her mouth. Her eyes went wide with shock.

Enrique remained calm. He sat silently for fully a minute, showing no anguish, his eyes boring into those of Sergeant Castro-Padilla. He lit a cigarette.

The latter met his gaze, likewise revealing no emotion.

"I suppose you're going to tell me how it happened, Sergeant."

"An army patrol caught your son and several other young fools stealing petrol from the Pemex pipeline. Stupidly, they took the patrol under fire. Unfortunately, my men opened fire ... without my authority, I should add. Your son and one other thug were killed. An unknown number escaped."

Rosa wailed and slid her chair back with such force that it fell over. She leapt up and ran from the room shrieking, "My children. I'm going to check on my other children."

The abuelo drank from his coffee and lit a cigarette.

Several silent moments passed again before Enrique leaned back in his chair and hissed, "I suppose you know, Sergeant Castro-Padilla, I have connections with some of your superiors in the army. I'll see to it that you are severely punished. You'd better watch your back, *cabrón.*"

"I've already been dressed down by both my company commander and my battalion commander. For my failure to discipline my soldiers ..." Again he smirked slightly, "I'm being reassigned to the outer boondocks of Oaxaca state. There's not much worse they can do to me."

"Don't be so sure."

"Oh please, señor ..." It was a young woman's voice.

At the doorway leading from the kitchen, Geraldo stood gripping the arm of the girl Castro-Paddilla had seen with him the night before.

Her voice quaked as she spoke rapidly, almost incoherently, "My name is Juanita Montero, my family is in Oaxaca ..."

Geraldo clasped his hand over her mouth, but jerked it away when she bit him.

"The town of San Aug ..."

Geraldo silenced her by dragging her away from the doorway.

Chapter Nine

October, 2018
Seattle

Lien held her first university essay and read the professor's green-inked remarks in the margin. Her heart pounded, but as she read and digested the words, she broke into a broad smile.

*Well done Ms. Le. You've dealt with a difficult subject in an academically respectful manner. This is a scholarly look at the societal problems spawned by the issue of social stratification. I particularly like the way you have developed your premises and argued convincingly to demonstrate linkages between socioeconomic status and the contemporary scourge of modern-day sex slavery. In arriving at a mark, I've overlooked the few problems with grammatical construction in this paper, since English is your second language. I have noted them in ink, however, in order that you may continuously improve your speaking and writing skills in this language. Congratulations on a fine paper. **A***

Bursting with pride, she stepped from the Jeep Grand Cherokee, practically levitating up the front steps and through the oak door of the house on Prospect Street. This was the payoff for hours of research, both on the internet and in the Odegaard Undergraduate Library.

"Grandfather! Catherine!" she shouted. She strode through the living room toward the kitchen. "I have the nicest present for Halloween. An A on my paper on social stratification."

Pete and Catherine both looked up from their work of putting oranges and apples into lunch bags to hand out to the gremlins that would soon be ringing the doorbell.

"Outstanding," said Pete. An equally broad grin creased his craggy face. "Can we read it?"

"Of course. I want you to."

"That's marvellous," added Catherine. "I'm so happy for you." She dropped her work and gave Lien a bear-like, but affectionate, hug. She brushed the bags of fruit to the side and the three of them sat at the table, beaming, reading the essay together.

***

When the moderate trick-or-treat traffic stopped, Lien went to her room and booted up her computer. She opened the bookmarked website for Saving Kids in the US and read through the non-profit's site for the fourth time. The more she understood the nature of their work and their track record of success — 152 kids rescued in five years — the more interested she became. Was there a way she could call on her experience rescuing trafficked children with the Green Gecko Children's Foundation to become involved in some way? She wouldn't qualify to work as one of their operators; she was not a retired law enforcement officer or special operations veteran. But could she volunteer in some other capacity? And could she support them part-time, thus finding a pathway for her passion, even while she pursued her degree?

A week earlier, when she'd told Paul she'd like to visit him in San Diego, he had responded enthusiastically, assuring her that he would find a vacant dorm room on campus for her stay over the Thanksgiving weekend. And he'd make arrangements for her to visit SKIUS, where he was doing part of his practicum several hours each week.

But when she and Paul had been friends in Hoi An, he had wanted more than friendship. Would he press her now for a more cozy relationship?

Many times over the past few years, when she could step back from her emotions, she had wondered if she was — as westerners call it — frigid. The thought of sex terrified her, almost sickened her. She had learned in counseling that this was a common accompaniment to PTSD among former trafficking victims. Although her fears were supposedly "normal" and to be expected, she still wondered if and when she would feel comfortable about her body. And she doubted that she could ever abandon her distaste for an act that for her had been brutal, invasive, and ugly. How could sex ever be an expression of love and tenderness? How could she ever see her body as a vessel worthy of expressing and receiving love and desire, and not as a dirty, used thing?

Yet still she hoped that someday she might love herself enough to share affection in a healthy sexual relationship. And Paul was a good man. Her Grandmother Quy had told her, "A good man feels the pain of others. A good man who loves you will never be afraid to let your light shine."

Her thoughts were interrupted by the soft chimes of her iPhone. She answered. "Paul. I was just thinking about you …" She listened to him speak and then interjected, "About that … I might be having second thinking … uh, second thoughts …"

"But why? I thought it was all set. I've got you a room and everything."

"I'd like to see you too. And I absolutely want to find out more about SKIUS. I hope I can help them and learn from them in some way. But I'm afraid … I'm afraid that you might want to love me. I don't think I'm ready for that yet." She sighed. There, she'd said it.

"I don't know what to say." A few seconds of silence hung between them. "I've … been in love with you for three years. I think you know that. I can wait, Lien. I won't try to rush you into anything. Please believe me."

"If I buy my ticket sometime this week, I'll still get the seat-sale rate. Let me think about it a little more. Please. Give me a few days. I'll meditate on it."

"Okay." He sighed. "But wait. How can you meditate on a problem? In the temple, I learned to focus on my breath and suspend everything else. To close my mind to wandering thoughts, especially judgements."

Lien's laugh was that of a single musical note. "Gee. I never imagined I'd ever have to explain meditation to a Buddhist monk," she teased. "But what I've learned as I've practiced and practiced is that if I think of a certain question before meditation, then go into mindful concentration on my breath, I don't really think about the question during the session, but somehow I have more clarity about the problem after meditating. Don't you think so?"

"I've never had that experience. I don't see how it could work."

"My last teacher told me that the last question you think of goes into something called … inertia, I think he said. It's like going on hold. Then when you've finished formally meditating the question and the open-mindedness of the session can merge together. Everything becomes clearer."

"That's beyond my scope as a former lowly novice monk. But I hope it works. And of course, I'm rooting that clarity means you'll come."

She laughed again. "I'll call you back in a few days."

***

Several days later, Lien decided. The risk was small that Paul would do anything to cause her discomfort or trigger her misgivings about herself. Giving Paul a chance, and learning more about trafficking, was worth the risk. She'd see him on the day before Thanksgiving.

Chapter Ten

November, 2018
San Agustín Etla, Oaxaca

In Juanita's hometown of San Agustín, as elsewhere in Mexico, *Día de los Muertos* was the day when the souls of the dead were believed to come down from heaven and visit with their living relatives. Throughout this time of celebration, many people painted their faces white or wore skull masks. These had no macabre intentions. Reuniting was a time of great joy.

People built colorful altars in their homes, decorating them with candles, flowers, pictures of their deceased relatives, and freshly prepared platters of the departed's favorite foods. In the streets, hundreds of songs, written and sung specifically for the dead, could be heard at all hours of the day or night. The repertoire of instrumental music was a mix of Mexican Mariachi and Latin American bolero. Furious blasts from fireworks and blanks fired from rifles punctuated the cacophony. Church bells pealed relentlessly.

The festivities extended into the cemeteries, where families played music and brought picnics to share with their ancestors. Mosaics of colorful flowers and images made of painted grains and seeds surrounded the graves. Some people would spend the night graveside to be close to the returning spirits.

Despite the festivities raging around them, the Montero family went about its daily routine morosely. It had been weeks since they had lost touch with Juanita; their anxiety and stress were all consuming. They barely ate and slept even less. Sofia plodded through the motions of making tortillas in a desultory fashion, the slap slap of her palms lacking their usual liveliness. Her drooping eyelids and taut facial muscles reflected the strain. Pablo half-heartedly tended to the maize in their small garden. The plot of long green rows would provide enough corn to feed a hundred people their month-long ration of tortillas. He needed to work through his melancholy and bring these golden ears to maturity. People counted on him not only for food but to provide husks for tamales and for children's dolls. Their son Carlos had trudged off with friends two hours earlier looking bedraggled and slump-shouldered.

It had been three weeks since the assistant dean at the Universidad de Guanajuato had advised them that Juanita had not been in class for seven school days. When a university official visited Juanita's rooming house, the proprietor said that Juanita hadn't occupied her room in over a week. "Aren't you concerned?" the official had asked. "No, it happens all the time with these students," the woman said. They'd go home to see their parents without telling anyone. Some would go off on forays with a boyfriend. Some had dropped out and hadn't bothered to tell anyone. But the dean worried. In the short time Juanita had been at school, she had gained a reputation as an enthusiastic and spirited student with an impeccable record of attendance in all her classes.

The Monteros had rushed to see Padre Sebastian, who told them he would pray for them and make some phone calls to colleagues in Guanajuato to see if they could help in any way. They visited the police station in town but the local authorities said they could do little except file a report with the *Policía Federal*.

Now Pablo stopped scratching the hoe between the maturing green plants. He removed his straw sombrero and pulled a blue and white bandana from a pocket of his denim overalls. He wiped perspiration from his forehead and absentmindedly stared at the green husks and yellow tassels of the maize. He heard a commotion and sensed movement on the other side of the stone wall demarcating his property.

A voice called out, "Pablo, we're going to the cemetery. Join us."

He parted the tall stalks of corn to peer at the small crowd of villagers who had now stopped near the fence, forming a semicircle. "*Dios mio*, how can I celebrate the dead when I don't know where my daughter is?"

"Pablo," another man called out. "Maybe you will feel better in the company of others and among the spirits of our dead."

A chorus of voices ensued.

"*Sí*, come Pablo."

"We'll take care of you."

"We must bring you and Sofia to commune with the spirits."

"It will be better. It will ease your sorrow."

Pablo pushed through the corn and at the stone wall addressed his neighbors sadly. "My friends." He looked down at the ground, "It is like my world is in an eclipse. The moon has blotted out the sun and we, Sofia and me, cannot find our way in the dark. How can we go to the churchyard to commune with spirits when we don't even know if our Juanita is a spirit or not?" Tears streamed down his cheeks. He used the blue and white bandana to wipe his face again.

A teen-aged girl approached the wall and reached over the top to stroke Pablo's forearm. "Señor Montero, if you and your wife come to the graveyard, you can pray to the saints for help to find Juanita. "

Pablo shook his head sadly.

Sofia, who had heard the murmuring voices from her kitchen, joined Pablo. "I heard you Huila," she said to the 13-year-old. "We've been praying night and day for three weeks. Padre Sebastian is praying. I know that many of you, our dear friends, are praying. But it feels like God is not listening. Going to the cemetery to be with the dead will only make our not knowing feel worse."

The girl touched Sofia on the forearm and drew back into the crowd, tears of sympathy and grief across her cheeks.

"Thanks to all of you for being so kind and loving," said Pablo. "But now please go to the cemetery without us."

The crowd shuffled on toward the cemetery, quiet and somber at first, but as they gained distance from the Montero farm, they became enthusiastic, but not joyous. Sofia and Pablo remained standing at the rock wall where they could hear the jabbering. Until they couldn't. They turned and walked into the small casa, where Pablo slumped into his threadbare upholstered chair, a habit that had become more frequent since depression and anxiety had taken hold of his life. Sofia resumed the slap, slap, slapping of making tortillas.

When they had pushed another lacklustre dinner of beans and rice and goat meat half-heartedly around on their plates, they stood together and washed the few dishes, not speaking. Carlos had still not returned. The sound of crunching gravel reached them. Then they heard a car door slam and looked anxiously out the open kitchen window. A tall man in pressed fatigues, trousers bloused into his combat boots, baseball cap in hand, trudged toward their door.

With his heart pounding apprehensively, Pablo moved to the door to learn what this was about.

Sofia remained in the kitchen, the knuckles of one hand in her mouth. This had to be about Juanita. But what? Sometimes they saw soldiers in green vehicles on patrol in town, but none had ever come to their door. She shuddered. This could not be good news.

With unspoken questions all over his face, Pablo stared at the big soldier who filled the doorway, almost blocking out the light of the late afternoon sun.

"*Buenas tardes,*" the man said. "I am Second Sergeant Castro-Padilla of the *Ejército Mexicano.*"

Pablo managed a weak, "*Hola, señor.*"

"I have some news about your daughter. May I come in?"

Pablo nodded, and Sofia suddenly appeared at his side, her hands trembling as they fiddled with her flour-covered apron. They didn't even think to ask the sergeant to be seated, so all consuming was their anxiety.

Sergeant Castro-Padilla understood. Abandoning his usual command presence, he said gently, "A week ago, I met your daughter ... I believe her name is Juanita ... very briefly. She was in the municipality of Tenancingo in Tlaxcala state."

A million questions raced through Pablo's worried mind. But Sofia reacted first, her voice trembling, her hand on her chin. "Is she okay? What is she doing in Tlaxcala? Has she been hurt? How did she look? Why hasn't she called us?"

"*Señora,*" he said, further moderating his normally booming voice. "I'll tell you what I know." As in pictures Pablo had seen of Napoleon Bonaparte in uniform, the sergeant tucked his right hand into the front of his shirt, between two buttons, before continuing. "As of a week ago, Juanita was in the home of a family known as the Rojas. They are a rich family, but they are involved in some shady businesses."

"What do you mean 'shady?'" Sofia interrupted. "Why is she there? Is she okay?"

Sergeant Castro-Padilla withdrew his hand from his tunic and raised his index finger to ask for silence. "Please madam, I understand your distress. Let me tell you what I know."

Both Sofia and Pablo nodded. Pablo said, "*Por favor.*"

"When I saw your daughter she seemed okay. She is well, I think. But ..." He affected a sad demeanor. "I must tell you the Rojas family, and almost everyone in Tenancingo, are *padrotes*. They're pimps. Their men roam all of Mexico to find girls. With the promise of love, they seduce them into traveling to Tenancingo to meet the family." He studied the faces of the Monteros, both of whom were wide-eyed with horror. "The girls are coerced into becoming *putas* and, after a time of training, go to work for the family, usually somewhere else in Mexico or even in *Los Estados Unidos.*"

Sofia crossed herself and cried incoherently, her voice like screeching tires. She fell into the ragged upholstered chair and ripped off her apron to cover her face. She sobbed *"Madre de Dios,"* over and over, begging *La Virgen de Guadalupe* for salvation.

Unable to find any words, Pablo stood dumbstruck, his tears washing his cheeks clean of the day's grit.

***

The tiny office was spartan, furnished only with a small table, three straight chairs, and a two-drawer file cabinet. The only objects on the table were a rotary telephone, and three partially filled teacups. A large painted plaster crucifix adorned one wall, the blood trickling from the nail holes a brilliant scarlet. A faded picture of Mary, *La Virgen de Guadalupe,* also in color, hung slightly askew on the opposing wall. The image portrayed the mother of Jesus standing, a long hooded robe covering much of her body, her eyes cast downward, hands before her breasts in the prayerful position.

Padre Sebastian sat beneath the crucifix, the black handset of the telephone held to his ear. *"Si, entiendo,"* he said into the mouthpiece. *"Vamos a tratar luego."* He looked across the table to Pablo and Sofia. "That was a housekeeper. She said no one else is available. She suggested we call back in 30 minutes. Let's go out into the garden and visit the Stations of the Cross while we wait."

The 14 bas-relief dioramas, each carved into a block of Mexican rosewood and resting atop a pedestal, were arrayed among the blooming bougainvillea and crotons along a meandering gravel pathway. The three, Padre Sebastian in black shirt and clerical collar, the Monteros in their rough cotton clothes, paused at each of the stations to meditate briefly. Padre Sebastian said a short prayer each time. When they reached the final spot — Jesus is laid in the tomb — Pablo crossed himself for the 14th time and Sofia fingered her rosary beads. The priest intoned the prayer again: "We adore you, O Christ, and we bless you. Because by your holy cross you have redeemed the world."

"Now," he said turning to the Monteros as he lit a cigarette, "let's go back into the parish office and make that call."

Juanita's parents again sat across from the padre and listened to his part of the conversation. After a few preliminaries, it sounded as though the padre had connected with a principal member of the Rojas family.

"Yes, yes. I am the parish priest of *La Parroquia de San Agustín Elta en Oaxaca.* With whom am I speaking?"

He paused to listen.

"I see, Señor Rojas. I'm calling on behalf the parents of a woman by the name of Juanita Montero ..."

Sofia sobbed.

"We understand she is a ... ah ... guest in your home. Is it possible to speak to her?"

A lengthy pause followed on the priest's part. The Monteros heard the buzzing of a long monologue on the other end of the line, but they couldn't make out the words.

"Do you know how we can reach her?"

Another pause.

"I see. Yes, I'll pass that on. *Adios.*"

He laid the receiver gently in its cradle, rubbed his chin for a moment, then lit another cigarette.

The Monteros watched him with wide-eyed apprehension as he took a long pull off the cigarette and slowly exhaled a column of smoke through his nostrils. They both knew full well he was trying to find some easy words to deliver bad news.

Chapter Eleven

November, 2018
Puebla, Mexico

With Juanita and two other women in tow, the pimp, Rafael, knocked at the door of Room 118 at the Motel Super. "Your room service." He spoke loudly enough that it could be heard on the other side of the door.

The door opened. Juanita stared into the face of a Caucasian man dressed only in a pair of red athletic shorts. A few black hairs sprouted from the center of his chest, more just below his naval. The stub of a cigarette dangled from his unsmiling lips. His head and crew cut were shaped roughly like a child's sand bucket perched on rounded shoulders.

"Come in," he said tersely, his voice unwelcoming.

The room, typical of those found in cheap motels the world over, had no art on the walls, only a smudgy window on the back wall, a double bed with a soiled spread, a sink on the wall opposite the bed, and a tiny bathroom off to the side.

"Are these my only choices tonight?"

"*Si señor,*" Rafael said. "These are three of my best. Take your choice."

He studied the nubile bodies.

Juanita felt dirty, like used dishwater, as his eyes roamed over her body. She scowled and slumped her back to make herself unappealing, and then flinched when the man touched her shoulder.

"I'll take this one." He moved his hand from her shoulder to stroke her breast.

She shrivelled away from him.

"She's a spunky one. I'll enjoy fucking her. Come on sweetlips, the bed's right here. Let's get to it."

As Rafael and the two other girls left the room, one of them said over her shoulder, "It's inevitable, Juanita, just relax and enjoy it."

It was anything but enjoyable. As he grunted and groaned over her, his foul breath on her face, Juanita tried to imagine herself somewhere else, by a brook in the mountains near her home, walking among the tall stalks of corn on her parents' farm, meditating and at peace with her soul during the ritual of the mass at *la parroquia* in San Agustín Etla. But this last fantasy brought her brutally back to reality. How could she be in the sanctity of the mass while being defiled in this sinful place? Surely, she would go to hell.

***

Juanita sat at the kitchen table of the small rooming house. She bowed her head and said a silent prayer. Three other girls, about her age, sat at the table chattering among themselves. Their minder, a middle-aged woman, well-worn and probably a retired hooker, set a platter of beans and rice on the table before them. She dropped four fried tortillas on top.

Iz, who sported a tattoo depicting a coiled rattlesnake on her bare shoulder, said to Juanita, "Get used to it *chica,* the food never changes. Breakfast is always this *mierda.* It reminds me of dog poop. But don't worry *compañera,* it will be followed by brewed coffee mixed with fried corn. Yum yum. Dog piss."

"But you can always add chile flakes to the coffee," said Rosita. "That will put fire in your belly so the men will like you better. That is if you don't fart while they're on top of you."

Everyone laughed except Juanita. Her intestines had been in a constant state of turbulence since arriving in Puebla. This was her fourth day with the same routine. They spent mornings and early afternoons in the rooming house tucked into an alley next to the freeway, two blocks from Universidad de las Americas. Midafternoon, she and one or two of the others would be delivered by Rafael to their first customers of the long afternoon and evening, usually at the Motel Super three blocks away, but sometimes to dormitories or fraternity houses. She was tired, bored, frightened, morose, and sore between her legs.

The three other girls seemed tough and sleazy to Juanita, seasoned whores. She longed to talk with someone who might understand her horror at being in this terrible situation, such a far cry from her village and her values. "How long do you think I have to be here?" she asked of no one in particular.

"Hah," snorted Iz as she slewed a tortilla through her beans, folded it over into a sandwich, and brought it, dripping red juice, to her mouth. "You'll be here until the Rojas family decides you're ready for the big time, like Mexico City or Tijuana. It could be a matter of weeks, or it could be months. Like I said a few nights ago, relax and enjoy it. Life's a bitch, but then you die."

Juanita had already learned that life, *this* life, was an avalanche of humiliation and pain. She scowled at Iz and looked toward the minder, hoping for a better answer.

The older woman silently took the pot of boiled coffee and corn off the burner and filled four cracked and mismatched cups.

Iz wiped the sticky red drool from her chin with the back of her hand. She looked a little older than the others, probably in her mid to late twenties. "I can give you a few dos and don'ts that might keep you out of shit in this life.

"Do make your customers happy.

"Don't make fun of them. And don't act like they repulse you. No matter how stupid. No matter how ugly. No matter how fat. No matter how hairy. And no matter how tiny their *pinchazo* is."

Rosita chuckled.

"Do make Rafael happy.

"Don't talk back.

"Do keep the appointments for your weekly health check. And do make sure your card is updated after each visit to the clinic.

"Don't ask the police for help.

"And do show them your health card if they demand it."

"Are we allowed to eat anything during working hours?" Juanita asked. "For the last four days I've had nothing all day after this miserable breakfast." Her body needed sustenance, even though she had little appetite.

"When you have a break between customers," Rosita said, "you can ask the motel clerk to bring you some fruit, or some corn, or a *bolillo con carne*. He will charge you about 20 pesos."

Juanita did the math in her head. She was only allowed to keep one percent of what she took from customers. That meant she'd have to take in 2,000 pesos to buy food each day. That meant servicing ten men.

Iz slurped her coffee, then said, "I know what you're thinking. You need to make one hundred US dollars in a night in order to eat. It can be done. Also, some of the *gringos* will give you a tip if you please them. Don't tell Rafael when you get tips. Hide the money somewhere."

"I don't know where I'd hide it. Rafael searches me each time the night is finished. He even checks in my bra."

"Your bra and your panties are too obvious. Even inside your *panocha* is too easy. Your *culo* too. The best place is on the bottom of your foot. Not in your shoes. Again too easy. Fold the bills in half and tape them to the sole of your foot."

"Where am I supposed to get tape?"

"There's tape in the bathroom here. Tear a strip off, roll it up with the sticky side inside and take it in your handbag or tuck it under your armpit. They won't search you on the way to work."

Juanita suppressed the wave of bile rising in her throat by swallowing a couple of times. She needed to find a quiet place in this apartment to pray. Maybe God could save her before she had to "work" again today.

***

Evidently God didn't hear. Four hours after breakfast, Rafael delivered her to the motel for a client who wanted a "nooner."

The client turned out to be two young and randy men, both wearing nothing but leering grins. She twisted abruptly and tried to get back through the doorway, but Rafael blocked her and pushed her deeper into the room.

A familiar voice from farther inside said, "It's okay Juanita. This is called two on one. It's part of your trade. The pay is better. The more you earn, the sooner we can have a life together and you can go back to university."

Her eyes adjusted to the gloom and she made out Geraldo standing in the doorway to the bathroom. "You ... you ... "

"Never mind darling, you don't have to tell me how much you love me now. But you be good to my two friends here. They've come a long way to see you. I've told them how special you are."

***

After three weeks in Puebla, Juanita was learning what to expect. Her initial defiance gradually gave way to hopelessness and then to resignation. It would be like this until ... until what? Would anyone come for her? Could her god hear her prayers?

One morning Iz told Juanita, "Prostitution in this country is regulated. Pimping and open solicitation are not legal. And since 2012, sex trafficking is also illegal. But don't count on the authorities to bust the pimps or help you out of this life."

"But why not?"

"*Chica*, Mexico is still a developing country. The laws on paper are one thing, but reality is another. Money talks louder than words, if you know what I mean, and it definitely talks louder than what's printed on paper."

"I have faith in the Holy Trinity."

"Hah. You're superstitious. Jesus and his mother are fairy tales. Forget the Bible. Read newspapers, instead, wherever you find them. Most of these people worship only money, and you and I are only small parts in a very big business."

"How can you say that ... that Jesus is a fairy tale? The Lord creates our destiny. There is a reason we're here now. He wants us to learn something from it. But in the end, he will help us out of this situation. You must believe. Then you will see."

Iz plucked a piece of green apple from the bowl at the table where they sat. She sprinkled chili powder on it, plopped it in her mouth, and chewed noisily. "My naive friend, God is a myth, not a divine character that creates our destiny. At this point in our lives, our destiny is in the hands of the cartels. We are at their mercy.

"They have been trafficking drugs and starting wars here for years. They own many of Mexico's officials. They put tons of money into the pockets of politicians, judges, police, and high-ranking army officers. The gangs that traffic us are also tied in with the big cartels. We're just commodities, like marijuana and cocaine. And guess what? They can only sell a kilo of cocaine one time. They can sell you and me again and again and again. We're very valuable to the *criminales.*"

"How do you know all this?" Juanita asked.

"I studied criminology at the Universidad de Mexico until I ran out of money. Then I became a *prostituta* to support myself."

"So you're doing this of your own will? You want to do it?" Juanita couldn't imagine anything that would make her choose this life.

"It's not that I want to. It's just that I need the money, as little as it is. Believe me, I plan to get out of this life."

"But why this? I'd rather sweep the street than do this. I'd rather sit on the street and beg. I would live with my parents and give them everything I earned. There is no shame in being poor. But this … "

"Grow up, chica!" She slammed her coffee cup on the table. "Who do you think decides who will sweep the streets or sit on them? If you were old and ugly, pregnant or deformed, these *cabrónes* would have you there already. And what if your father wanted more than you could earn? What if he sold you into this, as Rosita's father did? Don't be so quick to judge what you can't understand."

Juanita shrunk back in her chair, eyes wide. Rosita's father had sold her? Thinking suddenly of her own father, her eyes filled with tears. He would never force her to live like this. She was certain of it.

Then Iz's tone softened, "Juanita, your best chance to get out of this is for your family to send someone who can help you. Try to get your hands on a phone and call your family."

Later, in her tiny room, one of four partitioned off from the kitchen, she thought about Iz's advice. But how would her family know where she was? And did she really want them to know what she'd been forced to do? It would kill her father to know that she was now a *puta*. A dirty, shameful job. A sinful life. But if she prayed hard enough, would God intervene and somehow help them find her? Would He convince them she still had value as a human being?

Or had God abandoned her? She pulled the small crucifix from her neck and toyed with it between her fingers.

Chapter Twelve

November, 2018
San Diego

Lien stood near the baggage carousel in the San Diego airport, mesmerized by the bags trundling along like boxcars on a train, proud of herself for managing to get through security in Seattle. Grandfather and Catherine had said their goodbyes curbside outside the departures hall where she maneuvered from the check-in to the gate as if she had done it a thousand times. But her stomach fluttered as she prepared to meet Paul again after so many months of emailing and texting.

Before she left, she had talked to Catherine about it as they stood side by side in the kitchen preparing vegetables for yet another Vietnamese meal. Both Grandfather and Catherine had taken to these lighter, flavorful meals. Lien stopped slicing to stare out the kitchen window into the back garden. The November rains had slashed the remaining leaves from the trees, and she had helped Catherine rake them all and heap them onto the flowerbeds to compost during the grey cold months that were to follow.

"Hello. Where did you go, Lien?" Catherine chided gently, the rhythm of her chopping unbroken.

"I'm still thinking about meeting Paul again."

"Nervous?"

"Yes." She hesitated. "I'm excited to see him, but …" Again she hesitated. "What if he wants to get intimate?"

"Oh, sweetie." Catherine stopped her chopping to stroke Lien's shoulder. "I knew you'd be stewing about that." She started chopping again, more slowly. "I guess it's only natural given your experience in Cambodia, but remember what your counselor said: time will heal your wounds. I know it sounds hackneyed, but when the right, gentle man comes along you'll want to share your love for him physically."

"Hackneyed?"

"Sorry, another English expression to add to your vocabulary. It means an expression that is overused. So much so that it just rolls off the tongue. Anyway, you're much calmer, even when Grandfather gives you one of his famous hugs. I see a level of trust that wasn't there before."

"But he's an old man, and my grandfather. He wouldn't be thinking of sex."

"I should hope not!" Catherine said, laughing. "But the sexual aspect of a love relationship is complicated, and believe me, everyone worries about how it will be with a new partner, even when their lives haven't included the trauma that yours has." She laid her knife on the counter and took both of Lien's hands into hers. "Everyone has doubts about whether their partner will still be attracted after they've seen them naked. Everyone wonders if they'll do it 'right.' All I can say is that you'll instinctively know if you want to share your body with Paul. He's a good man and his training at the monastery has given him a respectful perspective. He practices kindness. And, he may only want friendship. I'm confident that you'll find your way together."

Now Lien wasn't so sure. But when her bag careened onto the carousel from the chute, she grabbed it and turned. And there he was, grinning and clutching a small bouquet of flowers.

He was more muscular than he had been — and his hair! When she had last seen him, serving customers at his new restaurant on An Bang beach, his head had been covered with short bristles, growing out from the shaven head he had worn as a novice monk. Now a shock of shiny black hair fell over his eyes. And his eyes sparkled just as they had then. In his San Diego State sweatshirt and stylish jeans he looked completely at home in California.

"Lien, great to see you," Paul said, proffering the flowers with one hand and gently touching her shoulder with the other.

Lien quelled her instinct to flinch and hoped that Paul had not felt the tightening of her muscles. "Thanks for coming to meet me," she said, finding her voice as she disguised her jitters. "The flowers are pretty. And I hardly recognized you with all that hair. You look so American."

"I thought the same about you," Paul replied with a smile. "Not about the hair, yours is as gorgeous as always. I meant the bit about looking so American.

You look good in jeans. The car is close by in the lot. We can get caught up on the way to campus."

He guided her across the parking lot to his beaten-up old Ford Mustang. As he loaded her suitcase into the trunk, he said, "We should be mounting a motor bike with your suitcase strapped on the back."

"I was just thinking the same thing." Lien giggled, her tension dissolving. They were old friends, good friends, and they'd had the same thoughts, twice within the first few minutes.

Paul drove confidently through the snarl of traffic exiting the airport and then onto Interstate 5 northbound. Lien gazed out at the sunny skies and spied a few palm trees that reminded her of her Vietnamese home.

"We're heading north," explained Paul. "But we'll turn east onto Interstate 8 in a few miles. The city center is behind us. The SDSU campus is on the northeast side of the city. But we'll leave the sightseeing for another day. I thought that you'd like to get settled in your room and freshen up a bit. I think you'll like the room and the security of the dorm. By the way, shall we speak in English or Vietnamese?"

"English, please. I need the practice."

"Good for you." The fingers of one hand drummed on the steering wheel as he drove. "My parents are having Thanksgiving dinner tomorrow. They'd like you to come. I know it's a lot to ask, but they'll love you." At the look on her face, he added, "Sorry, I didn't mean to lay the family dinner idea on you so soon."

"I hadn't thought about dinner with your family." Her voice sounded a little tremulous.

"It'll be a traditional American Thanksgiving dinner, with a couple of my aunts and uncles there too. My mom will add some Vietnamese dishes, to honor you, of course. And they'll want to speak Vietnamese. They've never felt comfortable with English and they'll be happy to have someone to talk to. You okay with that? The dinner?"

"I guess so. Do they know about me? My past, I mean."

"I told them that you're a friend I met in Vietnam the last time, and that you're here studying at UW. I said that you're doing a degree in social work like me and want to know more about the practicum I'm doing. The rest of your story is yours to tell."

"Thanks. I usually tell a shortened version of my past. Sometimes, when I say very little, people assume that I'm shy or have little spoken English. I'm not the traumatized girl of a few years ago, but when I include that chapter of my life, it tends to reroute the conversation."

"Nothing wrong with your English. Your vocabulary has really improved. 'Traumatized!' 'Reroute!' You sound like you've been at a university level in social work for ages. How are your courses going, anyway?"

Lien leaned back in her seat and took a deep breath. Paul was making it easy for her to relax.

***

"Oh, lovely," Lien exclaimed as they drove onto the campus of San Diego State University. The white stucco buildings and their red tile roofs all glowed in the bright sunshine. "It looks like a carefully planned little city, with the boulevards and gardens. At UW, there's a mixture of architecture. Many of the buildings are dark and old, with a few more modern. There's no consistency."

"I think I know what you mean. I've always fantasized about attending one of the old schools back east or even in England, where you have a sense that the ghosts of generations of scholars still linger in the hallowed halls — buildings of ivy-covered stone and manicured gardens uniformly solemn."

Parking presented no problem on this quiet holiday weekend. Paul carried Lien's suitcase and a paper bag as he led her towards Villa Alvarado. Nearing the desk in the lobby, she hesitated as the biggest black man she had ever seen rose from behind it. He stood at least six foot three and weighed about 300 pounds.

"Hello folks!" A big grin showcased his shiny white teeth. "How can I help y'all?"

"This is Lien." Paul said. "She has a permission slip to stay in Shawna's room for the weekend."

"Ah, yes, I see. Just sign in here. Show me some ID and we'll be all set."

Lien pulled out her UW student card.

"Ah, you're from Seattle. Sure hope you didn't bring any rain with you." The security guard pushed some paperwork toward her. "Now here's what you'll need while staying here. This here number is for the cypher lock to your pod."

Paul read the confusion on Lien's face. "A cypher lock is a coded key pad on the door to your pod."

"Pod?"

"The rooms here at Alvarado are grouped around a shared kitchen, so they're called pods. Don't worry, your bedroom will also have a lock inside the door."

"Now, here's the WiFi password for you, miss. And if no one's sitting at this desk when you come back at night, just push the buzzer on the outside door. It's on the right, and someone will come running to let you in."

"Thank you." Reassured by the man's friendliness and all of the security measures, Lien trailed after Paul, who was already heading down the hall.

"Here, you try the code." Paul handed her the slip of paper with the number.

The lock clicked and Lien opened the door on a nicely furnished small lounge with an open kitchen behind.

Paul placed the mysterious brown paper bag on the kitchen counter and opened it to reveal some tea, yogurt, and muffins. He blushed slightly. "My mom didn't want you to be hungry in the morning."

"That's very kind." Lien took the groceries and stowed them in the almost empty fridge.

"Hey, I thought I heard someone out here." A lanky young man with a booming voice ambled down the hall. "Paul, my man, is this your guest? Shawna told me you were coming." He turned to Lien with his hand outstretched, "I'm Rosco. I live here. The Monk is my friend." His thumb pointed in Paul's direction.

"I'm happy to meet you." Even to her own ears, she sounded uncertain.

As if to reassure her, Paul said quickly, "Let's see your room."

"Ok, just holler if you need anything," Rosco added, then he shambled back down the hall to his room.

"Don't worry," Paul said, showing her into her small, private room. 'Rosco's a sweet guy. And see, here's the inside lock." He pointed at it, then backed into the hallway. "Why don't you get unpacked, have a rest, and freshen up. I'll come back to get you for dinner. What do you wanna eat?"

Lien remembered the time she had seen Paul eating a hamburger, mustard smeared on his face and down his monk's robe. He had looked so very guilty. She laughed. "Let's have a hamburger."

"Great!" he said, clearly not getting the joke. "I'll come back for you at six. That should give you time. I'll treat you to the best burger you've ever had and show you something that you'll think is pretty cool."

As he left, Lien locked the door. She surveyed the neat small room, with pictures plastered on the walls and books piled on two desks. A note on one of the beds said, "Welcome Lien. This is your bed. The sheets are clean. Have fun with Paul. Shawna."

As she hung her few clothes in the closet, unexpected tears came to her eyes. Relief, excitement, fatigue, and confusion swirled through her mind. Everyone was so kind here, but her instincts remained vigilant. She had not expected a co-ed dorm, and she had not expected dinner at Paul's parents' place tomorrow night. Everything was strange, but pleasantly so. And most confusing to her was that although Paul's touch on the shoulder at the airport had made her recoil, strangely, she wanted more. Exhausted, she flung herself on the bed and was asleep in minutes.

A loud buzzing woke her. She saw a light blinking on the speaker on the wall.

"The gentleman is here to see you, Lien," the box announced. She recognized the voice of the guard in the lobby.

"Oh, I … I overslept. Could you tell Paul that I'll be there in five minutes?"

"Yes, Ma'am, I will." Click.

Paul stood in the foyer, laughing and chatting with the security guard, his hair flopping over his forehead. Turning to Lien he said, "Hey for a girl who just woke up, you look pretty terrific. Come on, our hamburger place is just over on Broadway."

"What's this cool thing that you're going to show me?" asked Lien, half afraid of what he might say.

Paul reached over and patted her elbow, "It's a surprise that will impress you."

Lien stared at her elbow. She hadn't flinched.

"Here we are," Paul announced as he drew into the busy parking lot of In N Out.

What a silly name, thought Lien.

The restaurant bustled with customers lined up at each cash register. Paul led them to the line closest to a dazzlingly white tiled wall. The staff moved quickly in their crisp white and red uniforms.

Lien was intrigued with the cleanliness and efficiency of the operation, surprisingly quiet given the number of customers.

Paul nudged her and pointed to the poster on the white wall. In the photograph, a pale woman with blond stringy hair peered through a hazy glass window. The caption read "Human Trafficking Hides in Plain Sight."

Lien's intake of breath was audible. She turned to Paul with large watery eyes. "*Troi oi,*" she gasped. "My god. What is this place? Why is this sign here?"

"Let's get our order and we can talk at the table."

At their table, Lien stared at her juicy burger wrapped in a wax paper envelope. It sat on a paper place mat, which read "Facts About Trafficking," and listed some shocking numbers and details about the trade in human life in the USA. The foundation named was Slave2Nothing. She couldn't breathe, never mind speak. Her hands lay motionless on the table.

"Oh Lien, I'm sorry," Paul managed to say. "I was so excited to show you how companies like this are developing social programs, and how foundations create awareness and raise funds. This one is called Slave2Nothing. It reminds me that our social work studies are not just academic for you. I'm an insensitive lout. Can you forgive me?" He placed his hand over Lien's, his eyes pleading.

Lien stared at his hand on hers, and raised her teary eyes to his. "I know that the problem of trafficking exists here in America. I bumped into Quyen on the UW campus. Believe it or not, she lived in the same place I did in Cambodia. So I should be used to the subject, but sometimes my sadness overwhelms me. Thank you for the apology. I know that you'll be an amazing social worker, but you need to work on your surprises." She managed a smile and left her hand comfortably beneath his.

***

Paul and Lien spent the next morning sightseeing around San Diego, and then Paul drove to his parent's house not far from the university campus. The modest house sat on a wide street of similar homes, with a pretty garden surrounding it. As they walked up the brick path Paul remembered his lesson on surprises, and told Lien what to expect.

"My uncles and aunties will be here, dad's sister and her husband and mom's brother and his wife. We're a pretty tight family, but not formal at all. I'm sure you'll be comfortable."

Laughter and the Vietnamese language filled the air as they walked through the front door. The uncles and aunties crowded around to be introduced, while Paul's parents waited for a quiet moment to say hello to this young woman about whom Paul had mentioned very little.

"*Chao Chu*," Lien said with a slight bow of her head as she extended her hand to Paul's father.

"Welcome to our home," he said smiling at her. "Please meet Paul's mother." He turned to the tiny woman at his side, who wore a traditional silk *ao dai*.

"*Chao Co,*" Lien said, with another dip to her head as she offered her hand.

Conversation erupted. "Where are you from?" "I hear you study like our Paul." "What did you see today of San Diego?" "How is the room at the university?" "How long you stay?" The questions flew at Lien in Vietnamese. She could only wait and smile.

"Okay, okay," said Mrs. Pham. "Let the girl get used to us before you ask all your questions. Come with me to the kitchen, Lien, and we'll leave these men to watch their football. I need some help rolling the spring rolls. I made them just for you. My family has become very American. They love turkey with their football, but I've been looking forward to the taste of home."

The aunties trailed after Lien and Mrs. Pham and made their way to the table in the breakfast nook where they had been peeling potatoes and carrots.

"Let's work here at the counter," said Mrs. Pham, tying an apron over her *ao dai* and handing another to Lien, who rather sheepishly covered her jeans and t-shirt. She hadn't thought about dinner out when she had packed the most basic clothes for the weekend.

The task of rolling the spring rolls was meticulous, almost an art form, but Lien and this gentle older woman had years of practice and were skilled and quick as they chattered in Vietnamese. Maybe it was the music of her native tongue, maybe it was the warmth of the kitchen and the sight of the two aunties laughing together over in the breakfast nook, but Lien relaxed into her conversation with Paul's mother.

"Now tell me," Co Pham asked, "where exactly are you from in Vietnam? I do miss my homeland but my husband will not return. He's angry still, or maybe afraid of the Communists. I know things there are different now and I'd probably not recognize anything, but I do like to hear about the place of my birth."

"I was raised by my father and grandmother in a village called Tuy Phuoc near Quy Nhon. Do you know it?"

"Beautiful place. Yes, I know Quy Nhon. Were your family farmers?"

"We grew what we could to feed ourselves, but Grandmother Quy was getting old and my father is in a wheelchair. It was hard, but I loved it. Going to school on my bicycle with my friend is a very happy memory."

"Then why did you leave this place?"

The question, reasonable that it was, rose up and smacked Lien in the heart. She had known it would come, yet froze as it was asked. She looked at this tiny woman beside her, whose countenance reminded her of the gentleness and wisdom of her own grandmother. She took two very deep, thoughtful breaths.

"Because we were so poor, we believed my uncle when he said I could work in Saigon. I was 13 years old. He sold me to traffickers and I ended up in Cambodia." There. It was out and Lien waited for the shocked reaction.

Instead, Co Pham put down her work, grasped Liens hands, and whispered softly, "When we escaped from Vietnam, we ended up in a refugee camp in the Philippines. The guards were evil men and told us women that if we did not do as they pleased, our children would suffer, we would get no food. Say no more my child. I know your nightmare. I have never told my husband or my son what I did to keep us alive."

Lien stood transfixed. How could this woman have lived such a secret her whole life? How did she survive and adjust to a normal life? She was filled with awe and a sudden feeling of kinship with Co Pham. In response, she did a very American thing. She embraced her.

Chapter Thirteen

November, 2018
Puebla, Mexico

"You ever hear of *La Merced* in Mexico City?" asked Rosita.

"What is it?" said Juanita.

"It's in the center of the city, famous as a red light district. Many sex tourists come there from all over the Americas, even Europe. You better hope Geraldo doesn't send you there. It's probably the worst place in Mexico to be a *puta.*"

They were walking back to their rooming house in the alley off Calle 22, having just been to the 7-11 a block away to buy cheap makeup — lip gloss and rouge — with the paltry handful of pesos their matronly minder had given them for the purpose. Low clouds hung drearily above the city, obscuring the snow-clad peaks of Popocatepetl and Ixtaccihuatl 50 kilometers to the west. Nonetheless, the temperature remained a balmy 19 degrees Celsius, with the scents of oranges and ginger hanging in the air.

During the preceding three weeks, Juanita had pretty much learned to cope with her situation. Sustained by her faith and her prayers, she had tried to rise above the depression and anger of her first days as an enslaved prostitute. But now, as she walked, and despite holding them in, her tears lay just below the surface. As she shuffled along in the grey morning, she ate a fried banana wrapped in a tortilla with mole sauce.

"I was there for a year," Rosita said. "The Rojas and the other trafficking gangs have boys on bicycles and men on foot all over the neighborhood. Their job is to steer the tourist *cabrónes* to the hookers on the street and in the love hotels that are all over the place. But they also keep their eyes on the whores. You're always watched. You don't get a minute to rest. You're expected to service 15 men a night and you work in the daytime too."

"Why are you telling me?" Juanita asked. "I don't want to hear this."

"Because you've been here almost four weeks now. You don't seem to fight it anymore. The customers like you. I think Geraldo will move you to the big time soon. That could mean to Mexico City. It could mean Tijuana. Or it could mean you'll be transported to the United States. If you have any say, you should ask to go to the US. I don't know, but I've heard that the men there are a little bit nicer than here."

"Rosita, I just want to go home or back to Guanajuato. I don't fight because I know it's useless. I'm still looking for a chance to escape. And I pray to my god everyday to help me be free."

But Juanita didn't hold a lot of hope for her prayers being answered. She carried her fear and anxiety with her all day and night. With every breath her dread was palpable, like a cancerous mass, pushing against her chest from inside. Some mornings, she would wake feeling happy, but only for seconds. As soon as she was fully conscious, the foreboding possessed her, the pressure in her chest, awareness that this would be another day of hell, another day to survive.

When Juanita and Rosita were within steps of their rooming house, a late model blue sedan approached them and pulled up at the edge of the lane. "Hey *putas,*" one of three male occupants said. Then, in English, "Let's go for a ride."

Juanita ignored them, but Rosita chose to be flirtatious. "What did you have in mind, boys?" She turned toward the vehicle and wiggled her jean-clad hips.

In the front seat, the one with a moustache that resembled a caterpillar said, "Just a little fun. You know, like go for a ride. Mebbe play some games."

"Maybe we could play hide the sausage," the driver said, and slapped the leg of his passenger.

Juanita felt a fluttering fear in the pit of her stomach. She dropped the remains of her fried banana onto the gravel. Her impulse was to dash into the rooming house, but she didn't want to leave Rosita on her own with these punks, no doubt American college kids from the nearby university. Not the vulgar men she had to service in the Motel Super, but still needing peer approval, in this case probably combined with a beer or two, and seasoned with testosterone. More than enough to lead to trouble. She clutched Rosita by the upper arm. "Come on. Let's go."

"Naw, let's just tease them for a while," Rosita said. "This could be fun."

Just then, the rear door of the car swung open and the third occupant emerged, a tall kid with rimless glasses and a patchy beard. "Look here, ladies," he said, with an idiotic grin, his speech slightly slurred. He arched his back and tapped the crotch of his blue jeans to draw attention to his arousal.

Juanita recoiled and took a step backward, gravel crunching under her feet. But Rosita stepped forward and thumped the bulge with a flick of her index finger. "Is that the sausage you want to hide? You won't have any trouble with that teeny-weeny. You could hide it anywhere, it's so small."

Emboldened by alcohol, the two young men in the front seat both convulsed with laughter in their bucket seats, the horn blaring as the driver rocked into it.

Juanita stood transfixed. The boys were clearly drunk.

But Rosita continued to egg them on. "Come on boys. Why don't all of you show me your meat. Let's see if any of you is a man yet."

"Ohhhh," squeaked the one with the caterpillar lip. "She wants to see our equipment. Sure *chica,* hop in the car. Both of you. Then we'll go somewhere for show and tell", his shrill laughter like a soprano's high notes.

At the same time, the guy from the back seat undulated, thrusting his hips in and out lewdly.

Rosita had tired of the game. She said, "You'd better cool down before you break that thing. Maybe you children should go back to your dorm now and write letters to your mothers. I'd rather make out with the artichoke on my kitchen table than with any of you juveniles." She turned abruptly, grabbed Juanita by the arm and steered her the few steps to the rooming house.

Put in their place, the boys did a U-turn in the alley and drove back in the direction of the university.

***

Juanita sat sullenly glaring across the table at Rosita. She said nothing as Rosita bragged to their minder about how she had put those *hijos de las putas* in their place.

The minder, sipping from her mixture of coffee and corn, nodded knowingly at the account, a hint of a smirk curled around the corners of her glossy red lips.

The drab gray walls of the kitchen, like the rest of the house, were sprayed with hairline cracks through the plaster, like random and asymmetrical spider webs. Cheap plywood cupboards occupied one wall and the two-burner stove next to the sink another. A half-sized refrigerator perched atop an open crate. A broom and mop leaned into a corner, a metal bucket nearby. An opening in one wall led to the four partitioned spaces where the girls slept. An open door in the opposite wall revealed a wood-plank landing with stairs that led up.

In the room at the top of the stairs, strictly off limits to the four prostitutes, their minder slept. The carnal moans and animal snorts emanating nightly from the old hooker's quarters suggested she had regular company, and the cloying bouquet of cheap aftershave pointed to Rafael as her boy toy, long after he performed his nightly count of the dollars and pesos they handed over to him.

And then, speak of the devil, he appeared in the kitchen, accompanied by Geraldo, whom Juanita had not seen in over a week. A small earthquake shook her when Geraldo leaned over and kissed her neck; an unseen hand seemed to squeeze her heart. Although his betrayal repulsed her, some small corner of her being still had a warm spot for him. She didn't know why. The bastard.

"My darling," he gushed, oozing honey and cream. "Rafael tells me that you're doing well. Soon we can go back to Guanajuato and make a life together."

Juanita's chair screeched as she slid it sideways to gain a few inches of space from him. She stared at the table, her lowered brows hooding her eyes.

The other girls sensed that some small drama might play out, and they sat forward in their chairs. The minder leaned against the stove and folded her arms across her chest, her eyes wandering from face to face.

Juanita flinched as Geraldo touched her shoulder.

"Listen," he said. "I need to talk to you. I have good news." Then to the room at large, "Leave us alone for a minute."

Chairs scraped against the floor. The three hookers rose and shuffled off toward their quarters clucking and chattering as they made their way to the partitioned area. The minder rolled her eyes, heaved her shoulders, and sighed heavily as she trod up the stairs, Rafael closely behind her.

When they were alone in the room, Geraldo plopped himself into the chair vacated by Iz and slid forward. He waited for Juanita to look at him, but her eyes continued to bore into the table. The other girls' chatter faded away and the room became silent, save for the soft hum of the refrigerator.

A minute passed. Juanita hunched her shoulders and made herself as small as she could in her chair. The only news she wanted to hear was that she'd be going home. But she'd learned to read the deceit in his voice and knew that wasn't what he'd come to tell her. She closed her eyes. Dear God, help me get away from this … from him … from these people. Make this not be real anymore.

"Juanita. Look at me." He lifted her chin with two fingers.

She opened her eyes, awash with tears.

"Listen to me," he said. An undercurrent polluted the tone, meant to be cheerful. He sounded insincere, oily. "Juanita. This is a good opportunity. I'm taking you to Tijuana. After a few days, maybe a week there, we'll go into the United States, the land of opportunity."

Juanita cried unabashedly. "No, Geraldo." Her voice throbbed. "No. I don't want to go anywhere but home or back to the university where I should be."

"You're not thinking clearly. You're just emotional right now. It'll be okay. You'll see. Tijuana is an exciting city. And the United States is clean, the cities are beautiful and prosperous. We'll make tons of money there, and in time you'll return to the university."

Juanita's sorrow turned to anger. "And just how many scumbags will I have to sleep with in Tijuana? How many per night, you bastard? How many slimy, rough dirtballs will you invite to paw my body ... to force their filthy *pinchazo* into my *culo* ... into my mouth? How many *gringos* in America will rape me ... sodomize me? How many Geraldo?" She paused for effect. "I hope you rot in hell."

She leaned her elbows on the table and dropped her face into her open hands, sobbing and trembling uncontrollably. "My God. My dear God, forgive me. *Madre de Dios,* deliver me."

Chapter Fourteen

November, 2018
San Diego

Friday morning dawned with brilliant sunshine, and by nine o'clock, when Paul picked up Lien, the temperature had reached 65 degrees. "It'll take about 45 minutes to get to Carlsbad," he told her. He took the Genesee Avenue exit ramp off the Interstate and turned onto the South Coast Highway. "This way's less frenetic than I-5 and much more scenic. We'll see the coast in several places."

Sure enough, as they cruised through the seaside communities of Del Mar, Solana Beach, and Encinitas, the vast blue Pacific spread impressively before them. With the window down, Lien inhaled the mixed fragrances of oxygen-rich salt air, jasmine, and oleander, seasoned with tempting aromas emanating from numerous taquerias dotting the roadside.

When they crossed a low bridge over a small saltwater lagoon on the north side of Carlsbad, Paul said, "Next, the city of Oceanside. That's our destination. The SKIUS office is there."

"Is it big? Do lots of people work there?"

"No. The office is no more than about 500 square feet, maybe 45 meters, with a total of around 15 licensed private investigators, all working on a volunteer basis. But many of them have work that pays, as well, so they can support their families.

"They're all retired military or police. We'll meet Andrew Zorbis today. He's a retired Navy SEAL. Another guy — I don't know if he'll be there this morning — is a former Green Beret who served three tours in Vietnam. He's older, but very dedicated to anti-trafficking.

"And here we are."

He swung the car into a small parking lot sandwiched between a diner, called Fred's, and a two-story frame building.

The SKIUS office occupied a front corner on the second floor of the frame building, with windows that offered a commanding view of the beach and the breaking surf across the street.

Andrew Zorbis stood to greet Paul. "And this must be the famous Lien, rescuer of trafficked children in China." He wore a tight black t-shirt and a pair of military-style dog tags. A silver cross dangled from a chain around his neck. Broad shouldered, but short, he wore his salt and pepper hair cropped. By the way it receded on both sides to leave a ridge down the middle, Lien judged him to be about 60.

"Actually, I was only involved in the rescue of one girl from China," she said. "So I'm not famous."

"The way Paul tells the story, you and two others conducted a bold penetration a couple of hundred kilometers into China. Then you raided a house where the victim had been held."

"It was really ... how do you say ... low key. And three years ago already."

"Still pretty heroic, I'd say."

"You used the word 'raid,'" she said, eager to move the focus back to him. "Is that what you do? Raid places where trafficked people are?"

"Oh no. We leave that to the police. But we gather intelligence about missing persons when we believe they've been trafficked."

"How do you gather this intelligence, Mr. Zorbis?"

"Please call me Andy. We have a number of ways. For starters, we're networked with lots of law enforcement agencies, police departments, sheriff's departments, the Department of Homeland Security, the FBI, as well as social service agencies. One of the most important of these is the National Center for Missing and Exploited Children, NCMEC as we refer to it. We're also very tight with a network known as the Trans-Border Anti-Trafficking Alliance, or TBAA. They're a coalition of over 60 government and non-profit agencies that combat human trafficking along the US-Mexico border region."

Paul jumped in, "TBAA is where I'm doing my practicum. That's where I heard about Andrew and these guys."

"Maybe this is a little too detailed?" Andrew asked.

"No, it's okay. But how do you actually *get* information?"

"We coordinate with our network. But we're also proactive in using technology, particularly social media, to obtain information about possible trafficked persons. Some of our investigators are techno whizzes. Old fashioned detective work fits in too. Knocking on doors. Making phone calls. Conducting surveillance. Would you like to see a case study of how we found one trafficking victim?"

"That'd be interesting," Lien said.

On his computer, he brought up an image of a chestnut-haired girl of about 16 or 17, her eyes obscured by a black rectangle on the screen. "This is Raven. Not her real name, but that's how we refer to her in the case study, which is available online.

"A police department in the Central Valley asked us to put some resources to work on finding her. Detective bureaus of police departments are typically too busy. With multiple caseloads, they sometimes don't have the resources for a thorough investigation of one missing person, especially if the person is a runaway and the level of danger is unclear. In Raven's case, her parents were concerned after she went on a date with an older guy and didn't return. According to the police, who'd interviewed several of Raven's friends, she had a habit of dating older men, sometimes as much as ten years older. So the police asked us to be involved.

"We sent two investigators to Raven's hometown to collect as much background information as we could. They interviewed her parents and her friends. She'd dropped out of school the year before, but we spoke to former teachers as well. What emerged was a pretty good profile of Raven and her pattern of behavior. I won't go into details on that. But we had enough information to think she may have been lured into what we call a 'Romeo scenario.' That's where a perp lures the victim with the promise of love and affection." He paused for that much to sink in, then said, "I don't know where my manners are. Would either of you like coffee or tea? A glass of water maybe?"

"Nothing for me," said Paul.

When Lien asked for a glass of water, Andrew went to a small kitchen alcove and returned with a mug of steaming coffee for himself and a bottle of distilled water for Lien.

"After the initial research," he said, settling back at his computer, "we turned to technology. We created a web page and a Facebook page on Raven and asked for help from our network in driving traffic to those pages, both of which had contact links for getting information to us. We also began monitoring Raven's own Facebook page and the Facebook, Twitter, and Instagram accounts of her friends.

"Through these efforts, we got an ID on the guy she had been seeing. Through the DMV, we obtained an image of his driving license and his auto plate number."

"What's DMV?" asked Lien.

"Oh sorry. Department of Motor Vehicles. We found an address for him in a seedy neighborhood of Seaside, California, on the Monterey Peninsula. We put the house under surveillance and eventually got a photo of Raven through a window. Her parents verified that the image was her. Now we had her located, but we had no way of knowing if she was there of her own free will or had been kidnapped. So we coordinated with the Seaside Police Department, shared our information with them and asked that they do a welfare check." He paused to take a sip of his coffee.

"It turned out that Raven had been forced into prostitution and was servicing customers at a cheap motel nearby. The police freed her, arrested two men, and notified us. Even though Raven was traumatized by her experience, she didn't want to return to her family. So, again through our network, we arranged a shelter for her, here in San Diego County, where she'd be safe and have access to counseling and therapy."

"I think it was actually the TBAA that arranged the shelter," Paul said. "Wasn't it Andy?"

"Yes. We worked through them. They did a preliminary assessment of Raven's mental condition and needs. Then arranged the shelter."

"What's TBAA again?" asked Lien.

"That's the Trans-Border Anti-Trafficking Alliance, where I'm working," Paul said.

"Every case is a little different," Andrew said. "Sometimes frustrated parents contact us directly. Sometimes we're asked to investigate if school officials suspect something is amiss. And, as in this case, sometimes we're asked to help the police."

Through a lump in her throat, Lien said, "Thank you Andy. I'm glad your organization exists."

"And because SKIUS is a volunteer organization," Paul said, "they don't charge anyone for their investigations. Andrew, for a similar case such as Raven's, how much would it have cost, say the parents, if they had contacted a commercial private detective agency?"

"Upward of 50,000 bucks. Probably closer to 75,000." Andrew's computer emitted a short series of beeps and a new screen opened. "Oh, how timely. Look at this you two. You're seeing a text dialogue between a hooker and a potential john." He swivelled his computer so they could all clearly see the screen.

hi. Would u like a date?
 you bet how much?
$100 starting price how big a party u want?
 just straight sex how old are u?
only 16 but lots of experience.
 sounds delicious can you come to here? i'm in la jolla.
I can take a cab or uber but that cost xtra $. how old are u?
 Cool I'm on the sw corner of nautilus and draper apt b. how soon will u b here? I'm 34.
im younger than other girls doing this but can make up for that with a really good time 4u.
 awesome I m really getting worked up

The hooker's part of the exchange suddenly changed its thrust:

This is the San Diego County Sheriff's Department. In California paying or accepting money for a sexual act is a crime. Under the provisions of Penal Code 647(b), both prostitutes and customers can be charged with a misdemeanor. Buying sex can also cause serious long-term harm to victims, as well as furthering the cycle of human trafficking. Details of this exchange will be reviewed further and you may be contacted by law enforcement.

 ok im outa here I didn't know honest

"Holy cow," Paul said.

Lien stared at the now blank screen with her hand over her mouth, eyes wide.

"You've just seen a law enforcement tool for discouraging trafficking and prostitution in general. They use artificial intelligence software, known as a chatbot, to train the computer to have a conversation with a potential john. In this case it has infiltrated a local sex chat room. We passively monitor some of these sites with a view to obtaining leads on the whereabouts of trafficking victims."

Too shaken to continue, Lien took a drink from her water bottle to compose herself. Then she said, "Paul, will you take me back to Villa Alvarado please?"

Remembering her manners, she looked briefly at Andrew. "Thank you, Andrew. I'm impressed with what you do."

En route back to the campus housing, Lien silently stared at the ocean out the right side window, before finally saying, "I'm confused about something. I guess I understand that the girl's part of that conversation was actually a computer, but it didn't sound like she was forced into prostitution. It was kinda like she did that of her own will. So that's not trafficking is it?"

"Well, did you notice when her side of the conversation morphed into the Sheriff's Department part of the blurb referred to 'harm to *victims*?'"

"Yes. But how is she a victim if she has chosen this for her job?"

"Most social service agencies and women's welfare advocates take the view that anyone who's 'in the life,' so to speak, whether trafficked or not, is a victim of something. Trafficking victims have been coerced, but others are victims of mental illness, addictions, or poverty, or abusive homes. Stuff like that."

Lien nodded. Then she silently watched the traffic for the entire 45 minutes it took to drive back to SDSU.

Just as they pulled up to Villa Alvarado, she said, "There is no other purgatory … but a woman."

Paul snapped out of his own reverie. "Huh? What's that? Where's that from?"

"It's a line from a play we read in English class, *The Scornful Lady*. I'm not sure what it really means. But it seems to fit today."

***

It took Lien several seconds after waking on Saturday morning to realize where she was. She blinked the sleep out of her eyes, rose to a half-sitting position in bed and gazed uncertainly around the room until her brain kicked into gear and she remembered. Of course, Villa Alvarado at SDSU.

Then she remembered the meeting at SKIUS and the upsetting text conversation they had all watched unfold on the computer screen. With a heavy heart, she went to the window to look outside and force her misgivings aside.

What a beautiful campus. And the balmy weather in San Diego felt more like home to her than cool, dreary Seattle in November. Wouldn't it be neat to transfer from UW to San Diego State? Of course, Grandfather Pete and Catherine would discourage that. But it was something to think about.

She had just sat down to her light breakfast when the speaker box on the wall buzzed. Paul's cheerful voice announced his presence in the foyer downstairs. "Hey Lien, are you about ready?"

"Just give me a couple of minutes, I'll be right down."

The Saturday traffic was light as they drove south toward downtown San Diego. Filled with the vitality of a glorious southern California morning, Lien confided, "This morning I had a wild impulse to see about transferring from UW to SDSU." She turned to watch for Paul's reaction.

The corners of his lips rose fleetingly. He glanced at her. Then his eyes went back to the roadway as he silently considered her news. "That'd be great. And you know what? Maria Gutierrez, the woman we're gonna see this morning, is on the faculty of the School of Social Work. She might be able to grease the skids for a transfer."

"Grease the skids?"

"Sorry. Another American figure of speech. It means make it easier."

"I thought Maria … what's her last name?"

"Gutierrez."

"Right. I thought Ms. Gutierrez was the executive director of this TBAA place we're going to this morning."

"She is. But she's also a part-time lecturer at San Diego State. She has her MSW from the School of Social Work and is working on her PhD."

"Do you really think she'd help me transfer? I mean … this is only a wild idea that I had this morning. I don't know if it's realistic."

"Well, can't hurt to ask."

Fifteen minutes later, they pulled into the parking lot behind a single-story, cinder-block office building. "Here we are," Paul said. "The Trans-Border Anti-Trafficking Alliance."

"And you have an office here?"

"More like a little table in a corner with a telephone. I have to bring my own laptop when I'm working here."

"What do you actually do for your practicum?"

"Anything I'm told to do … ha. Actually, I have to work 16 hours a week for my entire senior year. Maria's my field practicum supervisor. So far I've helped do preliminary needs assessments for freed and rescued victims of trafficking and other exploitation."

"But how do you actually do an assessment? Is there a standard set of questions, or do you just talk to them, or what?" She tried to remember how she had been "assessed" in the days following her rescue.

"There's a team of people involved, usually two or three. I assist a more experienced advocate. It's basically a series of interviews with the victim, and maybe others like the parents or the police. We try to decide what's best for the victim right away, like shelter, rehabilitation, counseling, mental health resources, or maybe to return home. It can go a lot of different ways, depending on the circumstances. But let's go in and meet Maria."

Maria Gutierrez was effusive in her greeting. "Welcome Lien. I've heard a lot about you. Paul has told me about your anti-trafficking work in Vietnam, as well as your own experience as a victim. You're obviously a very brave woman." In her fifties, she had beautiful brown eyes, shining with both intelligence and compassion. Her warm smile was welcoming.

"Thank you, Ms. Gutierrez, I ..."

"No. No. It's Maria, not Ms. Gutierrez."

Was everyone in California this informal? Calling an elder by their first name was unheard of in Vietnam. "Okay, Maria," Lien said shyly. "But Paul probably exaggerated about me."

"Oh, I don't think Paul's given to exaggeration. Let's have a beverage," Maria said. "We can go next door to a little cantina. You've already seen most everything there is to see of our humble office space. We also have a conference room, which will seat about 12 people, but it's in use for a workshop on child advocacy at the moment."

The cantina, about the size of the living room in a modest home, had three stainless steel tables, each with four straight armless chairs, and a counter with three stools. Behind the counter a fridge, a small microwave, a hot plate, and a sink. The menu consisted mostly of churros, burritos, and other microwaveable products, written in white chalk on a blackboard propped on an easel. Each table had a folded tent card describing the drink menu: coffee, tea, bottled water, Sprite, Coke, and Fresca.

Their three chairs scraped across the tiles as they sat. "Now," said Maria, "if you've had a chance to see our website, you have a pretty good idea of how we collaborate with other NGOs and arms of government to fight trafficking, help its victims, and punish its perpetrators. Our model is *Victim — Survivor — Driver*.

That means we seek to transition victims into fully integrated members of society. What else can I tell about how we work, Lien?"

For the next hour, Lien asked thoughtful questions and listened attentively as Maria familiarized her with not only TBAA's mission and purpose, but with its values, attitudes, and beliefs. When she learned that TBAA had another office in Tijuana, and was truly a trans-border endeavor, she once again felt the call to work for this compassionate agency.

Finally, Paul had a chance to speak. "Lien's just finishing her first quarter in social work at the University of Washington. She thinks she'd like to transfer to SDSU. Do you think that's feasible?"

Maria's eyes lit up. Then her smile changed as she clasped her hands together. "That's probably not feasible at the moment. For several reasons."

Lien hid her disappointment. After all, this was an impulsive notion, something she'd only considered this morning.

"First," said Maria. "You'd need to have completed two years elsewhere to be accepted as a transfer student at SDSU. You need 60 semester hours worth of credit elsewhere. Otherwise, regardless of how many credits you would bring from UW, you would start over as a freshman. Second, you would have to pass the SAT with a high score, and third, your high school GPA would have to be above a three point average."

"That would disqualify me right off," said Lien. "I didn't go to a conventional high school. I did my grade 12 equivalency in Vietnam. A totally different academic system."

"But you were accepted at the University of Washington."

"Yes. That was a long drawn out process. I had to have many documents translated and I needed a number of letters of recommendation. It probably helped that my grandfather Pete Trutch is an alumnus. He earned both his bachelor's and his master's degrees at U-Dub. They accepted me as a foreign student."

"Well, here's the other factor, Lien. As a non-California resident, out-of-state tuition would cost you over $20,000 a year." She turned sideways in her chair, put her hands between her knees, and said, "Listen. I think you should continue on at UW until you have two years under your belt, then consider transferring here. In the meantime, I'll make you an offer I think will be enticing."

Eyes wide, Lien gave her an enquiring look.

"If you'd like, you can work here for TBAA as a volunteer for the next two summers. That experience would supplement your academic learning with some practical experience and would also give you an opportunity to decide for sure whether you'd like to transfer. We could provide you with room and board in one of our transitional houses during the summers you're here. It would be modest, mind you, but adequate."

***

On Sunday morning, Lien stood at the entryway of Villa Alvarado with her small suitcase at her feet. They had covered a lot of territory in three short days, and her visit had turned out better than she could have imagined. But how had her time in San Diego passed so quickly? She had discovered the efficiency and dedication of the staff and volunteers in both the agencies she and Paul had visited. He was so fortunate to be augmenting his studies like this — being mentored by such passionate anti-traffickers.

Then Paul pulled up, flipped open the trunk, and threw her bag into the battered old car.

As soon as they were on their way again, she said, "I'm really sorry that we didn't have time for me to say good-bye to your parents. They were so kind to me. I hope I'll see them again. And of course I'd like to meet Shawna and thank her for letting me use her room."

"Well ... I was hoping to talk you into coming back for Christmas break. I'd come up to Seattle to see you, but the holiday season is just as busy at TBAA as any other time. Many of the residents in our shelters are Mexican and devout Catholics and it's a tough time for them. They miss their families, and of course they're questioning their faith because of what they've endured."

"I'd love to come down. I'll have to check with Grandfather and Catherine, though. They've been so generous to me, and I don't want to push it. But I'd also love to help if I could."

As they sped towards the airport, Paul said, "Let's think about it. We can always use another set of eyes and ears and I'm sure that you could help the girls in recovery."

Lien agreed, and gazed again at the palm trees waving in the slight breeze. As they had when she first saw them, they left her feeling nostalgic for her Vietnamese home. Her time in San Diego had sparked a longing for a warmer climate, and the thought of working alongside the experts at TBAA tantalized her. This was a place where she could gain the necessary knowledge and skills to help victims of trafficking. Girls like her, who wanted nothing more than to regain a "normal" life.

They faced each other on the pavement outside departures at the airport. Paul leaned towards Lien. She offered her cheek, where he planted a soft kiss.

"See you at Christmas," he said hopefully, as he walked backwards towards the car.

Lien watched as he drove off, her fingers on the spot where he had so tenderly left his message of affection.

Chapter Fifteen

December, 2018
San Agustín Etla, Oaxaca

Pablo and his son Carlos prepared their small herd of Creole goats for steering them to a neighbor's ranch a few kilometers down the dusty road, where they would be used for land clearing and imparting nutrient-rich microbes back into the soil. The split-hoofed eating machines were much in demand, as their wandering tended to till the soil rather than compact it. At the same time they recycled vegetation, with its moisture and nutrients, back into the soil by trampling in their own manure. They'd bring a tidy sum of money to the Montero family for a month's worth of work. Later in the new year, a number of them would be harvested for meat and sold at the market in town.

Pablo, standing on the road just outside the open gate to the goat pen shouted, "Keep them moving. Keep them moving, Carlos." From inside the pen, Carlos prodded the animals through the opening and onto the road where Pablo, using his voice, augmented by a staff, would turn them north, the direction of the neighbor's acreage.

Just as the last of the goats reached the road, Sofia came running from the direction of the house. Another neighbor, a matronly woman in a housedress, followed close behind. "Pablo," Sofia yelled, "Come quickly. There's someone on the phone for us at Señora Cortez's house. It's about Juanita. Come quickly."

"Carlos. Take over. Try to get the goats back in the pen." He dropped his staff and ran to Sofia and Señora Cortez. The three of them trotted to the Cortez house.

Pablo tilted the handset sideways so Sofia, standing close to him, could also listen to the other end of the conversation. "This is Pablo Montero," he said breathlessly. "Who are you please?"

A female voice came through the static on the line. "My name is Iz. I'm calling from Puebla with news about your daughter, Juanita?"

"Is she there? In Puebla? Is she with you?" Pablo asked. Sofia clasped her palm against her mouth, her fingers splayed so that one reached up to the bridge of her nose and another cupped her chin.

"No, señor. She was here for about four weeks. I'm calling to tell you that she has been taken to Tijuana. From there, she'll probably be taken into the United States. If you know of anyone who can help you to rescue her, someone should get to her in Tijuana, before they put her in the US."

Sofia went still. Then her knees buckled and she collapsed onto the stained tile floor of the Cortez kitchen.

***

While he waited for the phone to be answered on the other end, Padre Sebastian looked up from his desk to the plaster crucifix on the opposite wall.

While in seminary, he had read an essay on art as religious inspiration, and he had memorized a passage quoted from a homily delivered by a French priest to his Parisian flock in the 13th century. The words played through his mind now: *Oh see, Christians. Look, look! See how Jesus has his head leaning down to kiss you, his arms extended to embrace you!*

The scholarly author of the paper had opined, "Was there ever a clearer indication of the immediate power of the religious image to move and inspire? In encouraging his listeners to look up at a crucifix, so confident that they will find their bliss, the preacher seems to express extreme faith in the force and transparency of art, that famed 'Bible of the Simple'."

Sebastian had struggled many times, during his 14-year tenure as a priest, with the seeming contradiction between faith and science. Even now, he wondered how long Catholicism and science could coexist in a world where technology seemed more powerful than prayer. The philosophy of Thomas Aquinas notwithstanding, the best answer Sebastian could come up with was that science investigates the natural world, while religion deals with the spiritual world. Faith embodies the belief that the two can be complementary. An oversimplification perhaps, but it worked for him and it was the best he could offer to any of his flock who also posed the question.

His musings were interrupted by a guttural but gentle voice, "Good afternoon Padre Sebastian. This is Bishop Diego. What can I do for you?"

"Yes, Your Excellency. One of my parishioner families has reason to believe their 17-year-old daughter has been coerced into sexual slavery and may be headed for the United States to work as a *prostituta* ..."

"How do you know this girl didn't simply run away?" the bishop interrupted. "That happens with teenagers."

Sebastian pictured Juanita as she had looked during the celebration of her acceptance to the university. Full of exuberance, eager to head off to study, beautiful, wholesome, full of excitement. "I have known this family for years, Your Excellency. They are fine people. Good Catholics. The Monteros, farmers of corn and goats. The daughter, Juanita, is a good person, a loving daughter, and an excellent student. She was the first of her family to go to university. It was at the University of Guanajuato where she was lured away to visit the family of her boy friend. They live in Tenancingo, Tlaxcala."

"I see. And what evidence suggests that she's a sex slave?"

"Your Excellency, after she had been missing from the university for a number of weeks, with no call to her parents, a sergeant from the *Ejército Mexicano* visited the parents to tell them he had seen their daughter in Tenancingo. At that time she was in the home of the Rojas, notorious pimps and slave masters."

"And what else?"

"They came to me, I called the Rojas family only to learn that Juanita had been taken away from Tenancingo. They wouldn't tell me where. Then yesterday, the Monteros, who have no phone, received a call through a neighbor's telephone from a *prostituta* in Puebla. She told the parents that Juanita had been in Puebla but was now being taken to Tijuana and then to the US."

Sebastian heard a tea cup clack against the handset on the other end. After a slurp, the bishop asked, "Do you think that's credible, knowing that the girl in Puebla is a *puta* and all? How did she know where to contact the Monteros' neighbor?"

Padre Sebastian sighed and looked up at the crucifix as if asking for divine help in convincing the old bishop. "I can only imagine that Juanita has been begging others to help. But I know what goes on in Tenancingo. Just about every woman who leaves that town has been lured there with promises of love. After a few days, they are persuaded or coerced into becoming prostitutes. I find the story of the Puebla woman, Iz, very plausible."

"What is it you wish from me, Padre?"

"I know that you know people who are fighting against this sin of human trafficking. I'm hoping you can contact someone who may help."

"Very well, I'll call a woman named Maria Gutierrez, she's the executive director of the Trans-Border Anti-Trafficking Alliance. She can probably alert other member organizations of her network to be on the lookout for this Juanita on both sides of the border. Please email me a recent photo and her personal information."

"I will, Excellency. I'll go out to the Montero *casa* today to obtain the information."

"Okay, peace be with you, Padre."

"And with you, Excellency."

Padre Sebastian nested the handset in its cradle, rose from his table, and stepped outside the parish office. He tugged open the stubborn driver's door on his decrepit Volkswagen Beetle, and set out for the Montero home.

On the dirt road that led to the farm, he thought about the priesthood and his own life within the church. He had been ordained 14 years earlier at the *Seminario Pontificio de la Santa Cruz*, along with 15 other young men entering the vocation. Seven of those men, all under 35, were dead. Sebastian had attended the funeral of Father Gregorio Oberon, the most recent one to be gunned down in the never-ending violence between warring drug cartels, just five months before. A recent Vatican paper had proclaimed that Mexico was the most dangerous country in the world in which to be a priest, the message being that no one is untouchable and the priesthood, due to its wide-reaching influence, is seen by gangsters as a major point of reference. Murdering a priest keeps the peasants off balance and is somehow seen to promote their fealty to the drug lords.

How long would he be safe, Sebastian wondered. He habitually took the normal precautions of avoiding set patterns, changing his routes regularly when visiting parishioners, and never putting his appointment schedule in writing. He worried not for his own life, but for the souls of his flock and even those of the cartel men.

He was all too familiar with the fact that sexual trafficking of persons was closely linked to the cartels and that anybody who interfered with it was vulnerable to violence. Denying a trafficker his supply of victims was like taking cocaine from a drug dealer. Nevertheless, he would continue to do his part to rail against the scourge during sermons and catechism lessons. That human beings, all children of

God, could participate in anything as abominable as the sexual exploitation of children depressed him deeply.

Truth be known, he was depressed at the whole milieu of his vocation. Not only were traffickers and gangsters running amok in the countryside and punishing the church for its opposition, there was also the issue of the sexual abuse of children on the part of the clergy. Just recently, he'd read that over 150 Mexican priests had been suspended for acts of pedophilia over the past few years and several had been prosecuted.

He'd first encountered this scandal while in the seminary, when he'd narrowly missed becoming a victim himself. As a tender 18-year-old in his first year, he awoke with a start one night with the frightful, but surprisingly pleasurable sensation of someone fondling his genitals. He pushed the hand away, twisted violently over onto his stomach then threw the thin blanket off and leapt off the tiny cot. By the time he found the light switch, his assailant had gone. For the next month, he'd cautiously scanned the faces of the other seminarians, to see if anyone was eyeballing him during mass and the daily prayer sessions.

He never learned who had touched him. Upon ordination five years later, he remained distressed that there might be a pedophile among the 16 new priests.

He snapped his mind back to the present when the old VW crested a hill and the Montero farm lay ahead of him. On the dusty road in front of their casa, Pablo and Sofia stood waiting for him. As his vehicle neared them, he saw that the two of them clutched something and were staring wistfully at it — a large-format photo of Juanita. They both had tears streaming down their cheeks.

Chapter Sixteen

December, 2018
En route from Puebla to Tijuana

The orange and yellow bus pulled out of Puebla at a few minutes past eight in the morning. Seven women sat huddled in fear, under the watchful eyes of Geraldo and two other *padrotes,* as the vehicle got underway. Juanita noticed that Geraldo's demeanor had shifted away from his pandering, sweet-talking manner. There was no more "my love," or "my darling." A cold, strictly business side of him emerged as he lectured on rules, expectations, and how the women were to behave once they arrived in Tijuana. His voice became sharp, his commands firm. "You *will* be with at least 15 men every day. You *will* learn the dos and don'ts of the trade from the *madrotas,* the more experienced women. You *will* dress and make yourself up as they tell you to."

The first hot and sticky day on the road took almost ten hours with delays for construction in and around Mexico City. The only way to get air moving was to have all the windows down. But this only circulated the hot air. Heat pressed in on the girls and the *padrotes.* Sweating didn't help. Perspiration ran down their necks and backs like warm milk.

Juanita had suffered through the third day of her period, with no opportunity to stop and change her pad, so now sticky blood commingled with sweat to make her uncomfortable. She squirmed and scooted around her seat in a futile effort to get some relief. At least she wasn't pregnant, she thought. Maybe the minder in Puebla had put a powdered birth control substance in the food.

Geraldo, patrolling the aisle, noticed her distress. He went to the front of the bus and returned with a damp towel, taken from a cooler behind the driver's seat. "Here," he said with disgust. "Try to clean yourself up a little."

Finally, when they left the sprawl of Mexico City behind them and the bus gained speed, a breeze brought some relief from the relentless heat. Two of the women dozed off. Several others stayed glued to the windows, watching the distant mountains as the flat terrain of the Valle de Mexico rolled by. The suburbs of Mexico City receded and the vehicle picked up even more speed. A refreshing current of air swept in through the windows. But as the kilometers spun past, Juanita felt only the yawning chasm of despair, as though this new land she traversed carried with it acres of pain and loneliness. A hypnotizing flock of thousands of European starlings dancing over the plateau on her side of the bus failed to excite her, as it did several of the other girls. Oblivious to their exclamations of *ooh* and *interesante* and *fantástico,* she looked dully at the horizon and thought of home.

As they neared the city of Guadalajara, in rapidly descending darkness, Geraldo announced that the bus would drop him for a meeting in the Calzada Independencia. "It will occupy me until after midnight," he said. "Many parts of this city are unsafe at night, particularly for women. You'll be taken to the Costco in the Western part of town. You can eat in the food court and use the bathroom there and then you'll sleep on the bus in the parking lot. I'll rejoin you there."

Juanita despaired at this news. If it was so dangerous, why sleep in the bus? Would these other two goons keep them safe? Tentatively, she rose from the seat. Then, gripping the seatbacks in order to stay upright, she made her way to where Geraldo sat. A whimper of sheer frustration tore itself from her lips, "Geraldo, I must have pads or tampons."

"Miguel will get them for you when you get to Costco."

Thirty minutes after dropping Geraldo in what, to Juanita, was clearly a seedy part of the city, undoubtedly a red light district, the bus arrived and parked in a remote spot on the expanse of asphalt between Costco and another huge retail store called Mega. Miguel told them that they would use the washroom in Mega while he got them some churros and fruit from Costco.

Juanita, nearly hysterical, grabbed the young pimp by the sleeve and said pleadingly, *"Señor, por favor, necesito las compresas o las tampones."*

"Yeah. You smell like it. No way. I'm not buying menstrual rags in that store." Then to all of them, "Okay, *putanas,* my friend Beto will take you in to the bathroom." He jerked his thumb toward the other *padrote,* then stepped off the bus and strode across the lot to Costco.

As they began filing off the bus, the driver, easily 25 years older than any of the passengers, opened the first-aid kit stored near the dashboard and fumbled around in it for a moment. He gave Juanita a kindly nod when she stepped past him, and handed her a stack of thick three-by- six-inch sterile dressings.

Overwhelmed by the first act of kindness she'd experienced in many days, Juanita leaned down and kissed the back of his leathery brown hand.

***

By 11 the next morning, they were on Highway 15D passing near the town of Acaponeta in the northwest corner of Nayarit State. Geraldo stood up at the front of the bus and said, "In a few minutes, we enter Sinaloa. The cartels in Sinaloa and Sonora make them the two most dangerous states in Mexico. I want you to sit down and shut up. Avoid looking out the windows, and especially do not make eye contact with anyone outside the bus. We'll use the toll roads because they're the safest, but even so, it'll take two long days to get through both states. Cause me problems and I guarantee you'll regret it. We'll pick up extra security in Hermosillo, but until then, watch yourselves."

Juanita wondered what he meant by "extra security" but was afraid to ask. She searched Geraldo's face for more, but he abruptly sat down and faced the front. Several of the women exchanged questioning looks, eyes wide, eyebrows raised, mouths agape.

Within seconds of crossing the state line, the military stopped them at a checkpoint. Geraldo said, "We have to get off the bus. Stay cool. If the soldiers ask you anything, smile when you answer."

About a dozen soldiers, outfitted in fatigues, black boots, and helmets swarmed around the bus, assault rifles slung across their chests. Juanita had not seen many firearms in her life, so her heart raced. A flutter of fear filled her stomach. Nevertheless, she cautiously searched the eyes of the soldiers, wondering if she could find a sympathizer among them. One who might perhaps call a higher authority and orchestrate their liberation. If she found one with soft features and a caring face, maybe she could get a signal to him in some way. But she saw only vacuous, indifferent expressions.

The seven women, two of their minders, and the driver stood in a loose clump at the front of the bus, under the watchful eyes of two soldiers. A few yards away, a sergeant questioned Geraldo. Three other soldiers had boarded the bus to search under seats and among the meager possessions of the women.

Juanita couldn't hear what Geraldo or the sergeant said, but she could tell by their gestures and nods that this was not an adversarial encounter. She observed Geraldo reach into his hip pocket and produce a wad of pesos. The head soldier accepted the bribe without looking at the money. He shot a glance toward the girls and made a comment that caused both he and Geraldo to laugh.

Geraldo's response came just loud enough that Juanita heard it. *"Claro que sí."* Of course.

The sergeant called his soldiers off the bus. Then he winked at Geraldo and with a wave of his hand dismissed them all to go on their way.

In late afternoon they fuelled up at a huge Pemex station on the outskirts of Mazatlan.

"At least the washrooms are clean," Juanita said to Dolores, as the *padrotes* treated them to light food from the snack bar. She had read about Mazatlan in a magazine. It was famous for its fabulous beaches and world-renowned cliff diving. She didn't expect to see the beach, but when they reboarded the bus Geraldo told them that they would park for the night on Avenida del Mar, which ran along the beach of Playa Norte. This gave her a small lift. Her first ever glimpse of the Pacific Ocean might distract her from her misery.

Just past six p.m., the bus pulled up to the curb in front of El Acuario Mazatlan, across the street from the beach and halfway between the Centro Historico and the Zona Dorada with its glitzy high-rise hotels. The aquarium itself looked shabby and worn out, its tile façade stained with graffiti. A fountain, just below the *Bienvenido* sign on the fence, featured bronze statuary of two naked boys and a leaping dolphin. Carmen nudged Juanita, giggled, and made vulgar remarks about the boys' genitals. The corners of Juanita's mouth instinctively turned down. Her parents had taught her never to talk like that, and thinking of them turned her chest to lead.

Geraldo stood. "The aquarium is closed. But by special arrangement, we can all use the bathrooms just inside the gate. The guard will let us in. This is where we'll sleep tonight. In the bus again."

Minutes later, Juanita saw a late model sedan and a big pickup truck park at either end of the bus, bracketing it like bookends. Four men climbed from the vehicles. Although they brandished assault rifles, they wore civilian clothing. The acid taste of fear rose in her mouth as they took up positions on the sidewalk between the bus and the aquarium. One of the men had several days' worth of dark stubble on his face. He climbed onto the bus and stood near Geraldo, his features hard, his posture menacing.

Juanita's stomach lurched sickeningly, and she looked out the window on the ocean side of the bus to avoid this thug's eye.

Geraldo spoke over his shoulder from the front seat. "This is our security for the night. Don't worry, they're here to keep us safe."

But when Juanita looked toward the front, the *hombre's* dark, haunted eyes were clearly sizing up the youthful bodies on the bus. She shrunk as low in the seat as she could.

Rather than avoid his attention, her action attracted it. His eyes bored into Juanita and he walked toward her, the assault rifle draped across his chest rattling metallically, his heavy leather boots clunking. He approached to within six inches of Juanita and leaned forward until his face nearly touched hers. "Hey *chica*, you want to show me a good time?"

She recoiled at the blast of foul breath and spittle. She crossed her arms over her breasts and turned toward the window again, squeezing her body as close to it as possible.

He laughed, then reached down and gripped her chin between his thumb and fingers, turning her head forcibly back toward him. "What's a matter *chica*? I don't bite. Well, maybe just a little nibbling here and there. You'd like that."

Then his head jerked forcibly back and away from Juanita. His eyes bulged and he emitted a choking sound. Juanita watched with a mixture of relief and horror as he seemed to fly backwards a couple feet, until she could see that Geraldo had a tight grip on the back of the guy's collar, pulling his t-shirt into his throat, which caused more gagging.

"*Tu hijo de puta*," Geraldo spat out the words. "You are here for security. Nothing more. You and your *pendejos* are not to touch any of these girls. *Entiendes?*" He released his grip on the gagging man.

Still gasping and struggling for breath, the goon stumbled toward the front of the bus. As he stepped through the door, he turned and stuck his middle finger up into the air, sending his message of humility and defiance to all on board.

The driver, who had sat silently in his seat during the commotion, spit at the back of the man as he left the bus. Two of the other girls applauded lightly.

***

Saguaro cacti, their spiny arms bent skyward as though in prayer, dotted the landscape as the bus rolled northward through the state of Sonora. Out the windows the weary and apprehensive travelers could see a mixture of scrubby desert, rich well-irrigated farmlands, and in the distance to the east, the jagged mountains of the Sierra Tarahumara, a component of the thousand-kilometer length of Sierra Madre Occidental.

About an hour south of Hermosillo, Juanita, her limbs stiff, hair disarrayed, and body smelly from sleeping in the bus for two nights, made her way forward to where Geraldo sat in the front seat, right-hand side. She squatted down so that her face was level with his and said, "I want to talk with you, Geraldo."

"*Claro que sí, Juanita.*"

Her voice took on a somber, slightly angry tone. "Do you take pleasure in making girls and women fall in love with you and then betraying them? Do you enjoy it, Geraldo? Tricking them to become whores?"

He turned to look at her and raised his eyebrows. Juanita thought she caught a relaxation of the muscles in his face. "No. This is not fun for me. But it's my duty to my family. My role. And the money is good."

"Do you ever think that you're breaking hearts and ruining lives?"

"Juanita. I've been brought up to believe that the role of women is to please men and have children. I think women are answering their calling from God whether they marry and have one man for life, or whether they please many men."

"God has never said such a thing. The Bible says 'man is supposed to cleave unto a wife.' Singular — *one* wife. That means women should have only one man. What you're doing is forcing women and girls into sin and destroying them."

Geraldo turned to stare out the window. Billowing cumulous clouds brushed the peaks of the distant mountains. He swung back around to face Juanita. "*Mierda de toro.* I think the Bible also says a woman's body is a vessel for something. In the minds of most men it's a vessel for sex. That's just the way of the world. Maybe you should go back to your seat."

"Of all of the girls your family has lured into your despicable business, have you ever been in love? Do you know what it feels like?"

"I think with every girl I've helped I have a tender spot — something like love. Yes, I have felt love for all of them. And especially you." He smiled lasciviously.

"But not so much that you will quit ruining their lives. Not so much that you will turn this bus around and take us back to our homes. Not that we would be welcome back in our homes since you have caused us to become soiled, tainted."

"Juanita, the *Ejército Mexicano* killed my younger brother a few weeks ago. With him dead, there's no easy way for me to quit this business. If there were, I would want to marry you and return to the university with you."

"That will never happen, you bastard." She walked back to her seat past the other two slumbering *padrotes* and the six women, two of whom were also asleep.

***

For two and a half long days, there had been very little chattering between the seven women on the bus, each preoccupied with what lay ahead in Tijuana and maybe the States. But as they approached the southern city limits of Hermosillo, Carmen, who sat directly across the aisle from Juanita, said, "This is my home. I miss it so much."

Juanita saw the tears on her cheeks and reached across the aisle to stroke Carmen's forearm.

"But even if I could get off here, I wouldn't. I can't dishonor my family by being a whore."

"One day God will free you," offered Juanita. "And when He does, there will still be love in the hearts of your family."

They came to another military checkpoint with the same array of green vehicles, bristling guns, and helmeted, flak-jacketed soldiers.

Juanita once again shrunk into her seat. No doubt they would again be taken off the bus and made to stand in the sun while several soldiers searched the bus and the others stood around ogling the girls and lewdly joking among themselves.

But to her surprise, the senior officer, a *capitán segundo,* waved the bus through and it rolled on into the city, the capital of Sonora state. Juanita said to Carmen, "I wonder why all the checkpoints are manned by military and not police?"

Carmen said, "My uncle was a policeman. But so many people have been killed in Sonora in the drug wars, many of the police quit in fear. The federal government drafts soldiers to help control the flow of drugs. Soldiers can't just quit and walk away."

"But I have seen a few *policía.*"

"*Sí.* They probably belong to the units that work for — are *owned by* is more like it — the cartels and the gangs."

"How do you tell who's on whose side?"

"You can't. It's all mixed up. Even some units of the army work for the cartels, while others are loyal to the government. But that doesn't mean much when government bosses and politicians also cooperate with the gangs."

Just as they left the northern city limits, officials waved the bus to a stop on the shoulder behind two Mexican Army Humvees. Again, helmeted soldiers with assault rifles slung across their chests approached the bus. "Another checkpoint?" asked Juanita.

"Looks like it," said Carmen.

But rather than directing everyone to dismount the bus, the captain hopped up the steps, spoke briefly with Geraldo, then climbed off. He stepped into the nearest Humvee. All three vehicles then drove onto the macadam and started north. The military vehicles, each manned with a soldier and a .50 calibre machine gun in a rooftop hatch, took up escort positions to the front and rear of the bus. From his seat, Geraldo spoke over his shoulder, "Our security from here to Tijuana. We're driving straight through with only a couple of gas and toilet stops, about a ten-hour run."

Juanita wondered who this particular element of the *Ejército Mexicano* was loyal to.

Ten and a half hours later, at ten p.m., the little convoy rolled into the southern suburbs of Tijuana. Juanita smelled the faint odor of raw sewage.

Chapter Seventeen

December, 2018
San Diego

In the parking lot behind the Trans-Border Anti-Trafficking Alliance office, Paul Pham slammed the door of his Mustang and cursed at the steam rising from under the hood. This was the third time this month his car had overheated while driving to his practicum. Between his morning classes and his afternoon work at TBAA, he had little free time for errands and personal chores. But if he dropped the car off after classes tomorrow or Friday, and then used the Uber account his dad had given him, the bill would go onto his father's credit card.

He cast a last glance toward the hissing radiator and strode into the office. He had barely seated himself and opened his laptop when Maria approached him clutching a printed email.

"Good afternoon, Paul. I've got an important task for you. I've just had a phone call from an old acquaintance, a Catholic bishop in Oaxaca, Mexico. He also sent this email." She laid it on his table. "There's a fairly good quality photo of a Mexican national named Juanita Montero in there as well. I need you to get all this information out to our agencies first thing. This is your highest priority this afternoon."

"Sure. Should I use the group email list?"

"Yes. And be certain that the border people are included — Border Patrol, ICE, CBP Office of Field Operations, and Homeland Security Investigations. All of them. It's believed this girl is in Tijuana, but will soon be smuggled into San Diego County. I want to get Alejandra in our TJ office on it too. She'll get your email, but I'll call her as well."

Paul reached for the sheaf of pages and thumbed through them. "There's a lot of information about her here. Oh man, look at the picture of her. What a gorgeous young woman. What a shame if she's been trafficked."

"For sure. She has so much promise. Art, music, sports, a top scholar. Just started a scholarship at the University of Guanajuato this fall. It looks like she got duped into a Romeo caper."

"I'll get right on it."

***

Inside the San Diego Sector office of the US Border Patrol, a modern, clean, nicely landscaped building on Roswell Road in Chula Vista, the duty agent in the communications center read through the dispatch from TBAA. He assigned it a precedence designator of "Immediate" and relayed it to all stations in the sector, ensuring that every agent would be alerted at a pre-shift muster and be on the lookout for Juanita Montero. All Customs and Border Protection Officers at the official ports of entry would also see this alert, but it would be nested within the myriad others they received on any given day.

At the SKIUS office in Oceanside, Andrew Zorbis read the message from TBAA. He printed it off and pinned Juanita's photo onto a cork bulletin board, prominently displayed alongside those of several dozen other missing teenagers, mostly from southern California. Then he called Roger Upton, one of the volunteer investigators, and a retired watch commander at the El Cajon Border Patrol station.

"Afternoon, Roger. Andy here. Listen, we just got an alert on a young Mexican woman named Juanita Montero, age 17. It's believed she's in Tijuana in forced sex slavery but will shortly be smuggled into San Diego County."

"You caught me about six miles offshore, fishing for bluefins. You want me to pop into the office tomorrow morning to get up to speed on the case?"

"Nah. It's not really our case yet. I'll send you the lowdown on her via email. But you might want to touch base with some of your former USBP colleagues and suggest they stay tuned. You could ask them to let us know if they catch any intel about her."

"Sure. I can go over to El Cajon tomorrow afternoon. My buddies there can ask the other stations in the sector to be on high alert for her, as well."

"Okay. Good fishing. Take care, shipmate."

"Ten-Four."

At the Tijuana office of TBAA, Director Alejandra Gomez read the dispatch, her eyes darting across the lines of print. Then she read it a second time, more carefully. The corners of her mouth tightened as she studied the picture of the beautiful brunette. She called out to a staff member on the other side of the office, "Julia, print this picture and get it out to all our volunteer advocates on the streets in the Zona Norte. I want everyone to be on the lookout for this girl. Particularly along Calle Coahuila and the adjacent streets. Get some male volunteers to go into the strip clubs and watch for her."

Chapter Eighteen

December, 2018,
Tijuana

The Hotel Eduardo, a two-story fleabag in a back alley, was located a block off Calle Coahuila. Up the stairs on the second floor, Juanita's room measured a mere nine by twelve feet. The heart-shaped bed, with its glossy purple spread, dominated the floor space. A wardrobe leaned against the wall, leaving only ten inches or so of squeeze-by room between it and the end of the bed. The only other furnishing, a straight-backed wooden chair, doubled as a bedside table.

On each of the last seven days and nights, Juanita had been forced to service 14 to 16 customers for 30 minutes each. When the last customer departed sometime between three and four in the morning, she attempted to wash the shame and fetor from her body by wiping herself down with a face cloth in the disgusting bathroom shared by all four rooms on the floor. Then she cried herself to sleep on top of the bedspread, not wanting to crawl between the sex-soiled sheets.

On Wednesday morning, 12 days before Christmas, she dreamed of the liturgical season at her home in San Agustín Etla. In the dream, she had gone with her mother, father, and Carlos to *La Parroquia* for the blessing of the tree on the third week of Advent. Padre Sebastian, in his purple vestments, uttered the prayer before the nicely decorated balsam fir in the transept. Every eye of the congregation followed him as he walked slowly back to the chancel and stood in the pulpit. He delivered the homily, in which he reminded the children that the celebrated Christmas tree relates to many aspects of the Roman Catholic faith. In a voice trembling with reverence, he told them how the first parents on Earth were not allowed to eat from one tree, and how Christ paid the price of our redemption by hanging on a tree.

Following the mass, she and her family walked the three miles back to their modest farm, holding hands, their souls filled with the spirit of the Holy Trinity.

Then her dream took an ethereal turn as she found herself suddenly in Bethlehem attending the birth of Christ. Wearing her white communion dress, she slowly moved forward, hands steepled before her, to have a closer look at the holy infant. A warm sensation, like bubbly bathwater, washed through her slumbering body. But the serenity of the moment turned to horror when she peered over the lip of the cradle and found it empty, just as all the animals in the stable became devils.

She jolted awake to the reality of her situation — a whorehouse in Tijuana.

In the bathroom, under the dim light of a single bulb she went through the motions of starting her day. She used the toilet, brushed her teeth, and splashed cold water on her face, repulsed by the haunted image that peered back at her in the cracked and smudgy mirror — circles under her eyes, sallow skin, gaunt cheeks.

She did not have to don her work attire until 11:00, so she returned to her room and selected a pair of jeans and a loose-fitting sweater to wear for the next couple of hours.

Although she'd had no appetite for weeks, Juanita took her breakfast of beans and rice in a tiny room behind the reception desk along with two other girls. If she were to survive, she'd need to nourish her body. Neither of the other girls ate enthusiastically. One, a brassy redhead who had introduced herself as Valeria, had already been here when Juanita arrived and the other, a bleached blonde who hadn't yet offered a name, turned up two days after Juanita. From Mexico City, she had said. Juanita had not yet seen the fourth girl, who apparently lived with her pimp and only used her room during working hours.

After 15 minutes with only desultory conversation, Juanita pushed her chair back and walked through a beaded curtain into the dingy lobby. The clerk, actually a general factotum who doubled as doorman and bouncer at night, slouched in the tattered upholstered seat of a wooden armchair, where he smoked and read a tip sheet for the day's dog races at Agua Caliente. The other girls referred to him as Scarface, a reference to the long red welt on his upper lip, inadequately camouflaged by a droopy moustache.

Juanita avoided him as she headed for the stairs.

Not about to let the uppity little *putana* get away with shunning him, he growled in a gravelly voice, "*Ay, Coriña, como estas, hoy?* Your tight little ass looks good in those jeans, no?"

"Fuck off, Scarface." Valeria entered from behind the beaded curtain. "Leave her alone you dirtball."

"*Oye, besa mi culo.* I'm just expressing my affection. I love all of you *putas hermosas.*"

Juanita trudged up the derelict wooden staircase, careful to skip over the broken step a third of the way to the landing. She continued up past the second floor to the door that opened onto the roof, moving the fire extinguisher that held it closed. With a vigorous tug, she jerked the door open and stepped onto the roof. Already it was hot and muggy, the air filled with smog. This was her alone time, and she had learned to savor it, regardless of the pollution and sultry atmosphere.

She selected a south-facing spot, then got down on her knees. She crossed herself, placed her elbows on the dusty low wall and clasped her hands, palms inward. She asked first for blessings to be bestowed upon her papa, her mama, her brother, Carlos, and all the friends and neighbors of her family in San Agustín Etla. In a choked voice, with a few tears trickling down her cheeks, Juanita asked the Lord to forgive her life of sin and to help her be worthy of rescue and release.

Standing now, she placed her hands on the wall and leaned out to gaze over the rooftops toward the south, the direction of home and family. Oaxaca was far away, but still she pictured the beautiful apse of *La Parroquia,* wondering if her words could be heard from here. No wind blew to carry her supplications home. Oblivious to the clamor of traffic and the commotion of commerce floating up from the alley below, a sigh, almost a whimper, escaped her.

The startling crash of metal striking metal drew her to the other side of the roof. She peered into the alley. A motorcycle lay on its side, partially beneath the front bumper of a battered orange and white bus. The rider was on his feet, but obviously hurt. He held his left arm across his chest and applied traction by pulling on his elbow with the other hand. Passers-by mopped blood from his forehead and nose.

For the first time, she noticed the fire escape on this side of the building. A metal ladder affixed to the side of the building descended from just below the low wall around the roof down one floor to a metal landing. From the landing a set of iron stairs angled downward 45 degrees to another landing suspended about two meters above the alley.

Her mind raced. She knew that a Catholic church, *La Iglesia Inmaculada Concepción*, was a scant four blocks to the south. She could see it from her usual rooftop vantage point. If she could get down the fire escape to the lowest landing, could she safely drop two meters to the alley? There were garbage bags below the landing. Those would shorten her descent and soften her landing. Could she walk unnoticed to the church and seek refuge?

From a position on her knees, she gripped the lip of the wall and lowered one leg over the edge. When her foot connected with the top rung, she brought down the other leg. She allowed her full weight to settle, then took first one hand, and then the other off the rim of the wall to cling to the ladder. But as she moved down another rung, the top two bolts securing the ladder to the building façade pulled loose from the worn brick into which they had been bored years before. The ladder swung sharply outward.

Juanita shrieked and threw her weight forward. The ladder teetered momentarily, as though unable to decide whether to tip over or return to its setting. Gasping for breath, she thrust forward again. The ladder clunked back against the wall and Juanita found a secure grip with both hands over the lip. Breathing heavily, her pulse pounding in her ears, she held on and sent a plea to her god. Carefully she brought her lower foot back to the top rung and raised her opposite knee up to the top of the wall. Using all her strength, she pulled with her arms until she moved her weight off the ladder and brought the other knee safely up.

She sat panting and sobbing on the rooftop for another five minutes before she returned to her room. Almost show time. Time to take her place on the street.

***

By noon she had taken her position on the sidewalk along Avenida Ortega, one of six hookers per block on each side of the street. Wearing the stereotypical uniform of the *paradita* — tight miniskirt, three-inch heels, plunging neckline showcasing smooth cleavage, bare midriff — Juanita fit right into the Zona Norte milieu. She stood with the redhead, Valeria, near the open doorway to the Adelita Bar, good real estate for a street prostitute, and a popular place for sex tourists to fortify themselves with cerveza before approaching a sex worker.

Two young Americans with telltale GI haircuts, high-and-tight white sidewalls, strode toward the entrance and cast nervous glances toward Juanita and

Valeria. Juanita avoided eye contact and stayed silent while Valeria smiled coyly at them. She pursed her lips and made a *pssht* sound. —the acceptably subtle proposition, as solicitation was not permitted in Tijuana's regulated management of prostitution.

The men stopped. One, a fresh-faced youth with a spray of freckles across his nose, said, "How much, ma'am?"

Valeria looked around to see who might be listening. She had spotted surveillance cameras across the street, but they didn't have an audio capability. She partially covered her mouth with a hand. "Forty dollars."

Juanita glanced up the street. An identical scene was playing out in at least three other spots within her sightline, other hookers negotiating subtly with prospective mid-day johns.

The youth, with his short crop of sandy hair, asked, "Um, where would we go, ma'am?"

Again, she covered her mouth. "I have a room. I need another ten dollars for the room."

The second man said, "That makes 50. Is that for both of us?"

"No. Just one." She looked up at the security camera. Satisfied that the tiny red light was not illuminated, she lightly stroked the first boy's crotch. "This one."

A police cruiser motored past. Juanita looked hopefully toward its two occupants, but they were engaged in conversation, totally disinterested in the sidewalk dramas taking place.

Out of nowhere, Scarface appeared and leaned in to Juanita. "Come with me. You've been promoted off the street. We're placing you in one of the clubs tonight. It's a much better gig. Higher class *cabrónes*. We have to move you into a better room above the gentlemen's club. Let's go, *chica.*"

Juanita's skin prickled with apprehension. All along this journey, just as she had steeled herself to the reality of increasingly repulsive circumstances, along came a change, a change that always meant a descent into some further hell that offered very little chance of escape.

After a brief stop at the Eduardo to collect her things, Scarface steered her toward the glitzy glass and chrome façade of the infamous strip club at 2009 Calle Coahuila.

Tall polished brass letters in relief on the glass read:

Hong Kong Gentlemen's Club
Tijuana, Mexico
Open 24 Hours

To the left of the letters, in the same brass, and superimposed over the image of a dragon: the sculpted silhouette of a naked woman in a suggestive pose, similar to the ones often seen on the mud flaps of long-haul trucks. A flunky in a dinner jacket and a uniformed security guard stood on either side of the double-glass front doors.

Scarface held Juanita by the wrist and led her past the goons at the door and through the darkened showroom. Several men occupied about six of the thirty or so round, glass-topped tables. Near the low stage at the front of the room, subdued footlights and a heliotrope spotlight shone on the gyrating form of a pole dancer clad only in a G-string, her long dark hair swishing from side to side as she swung her body.

Scarface led Juanita to one side of the room, toward three highly polished wooden doors. Ignoring the two labeled *Hombres* and *Mujeres,* he took her through the third into a clean and airy vestibule containing a long table, decorated with a spectacular arrangement of white and yellow lilies. He pointed to a single leather upholstered chair and laughed. "That's where the meat inspector sits during busy hours."

Juanita ignored the comment.

Scarface guffawed and bellowed, "You know. She checks the johns for little sores or dripping dicks before they go upstairs. This is a healthy establishment." He laughed again.

Juanita remained unresponsive. *You're* the dick, she thought.

Up a carpeted stairway to the third floor, a well-lit, wide hallway cut a swath between at least ten bedroom doors. Several polished wooden console tables were evenly spaced along the corridor walls, and atop each a slender vase displayed a mixed spray of pussy willows and lavender. What a high-end hotel must look like on the inside, Juanita imagined.

Scarface pushed the door open on number 37, a room decorated in muted tones of ochre and beige. Furnished with a queen-sized bed, a dressing table equipped with an array of beauty aids, two chairs and an armoire, it was half again the size of her cubicle at the Eduardo. The doors to the armoire stood open, revealing an assortment of somewhat tasteful but provocative clothing: scant spaghetti strap dresses, hot pants, halter tops. A bouquet of long-stemmed roses adorned the night table by the bed.

"Look, there's an envelope with them posies," said Scarface.

Juanita squinted suspiciously as she lifted the flap. The note card read: *Congratulations. With love, Geraldo.*

So, he thought she'd be grateful that this favor had elevated her status. "Fuck that," she muttered, and then immediately regretted her words. That was her second ill-mannered response in less than five minutes. Was it so easy to become as crude as the people around her?

She dropped the note on the floor, sighed, and sat heavily on the bed. Would this depravity never end? She said a silent prayer.

Scarface turned to leave her alone. "One of the other *putanas* will show you what you have to do here. Welcome to the Hong Kong Gentlemen's Club."

Chapter Nineteen

December, 2018
Tijuana

The Trans-Border Anti-Trafficking Alliance branch in La Zona Centro occupied a modest office space in back of the Hospital Del Carmen, a clinic devoted to ministering to single mothers. Alejandra, the local TBAA director, and Sister Antonina Magdalena, on loan to TBAA from her holy order, sat side by side sipping tea, Juanita Moreno's picture and file spread before them on the scratched conference table.

"It's hard to be sure," said Alejandra. "But one of our volunteers spotted a woman who could be Juanita working in the Hong Kong Gentlemen's Club." She tapped Juanita's photo. "I believe that's one of the spots where your outreach efforts take you."

"Yes. The management allows me in every week to visit with the girls. In the mornings before it gets busy. Most of them are Catholic, of course, and most are receptive, even eager, for our visits. I usually pray with them and give them condoms. But I don't think I've seen this one there."

"Our volunteer went in undercover, posing as a prospective john. He'd never seen her before either. We think she's been there for less than a week. We only got word she was being moved from Puebla to Tijuana about two and a half weeks ago. So given travel time and probably some time for 'training,' the timing's about right. When will you go the club next, Sister?"

"I can go the day after tomorrow, in the morning. If she's open to it, I'll pray with her, try to get a sense of her state of mind and soul. Are you thinking of trying to spring her?"

"It's almost impossible to rescue a girl who's working against her will. She'll be under the control of *padrotes* from the Zona Norte. It doesn't matter whether she's on the walk or in a club. They're watched 24/7 by the *halcones*, the gossips and lookouts. The best we can do, I think, is offer her any support we can give her, hopefully through your visits. But you know, Sister — I probably don't have to tell you this — we don't preach. Just engage, support, and listen."

"*Listen, listen, listen.* That's my middle name, Alejandra. I have God sitting on my shoulder constantly reminding me. I don't preach to them. But I do pray with them."

***

"Sister, you're descending into hell again. You might get burnt."

The jibes of the security guard didn't faze Sister Antonina Magdalena. She strode confidently through the doorway of the Hong Kong Gentlemen's Club. "I'd prefer to think I'm here to drain the swamp, Jorge. But that would be mixing metaphors, wouldn't it?"

She wore a teal blue cotton sweater with colourful Mayan symbols embroidered on the yoke and down each sleeve. Along with her thick-framed glasses, she looked more the part of a young grandmother than a sister of a holy order. Her long black hair, clean and carefully brushed, was tied back to reveal tiny gold studs in her ears. She wore no other jewelry.

"*No entiendo*, Sister. What's a metaphor?"

"Look it up. I can only say I've never met-a-phor I didn't like." She grinned and hurried on.

A clutch of prostitutes sat around two tables drinking coffee, smoking and talking, but with no customers to perform for, the showroom floor was quiet. From somewhere off in another room a vacuum cleaner whined.

"*Hola, señoritas,*" the nun said as she approached the tables. "May the peace of the Lord be with you." She crossed herself.

Only one of the women, her glasses almost as thick as Sister Antonina's, followed suit by crossing herself, but several others chimed in with a chorus of "*Hola*, Sister."

Sister Antonina helped herself to a chair at one of the tables and reached into her shoulder bag. "I brought rosary beads for anyone who'd like some."

Several hands tentatively raised. A pimp, who had been drinking coffee and smoking in a distant corner, edged up to the group.

"Please join us, *señor,* I was about to say a prayer with the girls."

"Sure, Sister. Say it." He went through a rather abbreviated and sloppy motion of crossing himself.

She bowed her head. "Heavenly Father, please help the violators of these women be transformed and enlightened to realize the scope of their unjust actions. Allow them to see the value and dignity of every human person."

The pimp squirmed a little, but kept his head bowed in supplication.

"And Lord of Life, strengthen these women and those whose hearts have been broken. Fill us with the wisdom and courage to stand in solidarity with the victims so that we may all enjoy the freedoms and rights which have their source in your Son and our Lord, Jesus Christ."

Several voices, including that of the pimp, rang out on "Amen."

"Ladies," said Sister Antonina, reaching again into her handbag. "Is this one among you here?" She showed them the picture of Juanita.

Several of the women said *sí,* simultaneously.

"Will you take me to her?" She looked at the pimp to see if he would object, and he responded with a curt nod.

The door to room 37 sat slightly ajar. Antonina saw Juanita's back as she sat at her dressing table desultorily dabbing on makeup. She tap-tapped on the door. "May I come in?"

"Oh." Juanita started and turned toward her. "Who are you?"

"My name is Sister Antonina. May I speak with you for a few minutes? Visit with you?" Sister Antonina entered the room and sat on the bed. "It's okay, Juanita. I'm a friend. How are you?"

Juanita took a deep breath, as if she had been holding her breath previously. "Why are you here? Did you come from Oaxaca?"

"No, my dear. My order does social work to try to improve the lives of girls in your situation. I'm here to assure you that God has not forgotten you."

Juanita put a rueful hand on her forehead. "I pray every day, but I'm not sure that God hears me. My messages to him are colored by my anger and shame."

"To feel shame is normal. And neither I, nor anyone else, can tell you how to feel. But God does not find fault with you for what you are enduring. I hope you can take some solace in that?"

Juanita's upper lip curled slightly. "I have hate in my heart for the *padrotes* who have forced me into this life, especially for Geraldo. I thought he was my boyfriend. I don't think the Lord approves of my hatefulness."

"He understands, my dear. Believe me, He does." Antonina paused to let that assurance sink in and gauge Juanita's reaction. "Would you like me to bring you anything? Books? Tea? Snacks? Hygiene products?"

"Books maybe. Can you bring me something by Guadalupe Nettel?"

"Of course. Have you read anything of hers before?"

"We're … we *were* reading her first novel, *El Huésped,* in my Mexican literature class when I was … when I left Guanajuato. I finished it in Tenancingo. And could you bring me some pads or tampons too?"

"I'll try to find Nettel's latest for you. If it is not to be found here in Tijuana, I'll order it online and bring it for you next week. The pads or tampons are no problem."

"Gracias, Sister. I must also ask. Can you get me out of here?"

Antonina said softly, "I personally don't have the power to do that, even with God's help. But the NGO …that means charity… the charity I work with constantly finds ways to rescue girls from your situation. They know about you, and I'm sure you'll be released. Just have faith. Now, is there anything else I can do for you? Would you like me to contact your family?"

Juanita clamped a hand over her mouth. Her eyes filled with tears. "Oh yes … No. I can't have them know what I have become." Following a full sob, she said, "Can you just get word to them that I am alive, that I am okay? Don't tell them what I am doing or where I am. Please, Sister."

"Of course. We will do as you want. Do you wish to pray?"

"I … I guess so."

"May the precious blood of Jesus guide you, shield you, and be your protection against risks. Amen."

***

Sister Antonina walked back to the TBAA office feeling relief that, although both sad and thinner than in her photo, Juanita remained healthy and of sound mind. It was pleasant not to have received the kind of pushback that sometimes occurred when calling on these troubled women: *How do I know that I can trust you?* or *You have no idea what this is like. You cannot be of any help to me with your Jesus talk and your beads.*

She would brief Alejandra on the encounter as soon as she got back to the office. Alejandra would, of course, notify the main TBAA office in San Diego, who would in turn apprise the clergy contacts in Oaxaca. From there, Juanita's family would learn that their daughter was alive and well.

Chapter Twenty

December, 2018
On Board Aeromexico Flight 188, Mexico, DF to Tijuana

Padre Sebastian settled back into his aisle seat, one long leg stretched at the edge of the aisle, the other under the seat in front of him. The Christmas carols playing through his headset coupled with the white wine he sipped had put him in a mellow mood. He closed his eyes as the Boeing 757 climbed through 20,000 feet.

The call from Bishop Diego confirming that Juanita was in Tijuana had been welcome news. But her enslavement in prostitution was devastating. The visit to her parents, Pablo and Sofia, had excited a melange of turbulent emotions. He agonized over the half-truth he had felt compelled to tell them — that Juanita was alive and in good physical health but that the anonymous source of that information could not attest to her whereabouts or the circumstances under which she was living. Her parents were overjoyed to hear that she was well, but angry and frustrated that they couldn't know more. "Padre, how can we go on living in this hell of not knowing? You must help us to know," Pablo had begged.

Obtaining permission from the Bishop to make a trip to Tijuana had also been emotionally wrenching. "Sebastian," he had said with mock patience, "you can't even be thinking about going up against the gangsters and thugs and mounting some kind of rescue. You wouldn't have a chance and you know it. What do you hope to achieve by putting yourself in harm's way and going to a whorehouse four days before Christmas?"

"I simply want to convey her parents' love and that of the Lord. I want to see for myself what her circumstances are." His voice took on a trembling resonance. "I want to come back with sufficient insight into her situation, so we — the Church, the NGOs in the faith community, our educated and thoughtful parishioners — can put our heads together and devise a strategy that will persuade the authorities to take action to free not only Juanita, but others in her situation."

"You are not a secret agent, Padre. That's not your training. And you cannot know her situation with any precision without first taking off your shoes and putting hers on for a few days. You're in the wrong vocation for undercover work, not to mention the wrong gender. Nevertheless, I'll endorse this little ... um ... *reconnaissance*, under the condition that you tread very carefully and get back to San Agustín Etla in one piece. The rest of your flock needs tending on Christmas Eve."

"Thank you, Excellency."

"*Via con Dios, Padre.*"

He felt a light touch on his arm and opened his eyes to see a smiling flight attendant bent over him.

"Can I bring you another glass of wine, Father?"

"No, thank you. I'd better remain clear headed. I have some thinking to do. How long to Tijuana?"

She glanced at her phone "We've been in the air for 45 minutes. About another three hours 15 minutes."

He tried to visualize his encounter with Juanita. According to Bishop Diego, Sister Antonina Magdalena had met with Juanita at a place called the Hong Kong Gentlemen's Club. Would they even let him in there? And if so, would he be allowed to see her? A clerical collar would be out of the question. One option, of course, would be to wear mufti and pose as a looker during the floorshow. But would he be plausible as a john? He was probably older than the average whore chaser, and what about his soft, pious appearance, his delicate hands with the closely manicured fingernails and mannerisms? There was no time to grow a stubbly beard, impossible to develop calluses overnight.

Sister Antonina had evidently been able to walk into the club and meet with the prostitutes on a regular basis. The management probably saw her as harmless, but good for the girls' morale and welfare. Would they permit him to go in with her?

He skated through some other scenarios in his mind. Did Juanita ever get out of the club? Would a chance encounter on the street work? But with the *halcones* and snitches, probably not.

Could he ask the *policía municipal* to help him get a meeting? Again, probably not. Given what he knew about corruption and the power and reach of the gangs and cartels, many of the police would be complicit in the business.

What about the local priests? There was a Catholic parish in the Zona Norte, *La Iglesia Inmaculada Concepción.* Surely the local padres would know, and perhaps even minister to some of the local pimps and *pandilleros.* Could they exert some influence for him to meet with Juanita?

These thoughts tumbled over and over in his mind while he racked his brain for other possibilities until an electronic chime and an announcement let him know that they would land in Tijuana shortly. Sister Antonina Magdalena would meet him at the airport. He'd ask about the only seemingly viable option that had occurred to him — to accompany her on her visit to the club.

***

By six a.m., Padre Sebastian had finished a vigorous 45-minute workout in the fitness center of the Hyatt Place Tijuana Hotel. By 7:30, he had showered, dressed in casual attire, and breakfasted. Still he had two hours before Sister Antonina would pick him up.

He had been told that the Golf Club Campestre de Tijuana had the best café latte in the district, so despite the pollution, he stepped out onto Agua Caliente Boulevard. Even in this upscale neighborhood, many of the men he passed along the sidewalk looked shifty and coarse. He crossed the boulevard and walked on the south side, flanked by glitzy high-rise condominiums. High-end cars, their occupants well dressed, frequently came and went from this line of buildings.

On some of the narrow laneways and alleys between the buildings he saw many homeless people, including a family of three, living rough beneath cardboard lean-tos, their meager possessions piled into grocery carts. His heart lurched at the sight of a young mother huddled beneath a serape nursing an infant, her Mestizo origins betrayed by her dark skin and stringy black hair.

He stopped to speak with her and learned her name— Akna, a Mayan name, she said. She and her baby boy lived from moment to moment. At night they slept on the golf course, under the trees. A security guard let them in through a gate by the clubhouse.

"I'm a priest. When was the last time you ate?"

"Yesterday."

"Let me help you for today." He offered her a hundred-peso bill. I'm busy this morning, but if I come back later today, will I find you here?"

"I don't know. I don't know what will happen 30 minutes from now."

"I'll be back, Akna. God bless you." He touched her lightly on the shoulder then turned back onto the boulevard.

He arrived at the entrance to the clubhouse of the Golf Club Camprestre ten minutes later, still thinking about Akna. In his peripheral vision, he caught several pickup trucks heading north. Four or five tough-looking men in Kevlar vests rode in the back of each truck, brandishing assault rifles. Wondering whose side in the narco wars those *hombres* were on, he walked into the lobby of the club.

More of an atrium than a lobby, huge floor-to-ceiling windows overlooked several fairways and greens. The luxurious leather club chairs and love seats looked small by comparison. From a seat behind a reception table, a blue-suited man in his 30s greeted him and directed him to the terrace.

Seated on the veranda, he had a 270-degree view of the golf course, the Olympic-sized swimming pool and several red clay tennis courts. The hues of green, blue, and red contrasted sharply with the concrete and stucco buildings beyond the limits of the golf course. He noted the time. Eight-twenty. His walk had taken longer than he planned. He placed a quick call to Sister Antonina, and asked her to pick him up at the golf course instead of the hotel. Then he sipped his latte and sat back.

Even though Mexico had one of the largest economies in Latin America, more than half of its population lived in poverty. Regardless of all the rhetoric to the effect that things had never been better for Mexico and Mexicans, the country had virtually no middle class, stratified instead into the rich and the poor. Drug trafficking, people trafficking, violence, organized crime, and corruption had all increased the numbers of people displaced from their homes and their businesses. The old cliché that the rich get richer and the poor get poorer certainly couldn't have been more accurate. What chance did Akna and her street-dwelling neighbors have?

Tijuana, one of Mexico's largest cities, had the advantage of being part of the San Diego megalopolis, an economic powerhouse and a font of progressive social thought and cultural dynamism. Yet here, as in other cities of the republic, narco warfare, criminal enterprise, and government corruption drove violence, poverty, and fear. And one of his parishioners, a young woman from a simple Oaxacan village was now caught up in this dichotomy. He had intended his morning walk to feed his soul. Instead, he found himself deeply melancholic.

***

In the company of Sister Antonina, Father Sebastian walked through the doorway of the Hong Kong Gentlemen's Club at noon. He handed the smirking security guard a US $20 bill in passing.

Inside, the lighting was subdued. A solitary performer, wearing only a G-string, gyrated at the front of the low dais, her back to the few people in the room. Too early in the day for musical accompaniment, her routine consisted mostly of her bending forward at the waist, exposing the full round globes of her buttocks as she swivelled her pelvis. Three approving patrons, two Caucasian and a Mexican, sat at a corner table ogling her and drinking beer.

Padre Sebastian turned away to avoid gawking, but her dangling, swaying breasts, bare except for sequinned pasties covering her nipples, drew his gaze back. He turned crimson and glanced at Sister Antonina, who paid no attention to the spectacle. He cast his eyes around the rest of the room. Several dancers were indifferently eating a lunch of tortillas, along with wedges of some kind of meat pie, dripping red gravy. Near the garishly decorated Christmas tree on a back wall, two tough guys, bouncers or *padrotes* he reckoned, stood guard, their eyes darting about the showroom to take in the hookers, the customers, and now he and Antonina.

He looked more closely at the group of dancers to see if he could spot Juanita, but saw no one even faintly resembling her. Sister Antonina said, "Let's find a seat away from all the others. I'll ask one of the girls to go to Juanita's room and fetch her." They took a table near the front door.

Minutes later, when Juanita appeared in a doorway near the restrooms, he didn't recognize her. When Sister Antonina nudged him and said, "Here comes Juanita," his thick eyebrows arched upward in surprise. This couldn't be her. My God she looked skinny. Black eyeliner coated her lower lids and her eyelashes. Smudges of blue lay on her upper lids. With glossy red lips and huge hoops in her ears, she looked every bit a *puta*. It was her, though. Even her luxuriant chestnut-colored hair was gone, now frizzy and tinted orange. Shock and disbelief gave way to acceptance as she approached the table, where she had obviously recognized Sister Antonina.

As she neared the table her eyes widened. Her mouth opened and she whispered hoarsely, "Padre Sebastian. Is it really you? How did you … what are you doing here?"

He reached out and took her hand into both of his. "It's okay Juanita. I'm here to see you. To tell you that your parents love you."

He watched her hang her head and saw the tears on her cheeks. "Do they know … that I am here? Do they know what I'm forced to do?"

He shook his head sadly and continued to squeeze her hand.

She sat. Her shoulders slumped in resignation. "I'm so ashamed, Padre. I wish you weren't seeing me like this. I wish you hadn't come." She withdrew her hand from his.

"You needn't be ashamed, Juanita. You have done nothing to anger God."

"Are you here to take me home?" she half whispered and half sobbed.

Sebastian glanced at the two goons leaning against the back wall, who now watched their table intensely.

"I'm sorry. That's not possible now. If I even tried, I think we'd both be shot. That's not how God wants it to end."

Her voice took on a strident tone. "What is it that God wants of me? He's not answering my prayers. If he is a loving God, why do I suffer? Why does anyone suffer?"

Sebastian glanced over at the dancer then down at his hands. "That's a deep question. The only way I can answer it is to say that God sent his son to live among men so that he could experience suffering. His suffering on the cross took away the burden of our sins and suffering. He was resurrected. I think if you have faith, God will relieve you of your suffering. But you don't have to die for that to happen. Would you like me to hear your confession while I'm here?"

"That may not be a good idea, Father," said Sister Antonina. "Those men standing by the wall are getting fidgety."

Sebastian cast a quick look their way. They had edged closer to the conversation and had a menacing look about them.

"Juanita. I should go now." He reached again for her hand and held it tightly. "I must be back in San Agustín by Christmas Eve, but I'll try to come again tomorrow."

She fell to her knees before him, leaned down and kissed the back of the hand that held hers. "Please pray for me, Padre. Pray for all of these girls. God isn't listening to me."

Reluctantly, he rose and the two goons stepped back toward the Christmas tree. He gave Juanita a quick hug, then started toward the door with Sister Antonina Magdalena.

On the sidewalk in front of the club, he wiped his eyes. "Sister, I'm going to walk."

"Do you want to come over to the TBAA branch office and talk about this visit?"

"Maybe tomorrow. Now I want to stop in at *La Iglesia Inmaculada Concepción* and talk to the parish priest."

Fifteen minutes later, he stopped in front of the beautiful twin bell towers of the church and looked up to admire the graceful architecture. The sun, high in the early afternoon sky, glinted off the copper roofs and created the effect of dancing flames. A flock of English sparrows sunned themselves in the branches of a tree almost as high as the towers.

He lowered his gaze toward the open doors of the church just in time to see the whiskey bottle before it smashed into the side of his face. Knocked sideways, he fell first to his knees, then toppled over onto the sidewalk. A heavy boot caught him in the ribs. He coiled into the fetal position just as another blow struck him in the back of the head. His vision blurred and vomit rose in his throat. He became aware of blood streaming down the side of his face.

A boot hit him again, this time squarely in the groin. In excruciating pain, he writhed on the pavement, begging his assailants to stop. Another boot connected in the small of his back. At the same time a fist smashed into his nose. He vomited and desperately tried to wriggle on his belly toward the open doors of the church, blood now pouring from his nose as well as down the side of his face. A blow to his solar plexus immobilized him.

As the darkness of unconsciousness descended, a voice, spectral and detached, snarled, "You look after the souls, Padre. Leave the whores to us."

Chapter Twenty-One

Christmas Eve, 2018
San Diego

The waves, mere ripples, lapped gently against the shore. The morning sun shone dimly through a slight fracture in the pewter sky. A light drizzle settled on Lien and Co Pham like fine mist as they walked north on the packed sand of the La Jolla Shores beach. Ahead of them, the famous Scripps Memorial Pier jutted a thousand feet out into the Pacific, its reinforced concrete structure providing a platform for a variety of experiments that yielded data on ocean conditions and plankton.

"Thanks for walking with me, Lien. I love it out here with the sea air, and the sound of the gulls. It nourishes my soul. My husband isn't interested in walking on the beach. He'd rather drink coffee with his men friends so they can talk about their anger with the Communists now running Vietnam."

"It's my pleasure. I'm happy to walk with you. Despite the clouds, the air is fresh and the temperature's perfect. It's so gloomy and wet in Seattle this time of year."

Co Pham touched Lien's arm. "We're very happy Paul has chosen you for his … *friend.* We hope someday he will marry a Vietnamese girl. Maybe you."

Lien had arrived in San Diego the day before, for a four-day visit. She'd fly back to Seattle on Thursday, two days after Christmas. She hadn't expected to be involved in such a weighty conversation, and was taken aback, she said, "Co Pham, your son is my friend. But I'm not looking for a husband. I may never marry. I'm too … tarnished. That's the word."

"But if Paul were to choose you, we'd approve. I know about your past and so does he. But it doesn't matter. It doesn't affect who you are in your soul."

"Little by little, I'm learning that. But I have a long way to go."

They reached the pier and rather than walk under it and continue north where the shoreline became rocky, Co Pham turned back toward the parking lot where they had left her car. "Okay. I don't mean to be pushy. Just know that the Pham family cares about you as a person. Not about a past that was forced upon you. We'll see you for Christmas dinner at our house tomorrow. Have Paul bring you a little early so you can help me again, if you want."

"Of course I'll help in the kitchen," Lien said. "It reminds me of home in Vietnam when we're preparing food for a family celebration."

After Thanksgiving, when she had found the resolve to tell Catherine and Pete that she wanted to return to San Diego for Christmas, the news had not gone down well with Pete — especially when she added that she'd like to spend the summer as a volunteer at TBAA.

"You're 21," he said. "Obviously you can make your own choices. But you're here in the US under our sponsorship and we feel responsible for you. I feel particularly responsible to your father. I doubt he'd be keen on your chasing back and forth to San Diego to see a young man he's never met."

"Grandfather, I'm not about to *elope* with Paul. And I don't want intimacy with him, with any man. He's just a good friend. As Catherine said before I went down for Thanksgiving, he's a good man. He's gentle and he's a Buddhist."

"That's right. I did say that," said Catherine.

"I'm grateful for all you've done, and continue to do, for me. I don't want to disappoint you in any way. And I won't. Trust me."

"I agree that Paul's a fine man," Pete said. "It's just that you're not experienced in this culture yet. Southern California can be fast paced and dangerous for a village girl from Vietnam."

Catherine cringed. "Pete, Lien's hardly a village girl anymore. She's come a long way since then. There's nothing naïve about her."

"You've known for a long time that I want to devote my life to combatting child trafficking," Lien interjected. "I'll be better qualified to do that when I graduate if I have a chance to work in the field while I'm still studying. San Diego is the nexus of trafficking from Latin America into the US. And TBAA is a leader in helping victims. This is a fabulous opportunity for me, and the fact that Paul and his family are there to support me is a bonus."

"You almost lost me at 'nexus,'" Pete said, his eyes crinkling in the corners. "But, I should know better than to argue with the two women I love most in the world. Go ahead … with my blessing. I'll explain it to your dad."

***

Christmas day was filled with warmth and family at the Pham's home, and another sumptuous meal. After dinner, Paul took Lien to Westfield Mall to look at Christmas display windows. Then, after dark, they drove through the affluent neighborhood of Rancho Pensaquitos to see the elaborate and beautiful Christmas lighting displays.

Lien said, "What a fabulous day. And what a beautiful meal your mom put together. I was boiled away."

Paul grinned, "I think you mean bowled away."

***

The next morning, as Paul drove Lien through light traffic toward the TBAA office, she asked him, "How did Maria get into this kind of work? Do you know?"

"She said she was born very near the TBAA office, in what used to be called Barrio Logan, a blighted neighborhood. She suffered abuse as a child, and because her mother didn't enrol her in school, the county child welfare people placed her with a foster family when she was eight. They'd found her a good family, who saw that all her needs were met and that she obtained a good education. That inspired her. By the time she went to university, she had no questions about what she wanted to do. She wanted to work for the betterment of kids whom fate had treated cruelly."

"That's exactly how I feel."

"Yes," Paul said, parking in front of the TBAA office. "I think you're both interested in social work for similar reasons. You both approach the work very much from your heart."

"Merry Christmas," Lien said to Maria when they entered, surprised to see her in the office. "Don't you ever rest? Christmas was just yesterday! In Vietnam, the most important holiday of the year lasts for six or seven days."

"Welcome back Lien. Hi Paul." Maria tilted back in her chair to greet them. "I'm afraid misery doesn't observe holidays. Two of my staff and I have worked for the past three days arranging shelter for two recently freed girls. We placed one in a drug rehabilitation program and one is in transitional housing, temporarily."

"But you're making a difference. I just hope I can contribute in some way over the next couple of summers."

"You can for sure. These problems won't go away by next summer."

Paul broke in then. "I brought Lien here because I wanted to familiarize her with the Juanita Montero case. Even though it's not ours yet, I want her to know about Juanita. I think she'll relate to her."

"By all means show her the file. Please excuse me, though, I have a meeting with SKIUS up in Oceanside."

Paul led Lien to his table and opened a file folder. "I've printed all the electronic traffic about Juanita." He showed her the photograph and leafed through the emails, explaining how Juanita was a first-year university student who had been trafficked through Tenancingo.

"What is TBAA doing to help her? And where's Tenancingo?"

"Tenancingo is a town in South Central Mexico, where entire families traffic girls into prostitution all over North America. The Department of Justice has identified it as the leading provider of female sex slaves to the United States.

"Our Tijuana branch office is keeping track of her. The traffickers will move her to San Diego soon. When that happens, SKIUS will get involved in trying to locate her. Maria wants me to be the liaison with them. If she's freed, then we immediately start advocating for her."

"I hate to think about what she must be going through."

"I agree. Our colleague in the Tijuana office told us that the parish priest from her hometown in Oaxaca flew up to Tijuana a few days ago to reassure her. Minutes after he met with her, he was beaten within inches of his life. Now he's lying in Tijuana General Hospital. Hopefully he'll recover, but he has a severe concussion and a ruptured spleen. These traffickers are animals, Lien. We can't take them on. That's up to the authorities. But we'll do all we can to help her, despite the risk."

"Yes. This is the work I want to do. More than ever. You're right — I can relate to Juanita. Please keep me posted about her." She turned her head and tried to blink back tears without Paul noticing.

Chapter Twenty-Two

January, 2019
San Diego

Border Patrol Agent Don McBride was in a sour mood. Nearing the end of his ten-hour shift on line watch, he ached from sitting in his long-in-the-tooth patrol vehicle, and beads of sweat wet his chest and back. Though only a few minutes past nine in the morning, the temperature had already risen to well over 80 degrees. The bulky Kevlar vest he wore over his rough-duty uniform added to his discomfort.

The air conditioning in the Jeep Cherokee had quit working a month before but had not yet been repaired. "Waiting for parts," was the excuse. Normally, his vehicle would have gone to the GSA auction lot two years ago, but tight budgets had forestalled its replacement. Another 45 minutes and he could turn over the keys at the Chula Vista station and head for home, where Christina would have a late breakfast ready for him. The fact that the kids would have already left for school gave him a lift. He'd have some time alone with her.

Ten years into his career, Don kept to himself on the job, even when on interdiction patrols or manning checkpoints with fellow agents. He got along well with his colleagues, but as one of only a handful of non-Hispanics in the San Diego sector, he'd always felt a little weird. He had a working knowledge of Spanish and could use it on the job, but he missed out on much of the camaraderie with the team members. He didn't quite get the nuances of their repartee and badinage. Like an interloper. That's the word he'd been trying to think of.

His duty required him to be both a law enforcement officer and a humanitarian. Nine-tenths of the people he interdicted were simple, honest, religious, family-oriented folks, merely trying to escape appalling economic and social conditions in their home countries. Who could blame them for fleeing from oppression and violence to seek a better life in America? He was obligated to detain them and transport them to centers where they would await asylum hearings, most often in overcrowded, inhospitable facilities. He didn't enjoy taking them into custody. Nor did he like seeing the confusion, unhappiness, fear, and trepidation all rolled into one on their faces. Thirsty, hungry children with raw terror in their eyes clung to their parents. On the other hand, he had no compunction whatsoever about taking down the skinheads, smugglers, and traffickers who made their livelihood off the misery of others.

Recently, a journalist on a ride-along had asked him what would make the job easier. "I'm not much into politics," he'd said. "I leave that to the politicians, but I have to say I don't think a wall is the answer. If we have a wall 100 feet high, the migrants will get a hold of a 101-foot ladder. As it is now, the drug and human traffickers just tunnel under the border. No sir, the real answer lies in taking down the big cartels. Wipe them from the face of the Earth. They're the bodies responsible for the flow of drugs and trafficked human beings into our country. They're the bodies responsible for creating the strife that drives people to seek asylum in the US. They're the bodies responsible for the rampant corruption in Latin American countries."

Now he swiped at his forehead with a golf towel he carried in the vehicle and hoisted his armored vest by the shoulder straps in an attempt to get some air under it. He had just lifted the bottom of the vest and was giving it a shake when a radio call ordered him to drive to the Importaciones de Jesus warehouse. He was to meet a Ramon de Jesus and his nephew Roberto de Jesus to check out a possible tunnel.

He keyed his microphone, "Will proceed. Ten-Thirteen." So much for going off-shift in 45 minutes.

At the import-export warehouse, he took a statement from the nephew, Roberto, who had seen the couple running across Kern Street. He asked both Roberto and Ramon a few questions and took pictures of the tunnel and the fence behind it with his phone. He'd have to stick around for a couple hours yet, while he waited for Homeland Security Investigations to arrive and check out the tunnel. Once they'd gathered their evidence, they'd want to fill it in with concrete and he'd have to wait around for that to happen too. Was $44,913 a year really worth all this hassle? He should've finished his degree at SDSU and gone into banking.

The guys who dug this tunnel had been in a hurry. Usually they'd tunnel in until they cut into one of the city's wide storm sewers. Then they'd crawl in the sewer and wade to the manhole cover of their choice, using the built-in metal stairs to climb up and out. With hundreds to choose from they could emerge just about anywhere they pleased. In this case, they'd simply risen out of the ground just inside the border.

McBride looked up at the wall of the warehouse and noted three surveillance cameras. "Can we have a look at your surveillance videos while we're waiting for the investigators?" he asked Ramon. He knew an MQ-9 Predator surveillance drone worked the border from San Ysidro to Tecate. But no one had alerted him to any sightings, so it must have been somewhere else when this crossing occurred.

Don and the two de Jesus men sat in the warehouse office scrolling through the videos. After ten boring minutes of benign footage of the grounds and building walls, Roberto pointed. "There. There they are." Two shadowy black and white figures emerged from the tunnel entrance and ran between the buildings toward Kern Street.

"Can you play that back to where they emerge from the tunnel and zoom in on their faces?" Don asked.

Roberto manipulated the mouse to scroll in reverse then homed in on the two people climbing out of the tunnel.

Don studied the images, looking closely at their posture, facial expressions, body language, and movements. The young woman's face looked familiar, possibly someone he'd learned of during a morning muster at the station sometime in the past few weeks. "I'd say what we have here is either a trafficking situation or a person-smuggling situation. I'd bet money the male is trafficking the female against her will. You can read it all over her face. Mr. Ramon, you'll need to loan this footage to the HSI team when they arrive. Can you put it on a thumb drive for me?"

"I'll do it for you, Agent," said Roberto, eager to please. He'd known from the look on the girl's face when he had almost hit them with his truck that something was up.

Chapter Twenty-Three

January, 2019

Suite 3200, Edward J. Schwartz Federal Office Building, San Diego

Fred Benson, the senior agent in charge of the San Diego Field Office of Homeland Security Investigations, entered the windowless room. It took a few seconds for his eyes to adjust to the dim lighting and focus in on the console of computer screens. "We get an ID on that asshole from the tunnel near the de Jesus warehouse yet?"

"Yes sir," said one of the two agents seated before the console. "Facial rec software just positively identified him as none other than our old friend, Geraldo Rojas."

"So that scumbag's back to our turf again, huh? As I recall he was last seen in Guanajuato, seducing co-eds at the University."

One of the agents laughed. "Co-eds? Boss you're dating yourself. Does anyone besides you still say that?" Then getting serious, he added, "But yeah, I've got his page up right here. I'm about to update the 'Last known Location' line."

Benson stepped behind him and looked at the display screen, a page from the HSI Most Wanted web file. At the upper left, a full-color, head and shoulder picture of Geraldo Rojas appeared to have been taken from a driver's license. Immediately beneath the picture, his name: **Rojas, Geraldo Eduardo**.

There were only two other headers on the page:

Wanted For: Human Sexual Trafficking.

Last Known Location: Guanajuato, state of Guanajuato, Mexico.

The agent deleted the location description and typed in: San Diego County, California and/or Tijuana, Mexico.

Benson nodded his approval and said, "Drill down a level. Let's refresh ourselves on this turd."

The agent hit the button at the bottom of the screen labeled: **Read More**

A new page appeared, again with the picture of Rojas in the upper left corner followed by headers for his Age, Date of Birth, Place of Birth, Nationality, and Gender.

Benson quickly scanned the Summary, which read:

SAN DIEGO — On May 21, 2015, US Immigration and Customs Enforcement's (ICE) Homeland Security Investigations (HSI) and the FBI conducted search and arrest warrants for several individuals suspected of human trafficking for the purpose of sexual exploitation, following leads provided by the San Diego County Sheriff Department.

Since 2012, several members of the Rojas family, all from Tenancingo, state of Tlaxcala, Mexico, have conspired and brought multiple women into the United States from Mexico, Guatemala, and El Salvador all for the purpose of forcing them to engage in prostitution.

During the course of the investigation, two women were rescued and Rodrigo Rojas, a cousin of Geraldo Rojas, was arrested, convicted, and sentenced to 16 years in prison. Geraldo Rojas eluded capture and was believed to have returned to Tenancingo, where he continues to work in the family business of human trafficking. He remains a fugitive from justice in the United States. His younger brother, Miguel Rojas, also a trafficker was recently killed by the Mexican Army.

"Okay," said Benson. "Get the update on the wire. I want this to go to every law enforcement agency and anti-trafficking NGO in Southern California. Also pass it through our social media network portal. Get it out there on Facebook, YouTube, Twitter, Instagram, Linkedin, the works."

When the two agents acknowledged his instructions, he asked, "Now, what do we have on the victim that he dragged out of that tunnel?"

"Sir, our vic is the girl in that TBAA dispatch a couple of weeks ago, Juanita Montero from Oaxaca, a student at Guanajuato University."

"Shit." He turned to another agent who had followed him into the room. "Smitty get a press release out to the print, digital, and broadcast media. I want to make a public appeal for any information that might lead us to finding this girl, as well as the perp. Be certain to include the number for the HSI tip line and the national trafficking hotline in the release."

"Right away, sir."

Chapter Twenty-Four

January, 2019
San Agustín Etla, Oaxaca

Bishop Diego sat in one of the two chairs beneath the plaster crucifix in the small parish office. Across from him and behind the desk, his face still bearing bruises and contusions, Padre Sebastian perched awkwardly on the desk chair, obviously still in pain. He had spent a total of three weeks in the Tijuana hospital. Doctors had repaired his spleen and carefully monitored his cerebral function to ensure that the swelling in his brain receded. Fortunately, cranial surgery to reduce the pressure had not been necessary.

"Your parishioners will be happy to see you back," Bishop Diego said, "Father Julio did a commendable job in your absence, but your flock was concerned about you. Are you sure you're up to celebrating the mass this Sunday?"

"The sooner I'm back in the pulpit, Excellency, the better. What were my parishioners told about my … uh … injuries?"

"The truth, Sebastian. I drove up here myself to meet with them and explain what had happened to you and where. I told them you were beaten by traffickers for attempting to take the Lord's word to sex slaves in Tijuana."

"My God. What about the Monteros. Were they in the meeting? Do they know I saw Juanita?"

"They were not in the meeting. But they heard about it and came to see me here the next morning, just before I left to drive back to Oaxaca city. They prodded and probed. And I couldn't lie to them. I told them the truth. They were both distraught, knowing what Juanita's enduring, but they're relieved that she's alive and that you'd seen her." He reached into the folds of his clothing and pulled out a pack of Marlboros.

Sebastian glanced up at the plaster crucifix, taking note of the pained, but self-resigned facial expression of Jesus, the blood dripping across the palms of his hands and trickling from the wound in his torso. "*Madre de Dios,* the poor souls. I'll go out to their farm and console them."

Bishop Diego tapped out one of the cigarettes and placed it between his lips. His eyes swept over the surface of the desk. "Do you have an ashtray here somewhere?" But before Sebastian could answer, he lit the cigarette, took a deep drag and exhaled a billow of smoke, which spread across the small office in its rise toward the ceiling. "There's more you should know, Padre. My friend Maria Gutierrez, of TBAA in San Diego, tells me that Juanita's no longer in the Gentlemen's Club in Tijuana. Sister Antonina Magdalena has been to the club every other day for two weeks and there's no sign of her. They suspect she's already been smuggled into the United States."

"Oh no." Sebastian reached into a drawer, removed a small glass ashtray and slid it across the desk. "But is your friend's organization looking for her?"

"Yes. As are several other NGOs, and a number of law enforcement agencies in Southern California. They all have copies of the photo you provided. You need to know this too: the Monteros want to travel to Tijuana to find their daughter."

"But do they know that she's probably already left TJ?"

"I've told them. But they insist. They want to go anyway. They want to plaster posters of her all over Tijuana and San Diego. Even though I've told them they can't legally enter the United States without a visa, they don't really understand that. They seem to think that we — the Catholic church — can somehow get them across the border."

"Can we?"

"No Padre. It'd be difficult even for you and I to obtain visas to attend a Catholic conference in the US. It would require mountains of paperwork and could take weeks to be approved, if it ever would be."

"Hmm. I know these people, Excellency. They've been my parishioners for over five years. Making a trip to Tijuana, fruitless though it may be, would give them hope. They'd feel actively engaged in finding their daughter. They'd see it as their duty."

Bishop Diego took another long drag. After a pursed-lip exhalation, he said, "The members of this town are good people and compassionate Christians. They've taken up a collection to fund the Montero's travel to Tijuana. The diocese is prepared to augment those funds and I've already arranged for Sister Antonina

Magdelena to meet them and shepherd them around while they're in TJ. They leave by bus tomorrow morning."

Sebastian rubbed his chin stubble. He raised his eyes to the crucifix. "Bishop, I'd like to accompany them."

"Out of the question."

"Then at the very least, I'll drive out to their farm this evening and pray with them."

"I'd expect no less of you, Padre."

***

Padre Sebastian arrived at the Montero farm to find Pablo and Sofia in their living room piling a few meager possessions into an ancient piece of American Tourister luggage. Pablo was breathing rapidly. He was sweating and his hands were trembling. Carlos was saying, "Papa, maybe you shouldn't be going. All this worry is making you sick. I can go with Mama."

"No, no. I'll be fine." He looked absent-mindedly at a pair of blue socks clasped in his shaking hands. "The doctor gave me something to settle me down. I'll be okay. Besides, we need you to keep the farm going. The goats must be fed and the corn must be tended to." He stuffed the socks into a corner of the suitcase.

"*Además* Carlos, you're only 15," added Sofia. This business calls for adults."

"Why am I man enough to run the farm, but inadequate to protect my mother from danger on a trip to a rough place?"

"Please son. This situation is hard enough on all of us without arguing. You'll contribute to getting Juanita back by running the farm while we're away. And that does take a big strong man."

Pablo's face suddenly took on a pallor. He groped his way to the ragged upholstered easy chair and sat heavily into it. He pulled a white handkerchief from the pocket of his jeans and mopped his face.

"Father, can't you see, you're sick? Please stay here and let the villagers take care of you. Let me go with Mama."

"Your mother and I must go. And you must stay here. That's all there is to it. Padre, will you pray with us?"

"*Claro que si.* All powerful and merciful God, at every moment and in every place you are near to those who serve you; keep our brother and sister in your fatherly care, so that they will find you with them on their journey. Keep them safe. And, Father, bless not only Pablo and Sofia, but look after Carlos as well."

***

Sister Antonina Magdalena met Pablo and Sofia at the bus station in Tijuana and escorted them into the back seat of an Uber. From the front, she said, "I'll get you checked into a hotel then take you to the TBAA office here in town. They'll give you all the facts as we know them about Juanita."

Apart from having passed through Guadalajara during the hours of darkness on their long bus ride, this was the largest city Pablo and Sofia had ever seen. Their heads swiveled back and forth as they took in the sights, sounds, and general chaos of Mexico's sixth largest city. Traffic swirled by in all directions, and the presence of heavily armed soldiers and policemen in muscular trucks and jeeps made a sobering spectacle.

Although they didn't pass directly through the Zona Norte and its notorious red light district, they gaped at streetwalkers who displayed their bulges and curves beneath raised skirts and plunging necklines. A shot of pain pierced Pablo's abdomen as he tried to repress thoughts of Juanita dressed like that. He looked away, down into his lap, and clutched the stack of posters Padre Sebastian had printed for them on the church's ancient photocopier.

The bold header screamed **Ayudanos** in letters two inches tall. Beneath that, a color head and shoulder photograph of Juanita showed her luxuriant hair cascading over one shoulder, her hazel eyes dancing with green and gold tones in the irises.

Beneath the photo, the words *Desaparecido ya que Septiembre, 2018* stated the length of time she had been missing, followed by contact information for *La Parroquia de San Agustín Etla.*

So innocent. So full of life and light. His hands trembled on the posters; he refused to accept that his daughter could in any way resemble the street hookers he had just seen.

The vehicle pulled up to TBAA's office in the back of the Hospital de Carmen. Pablo and Sofia scanned numerous posters similar to theirs, taped to utility poles and plastered on the stucco walls of several buildings. To their horror, some of the posters also depicted crude crosses jutting from the desert sands, female names written on or under them. Inside, a photo in the hall showed a policeman examining a human femur and a few scraps of lingerie, apparently found in the desert. Behind him, a middle-aged peasant couple stood holding each other, the woman weeping.

As she held the door to the office open for them, Sister Antonina Magdalena said, "*Señor y Señora Montero*, I think Padre Sebastian already told you this, and I'm sorry to say it, but we think, Juanita has been smuggled into the United States."

Pablo nodded slightly. Sofia swiped a handkerchief along the corner of her eye.

"But that could be good news," Alejandra Gomez said, approaching them. "Law enforcement is much more … um … efficient in the US than it is here. The police at many levels know of Juanita and have her photo. Now, come in please. I want you to meet two people who've come over the border from San Diego today, to speak with you about Juanita."

Apprehensively, Pablo and Sofia entered the spartan office, where two men rose to greet them, a Caucasian in his fifties and a much younger Asian man.

Sister Antonina Magdalena introduced Roger Upton and Paul Pham, explaining in Spanish that they came from non-profit groups and were here to help. "Mr. Upton would like to ask you some questions about Juanita that he thinks may help in the search for her."

Pablo looked uncertain. "They're not from the police?"

"Mr. Pham works with us at TBAA on the other side of the border and Mr. Upton is a private investigator." She explained the role of an investigator.

Still uncertain, but willing to speak with them, Pablo asked, "Can we go into the United States with our posters? Can these men help us to look for our daughter?"

Sister Antonina Magdalena sighed. "Tomorrow, we'll take you to the American Consul General here in Tijuana. We'll help you apply for B visas to visit the United States. But even with documentation in order, it takes up to 50 days to have an interview with the immigration officials. So we can start the process, but let's hope Juanita's found and returned to us well before you'd be interviewed."

"Can these men take some of our posters to the other side of the border and put them up in San Diego?"

Alejandra translated the question.

"Mr. Montero, we can do that," Roger said, "but we can also do better. We'll get that poster into the social media, um … that means on computer networks, and spread it all over Southern California. Now, if I might, I'll ask you some questions, starting with a difficult one. Please don't be offended. Just understand that it's necessary for us to know this, if we're to help." He paused while Sister Antonina translated, then asked, "Is there any possibility that Juanita ran away? Or that she went off with her boyfriend of her own free will?"

Pablo and Sofia responded with bewilderment and hurt expressions. But when the nun explained why the question mattered, they answered emphatically, "No." They explained the visit from Sergeant Castro-Padilla and the phone call from the prostitute in Puebla.

Prompted by a list he had placed on the table top, Roger asked a series of questions. Did Juanita have a cell phone? Yes. Did they know the phone number? No. Did they know her tastes in music? Books? What did she like to do in her leisure time? Who were her closest friends? Any peculiar habits or patterns of behavior? How did she like to dress? What foods did she like? Dislike? Did she drink alcohol?

Finally, "Where can we reach you here in Tijuana?"

Sister Antonina Magdalena answered for them. "Through our office, here."

"Or," added Alejandra, "at the Hotel Aqua Rio, where they're staying."

"And how about if you go home to ... um," he glanced at his notes in the case file. "San Agustín?"

Sister Antonina Magdalena translated their indignant response. "They say they will not go home without their daughter."

The translation of every question and every answer, frequently followed up with further questions for clarification, made the process awkward and tedious for everyone. They took frequent bathroom and water breaks. After an hour and 30 minutes with Roger Upton asking questions and Paul Pham recording the translations on his iPhone, along with the occasional note, both Americans agreed that they had some useful data.

"With your permission, Mr. and Mrs. Montero, our organization will try to find Juanita. We can probably search more intensively than the police."

"Oh, *si por favor,*" they said in unison.

"I'll just need you to sign these." He produced bilingual copies of an application for services and a limited power of attorney. "The application gives us permission to search for your daughter, and the POA allows us to coordinate with police and government agencies on your behalf."

They hastily signed the documents.

"Just one final thing. I want to show you a still picture from a videotape made several weeks ago." Roger opened an iPad and showed them a facial close up of the girl emerging from the tunnel near the warehouse. "Is this your —"

Before he could finish, both Pablo and Sofia were on their feet. *"Si, si, si. Es nuestra hija. Ella es nuestra bebé."*

Roger closed the iPad. *"Señor* and *señora,* we'll find her."

***

The next morning, Roger flew to Guanajuato, where he interviewed a dean, and two of Juanita's university professors. Then he went to the home where Juanita had roomed. He asked the landlady if he could see her room, but a new tenant already occupied it.

"Were any of her possessions left in the room when she was … uh … when she disappeared?"

"They're in a box in the basement. Come, I'll show you."

Roger spent 30 minutes sifting through items of clothing, shoes, school papers, stationery, and a miscellany of small insignificant items. At last he found a phone bill, which gave him her cell number. Later, in California, he would ask a friend in the San Diego Sheriff's Department to officially request data from the Mexican telecom company, related to when and where the phone was last used.

He had gained little actionable information on the trip to Guanajuato. Regardless, he now had a much better sense of Juanita Montero.

Chapter Twenty-Five

January, 2019
Seattle

Recognizing the handsome face in the caller ID window of her phone, Lien answered before the ring tone could kick in. "Paul, I'm glad you called. I'm ready for a break. I've been studying for two hours." She shoved the textbook on cultural diversity and social justice to the side, and leaned her iPhone against the computer so she could see Paul's face as they spoke. "So, what's up?"

"I went across the border today, with Roger Upton, from SKIUS. We interviewed Juanita Montero's parents. They've come to Tijuana. It was exciting. I feel like I'm actually engaged in important human rights work."

"Take it easy. You're breathless already. You might have a scissor ... no, a seizure. You mean you actually went into Tijuana? What's it like?"

"Big, bustling, dirty in places, clean in others. In the central zone, where the TBAA office is, it's touristy, boozy, and colorful. Seems like everyone is in a hurry to get somewhere, except the hookers, who just stand around trying to look tempting." He stopped. "Oops, sorry to bring that up."

"It's okay Paul. I know the truth of that. But what was your role? What did *you* do there? Did you actually interview the parents?"

"No. This was a SKIUS thing. They know that Juanita has been smuggled into San Diego County so they're gearing up to try and find her. Roger Upton did the interviewing. I just went along as the liaison from TBAA. I recorded the interview and took a few notes. But it feels like I'm really in on the action, if you know what I mean. It feels good."

"What are Juanita's parents like?"

"I think they're poor and not well educated. But they're good people. I could tell they love their daughter deeply. They're desperate to find her."

"I'm excited for you. I hope I can be of some help in all this, come next summer."

"I can't wait. Four and a half months, and you should be here again."

Chapter Twenty-Six

February, 2019
San Diego

From her position near the doorway of a small, single-story pawnshop, Juanita watched three sailors swagger drunkenly toward her along the broken sidewalk on the east side of National City Boulevard. *Pendejos. Animales,* she thought.

Overhead, a sign read: Barrio Logan, Jewelry & Loans. Under the lettering, the ubiquitous symbol of the trade — three balls. At nearly 11 p.m., the shop was closed, but its neon glow made Juanita conspicuous in her leather miniskirt and stiletto heels.

Her *padrote*, Frank, stood in the shadows across the street. He gave her a barely discernible shake of his head, then tilted it to the left to point out a police cruiser sitting at the curb, its lights out, engine idling.

"Hey Sweetie, how 'bout some pussy?" One of the sailors approached her, encouraged by his peers.

"Not tonight. Closed for business." She turned abruptly to walk southward, away from the police.

She'd been on the circuit for 16 days now, and she knew the rules. Frank watched her constantly, or one or two of his assistants, or Tillie, an older, coarsened prostitute in Frank's coterie. At least 30 "Franks" worked in San Diego County, all of whom reported to Geraldo and the Tenancingo Ring. Seeking help from the police was impossible, given the scrutiny and control to which Juanita was subjected.

The three sailors tagged along behind her, fresh into Naval Base San Diego from a 66-day deployment on board the USS Pinckney. Their lewd remarks followed her as they proceeded, their courage bolstered and reinforced by a combination of alcohol and camaraderie.

"Hey darlin'. C'mon. We're fresh off the ship and we got big fat wallets."

"Yeah. Besides it's your patriotic duty to support us. Just give us some sugar."

Juanita walked another ten minutes before she turned on East Seventh Street. She walked a hundred yards farther and stopped in front of a shabby, stucco bungalow surrounded by red gravel. Now Arnie, one of Frank's goons, watched her from a Mustang GT parked at the curb. She crossed herself inconspicuously and turned to face the seamen. "Okay," she said in heavily accented English. "This is my house. You come in one at a time. Fifty dollars each."

"Blow job?" asked one of the gobs.

"No," she said, emphatically. Then she led the first of the sailors into the little house. Moans and grunts emanated from two of the three bedrooms. She opened the door to the third, just off the small kitchen.

***

At ten o'clock the next morning, Tillie shook Juanita awake, "C'mon honey. Get your white ass outta that bed. We're goin' to the mall to get your hair and nails done."

Juanita opened her eyes and sat up. "We already did that two weeks ago."

"Don't matter, girl. We're doin' it again today. Gets you more respek from the johns. Makes us more dough. Know what I mean?" She ripped the soiled top sheet from the bed, grabbed Juanita's wrist and pulled her up. "You just got time to say those prayers of yours 'fore we grab the 10:20 bus to Coronado."

Reluctantly, Juanita went into the tiny bathroom. She used the toilet and threw some water on her face, then recoiled at her own image in the mirror. Her face looked puffy, with light smudges of makeup smeared around her eyes. Her orange-tinted hair looked frizzy and disgusting. Hastily she said a prayer, though it did little good to pray these days. Nobody had been listening for the past four months.

Not only were her features hardening, but so was her attitude. She was no longer the defeated, submissive little wuss of two months ago. With rescue unlikely and God not helping her, she'd have to help herself.

In her window seat on the bus, with Tillie at her shoulder, she emerged from her sullenness to ask, "Tillie, how long you been in the life."

"Since I been 'bout 13, honey. I started in N'orleans, then to Las Vegas. I been here in San Diego for 'bout three years."

"Where's your home and family?"

"Ain't really got no family, Honey. I been all on my own since I was 'bout ten, know what I mean?"

Juanita nodded and turned to stare out at San Diego Bay as the bus glided across the Coronado Bridge. Although she wasn't sure about God any more, she did wish she could still talk with Sister Antonina Magdalena. At least at the Hong Kong Gentlemen's Club she'd had someone to confide in, someone to give her hope, however briefly. But she hadn't lost hope. Even on her own, with her faith waning, what would she have if she didn't have hope? And resolve. To get out of this life, she'd need unwavering determination. She'd have to make her own opportunity.

She turned back to Tillie. "Why are you still doing this? You ever try to get out?"

"Oh, I used to say all the time, I'm gonna make myself better and get a more respekful job. Maybe a husband. But I ain't gonna say that no more. This is my lot. I reckon I'll do this until the men don't come on to me no more. Then I don't know what. Maybe I'll get into the management end."

"Did you ever get sick? From sex partners I mean?"

"Oh, I've had the critchy crotch sometimes, but never no gonorrhea or nothing, know what I mean?"

Juanita took a deep breath. "Tillie, how can I make a phone call to Oaxaca? Can I get my hands on a cell from …"

Tillie grabbed Juanita's arm to cut her off. "Don' even think like that, bitch. They'll beat the shit out of you. Maybe even kill you if you try."

Juanita clenched her fists at her side and opened her mouth to respond.

"Shut up. Here we are. This's our stop."

***

The nail technician applied the last few brush strokes to Juanita's fingernails, then looked up. "Hold your hands still till those nails dry."

Juanita glanced toward Tillie. Although probably functionally illiterate, Tillie was leafing through a *People* magazine. Sotto voce, Juanita spoke to the tech. "You're Vietnamese, right? Are you Catholic?"

"No. I'm a Buddhist, but here in San Diego I attend a Protestant church on the base with my husband. He's an American. In the Navy."

"You live on the air base here in Coronado?"

"No. We have family housing across the bay at the San Diego Base."

"I live near the base right now. Do you know where is the closest Catholic Church?"

"St Mary's. It's on Seventh Street in National City."

Juanita's eyes widened. The bungalow was on Seventh Street too, so the parish couldn't be too far away. Maybe just a few blocks.

"Now your nails dry enough. You go to Maria's chair over there. She do your hair."

But Juanita barely heard the instructions as her mind raced. The nearby church could be her way of getting a message to Oaxaca.

Chapter Twenty-Seven

The fourth Saturday of February, 2019
San Diego

Juanita crossed National City Boulevard in the middle of the block. It was just past midnight and she'd already turned five tricks — four sailors from the USS Lake Erie and one marine gate sentry. She approached Frank and Arnie, who were huddled in a conference of some kind in the doorway of Star Automotive, an independently owned repair shop.

"Frank, I need to talk to you."

"Alright. Gun it, like shit through a goose. I don't have time for chit chat and neither do you. You need to be hustling."

"What I need is to go to mass tomorrow morning. I haven't been in weeks."

"Is your god gonna make you a better lay?"

"Please, Frank. I just need to pray. Even in Tenancingo, Geraldo let me go to mass with his sister."

"I really don't give a shit, as long as it don't interfere with work. What time's mass?"

"Eight-thirty."

"Holy shit, chica. That early? But it's okay with me as long as either Arnie or Tillie goes with you."

"Not me," said Arnie. "Last time I was in a church a nun washed my mouth out with soap."

"You'll have to persuade Tillie to go with you," Frank said. "Now, get back over there."

***

Tillie flipped her cigarette butt onto the sidewalk as they approached St. Mary's entry door beneath a terracotta-tiled eave. "Never been in no Catholic church before," Tillie wheezed. She chomped vigorously on a wad of pink gum. "It's too friggin' early to be up. Know what I mean? I ain't singin' or nothing like that."

"You don't have to sing. You just sit there. And you stand when everyone else stands, and you sit when everyone sits and you kneel when people kneel. You don't have to go up to the altar and take communion when everyone else does."

"Then you ain't going up either. I'm supposed to keep you by my side." Her voice rose shrilly, "How'm I supposed to kneel down in this tight red dress? My hoo hoo will hang out the back side."

"Don't worry. There's a little kneeling board that keeps you up off the floor. You're on your knees with your feet out behind you. I don't think your dress will rise."

As they entered, Juanita dipped her fingers in the font and crossed herself with the holy water. Tillie stood by her side and gawked around at the religious symbols and furnishings in the sanctuary, her jaw working furiously on the chewing gum.

Once in the nave, they found two vacant seats in a pew near the rear. Juanita, acutely aware of the turned heads and stares they were getting, stared piously at the large wall-hanging crucifix in the apse, her hands folded reverently in her lap.

Tillie responded to the rubbernecking by placing one hand behind her head and the other on her waist as she smiled suggestively at the parishioners. She blew a couple of little kisses at some of the Hispanic men, while their wives eyed her suspiciously.

Abruptly, the organ blared with the notes of the opening processional. All heads turned toward the center aisle where two boys of equal height, both Hispanic, and both in white and black cassocks, marched solemnly toward the apse bearing lighted candles. Following them, a slightly taller boy carried a long staff, topped with a bronze crucifix. In the rear of the procession, wearing a purple chasuble over his white cassock, a tall, clean-shaven priest advanced, a beatific smile on his face.

Tillie turned to Juanita, whose face radiated the joyousness of the processional. In a hoarse whisper, she asked, "You reckon that priest is buggerin' them boys?"

Heads turned again.

The rest of the liturgy went well. Juanita was reverent, completely caught up in the splendor and rejoicing of the mass. Still chomping on her gum, Tillie fidgeted and looked around at the people, the furnishings, the religious relics.

As the offertory hymn began, Tillie grew preoccupied with the priest and altar boys as they prepared bread and wine at the altar. As ushers started up the center aisle passing baskets for tithes and offerings, Juanita reached into a cubby on the back of the pew in front of them and withdrew two offering envelopes. She slid one of the envelopes into her blouse between two buttons and then pressed it upward under her bra. With the other envelope in her lap, she tapped Tillie and whispered, "We need to put some money in this envelope."

Still preoccupied with the preparation for the Eucharist, Tillie opened her handbag and withdrew a dollar bill. "This about all I got on me, honey. It'll have to do."

After communion and several hymns, the mass ended with the priest and altar boys ceremoniously parading down the center aisle with the organ playing the recessional music. The congregation then filed out, past the priest who stood under the eave shaking hands and making small talk, mostly in Spanish, with his parishioners.

"That was real nice," Tillie said to the priest, offering her hand. As they gripped, she bent her middle finger inward and stroked his palm a couple of times.

He pulled his hand free and flushed a deep crimson, his eyebrows lowered in indignation.

Tillie stepped onto the sidewalk laughing. She lit a cigarette.

***

Juanita stood on a chair and carefully removed two of the three knurled thumbscrews securing the glass dome to the light fixture on the kitchen ceiling. It was ten a.m. Two of her three roommates were asleep in their beds. Tillie, still in the red dress, dozed in a tattered upholstered chair in the bungalow's tiny living room. Arnie was sitting in his GT at the curb on Seventh Street to keep an eye on things. With luck, he wouldn't come bursting through the door, and the others would remain asleep, while she secreted the offertory envelope inside the globe and replaced the thumbscrews.

She had just returned the chair to its place at the formica table and was wondering where she might get her hands on a pen or pencil, when she heard the front door open.

Arnie's voice boomed through the house, "Hey, you bitches, get yourselves out of bed and get made up. Red alert. A destroyer tied up about two hours ago. The *Higgins*. In another hour there'll be 200 sex-starved squids prowling the streets of National City. Get out there and help them spend their money." He burst into the kitchen, his cell phone held to his ear, "Yeah Frank, I'm rousing 'em. They'll be on the street in 20 minutes, bro."

Two hours later, Juanita led a drunken petty officer second class into her room in the bungalow. She sat on the bed. With slow and graceful hands, she pushed each of the buttons of his khaki shirt through its buttonhole while he stood before her on wobbly feet, murmuring slurred suggestions. She deftly lifted the flap over his breast pocket, removed the ballpoint pen and let it drop to the floor, where she pushed it under the bed with her toe. If one of the *padrotes* found it later, or Tillie, it would look as if it had been carelessly dropped by a client, rather than deliberately concealed.

Before the others woke the next morning, it took Juanita only a few minutes to scrawl a brief note onto the back of a utility bill that had been left at the door.

She read it over hastily.

Padre o hermana,
Por favor envíe esto al padre Sebastian de la Parroquia de San Augustin en Oaxaca. Me
llamo Juanita Montero. Soy un prisionero sexual en una casa en
Calle 7 cerca la avinida B. Por favor ayúdame.

Again, while the others slept, she slipped into the kitchen, removed the thumbscrews securing the glass dome over the light and slipped the note into the offertory envelope.

"Watcha doin' on that chair, girl?"

Juanita started at the sound of Tillie's shrill, wheezy voice. She struggled to regain her balance, then stepped off the chair and held up her hands so Tillie could see the grit and dust on her fingers. "Just cleaning the light fixture, Tillie. It's disgusting."

"You're crazy, girl. It's not even noon yet and you're up jivin' around like a dog shittin' watermelons. Don't make sense. Now you go back to bed. Them sailors off the Higgins still on liberty. Today's another busy day. Know what I mean?"

***

It was three weeks before Juanita had a chance to return to St. Mary's. While the communion preparations at the altar once again preoccupied Tillie, she slipped the envelope containing the missive into the collection basket.

***

That afternoon, the Reverend Juan Barella, a transitional deacon, opened collection envelopes in a small office off the rectory. One envelope contained no money or check, just a folded yellow sheet of paper, an invoice for gas and electric power from SDG&E for an address farther west on Seventh Street. He turned it over and read the note from Juanita. Fluent in Spanish, he immediately grasped its significance.

He entered the rectory where Father Ruiz sat sipping coffee as he worked on the Sunday crossword. "I think you'd better see this, Father. I found it in a standard collection envelope in today's tithes."

"Good Lord," said the priest. "Do as she wishes. Find an address for the parish in San Agustín and mail it, express post. Also, let's photocopy it and send it to the National City Police Department."

***

Once it reached the NCPD's headquarters on National City Boulevard, the note languished in a pile of unopened mail in the departmental mailroom for three days before a clerk opened it. Uncertain where to send it, the inexperienced clerk let it rest on the table top for two more days until she decided to route it to the Investigations Division. It landed in the in-tray of the clerk to the administrative assistant where it lay for eight more days while the clerk enjoyed her honeymoon in Ensenada.

Chapter Twenty-Eight

March, 2019
San Agustín Etla, Oaxaca

Padre Sebastian spoke into the phone. "Your Excellency, I've just received an envelope from a Catholic church in San Diego. It contains a note from Juanita. She's there. She's in a house near the church."

"Is there a date on the note?" asked Bishop Diego.

"No. But the envelope is postmarked February 28. It took over two weeks to get here."

"Then we don't know for sure if she's still there. But scan that note and email it to my friend Maria Gutiererez with TBAA in San Diego. I'll send you a link with her email address." He paused for a moment. "There. The link should be on your screen momentarily."

"We don't have a scanner in this poor parish, Excellency. But I can quote the note from Juanita word for word in the email."

"Yes, do that. But if Maria can persuade the authorities to act, the note in Juanita's handwriting may be useful. Fax it to me. I know you have an old fashioned facsimile machine. I'll scan it and email it. Let's hope Maria can persuade the authorities to get involved. And let's hope they act fast before Juanita gets moved again. That's the style of the traffickers. They keep their women moving from place to place."

"One more thing, Excellency. I went on Mapquest and found the intersection where the house is located. It's about four blocks from St. Mary's Catholic church. It's also about three blocks from a huge US Naval base. The satellite view of the Navy base shows at least 15 ships tied up to the docks.

"*Sí.* I see the relevance. Start your fax and get that note to me as fast as you can."

It took ten minutes for the ancient fax machine to get warmed up. With agonizing slowness, it took the document in through its feeder and finally got it on its way. Padre Sebastian picked up the phone again. "On the way, Bishop."

"Okay, it's coming through. Listen, do you think we should advise Pablo and Sofia Montero of this development? You know them better than me. Would we only build false hope? They're still in Tijuana. How do you think they'd react? Would they do anything crazy?"

"All due respect, Your Excellency, I think it's our sacred obligation to advise them. To reinforce the hope they've been clinging to. And then we pray the hope isn't dashed."

"That's what I hoped you'd say. Why don't you see if you can reach them through the TBAA office in Tijuana? Or through Sister Antonina Magdalena?"

Chapter Twenty-Nine

March, 2019
Oceanside, California

Andrew Zorbis stepped onto his front porch and took several deep breaths. He stood facing the east, where the breaking sun cast a soft, yellow light across the rooftops and spring foliage of the leafy neighborhood. The streetlights along Michigan Avenue were beginning to dim. The district was quiet, save for the yowl of a tom cat several houses away.

Andrew had a big day ahead of him, starting with a meeting in the SKIUS office at 7:30, in little more than 90 minutes. He'd barely have time to practice his morning meditation, a habit he had developed while serving as a Navy Seal on clandestine operations in Southeast Asia. He rolled out his tatami mat, sat in the lotus position, legs crossed, each foot resting on the opposite thigh, back ramrod straight, and concentrated on his breath.

Thirty minutes later, he joined Dora, his wife of 24 years, for a breakfast of fresh fruit, granola, and two slices of toast slathered with butter. They'd met in college at Colorado State, married when he graduated and she was in her last year. Together they had embarked on the peripatetic life of a career Navy Seal. Maintaining her own career as a school teacher was a challenge as they moved from one base to another. But she'd landed jobs, usually as a substitute, in the dependent schools on the posts. For Dora, the toughest aspect of their marriage was the frequent, short-notice deployments of his team on missions, the duration of which he never knew, the purpose and details of which she was not authorized to know, and the locations only vaguely described to the families of team members.

"I have a meeting with several of our investigators in just under an hour," Andrew told her. "We have to get moving on a case involving a 17-year-old girl from Oaxaca. We believe she's now here in San Diego County." He kept his comments deliberately vague, not because further details were restricted or classified, but from the long-ingrained habit of keeping details held close to the chest, in the interest of operational security.

Dora knew better than to probe too deeply. "The poor girl must be terrified. But if anyone can find her and rescue her, you guys can. I pray you can solve this one in a hurry."

***

Four men and a woman sat at the conference table in the SKIUS office, a couple with open laptops or iPads. Steaming coffee cups, glasses of water, and ruled notepads littered the tabletop. The woman wore a crisp blue uniform with three white chevrons on each sleeve, and a gold and blue badge above her left breast. Andrew introduced her as Sergeant Allende of the National City Police Department. With a remote, he activated a wall-mounted computer screen and brought up an image of a run-down bungalow, off-white stucco with faded blue trim on the gutters and around the windows. "Sergeant Allende will bring us up to speed on what they have."

"Right," she said. "We've had this house, at the corner of Seventh Street and B Avenue under active surveillance for 24 hours. This is the house described in Juanita Montero's note to the church. Although there's been a lot of coming and going, mostly youngish men and a few women who appear to be hookers, we've seen no evidence of anyone underage, or of anyone held against their will. We have neither the resources nor the justification to surveil it indefinitely, so we're pulling our man off the stakeout within the hour. It'd be nice to leave a mini-surveillance camera somewhere across the street, but since the utility lines are underground, SDG&E can't help us with that. No poles."

One of the men, Roger Upton, looked up from his iPad. "What about planting a cam on a parked vehicle?"

"Probably couldn't do it without arousing suspicion," she said. "Parking on Seventh Street is limited to four hours. Plus, we're not the only ones surveilling the house." She picked up the remote and brought up an image of a Mustang GT with a single male occupant, parked near the bungalow. "This is a pimp known to us. He goes by the name Arnie. He and a couple of other dudes keep an eye on the house to make sure their women mind their Ps and Qs."

Andrew spoke. "There is evidence, in the form of the letter from Juanita, that she is, or was, being held in the bungalow against her will. Further indications support that, based on the NCPD's observations that this is an active whorehouse. Now we need actionable intelligence that proves Juanita is a sexual slave being held there. Once that has been established, we can suggest that the police raid the house."

"Sounds like you're suggesting either a sting or an undercover caper, shipmate," said one of Roger's teammates.

"Exactly. I'd like a couple of you to start unobtrusively talking to neighbors. And Roger, I suggest you get yourself into that house as a john. See if you can talk to Juanita. It would be a big help if you could plant a camera or recording device in the house, but at the minimum, go in wearing a body cam to record the evidence you collect, if any."

***

Just past 11 p.m., Roger Upton walked up the short sidewalk that dissected the front yard and knocked on the door. He wore a khaki uniform with the insignia of a senior chief petty officer on his sleeve.

The porch light came on and the door opened. "Well, lordy if it ain't a bigwig of some kind," said Tillie. "Watcha want, honey?"

He wobbled a bit, leaned against the door jamb and said, "A date. Preferably with a chicana, if you got one here." He reached up and straightened his horned rim glasses, which had become slightly askew. He pinched the left temple piece just forward of his ear, activating the miniscule video camera hidden in the frame.

"That about all we got, honey. Except for me that is. How 'bout a little dark meat tonight?"

"No offense sweetie. I think you'd be great. But all I could think about on board that ship for the past few weeks was a spicy little Mexican. Think you can dig one up for me?" He tottered slightly.

"You just come in and sit right down, chief. That's what you are ain't you? A chief? I'll call Juanita off the street to come right home for you. She's something else, know what I mean?"

Roger's heart skipped a beat. Maybe this would work on the first try.

Tillie led him to Juanita's room. "You just have a seat right there on that there bed. She'll be here in no time."

Roger stood when Juanita entered the room. He smiled and said, "Hello, Juanita." She looked surprised, perhaps not expecting to see a client his age, or one that would stand to address her.

Her expression changed to one of cynicism. "I don't do anything special. Just regular sex. Fifty dollars."

"I don't want you to do anything special, Juanita. In fact, I'm not here to have sex with you. I'm here as a friend."

A cloud of suspicion blanketed her face. She narrowed her eyes.

"Really. I'm here to help you escape. I've seen a copy of the note you dropped in your church."

Now her brows shot up. "How ... Who are you?"

Roger saw much of the tension drain from her shoulders. "I'll tell you in a minute and we must be fast. But first I need to ask you two questions. Are you Juanita Montero?"

"Oh yes, *señor*. From San Agustín in Oaxaca. But ..."

"Shh. Juanita, I'm recording this through a camera in my glasses. I need to hear you say that you are not here because you want to be here."

"I don't want to be anywhere but back home ... or in Guanajuato. I was tricked. I was forced to become a *puta* for about five months now. How can you help me escape?"

"Let's keep our voices low. My name is Roger. I'm a private detective. My agency has volunteered to find you and arrange your rescue. I met your parents several days ago in Tijuana. They signed papers authorizing us to help you."

"My parents are in Tijuana? How ... Do they know what I'm doing?"

"Yes. But they know you've been forced into it. They love you very much and want us to free you."

Tillie's shrill voice came from the other side of the door. "Honey, you okay in there? I don't hear no sounds of wild sex. Sounds like you're just talkin' with that there john."

"*Sí.* It's all right Tillie. This man wants to talk awhile first. He's been at sea and has been lonely. He just wants to talk a little before we go at it." She sat on the bed and bounced a few times, causing the springs to squeak, at the same time she lip synched for Roger to make some noise that sounded pleasurable.

He groaned audibly several times.

Juanita said, "Oh boy. Here we go. Here we go." She feigned breathlessness.

Tillie shouted as she ambled away from the door, "Time is money. You charge overtime for every minute."

"I'd better leave in a couple of minutes, Juanita. The next thing that will happen is we'll show this video to the police. They should raid the house and rescue you within the next couple of days."

"Wait. We need to muss you up a little before you go out there." She yanked on the front of his shirt, pulling it partway out of his pants, and forced some wrinkles into the starch by squeezing it between her fingers. She ran a hand roughly through his hair, disarranging it. "Okay, go now. But hurry back."

Chapter Thirty

March, 2019
Tijuana

The Agua Rio was a modest but clean hotel on Avenida Constitución in the Zona Centro, its three stories of rooms arranged in a U-shape around an asphalt parking lot. It offered little in the way of amenities, save a continental breakfast, which tasted like cardboard seasoned with frijole sauce. Pablo Montero, still suffering symptoms of alternating anxiety and depression, had slept little. The first tentative jingle of the telephone jolted him out of his light slumber and sent adrenaline charging through his body. He leapt from the bed, snatched the phone out of its cradle, and said, "Hola."

"*Señor Montero, soy Alejandra de TBAA.* May I come over to see you and Sofia? I have some news and something important to show you."

Sofia stirred and asked, *"¿Quién es?"*

Pablo covered the mouthpiece. "It is *Señora Gomez,* at TBAA." He spoke into the phone. "*Sí, sí.* Come over. We'll meet you in the breakfast room."

Thirty minutes later, Pablo and Sofia sat in a corner of the tiny eating space. Pablo's callused hands fidgeted endlessly, alternately reaching up to rub his stubbled chin, tug at the fabric of his trousers, or rub his knuckles with the thumb of the opposite hand. Sofia nibbled on an apple, her gaze darting around the room to take in the three other diners as they munched their way through what, with lots of imagination, passed for breakfast.

Alejandra entered and strode directly to the corner where Pablo and Sofia sat. Borrowing a chair from another table, she arranged herself so she could look them both in the eyes. She forced a smile. "Juanita has been found. She's in a house in

National City. That's a suburb of San Diego, about 30 kilometers from where we sit."

Both of their eyes lit up and Pablo emitted a little "Oh." Sofia crossed herself and called upon the Vigin of Guadalupe, *"Madre de Dios. Gracias. Gracias."* Her eyes filled again with tears, this time though they were tears of joy.

"When can we see her? Will someone bring her here?" Pablo was out of his chair and shifting from one foot to the other, his hands trembling even as he clutched them to his sides.

"Not yet." Alejandra's smile twitched. "She's still being held by the *padrotes*. But *Señor* Upton, the private investigator you met a few days ago managed to get into the house. He couldn't rescue her. But he spoke with her. She's okay. She's strong and she's fine."

"But how could he see her? Why could he not rescue her? How did he find her?" Sofia, now on her feet, also trembled with emotion.

The three other diners in the breakfast nook, all men, politely stuck their noses deeper into their newspapers.

Pablo sunk back into his chair and slumped, deflated.

Alejandra opened her briefcase and pulled out a photocopied document. *"Señor* y *Señora* Montero, two days ago, your parish priest in San Augustín received this note. It was emailed to us. The police in National City also have a copy of it. Would you say that this is Juanita's handwriting?"

Sofia peered at the note. Pablo craned his neck to read it as well. As though they had reached up off the paper and hit her hard, the words *prisionero sexual* smacked Sofia like a hammer. She recoiled from the paper and broke into sobs. "Yes, yes, It's her writing. I knew in my head what she had been forced into, but my heart could not believe it. My baby. Oh my poor baby."

Pablo too was crying but could only mutter, *"Mierda. Mierda. Cristo auyda su."*

"But it is good news that she's been found. She's well and she's strong," Alejandra repeated. "As we speak, the detectives and police are planning how to rescue her. I'm sure she'll be safe very soon."

Sofia looked up from her lap. She held her head high as she wiped away tears. Pablo nodded.

Alejandra removed a laptop from her briefcase and popped a USB drive into the port on the side as she fired up the computer. "Mr. Upton had a camera hidden on his person when he went into the … house where Juanita is. He managed to get some video of her as they spoke. Can I show you?"

They watched the short clip with expressions of despair and joy as they saw their daughter speaking confidently and projecting strength. They didn't understand the English words she spoke, but clearly caught the drift of her meeting with Roger Upton. They looked puzzled when they heard the voice of Tillie, speaking in her patois through the closed door and then watched Juanita bounce on the bed causing the springs to squeak. But they understood when they heard the voice of Roger Upton, whom they could not see, as he moaned sensually. The strength and cleverness of their daughter buoyed them momentarily, but her situation left them distraught.

All of this Alejandra read in their faces. "Pablo and Sofia," she said, "the last words of Mr. Upton in that video, spoken in English, tell Juanita that she will be rescued within the next couple of days. We should embrace that and hope for it."

"Oh *mi dios*, let it be so."

Chapter Thirty-One

March, 2019
Seattle

Lien's computer screen was split into two views. Paul Pham's uncharacteristically somber face filled the left panel. He leaned into his elbows and his right eye twitched. On the right a video played of the front of a stucco bungalow, off-white in color with pale blue trim.

"Paul. What's the matter? You look worried … or scared."

He removed his hand from his face and took a slurp from a coffee mug with the TBAA logo. "There's good news and bad news about Juanita, Lien."

"Tell me."

"The good news is that Juanita managed to get a note to a Catholic church in National City. It described where she was being held — a small house near the San Diego Naval Base. The one you can see on your screen. The note was passed to the police and to SKIUS." He told Lien how Andy Zorbis had sent one of his investigators to the house, wearing a video camera. "That was two days ago. She was all right then."

"What do you mean 'then'?"

"The police went to the house yesterday." He lifted the cup to his lips again, as though to fortify himself for what he would say next. "Here's the bad news. It was empty. No one was there, not Juanita, no other hookers, not a pimp to be seen. Everyone just gone. They left nothing in the house. No personal possessions, no luggage, no items of clothing, no toiletries. Nothing."

"Oh Paul, what does it mean?"

"Maria tells me these operations move around frequently. They shift locations, depending on the client demand and to what extent the police are sniffing around.

The police think this little band of four or five hookers and several pimps have gone somewhere else, probably in the North County region around Escondido or close to the big Marine base at Camp Pendleton."

"Oh my gosh. Now what? How will she be found now?"

"The US department of Homeland Security has broadcast a photo of Juanita and also of her pimp, a guy named Geraldo Rojas, to all the social media. They also sent it to other law enforcement in Southern California. Someone will spot her and report to the authorities … I hope. Also, the SKIUS guy who got into the house, Roger Upton, he got some good footage of Juanita. That's been turned over to the local television stations. Ten News is doing a seven-minute spot on both their nightly newscasts, 5:30 and 10 o'clock. Watch the right side of your screen. Here it is."

Two broadcast journalists, one man, one woman, appeared on the screen, ensconced behind the news desk. The woman spoke first:

"Little known to many county residents, National City Boulevard is part of what's known as 'the circuit.' Hookers are rotated between several locales in the county. In National City, many of their clientele are servicemen from the sprawling San Diego Naval Base. Ten News has learned of a tragic story about a young Mexican woman, kidnapped from her university campus, forced into prostitution, and smuggled into San Diego." The colored picture of Juanita appeared on the screen. "Ten News reporter Rosey Robertson has the story."

The screen flipped to an image of a journalist in a red pantsuit, holding a mic. Behind her, the bungalow on Seventh Street.

"Good evening, David and JoAnna, this house behind me on Seventh Street in National City was an operating brothel until just a day or two ago. Police and social service agencies learned that …" she glanced down at a note card in her hand. "Juanita Montero, age 17, of Oaxaca, Mexico, was held here as a sexual slave."

She described how the note had been left in the offering basket of the Catholic church, and the ensuing events.

"News of Juanita and her plight has become viral on social media sites. She has become somewhat of a cause célèbre, demonstrating that sexual trafficking happens not only to poor and marginalized youth, but to anyone." The screen filled with footage of provocatively attired girls on the stroll and pimps in high-end cars patrolling the area around the naval base.

"The police have appealed to the public to call this tip line number if anyone spots Juanita or knows anything else about girls held as sex slaves." A ten-digit phone number appeared in a banner at the bottom of the screen.

"Back to you, David and Joanna. Rosey Robertson, Ten News, reporting from National City, California."

"*Troi oi.* As my grandma Quy would say, this is making my blood run cold."

"Well, let's hope she's found fast. Here's another bit of hope. Do you remember going to the In N Out hamburger restaurant just before Thanksgiving?"

"Of course. How could I forget?"

"They have posters with a picture of Juanita, with an appeal for help in both English and Spanish, in all 347 of their locations. They include the national tip number for trafficked kids as well as the local number for SKIUS."

Chapter Thirty-Two

April, 2019
Seattle

Pete Trutch looked up from the computer screen and stared pensively through the glass on the rain-streaked French doors, into the darkness. He could barely make out the lights on the Space Needle and one or two of the skyscrapers in downtown Seattle. To the southwest, the red and green navigation lights of a ferry shone through the gloom obscuring the waters of Puget Sound. The article he had been reading in the online version of the British newspaper, *The Guardian,* troubled him deeply.

He sensed Catherine's presence in his study and rotated his desk chair around. Her entrance into the room lifted his spirits. He smiled at her and accepted the cup of steaming tea she offered.

"What are you working on, dear?"

"I've just read this article. Look at the image." A glitzy salmon-colored house with purple trim filled the screen — a mansion with oddly shaped rooflines, cupolas, and turrets. The caption read: *One of many gaudy houses in Tenancingo, in the state of Tlaxcala, a hub of sex trafficking.*

"What is it? Where's Tenancingo?"

"It's the town southeast of Mexico City that Lien told us about. The whole town is involved in sex trafficking. It's regarded as the core for trafficking sex slaves into the US."

"I remember her telling us. That's where that girl she's interested in, Juanita, was forced into sex slavery. Isn't she now somewhere in California?"

"That's what they think. This article was written in 2015. They sent a news team to Tenancingo to write an exposé. They did a brilliant job reporting on the town and its reach in North America." He purposely neglected to mention the threats and harassment the team of journalists faced while on the ground there.

Catherine searched his face and eyes. "I hope you're not thinking what I think you're thinking."

He flushed, but didn't say anything.

"You would never fool a polygraph, Pete. Your face tells me that you are, in fact, thinking about going to this Tenancingo place to research another book on trafficking. May I remind you, you're well into your seventies? Cancel that train of thought right now. I won't support it. In fact, I damn well won't stand for it."

"I'm merely indulging in a pipe dream at this point. I wouldn't think of going there without your full support. But I will do further research on the Tenancingo Ring, as it's called. This entire town makes a cottage industry out of victimization. I'm particularly interested because of Lien's empathy with the victim, Juanita. When I know enough about it, I want to add my voice to the outrage by writing about it. For now, I can do the preliminary research right here, from this study. On the internet and through some phone calls."

"Who would you call?"

"For starters, the two non-profits in San Diego that Lien told us about." He glanced down at an open page in his notebook. "The Trans-Border Anti-Trafficking Alliance and Saving Kids in the US. If I need more depth after that, I'll check with some of the law enforcement agencies that would know about Tenancingo."

"Would you know where to start? In the federal government alone, there must dozens of agencies interested in trafficking. The DEA, FBI, BATF, Homeland Security, Coast Guard, just for starters. And a myriad more at the state and local levels."

"I've learned that the office of Homeland Security is the coordinating agency. Homeland Security Investigations — HSI. All law enforcement involved in international trafficking of humans into the US goes through them. I'll start with the Office of Public Affairs for HSI."

Lien joined Pete and Catherine for dinner that night. After some light banter about her studies and the friends she had made at the UW, Pete asked, "When Paul Pham told you about this Tenancingo place in Mexico, how much did he actually tell you?"

"He said that US authorities call it a hub. It sounds worse than Svay Pak, and that was awful."

"It's been going on for generations in the state of Tlaxcala, since the state lost the basis of its economy, mining and ranching, back in the 60s. Now, apparently, boys are taught to be pimps from the time they're in grade school, and girls are encouraged, sometimes forced, to sell their bodies as early as age ten or eleven."

Pete felt the toe of Catherine's shoe strike his shin under the table.

"Oh Jeez. I'm sorry, Lien. We shouldn't be talking about this. It's just that I've been doing some research on this Tenancingo thing, and I'm almost obsessed with my anger at the whole business."

"It's okay, Grandfather. I don't want to forget about my past, and I can't hide from this problem. I want to do work that will help trafficking victims. That feeling was so strong when Paul told me about Juanita Montero and showed me her picture. I've never met her, but I feel like she's my sister."

"I know," said Trutch. "Do you have a copy of her photo? Could Catherine and I see it?"

"Of course. I'll run upstairs and get it."

Catherine put her hand over her mouth when they saw the image. "So innocent looking," said Trutch.

"He wants to write another book," Catherine said. "I'd applaud that, but he's hinting at going to Tenancingo for field research." She rolled her eyes. "We don't want him to get near that place, do we Lien?"

"Why don't you and Catherine go to Mexico for a couple of weeks, to escape the winter gloom in Seattle? Not to Tenancingo. You could go to Mexico City or San Miguel or some other place with a good library. Do your research there. You'd probably learn more about Tenancingo in Mexico than you would online from here, and you wouldn't have to visit the dangerous places."

"I could go for a week or two in the sun," said Catherine.

"A good idea, sweetheart. How soon can we be packed?"

***

The next afternoon, Trutch sauntered into the living room, where Catherine and Lien were playing cribbage. "Okay, we've got reservations. We leave on Friday. How does four days in Mexico City and then a week in Cancun sound?"

"Wow. That was fast. No flies on you, Colonel Trutch. Can you research Tenancingo while we're in Mexico City?"

"Yep. For starters, I've got an appointment with the SAC of the Homeland Security Investigations attaché office. At the embassy. And I managed to get us a room overlooking Chapultepec Park at the Marriott on Paseo de la Reforma. And two museums are within walking distance. You can visit them while I'm working."

"You've been out of the army for over 20 years, and you're still using acronyms and initialisms. What's SAC?"

"Sorry. Special Agent in Charge. Get this, Lien. He's of Vietnamese ancestry. His last name is Nguyen."

***

"Mr. Trutch, owing to the reach and power of the cartels and gangs, Tenancingo is protected by *un velo de impunidad,* a veil of impunity." Ken Nguyen leaned forward in his chair and placed his hands on his knees. "Your wife is right, sir. Visiting there is definitely not a good idea. Journalists and documentarians have had bad experiences there. For that matter, our own experience there has been somewhat … uh, dicey."

"You've been there?"

"Tenancingo, and several other locations in Tlaxcala are under constant surveillance. I can't say any more about that. But on a couple of occasions, we've conducted what you might call ground reconnaissance within the town. We've gone in incognito, or so we thought. Four of us went in an old van, equipped with a couple of hidden video cams. We didn't blend in well. Both kids and adults harassed us, until we figured we were in danger and sped out of there."

"I'm convinced. I don't want to go there. But I need to get a good feel for the place."

"Have you tried YouTube? Several years ago a production company called the Fusion Group got several of their people in, when they were filming a documentary called *Pimp City.* They fled for their own safety, but they did get some good video footage."

"And I can find that on YouTube?"

"Yes. But I have a copy of it downloaded on my system. And I happen to have a couple of free hours. Let's watch it together. I can add some comments."

It opened with a view of the highway into the town of 10,000 people, shot through the back window of a sedan. The camera panned to the face of the narrator, Mariana Van Zeller. Past Mariana's pretty face, a row of one-story buildings dotted the highway.

She began her narration: "We are arriving in Tenancingo. Our guide tells us many of these low buildings are whorehouses. This is the on-the-job training ground for girls forced into prostitution. We cannot use our guide's name. She doesn't want to be on camera because she has to drive here often. She won't tell us what her usual business here is. She has also asked us to be very careful with the cameras."

The next scene showed Mariana on the street in Tenancingo, her colleague surreptitiously filming her with a hidden body camera. "We've arrived here on the actual day of Carnaval. Oh wow. So look at that. You can see the men with masks. They're, uh, all dressed up as devils and evil characters. They're actually whipping each other. You can see they have these rope-like whips that crack and snap as they whip each other."

Behind Mariana, the video showed men and boys dressed in red or black robes and devil masks flailing at one another's feet and lower legs. Among the whoops and hollers of the participants, the snapping and cracking of whips could clearly be heard.

"I don't know if they're showing off for each other or for us. They're paying a lot of attention to me and commenting on my blond hair."

A brief exchange occurred in Spanish between Mariana and one of the men. Several other men laughed boisterously. "He just said he wants to marry me. I think we'll move on down the street."

Mariana walked past rows of pastel-colored buildings, rendering a running commentary as she went along. "Our guide tells us that behind the costumes, there is something far more sinister about these men. Most are tied to the sex trade. They are *padrotes*, or pimps, and kidnappers who force women into prostitution. Here's another group right over here. They're running toward us."

The camera revealed a group of costumed boys, mostly younger than 12, brandishing whips as they ran toward Mariana and her cameraman, and then past them. "We're told that nine out of ten of these boys are already planning to be pimps when they grow up. Often times that isn't even a conscious decision. Boys as young as five just know that's what they'll be. That's what's expected of them." Marianna jumped and put a hand behind her back. "Whoa. I just got whipped right in the backside. I think we'll move again."

One man in a black robe and clown mask loomed over the others as he approached Mariana and began talking to her. Others in the crowd could be heard yelling and whooping. "This man is telling me he just got back from New York. He works there all the time, but comes back for Carnaval to show off his success. I just asked him if there was a lot of alcohol involved here today and he said, 'Yeah, man,' and pulled a flask from under his robe." One other man poked the one with the clown mask. "Now the others are telling him to shut up, to quit talking to us."

The camera panned 360 degrees around the street, clearly depicting the revelry and debauchery. Virtually all the men and boys were drinking openly from cans or bottles. Several of them came up to Mariana and spoke. One, wearing a skull mask, put his arm around her shoulder and tried to get her to take a sip of beer. "I'm not too sure it's really safe here. There's an awful lot of drinking going on. Some of these men are telling me it's okay if we film — I guess they spotted the body cam — but only if we talk just about the Carnaval, nothing else. They don't want any other news getting out of this town. So it's pretty obvious to me that everyone here knows there is a not-so-hidden secret here in this town, and that's sex trafficking. Whoops, I probably said that a little too loud. We're getting kind of a big audience here. I think we'd better move on again. It's becoming obvious we're not welcome here. I think we'll try to slip away from the frivolities of Carnaval and move into more of a residential area. I'd like to get some footage of the houses. They're called *calcuilchil*, that means houses of ass, in the local Indian dialect."

The next scene opened in a residential neighborhood of tasteless, gaudy houses. The camera panned up one side of a narrow, partially paved street.

Ken Nguyen paused the video. "There. Look at that one."

Trutch stared at one of the most outlandish pieces of architecture he'd ever seen. Mustard-colored with a crenelated cupola on one side of the roof, the weirdest features were several life-sized gargoyles and two pink angels peering down into the street from just above the second-story gutters.

"That's the Rojas' family house," Ken said. "The men of that clan make frequent trips into the US, taking enslaved women with them. We've been itching to bust those dickheads for a long time. The eldest son, Geraldo, is on our most wanted list of traffickers."

"Most wanted list?" asked Trutch. "Can members of the public get a look at that list? It would be interesting background for my research."

"Sure. It's on our website. Just google ICE Most Wanted." He restarted the video.

Mariana was now in front of the Rojas house, walking slowly as she spoke sideways to the camera. "We're told this is the Rojas house. Notorious traffickers and pimps. We're just gonna try to walk by the front. We can't really be too obvious staring through the gate, but I think you can see through the grilled gate to my left is a beautiful courtyard. It looks like the whole castillo is built in the Spanish style, around a series of courtyards. But the exterior style is really not Spanish. I don't know what you'd call it other than garish. There. There, someone inside the grill is watching us. And a neighbor just came out. He's watching us."

The camera pointed in the direction from which Mariana had been walking. A white sedan was blinking its lights. A man leaned out the passenger window and yelled, *"Ven. Ven rapido. Mas personas."*

"He's saying, 'Come quickly. More people are coming out of the house.' I'm gonna … oh oh … we're gonna head for the car."

The camera continued to roll as both Mariana and the cameraman got into the car. The interior of the vehicle looked upside down and sideways as the body camera followed its operator through the contortions of climbing in. The female guide/driver shouted, *"Vamanos. Vamanos."* The squeal of rubber could be heard as the vehicle sped away from the house in reverse.

"Now there are about 15 men lined up along the street shouting threats. We've gotta get out of here," whispered Mariana.

Following a break in the filming, Mariana can be seen sitting in the rear of the car again. Out the window behind her a blur of low-rise buildings passed by. "We decided to leave Tenancingo for our own safety, but I think we've got some good footage."

Ken Nguyen clicked the video off with a remote. "Now you've seen something of Tenancingo."

"I sure have. That's one gutsy woman."

"You bet. Reporters and journalists are frequently shot for revealing the underbelly of the Mexican mafia and exposing corruption in the various levels of government. There's a lotta money at stake here; sex, drugs, corruption, violence. Not pretty."

"Is there any hope that this web of evil can be broken?"

"It can probably never be completely eliminated. The corruption is too entrenched. And as long as there's a demand for drugs and sex, the cartels, in some form, will provide the supply."

Ken Nguyen's computer chimed. He clicked on an icon on the screen and hastily read the bulletin. The corners of his mouth curled into a shape somewhere between a forced smile and a grimace. "Well, looks like Geraldo Rojas can be removed from the most wanted list."

Pete leaned forward. "Arrested?"

"Shot dead. Got in a beef with the police in Oceanside, California. Unfortunately, one of his victims, a young female, was killed in the crossfire."

Trutch felt a flood of numbness take control of his body. His mind flashed to the chestnut-haired, wholesomely beautiful girl in the photo Lien had shown him several nights earlier.

Chapter Thirty-Three

Three days earlier
San Diego

Geraldo showed up with Frank at the bungalow in National City on a Saturday and announced that the four women would be moving. "Time to move on, *mujeres*. We're heading for North County. This time of year, there's money to be made there."

Juanita felt the cold hand of panic clutch her gut. The detective who had come to her room had said she would be rescued soon. How would they find her if she moved? And where was North County? She grabbed Geraldo's sleeve. "Where? Where we going? And why now?" Her eyes were wide with terror. "The church is here. I need to be close to the church."

The other three hookers looked on with curiosity as Geraldo grabbed both of Juanita's shoulders and gave her a shake. "Listen, Juanita. You're in the life. This is your lot now. Don't make trouble. The consequences wouldn't be good. The fields and deserts are filled with the bones of *putas* who thought they were smart enough to defy my family." His voice moderated slightly, "Besides, there are churches in Oceanside and Bonsall as well as here."

Juanita wrenched herself free of his grip. She turned tearfully to Tillie, "Tell him we have to stay here," she pleaded. "Tell this *pendejo* we're doing fine here. We have plenty of customers here. We don't have to move."

Geraldo struck her across the face with the back of his hand, catching her totally unaware. He had never hit her before. "Don't ever call me stupid, bitch. Don't you dare give me any shit. Ever again."

Tillie moved to Juanita and embraced her in a huge hug, almost smothering her with her ample bosom. "Child, don't you be no uppity whore. Believe me, I've seen foolish hookers get hurt bad. Geraldo ain't kiddin' about bones in the desert. You just do as you're told now, know what I mean?"

"All of you. Get your shit," Geraldo said. "I've got a minivan out here. We're leaving now."

***

The drive to Oceanside took 55 minutes. At nine p.m. Geraldo pulled into a restaurant with a sign reading Fred's Oceanside Kitchen, next door to a wooden frame building identified as Wavecrest Office Building. Frank hopped out. "I'm gonna get some food for you. If anyone has to use the can, it's just in the door and to the left. Tillie'll take you." Moments later he returned to the van with a bag of burgers and several orders of yam fries.

"Okay, here's the deal," Geraldo said, swivelling in his seat as the burgers and fries were distributed. "We're just a few miles from the big Marine Corps base at Camp Pendleton. The jarheads there are the main customers. You stay in a two-bedroom mobile home in an RV park a few blocks from here. But you won't take johns home. There's half a dozen hotels within a few miles of the base. That's where you go with these guys. You pick them up on the street or in the bars and you take them to Day's Inn, or the Worldmark or Harbor's Inn. You always make sure the client pays for the room. But once you got it, you keep it all night, so you can bring more johns in during the night. Night clerks have to be tipped when you come through the door late at night, so always make sure your john takes care of that. Now eat up, then I'll take you up to the Sandy Beach RV Park. You'll have a few minutes to get settled. Then you hit the streets. On weekends the jarheads like to get an early start. Frank and I will be watching you. And we've got a lot of other *padrotes* who'll be keeping their eyes on you too. So no funny shit."

The Sandy Beach RV & Mobile Home Park was on Carmelo Drive, about six hundred feet inland from the long expanse of beach. About 40 rundown house trailers and travel trailers occupied gravel lots with a smattering of shrubs and potted plants. Three paved lanes made up the boundaries between the rows of trailers and created the illusion of orderliness. Along the lanes, an assortment of pickup trucks and middle-aged sedans were haphazardly parked. A smattering of kid's tricycles and plastic toys rounded things out. Geraldo pulled up to a neglected, 40-foot, black-metal mobile home with rusted panels and smudgy windows. A small wooden sign, displayed on a post at the front of the parking pad, read:

The Montagues
Roger and Wilma

Juanita cast her eyes despairingly around the premises. From the shabby neighborhood, the roar of traffic on the nearby San Diego Freeway was dizzying. She wondered who the Montagues were.

Frank provided the answer. "The owners live in Riverside. They use this as their vacation pad about four months of the year. So we've rented it for a few months. Don't no one mess it up more than it already is. And don't bring no johns here. Turn your tricks in the hotels and motels, or even on the beach if you want. Just bring the money here every night."

Geraldo jerked open the flimsy door of the trailer, knocking a bird's nest off the frame as he did. "Okay *putas*. Go on in and drop your things. Then get yourself fixed up for work. Frank will show you the stroll as soon as you've got your war paint on. Tillie, you come with me in the van."

***

"Where we goin', boss?" Tillie asked, as she climbed into the van.

"First, you and me are gonna have a little sport right on Harbor Beach. Then we're going to check on some of the other girls."

"I don't want no sand in my hoo hoo. Know what I mean, boss?"

"Don't worry. We've got blankets."

Geraldo parked in Beach Lot 12, near the Harbor Pelican Deli and Mart. They walked across the asphalt, past an idling police cruiser, and onto the sand. At least a dozen other couples rutted and groaned there already, undoubtedly off-duty marines and their pay-for-pleasure strumpets. The beach was dark, without benefit of a moon, but they could see the aura of San Diego's lights to the south. Ahead of them the ocean lay black and brooding, wavelets gently lapping the shore. Geraldo spread the blanket. Tillie dropped her trousers and got onto her knees, head down, resting on her folded arms.

Minutes later, back in the van, they headed for the action, the Saturday night meat market spread along North Coast Highway, Cleveland Street, Mission Avenue, and Pier View Way.

On Mission Avenue, near Ditmar Street, they pulled to the curb to converse with a group of streetwalkers, all part of the Tenancingo coterie.

"How's business, *chicas?*"

"Bueno. I've turned seven tricks and it's only 11:30."

"Not bad, Geraldo. Yesterday was payday on the base."

"Good. Good. I'll take the cash off your hands so you don't have to worry about carrying too much around." He collected several hundred dollars and stuffed it into a front pocket of his Levis.

A black and white unit of the Oceanside Police Department pulled up to the curb behind Geraldo's van. The cops put a spotlight on the covey of hookers, but made no motion to dismount their vehicle.

"They're just harassing us," said Geraldo. "Maybe seeing if any girls are familiar to them."

"Assholes," muttered Tillie.

"It's bullshit, that's what. *Mierda de toro.*" Geraldo yanked open the driver's door and stepped onto the street. "This is *bullshit,*" he shouted at the cops.

An amplified voice blasted out from a speaker behind the grille of the police car. "Sir, get back in your car. Get back in your car right now. We could perceive your behavior as a threat. *Get back in the fuckin' car.*"

"Don't you *cabrónes* have better things to do? Fuck off!" He slid back behind the wheel and slammed the door.

The cruiser pulled out and slowly cruised past the van, both occupants staring hard at Geraldo as they passed. Geraldo's eyes found the lettering on the side of the other vehicle: Oceanside Police, in block letters on the door.

Geraldo and Tillie waited another five minutes before they pulled out from the curb. They continued cruising the streets of Oceanside, stopping periodically to check up on other streetwalkers. At midnight, they drove several miles up the Coast Highway to the main gate of Camp Pendleton. They pulled into the off-base turnaround, just before the security checkpoint, and rolled up to a group of off-duty marines looking for rides into Oceanside.

"Hey. You *cabrónes* looking for pussy? Hop in. We'll take you to the action. Fine stuff."

Three men with white sidewall haircuts climbed into the back. Tillie turned in her seat and flashed them her most sexy smile. "We're gonna fix you up good, boys. Know what I mean?"

At three a.m., just as Geraldo was wrapping up business with another of his hookers on North Pacific Street, a blue flash refracted off his side mirror, followed by the short, abbreviated wail of a siren. He peered into his rearview mirror. "*Mierda*, now what do the assholes want?"

He pulled to the curb just opposite the Blue Whale Motel and reached across in front of Tillie to open the glove compartment so he could find the vehicle rental contract. A bright spotlight illuminated the interior of the vehicle and an amplified voice boomed, "Keep your hands where I can see them, sir."

Geraldo placed both hands near the top of the steering wheel.

"You too, passenger. Both hands where I can see them."

Tillie laced her fingers behind her head.

Through the side-mounted mirror, Geraldo watched the cop cautiously approach, his handgun drawn and aimed with both hands toward the vehicle. Through the other mirror, he could see another cop, his weapon also drawn, take up a position just opposite the back door on the right-hand side. Geraldo pushed the button to lower his side window.

"I said keep your hands where I can see them." Without the amplification of the police vehicle's speaker, the voice sounded shrill, almost adolescent.

Geraldo quickly put his hands back on the wheel. "... the fuck did I do wrong?" he asked the cop who arrived at his now partially opened window.

"Just keep your hands where I can see them. I'll ask the questions." He turned his head toward the microphone hooked through his left epaulette and spoke into it. "X-ray one three to radio. Request backup, North Pacific and Neptune Way. Uncooperative driver. Request ten-twenty-nine on California plate six, x-ray, victor, tango, eight, eight, zero."

"*Cabrón*, asshole. I'm not uncooperative. I just asked what the fuck did I do? Why did you pull me over?"

"Keep your hands on the wheel and climb out of the car slowly."

Geraldo reached for the door handle.

The cop yelled, "Keep your fucking hands on the wheel."

Geraldo responded, "You want me to get out I need to open the door."

"I said keep your hands where I can see them." There was not only menace, but panic in his voice, as if the cop suddenly realized he had bitten off more than he could chew.

Tillie moved toward Geraldo.

The other cop shouted, "Stay where you are passenger."

Geraldo jerked up on the handle and flung the door open.

The cop fired four shots in quick succession. Geraldo slumped. Tillie screamed, "You bastard. You killed him."

The cop, now berserk on adrenaline, fired two more shots, both striking Tillie in the sternum, one just above, and the other directly into, her heart.

Lights came on in buildings on both sides of the now eerily silent street. An acrid mist of gun smoke hung in the still air. Then the wail of distant sirens crept into the stillness. "Fuck," said the cop on the passenger side. "You've killed them both, Sean. We're in deep shit."

The shooter dropped his Glock 22 onto the pavement and staggered backwards. He muttered to himself and made a couple of pirouettes. *"Fuck. Fuck. Fuck."* He slammed his fist repeatedly into the rear quarter panel of the police vehicle just above the spot where the italicized lettering read, *Service with Pride.*

Chapter Thirty-Four

April, 2019
Oceanside, California

Andrew Zorbis convened an emergency meeting with six of his investigators in the SKIUS office on the second floor of the Wavecrest office building. "Okay, gentlemen. Here's the deal. The Oceanside PD is giving us full cooperation and anything they have that may help us find Juanita Montero. They've been collecting security videos from local businesses in the three days since that asshole, Geraldo Rojas, was killed. I want you all to watch this one.

"It's about a five-minute excerpt from two cams in front of a local restaurant, one facing the parking area and street and the second a pole-mounted unit showing the front of the restaurant and the parking area." He directed their attention to the wall-mounted computer screen. The field of view was split so that footage from both cameras could be seen simultaneously.

The opening scene, apparently from the pole-mounted cam, showed four cars parked immediately in front of the restaurant, one vehicle a grey minivan. A male occupant stepped out of the driver's side door and went in through the restaurant door immediately below the café sign. The heads of several females could be seen within the vehicle.

"Holy shit." One of Andrew's investigators pointed at the café sign on the screen. "That's Fred's right next door to us. They were there, that close."

Andrew stopped the video and said, "That's right. The time stamp shows 21:05. The irony is that both Roger and I were here, in the office, at that time on that night. If we'd known that Juanita was so close, we could probably have snatched her then and there. But we didn't and we didn't, so it's moot. Keep watching the video. You'll see Juanita in a minute. I want you all to get a really good look at her." He hit play and the video resumed.

The scene remained static for about two minutes. Then another vehicle pulled into the stall next to the minivan. Several teenaged boys in the Plymouth Fury noticed the load of women in the minivan next to them and behaved accordingly, like horny adolescents. There was no audio, but the camera at the front of the parking lot clearly showed their leering grins and lewd gestures.

The rear door on the right side of the minivan opened and a young woman stepped out, followed by a black woman who climbed out of the front seat. The two walked toward the restaurant door.

'Okay, the one that just climbed out of the back is Juanita. Apparently she's being escorted to the loo," Andrew observed. From the store-mounted camera, a good full frontal likeness of Juanita dominated the screen.

"That's her all right," said Roger Upton. "And the Black one's the one who greeted me at the door of the cathouse in National City. Her name's Tillie. She's the one who was killed with Geraldo the other night. Andrew can you freeze that with a close-up of Juanita's face, please?"

With the frame frozen, Roger said, "Okay, please note that her appearance is much different than in that head and shoulders portrait we've all seen. Her hair is shorter and, although you can't really tell in this video, it's tinted kind of orange in front. Also her face is a lot gaunter than in her portrait. Andy, let's print this frame and spread it around the local neighborhoods. Maybe even get it posted on bulletin boards in the Exchange and recreation facilities out at Camp Pendleton."

Andrew said, "I'm not sure that distributing the image widely is a good idea, Roger. I wouldn't want the bad guys to know there's a more current picture of her available to the public. Let's circulate this pic among our members only. The police already have it, of course."

The remaining few minutes of the video depicted Juanita and Tillie returning from the washrooms and Geraldo emerging from the diner carrying a bag of food. Once he climbed back into the van, the front camera captured him as he swivelled around in his seat and spoke to the women, scowling. The video ended as the minivan drove out of the parking lot.

"Okay, now you have a good idea of the current appearance of Juanita," Andrew said. "Oceanside PD wants to know where these girls are stashed. Problem is, hundreds of hookers are housed in low rent hovels and cheap motels around Oceanside. Naturally, we want to know where to find Juanita and how to rescue her.

"Homeland Security has made a drone available six or seven hours a day to the Oceanside PD and the San Diego County Sheriff's department to aid in the search. But, it won't be easy. Given the television publicity and proliferation of posters about Juanita Montero, she's probably become a burden to the pimps. At the very minimum, they'll modify her appearance again. It's possible they'll keep her out of circulation for a while." He paused. "God forbid they decide she's too much of a liability and dispose of her."

The room went silent. Andrew swirled the black liquid in his coffee cup. Roger stared at the darkened screen, held his opened glasses in his hand and bit down on the stem. Faces around the table grew somber, each man's thoughts clearly grappling with the possible dire outcome.

Chapter Thirty-Five

April, 2019
Tenancingo, Mexico

The richly polished walnut casket, adorned with a huge spray of white roses and purple iris sat front and center in the chancel of *La Parroquia de San Miguel Arcangel.* At the foot of the catafalque an A-frame easel presented a wreath of white lilies a yard in diameter. To the rear of the casket, within the apse, the altar table was covered with roses and the same white lilies. The scent of the floral tributes wafted over the first few pews. To the left of the casket, another easel displayed a one-yard square portrait of Geraldo. Dressed in a garishly-decorated brocade jacket, he sat on an elaborately tooled black saddle, astride a black stallion. Three priests, each in different colored vestments — violet, black, and white — and flanked by a phalanx of altar boys, stood reverently between the casket and the altar. In the pulpit, a female soloist, accompanied by the robust strains of the 200-year-old parish pipe organ, sang *Aqui Estoy Dios*, her trembling soprano voice reverberating in the vast chamber.

Every pew in the church was filled. An overflow of mourners stood along both walls of the nave, beneath the stained glass windows and stations of the cross. At the rear of the great hall, the narthex too was jammed elbow to elbow with standers. The crowd spilled down the stairs and onto the grounds surrounding the church, where they listened to the mass through portable loudspeakers, set on tripods by the local army unit.

In the north transept, the choir waited patiently for that part of the service when they would contribute to the requiem mass. Across from them, in the south transept, sat Geraldo's family — Enrique, Rosa, Abuelo, Martina, and a host of aunts, uncles, and cousins — the women dressed in black. Rosa dabbed at her moist eyes with a handkerchief, while the others pensively listened to the soloist. Enrique fidgeted in his seat and shot a glance toward Martina, beside her mother. She would have to take over now. Running the operation north of the border. Was she up to it? Enrique wondered.

She'd always been a headstrong girl, a bossy tomboy during her formative years, and an opinionated girl during her teens. Naturally, many of the adolescent boys of Tenancingo thought her an assertive bitch rather than a natural leader. Certainly she had the intelligence to take over the business in the US, but did she have the temperament? Was she too impulsive? Not sufficiently deliberate or calculating? They had little choice really. She'd have to go north and earn her stripes. It would be a sink or swim situation. This would still leave the family without a Romeo to woo new *puta* candidates in Mexico and other Latin American countries. They'd have to rely on other Tenancingo charmers to lure young women to their lair.

The soloist ended with a long cadenza that showcased the full range of her voice. She bowed slightly to the congregants, then surrendered the pulpit to the priest in purple, who delivered a stirring eulogy that left numerous people in tears. Several other eulogies, delivered by lay members of the community, followed. The funeral ended with the 40-member, mixed male and female choir singing a stirring rendition of *No Me Digas Adios,* their rich voices resonating throughout the old building. Many in the congregation sobbed openly. "Go in peace to love and serve God," said the head priest, signifying the end of the mass. The long parade of grieving townspeople would now follow the horse-drawn carriage as it conveyed the casket to the nearby cemetery.

***

Martina nodded solemnly. "*Si, Papa.* Don't worry, I can manage things in San Diego. I've been there before with Geraldo. I know the turf. And I still have a valid US visa." Still in their funeral attire, she and Enrique sat side by side on a stone bench in the courtyard of their *palacio.* They suspended the conversation momentarily as a female *ama de casa* brought them each a glass of tequila.

When she had left them, Enrique placed his palm on the back of Martina's hand and said, "But don't be too cocky, my precious daughter. Law enforcement in the United States is a different animal than it is here. The cartels and gangs don't have the police and the politicians in their pockets the way we do in Mexico."

Martina licked the salt off the rim of her glass and said, "Papa, give me the latitude to run things the way I see fit. I'm capable. I'm tough. I can do it as well as a man could. Give me the chance to prove it."

"We don't have much choice. You're out of brothers. I'm out of sons. I'm known to the police in the US. Because you're a woman, they won't have you on their radar the way they did Geraldo. But remember this. Other Tenancingo families have assets in the US. We're all part of the same network and I expect you to cooperate with them. They'll look down on you because you're a woman. Even some of the *padrotes* who work for us will resent your role. You have a delicate road to walk, *mi hermana*. You cannot be too pushy, but you can't be submissive either."

"I can do it *Papa*. Mexican machismo is bullshit and hot air. If I must stand up to pee in order to prove I am as good as any man, I will."

Chapter Thirty-Six

April, 2019
San Agustín Etla, Oaxaca

Padre Sebastian parked his battered Volkswagen in front of the stone fence surrounding the Montero property and made his way on foot past the tall maize and toward the front of the small house. *"Hola, Carlos. Estás aquí?"* It had been a hot and dusty drive from town, and his voice sounded croaky. He cleared his throat and shouted again with a more sturdy voice, "Hello Carlos. Are you here?"

"I'm here, in the shed by the goats. Who is it?"

"It's me. Padre Sebastian."

Carlos stepped out of the shed wiping his hands on a denim rag, a smile on his face. "Hello Padre. I'm happy to see you." He offered his hand.

But instead of taking it, Sebastian gripped both of Carlos' shoulders. He forced a sad smile and said, "Let's go in the house. I have something important to tell you."

In the tiny kitchen, Sebastian took a long drink of water and set the glass on the table. "Carlos. It's about your father. He's in the hospital in Tijuana."

Carlos' eyebrows shot up. "What's happened? What is it?"

"They don't know for sure yet. They're doing some tests, some kind of imaging of his head. They think he may have had a stroke, Carlos. His face sags a bit on one side and he's having trouble finding his words. Your mother is with him in the hospital."

Carlos' lip quivered. "I must go there. I must go to Tijuana. Can you take me to the airport in Oaxaca? Can you lend me some money to fly there?"

"The church has already bought you a ticket for tomorrow morning. I'll take you then. Now, let's talk to your neighbors and make sure someone will feed the goats and take care of things here. I must go back to the church tonight for vespers. I'll be back to pick you up at five a.m."

"Papa didn't look good before he and Mama left here. It's the stress about Juanita. It's making him sick."

"Yes. And he may have had some bad news today about Juanita that made him more sick. The police in San Diego learned where your sister was being held. They raided the house last night — they went in to rescue her — and they found the house empty. Right now no one knows where Juanita is."

"Ohh Jesus Cristo," Carlos moaned. He hunched forward, leaning on his knees.

***

Alejandra Gomez, of the Tijuana office of TBAA, and Sister Antonina Magdalena were in the crowded hospital room, along with Sofia, when Carlos arrived. They sat in folding chairs, trying to talk with Pablo, who looked frail and white beneath the blue sheets, an oxygen tube in his nostrils and an IV solution dripping into a vein on his right hand. His eyes moved around the room from person to person and even brightened slightly when Carlos entered, but he said nothing.

Carlos gave his mother a quick hug then bent over his father's bed. "Papa, Papa," he said softly, tears glistening. "Can you hear me?"

Pablo's eyes moved to Carlos. He opened his mouth and attempted to speak but emitted no sound. He twitched a finger on his left hand.

Carlos hugged his father, then looked up at his mother who stood at the foot of the bed. "I will go to *Los Estados Unidos*," he announced. "I'll find Juanita."

Sofia looked horrified. "No. You can't. The *gringos* will put you in jail."

"Excuse me, Carlos. I'm Sister Antonina Magdalena. And this is Alejandra. It's not wise to try to go into the US without a visa. You will certainly be detained by the *migras* and put in detention, possibly for a long time."

"I don't care. I'm going to find my sister."

"The police and the volunteer agencies will locate Juanita. Lots of people are looking for her. And they have technology to help. You're not trained or equipped. You don't know the United States. What can you do, Carlos?" asked the nun.

"I can use my wits. I can follow my instincts. I'll find her. I know I will." Angry tears spilled from his eyes.

Alejandra said, "Carlos, what would you do even if you found her? You would be putting yourself and your sister in great danger. These people who have her are ruthless. Many trafficking victims have been severely punished because they've been belligerent. Some have even been killed."

Sofia sobbed and swiped at her eyes with a handkerchief.

Alejandra said, "Carlos. Let's leave this room. Please come with me to the lounge down the hall by the nurse's station. I want to talk to you without upsetting your mother."

"Okay *señora*, but you won't change my mind." Both his hands curled into fists and sat knotted at the seams of his trousers.

Alejandra poured hot water into a cup and added a teabag from a tea and coffee service sitting on a small corner table in the lounge. "Would you like tea or coffee?" she asked Carlos.

"No."

She turned and took a seat on one of three inexpensively upholstered chairs in the lounge. Carlos remained standing, poised to leave abruptly. "Listen, Carlos. You're upset right now and speaking impulsively. I know you're smart. Please calm down and use your common sense. You can't get into the United States without a visa, something that could take months to obtain. If you try to sneak in you'll be caught. You can't fool the surveillance cameras, dogs, drones, and electronic sensing devices along the border. If you get caught you'll be detained in a prison for a long time until a judge decides to deport you back to Mexico. You can't help Juanita from jail, much less find her."

Carlos stood motionless. Silent. Glaring.

"A private detective agency is working very hard to find her. They have reason to believe she's still near San Diego. Between them and the police, a lot of resources are being brought to bear. They're confident they'll find her. And they certainly have a better chance than one young man, who doesn't speak English, working alone in a strange place."

"I'm going. I'll find a coyote to smuggle me across."

"Then you should know this, Carlos." Sister Antonina Magdalena's voice filled with compassion. "Up to 50 percent of the illegal migrants who attempt to elude the US Border Patrol die in the deserts of California and Arizona. Often, their coyotes die with them, without ever making it to safety. There is a cooler in the medical examiner's office in Tucson, Arizona, which, as of yesterday, held the remains of over 140 migrants found in the desert. Many are never found." She touched him on the elbow. "Carlos, many are arrested and treated like animals; many others *die* like animals."

"I'll be okay. I can get maps and stuff."

"Won't you take some time to think this through? Think about what I said. Stay here in Tijuana to help your mother cope with your father's illness … at least until they know more about his condition and what may happen with his health."

"I'm going. I'm going to find my sister."

Alejandra stood and faced Carlos. She raised her index finger. "What will you do about money? It would costs hundreds of dollars, if not thousands, to hook up with a coyote."

"I have money. I sold our goats to the neighbor."

Chapter Thirty-Seven

May, 2019
Oceanside, California

"Get some peroxide and some ammonia. We'll have to bleach the shit out of this girl's hair," Martina shouted into her cell phone. "Bring them back here now, within an hour. And pick up a pair of drugstore spectacles. Something with a heavy frame but still sexy, if you can manage that. I can't believe you idiots have not already changed her appearance since the posters and TV publicity hit the street." She threw the phone onto the plastic-covered settee, reached for the bottle of tequila on the counter and poured a healthy dollop into a smudgy glass. "Jesus. What a dump. I can't believe that brother of mine chose a trailer, for fuck sakes. There's not enough room to turn around and face the other direction in this place … and there's three of you living here?"

Juanita sat on the other corner of the L-shaped dining settee and stared without saying a word.

"Just look at this filthy glass. This is a pigpen. How many days did they have you working after that television news spot came out?"

"I don't know. I haven't seen any television. We moved here five days ago. I've worked every night."

"The stupid bastards. Frank should know better. You're not going onto the street tonight. I'll whack some more of your hair off, bleach it blonde, and restyle it. And you won't be working in Oceanside or around the Marine base for the next little while. I have a new set of clients in mind. They won't be as likely to recognize you from the publicity as the marines might."

"It's nice to see you too, Martina," said Juanita, her voice laced with vitriol. "Too bad about Geraldo. I was in love with him a few months ago. The bastard."

"Let me explain something to you, Juanita. Like it or not, you work for us. And you stay alive, or die, at our discretion. I've never liked your attitude and I'm now the boss of the Rojas family businesses in California. You exist for the sole purpose of earning my family money. Someday, if you live long enough to get old and are no longer attractive to our clients, you could be freed. But unless you please me and our family, you could also die. So, think about your attitude."

"You don't scare me, Martina. Threaten me all you like. But I have God in my corner. He'll see me through this." But was God really in her corner? After all, she hadn't heard much from him lately.

***

An onyx-black GMC Savanna 1500 minivan, a replacement rental for the van in which Geraldo and Tillie had been killed, now held in evidence, headed east on Mission Road, just southwest of Camp Pendleton. The sun, well into its descent toward the Pacific Ocean, cast long shadows on the road ahead of the vehicle. Fertile farm country, punctuated here and there by clusters of suburban tract homes, rolled by on both sides. Juanita felt a hint of renewal at seeing farmland again. The earthy smell of the countryside surfaced, and with it some pleasant anchors deep within her memory.

But in other places, scorched earth and the burned-out frames of farm buildings provided mute testimony to the infamous Lilac fire, which had devastated parts of Northern San Diego County in 2017. Juanita and four other women stared out the windows at the unfamiliar landscape. All had been picked up from houses in Oceanside. All wondered where they were going and what new clientele they were about to meet.

Martina sat in the shotgun seat, one eye on the road and the other on the GPS. About 12 miles east of Oceanside, at a community called Bonsall, she instructed the driver, Arnie, to pull onto a gravel road heading south. On one side of the road, small fields of thyme and marjoram offered herbaceous aromas, which seeped into the vehicle. On the other, acres and acres of tomato bushes grew, espaliered in wire cages, bright red beefsteaks and Romas, yellow taxis and green zebras, brilliant orange grape tomatoes, all ripe and ready to be picked, the first of two annual crops grown in this part of California. A billboard depicting a smiling and bearded Sikh in an orange turban indicated they had entered Harry Patel & Sons Farms.

With a hand-sketched map in her hands, Martina directed Arnie to pull over at a dusty row of 12 identical cinder block huts, featureless except for small windows flanking the doorway and a flat wooden roof. Near where the van had parked, and all dressed like itinerant farm workers in Levi's, rough calico shirts, and dirty Stetsons or baseball caps, about 30 slim-waisted Mexican men milled about, smoking and joking,

The last three buildings in the row, each with token window boxes and desultory flowers, were obviously reserved for families. Women and runny-nosed children idled in front of the houses, the kids harassing a dozen or more mangy mongrels.

A wrinkled and weathered man in his 40s stepped from the clutch of men and approached Martina. They spoke in Spanish for five minutes, the man jerking his shoulders while gesticulating and pointing at the hutches. The sun was nearly down now, and from the van Juanita had trouble making out the man's features. She strained to see him better, and hoped that he, and the younger men, were kind.

Martina turned to the rear of the van and said, "Okay, *putas,* each of you go to one of those houses. Show these *granjeros* a good time. Fuck like your life depended on it. It could."

Juanita stepped around a pile of dog feces and entered the first house in the row. She stood in the doorway and waited for her eyes to adjust to the dim light inside. A male voice from a corner said, "Come to me, *señorita.* "

She had trouble seeing through the unneeded prescription in her glasses but by straining her eyes, she made out his dim form on a cot in the corner.

He was the first of seven that night.

Chapter Thirty-Eight

May, 2019
50 miles east of Tijuana

A yellow Volkswagen microbus coughed and wheezed up a final rise and ground to a stop amidst clumps of mesquite and creosote in the gravel yard of a gray stucco bungalow. The front seat passenger, a short, stocky *hombre* wearing a vented straw cowboy hat and a coarse stubble of beard, stepped out and slid the back door open. It stuck midway, but the man gave it a shove with his shoulders until it creaked and groaned the rest of the way open. "Okay, *gente*. Into the house. Quickly. Bring all your gear. We wait inside until it's good and dark. About two more hours. *Vamanos.*"

Carlos was the first to step down onto the crunchy gravel, and was followed by nine others, a couple with two daughters around eight and ten, four men in their 20s or early 30s, and a wispy, frail-looking woman of about 20. Except for the family of four, none knew the others' names, nor did they know the name of the coyote or his driver. That was how Straw Hat and the driver wanted it.

Unknown to Carlos or his fellow travelers, they were in the tiny hamlet of Jacumé, a mere 30 yards from the wall separating Mexico from the US. On the other side lay the gritty town of Jacumba, population 560. It had taken them five hours to drive the 50 miles from the east side of Tijuana, alternating between Mexico Highway 2 and the extensive web of dirt roads hugging the border, a circuitous route designed to avoid the *policía*.

Carlos had linked up with this group in the shipping bay of a poultry processing plant near the airport, after having spent several days making inquiries about coyotes in the cantinas and taquerias of the Insurgentes district. Being tall for his age, he was not hassled or asked for ID in the dives, known for their lax enforcement of Mexico's drinking age of 18. He didn't drink alcohol anyway. On the third afternoon, as he emerged from a 7-11 on Calle Jose Gonzales, a skinny, shoddily clad boy not more than ten years old grabbed Carlos by the arm and said, "Come with me *señor*. I have a friend you need to meet. He can take you to America."

The meeting took place in the men's restroom of a bowling alley. The boy led Carlos in and pointed to a man in a straw hat standing at a sink admiring himself in the dingy mirror while picking his teeth with a gold toothpick. Without turning to look Carlos in the eye, the man said, "You want to go to *Los Estados Unidos? Tienes dinero?*"

"Yes. I have money."

"*Bueno*. Tomorrow at noon come to the 7-11 where the boy met you today. Bring four thousand US dollars." He cocked his head slightly to the side and worked the toothpick between two molars.

"*Señor*, I have 750 US dollars."

"Bring 700 dollars. You can sign a paper for the rest. You'll have to work in the US to pay us back. *Entiendes?*"

"Si." Carlos trembled with excitement. He would find his sister.

"With the other 50 dollars buy yourself some shoes with good soles, running shoes are fine. And fill your pockets with light, dry food, tortillas and dried fruit. Bring two one-gallon jugs of water. You can buy those at the 7-11. Once we get past the border, we'll be walking a long way, through the desert mountains. Travel light."

Now, as Carlos took a step toward the house, weighted down by the two eight-pound jugs of water tied to a length of rope and looped over his neck, he noticed for the first time the dark looming border wall. In the dim light, it did not appear that formidable. About three meters tall, he estimated, and constructed of corrugated steel panels. He wondered how they would breach it. Ladders? A tunnel? He detected no razor wire along the top, a feature prominent along the border fence within Tijuana.

The inside of the house was unfurnished and illuminated by a single kerosene lantern. Long shadows played off the walls as the group silently went about arranging their goods for easy carriage. The family of four settled into a corner, crossed themselves, and then prayed together briefly, before they huddled to catch a short nap. Each of the other six found a spot to alight and sat silently, keeping their own counsel. The two coyotes smoked and whispered to each other. From outside somewhere the mournful howl of a wolf sent a shudder down Carlos' spine.

Carlos dozed, but at eight p.m. a swift kick to the foot rudely woke him. Straw Hat stood above him, now decked out in a military web harness for carrying his water and food. "Time to go, *gente*. Everyone up. We have a lot of ground to cover while it's still dark and cool. It's only 85 degrees out there now. In 12 hours it will be over 100. I'm taking you to where a van will pick you up and take you to the load house in San Diego."

"What's a load house?" Carlos asked.

"Don't worry about it, *cabrón*. It's a place where the driver delivers his load."

"But we're walking in the desert? Those two children over there. I don't know how they'll do on a long walk in the desert."

"That's not your problem, *cabrón*. You ask too many questions. It depends on where the *policía* and the *migras* are. The trip gets longer if we need to circle to avoid them. And we must avoid the two main highways, Highway 80 and Interstate 8. We'll meet our driver in a village called Pine Valley. Now enough chatter. Let's move."

Carlos stepped out of the house and was momentarily blinded by the brilliant dazzle and spewing sparks of an oxyacetylene cutting torch — someone cutting through the border wall. As he approached, shielding his eyes with his palms, he saw the driver of the VW. To the right of the panel being cut, white painted graffiti read: *Sin Fronteras*. Without borders.

A square of corrugated steel fell from the bottom of the wall and onto the ground. "Through here, quickly," Straw Hat said. "There's a dirt road running along the wall just on the other side. Run quickly across that road and hide among the boulders and mesquite. When everyone is through, we'll start up an arroyo that skirts the little American town."

By the time they started up the dry riverbed, with Straw Hat setting a brisk clip, Carlos was sweating heavily. Tempted to take the first swig of his water, but knowing it would be prudent to conserve, he resisted. He swiped at his forehead with his shirtsleeve. On his right, a few lights twinkled among the smattering of houses in Jacumba. This was his first glimpse of the United States. It looked very similar to the village of San Agustín, he thought. Except there was no church steeple presiding over the cluster of buildings.

As the town of Jacumba receded from view, the gully inclined slightly, slowing the group's pace. The family of four had already fallen back from the rest of the group, the older of the two girls staggering. The group left the streambed and entered an area strewn with sharp outcrops of basalt and loose boulders, making footing tricky. The landscape was pimpled with organ pipe and saguaro cactus as well as mesquite bushes, whose vicious thorns snagged their clothing and tore at their flesh.

They crossed Highway 80 and gained altitude steadily for about two hours, clambering into the high desert terrain of the Jacumba Mountains. Carlos continued to sweat heavily and he felt the first blister on his feet. The rope, from which his 16 pounds of water dangled, chafed the back of his neck.

Straw Hat called for a break at 10:30. He sat down heavily, leaned on the trunk of a Joshua tree, took a long swill of water and checked the GPS on his smart phone, ignoring the others.

With the ambient temperature still in the high 80s, Carlos slaked his thirst for the first time, downing almost 30 ounces of his water supply, and he did his best to mop his sweat with the now-soaked sleeve of his cotton shirt. He glanced at Straw Hat and wondered how long the battery on that phone would last and whether or not he could navigate this wilderness without it. He went to Straw Hat and sat down next to him. "I think you should know that the family is struggling. I don't think the two girls can go much farther. They're both stumbling over their own feet."

Straw Hat took a long pull on his water jug, then turned to stare at Carlos. "Once again, *cabrón,* they're not your problem. Everyone is tired already. But we have a long way to go and this will be a furnace in the morning. Some may not make it. We usually lose a few people. If not to the desert, then to the militias that patrol the border."

"Who are the militias? Are they the same as *migras?*"

"I told you, you ask too many fucking questions. The militias are not police and they're not border patrol. They're more like volunteers who own all-terrain vehicles and have guns. They think it's their job to keep us "undesirable" Mexicans out. We're riff raff. Sometimes they shoot migrants. And they've been known to rape the *chicanas.*"

For the first time, Carlos noticed that Straw Hat carried a pistol among the other tools in his web harness. "Then why do you do this dangerous work, señor?"

"For the money, stupid. I have an advantage. I know this country on both sides of the border well. I grew up in Jacumé, that little village we started from. In the 1990s the border was just a two-strand fence, with many openings. People on both sides could pass without being hassled. My family and all the others in Jacumé would cross the border for shopping, for visiting the health clinic, some of the kids even went to school there. I used to cross all the time to screw this one girl who lived on the Jacumba side. Then after those Arabs flew into buildings in New York and Washington, the fence was strengthened and turned into a wall. Now if the people of Jacumé want to visit a relative in Jacumba they must have a visa and drive or hitchhike 40 kilometers to Tecate, to cross. That pisses me off, but it created an opportunity for me to make *mucho dinero*. Now, shut up and rest, *pendejo*."

Three hours later, with several now struggling, the group reached a point where they could hear the truck traffic moving along Interstate 8, still a half mile to their north. Straw Hat halted in another dry streambed and waited for the stragglers to catch up.

"We have to cross the freeway in about another half hour. Stay together now. We'll stop at the fence, wait until there's no traffic eastbound, then rush as a group across the two lanes. Crouch down in the wide median and wait till we can cross the other two lanes without being seen."

Carlos looked back to check on the plodding family. Both girls shuffled forward, dragging their feet, their heads hanging. The mother fussed over them, placing her arms alternately around one or the other's shoulders, saying encouraging words, kissing their cheeks, but she also staggered and tripped.

"Señor, how much farther tonight?" asked the father of the girls. "My daughters are both having a hard time. They've used all their water. And my wife is sick."

"You'll have to share your water with them. We can't stop until midday tomorrow. Then we'll try to find some shade and wait until night again. I think we'll reach the place to meet the driver in two more nights."

The father shook his head sadly. Carlos sidled up to him. Even though he had emptied half of one jug already, he said, "I'll share my water with your girls."

By seven a.m., a blazing orange ball of sun rose just above a ridgeline to the east of the struggling group. They were moving north along a low ridge, the backbone of the Jacumba Mountains. Great heaps of rugged topography rose around them on all horizons, sharp and angular mountains thrust up and folded, buttes and mesas, massive boulder fields.

The temperature was already well above 90. The 11 people had been trudging through the craggy desert mountains for 11 hours and had traveled only six and a half miles. Carlos had trouble producing saliva, and his skin was hot and dry. He had used half his water and had thrown one empty jug into the desert.

Others were doing worse. The wispy woman was now a hundred yards behind him, staggering drunkenly. Behind her, the family of four stumbled and reeled, the father now carrying the ten-year-old piggyback. Ahead, all four of the men lurched and wobbled as they plodded on. One discarded his now empty water jug. Even Straw Hat appeared to dither a bit. He called for a halt and instructed his charges to find what shade they could, eat something, and conserve their energy for one hour.

Carlos plopped into the scant shade of a manzanita shrub, took another pull from his remaining jug and ate a handful of dried apricots. Nearby, the father laid his ten-year-old onto her back. The mother squatted at her shoulders and lifted her head, while the father poured the last of their water into her mouth.

They resumed the march at eight a.m. By 10:30, the monstrous heat had risen to 102 degrees. Carlos felt dizzy and his fingers swelled. The air, thick and dry, clung to him with an intensity that hurt. His cotton shirt and denim trousers had shredded in places from the relentless clawing of the mesquite thorns. Well into his second jug of water, he now carried it by its handle, alternating the weight between his puffy hands.

At 12:15, with the sun at its apogee, directly overhead, the bushes and boulders surrendered much of their shade. The temperature was 108. Straw Hat called for another break. "A few hours," he said. "Try to find some shade. Eat and drink."

Carlos slouched back to where the family of four had plopped down. He got on his knees and asked, "How's everyone doing?"

"Not well," the father said. "We're out of water, my daughter is delirious and my wife has cramps all over her body."

"Take more of my water." Carlos passed his jug to the group and encouraged each of them to take a few swallows, fully realizing that he couldn't continue much longer without a resupply. He'd just have to assume that Straw Hat had looked after that. Surely there'd be a cache somewhere ahead. He squirmed as close as he could to the trunk of a manzanita and sought its meager shade.

Then, its rotor blades thwacking louder than the engine noise, at an altitude two hundred feet above the terrain, a green and white helicopter rose over the ridge to their east and headed straight for them.

"Border Patrol," shouted Straw Hat. "Everybody freeze. Don't move."

But the Black Hawk slowed and came to a wobbly hover a hundred feet above them, the beating blades producing a downwash that felt good. From the rear door a crewman lowered two cases of bottled water to the ground on a nylon strap. An amplified voice said in Spanish, "Stay where you are. You will be rescued shortly. We're low on fuel and must leave, but a ground unit is on the way." Then it abruptly accelerated and flew off to the west where it disappeared behind the long spine of the In Ko Pah Mountains.

Straw Hat rose to his feet and shouted to the group. "He means arrested, not rescued. *Vamanos*. Grab a couple bottles of water each and follow me."

"We can't go on. We'll wait for rescue," the father croaked.

"Suit yourself."

The 20-year-old woman, looking more frail than ever, said, "Me too."

"Fine." He gestured to the other five men. "Grab four bottles each and let's go."

"Shouldn't we leave some for the them?" asked one man, jerking his head toward the spot where the family and the other female sat.

"Fuck 'em, Mateo. You heard what the helicopter man said, the Border Patrol is on the way by ground. They always carry plenty of water in their vehicles. The helicopter will be back too, as soon as he refuels in Campo." Straw Hat tore open the two cases, grabbed four bottles for himself and stuffed them into his web harness. He set off down a scree slope toward the shallow valley on their left. Carlos, Mateo, and the other three men followed, stuffing bottles into available pockets. Carlos shoved two bottles into his front pockets and two into his hip pockets, but he knew that in this heat, four 12-ounce bottles wouldn't keep him hydrated another day. He gurgled down the last water in his gallon jug and followed Straw Hat down the slope, lurching and sliding through the debris of a million years worth of geologic activity.

Somewhat rehydrated and energized by a rush of adrenaline, he felt stronger and more focused than he had an hour earlier, and he stumbled down the slope without losing balance.

At the bottom, Straw Hat halted and checked his GPS. "We need to be heading west now, over that next ridge line." He pointed toward the long rim of the In Ko Pah Mountains. "But first we have to find a hiding spot. That helicopter will be back in about 15 minutes."

"What about there?" One of the men pointed toward a craggy outcrop 300 yards north of them. It appeared to have an overhanging ledge of rock that would provide both shelter from the sun and concealment from aircraft. They made for it.

Just as they clambered under the granitic sill, the newly exhausted men heard the beating blades of the Black Hawk helicopter as it crested the ridge to the west and began a search pattern. It swept directly over them, its engine roar thunderous, its blades slapping like the wings of a great bird.

Carlos and the others pressed as far back into their little shelter as possible. When the noise abated and the shelter became eerily silent, their leader said, "He'll go back and forth and up and down, searching for us until he runs out of fuel again. About two hours."

"We've been together for a night and a day now. What's your name?" Carlos asked.

"It doesn't matter. We're not going to be friends when this is over. If you must, you can call me Paco."

Soon they heard the high-pitched whine of several small engines from the ridge they had left. "The Border Patrol in ATV's," Paco said. "Everybody stay put." Just then his cell phone emitted a shrill beep, a warning. Low battery.

Chapter Thirty-Nine

May. 2019
Escondido, California

Two laborers from the Patel farm, Hector and Clara Vasquez, left the clinic just as two ICE agents arrived in a US Department of Homeland Security vehicle. The couple, both in their late 30s, walked with a slight stoop from years of farm labor, but they looked comfortable and confident together. Nevertheless, the agents, a man and a woman, stepped in front of them, clearly prepared to challenge their legitimacy as immigrants.

Hector beat them to the punch. He withdrew their H2A Guest Workers visas from inside his vest pocket and held them out to the agents for examination.

The woman snorted, but stepped back to let them pass. The two agents then swaggered in through the door under the sign reading, Dr. Julio Bautista, Health Care for Migrants.

Relief for Clara's recurring back pain demanded biweekly visits to the clinic. There she obtained Oxycontin, the powerful drug which provided just enough relief that she could work in the tomato fields alongside her husband. It wasn't the first time they'd seen Immigration and Customs Enforcement officials checking for undocumented migrants in Dr. Bautista's practice. They'd been in the waiting room before when the receptionist spotted the agents. She had hustled a number of waiting patients into a bathroom, instructing them to lock the door from the inside.

Now Hector and Clara walked to the nearby In N Out restaurant, where they would celebrate their weekly day off with a juicy cheeseburger before catching a bus back to the labor camp at Harry Patel & Sons Farms.

Hector finished his meal and savored a cup of rich coffee, laced with cream and sugar, while Clara picked at the remnants of her french fries and absently watched the other customers. She had just reached for another fry when an image caught her attention on the tabletop. She shoved aside the recyclable cardboard container holding the fries and studied the paper place mat. She turned it this way and that to check it from different angles, and even pulled a pair of cheap reading glasses from a pocket to examine the placemat more closely. "Hector, look at this. Look down right here." She pointed to the right hand side of the mat.

Lowering his head to look at his own mat, Hector said, "*Que?* I don't see anything. What?"

"Look at the middle picture."

Three head and shoulder portraits of women were arranged vertically down the right-hand edge of the place mat. Hector focused on the middle one. "What about it?"

"People are looking for her. She looks like one of the girls who came to the labor camp the other night. *Las putas.*"

Hector studied the picture. "Nah. None of those girls had hair that long."

"Cover up the hair with your napkin. Just look at the face. I think she's the one that went into unit one as we were walking past on the way from the washing machines."

"That one had short blond hair," he said.

"Just cover the hair and look again. She could have changed the color of her hair. Look at the teeth and the eyes."

Hector ripped his napkin into three pieces and used them to cover the top and both sides of the woman's hair. He studied the face from several angles, paying particularly close attention to the eyes and high cheekbones. "You may be right." He read the Spanish words directly beneath the English on the poster. "She's missing, believed to be forced into working as a *puta*. She could be the one. "

"*Si*. And there's a phone number. I think we should call it, Hector."

"We shouldn't get involved. It's none of our business. Besides we don't need any extra attention from the *policia* or the *migras*. They could decide to send us back to Mexico."

"But we have our papers. We're not *illegales.*"

"You never know about those *hombres*. They could deport us anyway."

"Hector. Think about this girl's parents. Think of the pain they must be in, not knowing where their daughter is."

Pain gripped his belly as he thought about the daughter they had lost to a drunk driver four years earlier. "I guess we don't have to say who we are. Maybe the restaurant will let us use their phone."

Chapter Forty

May, 2019
In Ko Pah Mountains, California

The six men talked very little during the course of the long afternoon. Just enough that Carlos learned their names. In addition to Mateo, his companions were Manny, Salvador, and Francisco, whose manicured fingernails seemed incongruous with their circumstances. Carlos wondered if he would be up to the rest of the journey. Dark had fallen again, but still the desert floor burned their feet through the soles of their runners. All six of the men were low on water again, having sipped from their 12-ounce bottles all through the arid afternoon beneath the rock overhang. Carlos had one bottle left and several of the others were on the last fraction of their remaining bottle.

Paco had turned off his cell phone to conserve the waning battery while they rested in the shelter, but now he needed its GPS again. In the darkness, amid the repetitive landforms and shadows of the high desert, they could easily become disoriented, with fatal consequences. The intermittent but strident pinging of the phone's battery warning had several of the men in a state of near panic as they moved ever so slowly, scrambling through boulder fields.

Carlos had been careful to take only sips of his remaining water, but by nine p.m. he thought to hell with it, and took one long pull, then another.

"Holy shit. What stinks?" asked Salvador as a vile odor filled the air.

Manny's foot touched a soft irregular-shaped object. "*Mierda.* It's a big snake."

"It's a body." Francisco lit a wooden match and held it briefly over the rotting remains of a human being.

Paco used the flashlight in his cell phone to scan the immediate area just long enough to determine that they'd found not one, but two bodies, before the battery warning forced him to turn it off.

Both sets of remains had been partially eaten by birds and desert animals. Their clothes, hinting at a man and a woman, were in tatters. An empty plastic water jug lay nearby.

"Shall we check them for identification?" Carlos asked.

"Not worth getting your hands dirty," Paco said. "Clearly they're *illegales*.

"What about burying them?" asked Francisco.

"No. We've got to keep moving."

They trudged on to the west, using the waning power of the GPS only intermittently. By midnight, they'd drunk all the water and Carlos again struggled to maintain his balance. His ears and eyelids burned from exposure to the sun during the long afternoon. His dehydrated lips were dry and flaky. He tried to wet them with his tongue, but again he couldn't produce any saliva. The desert air, as thirsty as any of the travelers, sucked up his sweat as fast as he exuded it. His breathing became labored as the reduced fluid in his body made it difficult to transport oxygen.

At 1:15 a.m. Paco checked the GPS again to ensure that they were still headed west. The instrument emitted an abbreviated chirp. A red light flashed for part of a second and then went out, as though it had changed its mind. The screen went black.

"Shit. It's dead."

"Maybe we should stop for the night." This came out of Mateo as more of a moan than an expression of opinion. "We'll get lost without the GPS." He sat heavily onto the ground.

"No. We keep going. We'll take it slow and easy."

"I'm not going. I'll wait here for the *migras* to find me," said Mateo, his voice now a self-resigned sob.

"Fine. The rest of you, let's go. Stay close together and take small steps. We'll move slowly toward the west. Without the GPS, we'll have to keep going in the daylight when we can better fix our position and direction, but I think we'll be at Pine Valley by noon."

The remaining group of five staggered and stumbled for another three hours, each showing increasing signs of dehydration. They had difficulty speaking and Salvador, when he tried, managed nothing but a string of consonants.

Carlos' mind circled. I can take this one more step, he thought. No, I'll rest a minute and then catch up. One more step. I think there's water over here. There is no water. I can take this one more step. He stopped to urinate. A tiny bit of precious fluid drained away. I can take this next step, his muddled mind decided.

At about four a.m. the group came to a stop when they heard a strange buzzing. "Keep moving. This way," Paco said.

"No listen. It's traffic … trucks."

Carlos heard the faint noises then. A shot of adrenaline coursed through his system and his sluggish mind leapt into gear. "It's the Interstate. We've been going in a circle."

"No. Can't be. We're going west."

Paco's mind was just clear enough to make an important decision. "It's the Interstate. Let's move closer to keep it in sight … then walk west. Stay on track without the GPS. But far enough … away … not to be seen."

After grumbled assent, the men stumbled in a ragged formation toward the direction of the traffic noise.

It wasn't long before they came upon another body. They covered their noses and staggered past without comment, too tired and stupefied to care much. And another body a few hundred meters on.

At first light, with the freeway in sight, as they moved parallel to it, Carlos was the first to notice the huge green sign with white lettering hanging over the westbound lanes. The letters blurred and the sign seemed to dance around before his eyes, but finally he made it out:

Pine Valley 17
Campo 26

His overheated and muddled brain couldn't comprehend the fact revealed by the sign. He fought to make sense of it. He closed his eyes tightly in the irrational hope that visualizing the lettering with his mind's eye would give it some clarity. Instead, an image of his sister appeared. Her eyes danced and her smile radiated warmth, as they did at her birthday parties. It was too much to bear. He opened his eyes again and staggered on a few feet. As he looked back toward the sign the meaning crystalized for him: Pine Valley 17; 17 kilometers. They'd never make it. *He'd* never make it. How far had they walked already? Maybe 15 or 16 kilometers.

They couldn't have that far to go. He stumbled toward Paco, who stood gazing at the sign himself. "That can't be, *hombre*. Not another 17 kilometers."

Paco cast his eyes downward. "No. Not kilometers. It's miles. Seventeen miles."

Carlos' numbed mind struggled with the change in frame of reference. What did that mean? How far was 17 miles? He wrestled with the formula he had learned in grammar school. Was the multiplier 1.6 or 0.6? He tried 1.6. What was 1.6 times 17? His overheated, oxygen-deprived brain had difficulty with the process. The gears wouldn't mesh. It had to be over 20. He couldn't make it 20 kilometers. Then it clicked for him. Just over 27 kilometers. No way. He sat hard on the ground and put his hands to his face, struggling for breath.

The five men were all sitting on the gravelly ground now, Mateo slumped against Manny. Weakened, dehydrated, and demoralized, none was up to continuing. Carlos had cramps in both legs. His abdomen felt like he had to defecate, but he had nothing to pass, not even gas. An image of Juanita again swam before his face and a hint of resolve spurred him to his feet. With his thick tongue he managed two simple syllables, "Let's go." But his wobbly legs barely inched forward. His brain screamed, *water, water, water.*

Carlos looked back to see if any of the others were getting up. Paco rose to his knees and got slowly onto his feet, leaning heavily on the trunk of a saguaro cactus, oblivious to the sharp spine that perforated his hand. A third man, Francisco, struggled to his feet. With help from Carlos, Salvador too rose. The other two remained on the ground, one now prone, a thin stream of vomit running from his mouth, spilling more of his depleted fluid.

The sun rose fully over the eastern horizon and the temperature hit one hundred. It took the three men two hours to stumble and stagger less than half a mile along an intermittent path paralleling Interstate 8. They stopped and gazed at a small sign on a metal stake:

Campo Indian Reservation
Campo Kumeyaay Nation
No Hunting No Camping

In their bewildered states, none of the men comprehended the words at first. Their brains could only manage one message — water. More impulsive than cognitive, this thought blotted out all other conscious and subconscious ideas. The words swam before his eyes as Carlos stared at them through blurred vision. Even their wave-like motion before his eyes triggered the mirage of blue, cool water. A single rational thought penetrated the fog enshrouding his brain and he staggered to where Paco stood, dazed and wobbly, to tell him.

"There ... there ... hasta..." He grabbed Paco's shoulder for support as his thick tongue and cotton-dry mouth attempted to form elusive words. Both of them tumbled to the ground, clutching each other. Carlos tried again, "There hasta ..." He could hear his own words echoing. "...people ... water."

Paco's eyes had glazed over. He didn't respond, just stared blankly, as though focused on an object thousands of yards away.

With a herculean effort, Carlos hauled himself to his burning feet again. He took a tentative step or two past the sign. His befuddled mind goaded him to drink his own urine. He fumbled with his zipper and, while staggering through a slow-motion pirouette, managed to pull out his penis and form a cup of sorts with his hands. He managed to produce a few drops — orange and bad smelling — and licked them up with his swollen tongue.

He turned to look back. His mind barely registered that all three of the others were on the ground, Paco twitching, the other two motionless. Carlos lumbered forward with baby steps, tripping and falling as he went. Soon he heard another strange buzzing, a whirring that echoed through his head. He cocked and swivelled his head as he tried to determine the direction from which it came. Abruptly he realized that the terrain beneath his feet had become more even and level. He was on a dirt road running perpendicular to the direction the group had been moving.

The whirring seemed to be coming from the right, away from the freeway. He turned in that direction and bumbled off to the north. His warped perception conflated with his imagination and he saw Juanita, through distorted vision, standing before him on the road, motionless but smiling and speaking to him. The whirring became louder and morphed into words. *Drink, Carlos. Have some water, Carlos.*

He no longer sweated. His entire body burned with fever and sun damage. His clothing felt like sandpaper and he tore his shirt off as he approached Juanita. In his delirium, he saw the ground open in front of her. A huge fissure appeared, luring him forward. Water. There would be water in it. He stumbled and fell over the top of the crevasse to lay at Juanita's feet. He threw his arms around her ankles

— a solid metal post. He looked upward through bloodshot, filmy eyes and saw the huge blade of a windmill swishing above him.

His mind shut down without his seeing the sign on the metal post:

Kumeyaay Wind Farm – Turbine 16.
Report damage or vandalism to
Live Oak Trading Post
1 mile south at I-8

Chapter Forty-One

May, 2019
Bonsall, California

Andrew Zorbis and Philipe, one of SKIUS' Spanish speaking operatives, drove up the long driveway and came to a stop under a low portico in front of an expansive hacienda-style house. A smiling Sikh met them at the front door. "Hi. I'm Harry. Let's go into my office. I'll have someone bring us some tea."

They passed through a large but minimally furnished living room, through a door on the far side, and into a richly paneled office. A tall floor-to-ceiling window behind the massive desk afforded a grand view of the tomato fields. A half-dozen Mexican pickers labored in the distance. Mr. Patel courteously offered his visitors two comfortable leather chairs facing the desk, and then took his own place behind it. "What can I do for you, gentlemen?"

"It's good of you to see us on such short notice, Mr. Patel. We're here to — "

"Harry, please."

"Okay, Harry. Thanks for seeing us." Andrew handed him his business card and repeated what they had discussed on the phone, that the agency had received a tip from an anonymous migrant couple reporting they'd seen the subject of one of its cases apparently working as a prostitute in the labor camp of this farm. They were here to see if they could obtain more definitive information that might lead to the girl's rescue.

"I'll help any way I can. I'm a straight shooter where the law is concerned. I will not employ undocumented migrants, in fact I go out of my way to help potential workers obtain and maintain their temporary work visas. I want my workers to be happy and fulfilled, so I do turn my back where sexual visits after working hours are concerned. But if a kidnapped woman is being raped on my property, I want her freed and the perpetrators arrested. What can I do to help?"

"Would you know the couple who called us, Harry? And if so, is it possible we could talk to them?"

"I have only three married couples living in the labor camp at the moment. Hector and Clara Vasquez visit the migrant clinic in Escondido every week, so if the call came from there, it had to be them."

"Is it possible for us to talk with them? We'd only need a couple minutes. We want to show them a more up-to-date photo than the one they saw on the poster."

"I can send someone to the fields to bring them here. You can meet with them here, in my office."

"That might intimidate them. Is it possible we can make it low key and just talk to them out in the fields?"

Harry grinned. "If you don't mind bouncing along a couple of dusty, bumpy roads in my less-than-clean pickup truck. I'll take you out there and you can visit with them in the truck. I have a crew cab, so there is a back seat. I'll get out to glad hand and chat it up with some of the other workers. You know, management by wandering around."

Hector and Clara were both fidgety when they first climbed into the truck and sat in the back seat. But Philipe, speaking Spanish, put them at ease when he explained that he and Andrew were not the law, just private detectives interested only in freeing the girl they had reported to the agency. It helped too that he was from Mexico and had originally come to the States as an undocumented 12-year-old who also worked in the fields. He didn't bother telling them that he'd been a Navy SEAL for 20 years.

With the rapport now cemented, Andrew handed them a copy of the frame printed from the video cam in front of Fred's Oceanside Diner. With her hair much shorter and her face gaunter in this picture than the year-old head and shoulders portrait, the couple nodded. "*Sí. Sí,*" Clara said. "It's the one. But her hair is yellow now."

"And she was wearing glasses," added Hector.

"When exactly did you see her?" asked Philipe.

"Two days ago. That was the first time. She came in the van full of *putas* that comes almost every night. She was with them again last night too."

"Does the van stay here while the women are … uh working?"

"*Si, si.* It waits for two or three hours. Usually there are two men waiting in it. But for the last two nights, it's been a man and a woman, the woman is a *chicana.*"

"*Muchas gracias. Muchas gracias mis amigos.* That's a big help."

As Harry drove Andrew and Philipe back to the house, they explained what action they would like to take, being very cautious not to say exactly when.

"Of course," Harry said. "Do it with my blessing."

Chapter Forty-Two

May, 2019
Campo Indian Reservation, Kumyaay Nation, California

The radio message on the Campo Field Office's Romeo network was succinct and urgent, but all too common. "Kumeyaay Wind Farm supervisor reports cluster of bodies, four possibly five, one mile north of Live Oak Springs on the windmill service road. Ten-Twenty-five."

USBP Agent Don McBride, on loan from the Chula Vista station for the last three weeks, had been patrolling the network of dirt roads south of Interstate 8 and enjoying it. At least this station had supplied him with a newer vehicle, a trail-rated Jeep Wrangler, with a powerful off-road package. And the air conditioning worked like a charm.

He keyed his microphone and said simply, "Roger, 10-13." He flicked the switches for blue lights and siren and stepped down on the accelerator pedal, careful not to overdo it. Fishtailing on a gravel road could be perilous. He passed the Tribal Community Center and Fire Station doing a cautious 50 miles per hour, but four miles north at the Golden Acorn Casino he turned right onto the on-ramp of I-8 eastbound and accelerated to 85. Three minutes later, when he turned onto the Kumeyaay Wind Farms Service Road, he extinguished his siren, relying only on the blue lights to forewarn any oncoming traffic.

A few hundred yards short of Tower 16, a tall Native American wearing a grey hard hat stood next to an ATV. He flagged down Don.

"Mornin' Don," he said. "Four bodies, over yonder, between the cacti." He jerked his head toward the east. "Probably all illegals."

Don climbed out of the vehicle. "Can you show me?"

"Follow me. Hotter'n a pepper sprout, ain't it? Gotta be a hundred in the shade."

"Yes sir. How'd you find 'em, Bill?"

"I was just heading north to check on the turbines. Telepathy signals shows one of em's acting up. It's been runnin' too slow. I stopped here to take a leak and noticed a slew of ravens lifting off just a bit further east. I knew what it meant, but went on up to check anyway. It's not a pretty sight."

They crested a small rise and Don saw the first three bodies, sprawled out on their bellies, claw-like hands reaching forward as though they'd been trying to drag themselves farther. He felt a chill. The hair at back of his neck stood out straight. He hated this part of his job.

A vented straw Stetson lay nearby. The nearest body wore a military-style web cargo-carrying vest. Don bent down to examine him. Then stood and had a cursory look at the other two. "How long ago did you find them?"

"About 45 minutes ago. I called you guys right away."

"Yeah." He let out a long sigh. "I'm no doctor, of course, but I'd say they've been dead at least two hours. Ravens have had a pretty good go at them. And they're starting to bloat already."

"Yeah, the others too. Just about another two hundred yards into the desert. You wanna see them?"

"Yeah, let's go look. Then I'll call it in and get a wagon out here to pick 'em up." He glanced back down at the guy with the web gear and, for the first time, noticed the handle of a pistol poking slightly out of the mesh.

"Oh shit. I'm calling it in now. We'll need an ME and the Sheriff's crime scene investigators out here. We could have a murder, or murders, on our hands." He reached for the mic on the shoulder loop of his armored vest.

He made the radio call and then pulled a pair of thin blue latex gloves from a zippered pocket in his vest, snapped them into place on his hands and bent down again to examine the body more thoroughly. In a pocket of the web vest he found a wad of money, mostly greenbacks but quite a few pesos in large denominations as well. "Looks like we've identified the coyote. "Show me the other bodies, Bill."

At the sight of the other two, Don had to step away to empty the contents of his stomach. They were both on their backs looking straight up, but unseeing, through empty eye sockets ravaged by the ravens. One man was bare skinned and charred black from the waist up, his shirt torn open and spread to the sides like he had been trying to get the fabric off his skin. The other man's mouth gaped open, filled with a wriggling mass of black flies busily laying eggs.

"All right." Don wiped at his mouth and tried to regain his poise. "Let's get back to the road. That call I made will've been monitored by dozens of scanners. Every journo and hackette in eastern San Diego County will be on their way here in minutes with cameramen in tow."

By the time they reached the road, two other Border Patrol vehicles had arrived, and behind them, farther to the south, the cloud of dust suggested dozens more vehicles on this barely used road.

Don gave the three other agents a hasty briefing. Two of them set out to preserve the integrity of the crime scene by fending off the reporters. The third, along with Don, would remain and try to hold back the journos.

Then Bill said, "There's one more up the road a few hundred yards at Tower 16. Maybe you'll want to get up there real quick too."

Don and Bill drove the short distance to Turbine 16, where the prone form of a fifth man sprawled at the base of the tower, his arms around it as though imploring a lover not to leave. As he stepped from the vehicle, Don could see that this one too was shirtless, with numerous purplish patches on his flesh. The abhorrent task of examining him for any signs of life lay before him.

He bent down and without touching the victim leaned in close in to check his face. The man lay with his face to the side, the dry and swollen lips cracked like segments of grapefruit. A young one, Don thought. Even with the skin darkened and hot to the touch, there was a youthful texture to it. He noticed the soft, almost feminine, eyelashes and gently lifted one to examine the eyeball. Fully expecting to see it glassy and staring nowhere, he jumped back when suddenly the pupil constricted to a pinpoint.

"Bill!" he shouted over his shoulder. "Bring me the first responder kit and a couple of bottles of water from my Jeep. This one may be alive."

He leaned down and put his cheek next to the victim's face to see if he could hear any signs of respiration. None. He pried the hands off the pole and checked for a radial pulse on the left wrist. He could find none, even after moving his two fingers laterally across the wrist several times in an attempt to find a viable artery. No pulse along the edge of the thumb either.

Bill squatted down next to Don with the canvas bag and two chilled plastic bottles of water. "Here ya go, Don. Anything I can do?"

"Yeah, I'm gonna call a medevac chopper. See if you can find a carotid pulse. Use your forefinger and middle finger together. When I get back, we're gonna roll him onto his back. We may have to do CPR. D'you know how?"

"Of course. We all have to learn industrial first aid. What do you think we are? Ignorant savages?" He grinned and gave Don a quick pat on the shoulder. "Just go make your call, I'll take over with the assessment. Let's save this poor guy's ass."

Minutes later, Don came trotting back to the base of the tower. "How we doing, Bill?"

"I've got a carotid pulse. Faint but rapid. It's a heartbeat. Let's see if we can get him into a recumbent position and get some water into him."

"Good work." Don pulled a folded blanket out of the first responder's kit and together the two of them rolled Carlos over onto his back and lifted him to lean his neck and shoulders against the blanket folded at the bottom of the pole.

Four or five vehicles came roaring down the service road and braked to a stop just ahead of Don's patrol vehicle. "Shit. The press." Don stood to intervene. "They got through from the north somehow."

"Yeah. There's a northern connector to the service road. Another dirt road leaving the freeway back at the Williams Road interchange," Bill said. "I can manage here. Go shoo 'em off."

Don stepped in front of the lead vehicle just as doors opened on several cars and reporters and cameramen tumbled out. He waved both his arms over his head and shouted, "Get out of here! Back off! Get back in your cars and pull back. We've got an active situation going here. Lives are at stake."

A chorus of voices, male and female, gobbled like turkeys. "Agent, how many bodies are there?" "Are there coyotes involved?" "How many wetbacks?" "Did they tunnel in?" "Agent, what do you think of Donald Trump's plan for a wall?" "Are any alive?" "Where will they be taken?"

Don opened his car and pulled out a portable electric bullhorn. "I said, get back. This is a police matter. You can get a press update in Campo. I'm ordering you now to get back in your vehicles and turn around."

But the shouts and chants continued on a tiresome theme. "It's a public road, Agent. We can be here." "You've no authority over us." "The public has a right to know." Several video cameras and a number of smartphones, held aloft, were already rolling and pointed at Don.

Don turned up the volume on his bullhorn. "This is not a public road and it's not public land. You're on the private service road of a Native-owned corporation and you're trespassing on reservation property. I've got a helicopter enroute on a life-saving mission and all of you are right where he needs to land. Now, get in your vehicles and back away."

Then three police SUVs, two San Diego County Sheriff jeeps and the only Campo tribal police vehicle approached from the south. They came to a dusty halt. A sheriff's sergeant stepped out of the lead vehicle and said to Don, "ME's on the way. We're here for traffic control, what else do you want us to do?"

"Just try to keep these assholes back." Don pointed to the small mob of journalists. "I've got a chopper inbound and need a landing zone here."

"Roger that," said the sergeant. He climbed back into his vehicle and edged forward toward the reporters, speaking through a speaker. "Get back. Move back. There's a helicopter trying to land. You people are interfering. You'll be arrested for obstructing justice, if you don't move back." Both sheriff's vehicles edged up to the crowd, while the Tribal policeman backed his vehicle to the south and then turned crosswise in the road to form a roadblock from that direction.

The vehicles slowly backed up, but most of the journalists, while also stepping backwards, stayed on the road and crowed questions until the clattering of rotor blades and the high-pitched whine of turbine engines overpowered them.

The California Army National Guard Black Hawk helicopter circled the makeshift landing pad twice, then settled down with the rotor blades churning up a huge cloud of dust.

Don stepped toward it, elbow crooked over his face to protect himself from flying grit. As the big engines whined down to an idle, the back door slid open and two medics in Nomex coveralls and flight helmets stepped out, one carrying a folding litter, the other a huge canvas bag of equipment. They both raised their visors as the approached Don. The leader said, "I'm Specialist Becerra, 164th Medical Company, California National Guard. This is PFC Jones. What have we got, sir?"

"Don McBride, Border Patrol. A male Chicano about 15 or 16, unresponsive and in advanced heat exhaustion, possibly early stage heat stroke. Temp sky high. Pulse weak but tachycardia. Respiration undetectable. We're trying to rehydrate him orally, but the water is mostly dribbling down his chin."

"Okay, let's see if we can get an IV into him. Veins are probably pretty empty and collapsed out, though." He knelt by Carlos, where Bill held his head up and was trying to dribble water into his mouth.

"Jonesy, see if you can find a superficial vein in the antecubital area. I'll assess vitals."

Jones palpated and located enough of a vein to insert a full-length IV needle and attach it to a feeder tube. He hooked it to a plastic bottle of Ringers lactate and held it over Carlos' chest. Meanwhile, Becerra ran a topical thermometer over the forehead. "Jesus Christ. 105 degrees. Let's start another lactate in the other side." He palpated the other elbow and found nothing, but then located a prominent vein in the back of the hand and inserted a large-bore butterfly needle and hooked it up.

He spoke to Bill. "Chief. Oh. Excuse me, that was racist as hell. Forgive me, I don't know your name. Can you hold this bottle up while I finish his vitals?"

"No offense taken. Happens all the time. My name is Bill."

"Christ," Becerra said. "BP is only 35 over 15, respiration about 5, pulse still fast. Let's get him onto the litter and into the chopper."

Becerra and Don managed the litter while Jones and Bill continued to hold the IV bottles overhead. As they slid Carlos into the chopper, the co-pilot stepped back between the cockpit seats and hooked the IV bottles to overhead racks as Becerra and Jones strapped the litter down.

Don and Bill stepped back from the chopper as the engines spooled up and the dust flew. Becerra strapped himself into a jump seat and raised his thumb into the air. He shouted over the whining engines, "Thanks, gentlemen. We're taking him to Chula Vista. If he survives this flight, I think he's got a 50 percent chance of making it."

The chopper lifted to a low hover, did a pedal turn of 180 degrees then its nose dipped as it scudded off to the southwest until it had sufficient headway to ascend into the sunlit sky and head toward Chula Vista. The dust wafted off and the wailing turbines receded.

Don, overcome with emotion, gave Bill a hug. "Thanks, buddy. I couldn't have done this alone."

"No problem, my friend."

Don strode to his vehicle as the journalists again shouted questions at him. "Is he going to make it, Agent?" "Were they all tonks?" "How many dead?"

He stopped, turned toward them and snapped curtly, "They were human beings. We don't use the term 'tonks' and we don't say 'wetback' either. Catch the press briefing this afternoon." He wondered how many of them even knew the origin or the term 'tonk,' a bad joke alluding to the sound made by a flashlight striking a migrant over the head.

Then he climbed into the Wrangler and wept for five minutes before he called in his report on the Romeo network. Sometimes he hated this job.

Chapter Forty-Three

June, 2019
Bonsall, California

Two members of the San Diego County Sheriff Department's Special Response Team slid into the muddy water of the roadside drainage ditch, their CAR-15A2 assault rifles held high and dry. The stagnant water smelled foul and mud oozed into their boots. They both wondered how long this boring wait would last and hoped for the action, with its attendant adrenaline rush, to start soon. Neither really expected a firefight, but you never knew. If the perps were armed and desperate enough to attempt an escape, they might try to shoot their way out. The SRT's presence was intended to prevent that, but also to serve as a buffer, hopefully to prevent any innocents being hurt. They were an added measure of security. Extra meat.

The senior of the two, 27-year-old Simon Hobbs, whispered into the voice-activated mic attached to his Kevlar helmet by a swivel boom, "Whiskey Two in position."

An acknowledgement, just two soft clicks like a toy snapper from a child's Crackerjack box, sounded through his headset. Over the next few minutes, three other two-man elements reported that they too were in position. Again, each transmission was acknowledged with two metallic clicks. When the last of them ended, the evening was eerily silent except for the murmur of a few male Spanish voices on the other side of the road. A sliver of moon, waxing its way toward a new phase, hung in the south.

Simon had participated in many anti-sex trafficking operations, almost all of them stings designed to entrap the traffickers, involving the coordinated efforts of multiple federal, state, and local law enforcement agencies. The SRT's role in these ops was to apply the judicious use of armed force, should it become necessary. But nine times out of ten they were nothing more than exercises in boredom and futility. He itched to be part of an actual takedown — to bust some of the scumbags who made their living off human misery — and he fervently hoped that tonight's operation would result in a jackpot.

A shiver ran through Simon as the sweat evaporated and his body cooled from the two-mile jog. The team had been dropped by their Bearcat armored vehicle on Mission Road and had made their way, on the double, along the dirt tracks of the farmlands to their position just across the road from the Harry Patel & Sons Farms' labor camp. The two older civilians, private detectives named Roger and Philipe, had trotted in with them and kept up without any problems. Simon was impressed.

***

Roger Upton and Philipe strode across the gravel yard of the labor camp and approached the group of men huddled around a fire and chatting in Spanish. Philipe asked where he might find Mr. Patel.

"He's right over by there by unit six talking with our foreman."

They found Harry talking to an older, weathered worker, probably in his 40s. Patel greeted Philipe by name and introductions were quickly made. Gripping Upton's hand, Harry Patel said, "This is my lead hand, Arturo. He's on board with the plan. Mr. Upton we're setting you up in the first of the quarter's units, unit one. Arturo will take the two of you over there." He looked at his watch. "Just past 7:30. That van should be here in about ten minutes. I'm going to stay out of sight when it arrives. But if you need me I'll be right down there at the family units."

Arturo led the two of them to the nearest cottage, unit six, and then along the rear of the row until they were just past unit one. They slinked along the north wall of the cottage and then turned the corner to the front. Roger and Philipe made straight for the doorway as Arturo strode up to the group of men around the fire, and engaged them in ribald chatter about the *putas* soon to arrive.

The interior of the unit was dark. Roger and Philipe both swung the beams of their red-filtered tac lights around the space to get the lay of the land. There were two bunks along each of three walls. The fourth wall held a sink on a two-by-four frame, a half-sized refrigerator and a double row of pegs from which various and sundry items of farm apparel hung. A crude table and four chairs occupied the center of the room.

The two sat on a bunk and waited.

Ten minutes later, the crunching of gravel announced the arrival of a vehicle, and was soon augmented by appreciative murmurs and a few catcalls from the group of *vaqueros*.

Feminine giggles erupted, and with them the chorus of men's voices rose in tempo and volume. Roger and Philipe rose from the cot, moved across the room and stood, back to the wall on each side of the open doorway. As they waited, both tensed for action, Arturo's voice rose above the others as he made the cottage assignments to the clutch of prostitutes now milling about the yard.

Soon the voice of a man, cooing and teasing, full of anticipation and sexual energy could be heard nearing the unit. Two sets of feet agitated the gravel, one pair clumping and the other scuffling.

The first form to cross the threshold was the young woman, followed closely by the farm laborer, who was holding her hand. From his side of the doorway, Roger Upton grabbed the other hand of the girl and quickly pulled her toward him. With his free hand, held a finger to his lips, "Shhh. Juanita. It's Roger Upton. We're here to free you."

At the same moment, Philipe threw one arm around the farm hand's chest, jerked him up against his own torso and held him tightly as he clasped his other hand over his mouth. "Don't say a word. Don't utter a peep," he said in his most threatening Spanish tone.

Except it wasn't Juanita. She jerked loose of Roger's grip. "*Que pasa? Que pasa?*" she shrieked. "*Que mierda estas haciendo?*" She pirouetted and stepped back outside the door.

"What the hell? Who are you?" Roger shouted, following her out through the doorway. His mind raced through the options and he decided he'd have to take a risk. He shouted, "Juanita! Juanita, where are you? It's Roger Upton."

The headlamps of the black GMC Savannah immediately came on and flooded much of the yard in xenon high-intensity light. Most of the crowd froze in their tracks and heads turned toward the voices of Roger and the hooker.

A female voice from the van screamed. "What the fuck is going on?" The engine started and the transmission clumped as the driver threw the vehicle into reverse.

***

"Get out of here! Get out of here," Martina shouted at the driver. "It's a raid of some kind. Start it up. Go!"

The driver had cranked the engine the minute he realized something was amiss around the first cottage. Gravel spewed everywhere as he raced the vehicle out of the yard in reverse and spun the rear around on the road. He slammed the transmission into drive, but before he could hit the accelerator, two powerful tac lights mounted under the barrels of CAR-15A2s blinded him. SRT members stood to the front and on each side of the road. In the next instant, another helmeted SRT team member violently smashed his side window. "Hands where I can see them!"

The driver jerked his head around to find a weapon aimed directly at his head.

From the passenger seat, Martina screamed as her side window was also smashed in. Now several voices yelled, "Hands where we can see them." The driver's door was jerked violently open. A pair of strong hands gripped him by the shoulder and neck, and in one motion pulled him from the vehicle and threw him to the ground. Another pair of hands reached in, moved the shift lever back to park and turned off the ignition.

On the passenger side, Martina was removed only slightly less violently and instructed to lie face down in the gravel. She complied, getting down on her own, first to her knees then down on her elbows and lowering her chest, before she could be roughly thrown to the ground.

"Face down. Hands behind your back." A strong hand pushed on the back of Martina's head until her nose touched the gravel, then wrenched her head sideways forcing her cheek and her ear into the roadbed. She heard the click before she felt the tight handcuffs squeeze first the skin of one wrist, and then the other.

Simon Hobb's disembodied voice said, "You have the right to remain silent. Anything you say can and will be used against you in a court of law. You have the right to be represented by legal counsel. If you cannot afford a lawyer, one will be provided for you."

She couldn't help the crying. This wasn't the way she had envisioned her job as the Rojas family boss in America.

***

The farm hands and hookers now stood apart in two clumps of confused onlookers. It took Juanita a moment or two to grasp the situation and recognize the voice that had just called her name. "I'm here. I'm here." She stumbled toward the sound of Roger's voice near the first cottage.

For a second Roger Upton didn't recognize her. The straw-colored hair didn't compute. But the voice was hers. He grabbed her by the hand. "C'mon. Let's get up to the road where the police are. You're safe, Juanita."

They stepped onto the gravel road and were immediately surrounded by four more SRT members. One approached Juanita, and shone a penlight into her eyes. "I'm the medic, miss. Are you feeling okay? Are you hurt anywhere?" He examined both eyes, then checked her pulse.

"I'm okay. Just confused right now."

Two pairs of headlights approached from the north as the armored vehicle and a sheriff's department sedan sped toward them. Roger said, "Here's our transportation, Juanita. We're taking you downtown where some nice people will take care of you."

When the vehicles stopped, a deputy sheriff climbed out of the front passenger seat of the sedan and moved to the rear seat. Philipe climbed in front beside the driver and Roger and Juanita slid into the back, joining the deputy.

The driver turned and looked over his shoulder. He smiled at Juanita, the first smile she'd seen in many days, other than the leering grins of the mindless johns. "Everybody buckle up and let's get this young lady out of here."

Suddenly overcome, Juanita felt her hands tremble. She tried to speak, but the words dissolved into sobs, "Th …. Tha …" Gasping and crying compulsively, she couldn't get the words out.

"*De nada,*" said Roger softly, gently squeezing her hand. "It's over, Juanita."

Chapter Forty-Four

June, 2019
Seattle

Lien pushed back from her desk, rotated her sore shoulders a few times, and stretched her neck in small circles. She wandered over to the window. Grey clouds hung in the air and a sprinkling of rain spattered on the windowpane. Catherine's prized roses below in the garden loved this rainy weather, and their perky pastel heads added a little color to the dreary evening. No wonder that roses grew in the higher elevations near Dalat at home, she thought.

The small red light on her bedside alarm clock read six p.m. In Vietnam at this hour the flamingo sun would be inching towards the horizon, turning the waving rice a soft gold. An evening zephyr would be fanning away the heat of the day. The sky would soon be black. But not here in Seattle. The light would last until nine p.m. despite the clouds. This phenomenon still surprised Lien. She flung a sweatshirt over her t-shirt and padded down the stairs where she found Grandfather Pete in his favorite worn leather chair by a warm fire, reading the newspaper, his glass of Scotch close at hand.

"Ah, there you are, Lien," said Pete. "I was wondering when you'd surface. You've been up there at your computer all afternoon."

"It's been a long day at my desk," confessed Lien. "I'm just finishing an important paper for my contemporary social problems class. The process is painful. I read the research online, and translate it all in my head to Vietnamese. Then, when I decide what to use and how, I write it in my head in Vietnamese and translate it back into English and type it up. And footnotes are a nightmare for me. I have to finish this paper by tomorrow."

"Does Google Translate help at all?"

"Sometimes I refer to Google to make sure that I've translated the terminology correctly, but it's not that helpful in translating long passages. I wish there were more research online in Vietnamese. Universities in Vietnam offer degrees in social work. Some of the social workers with Green Gecko were trained at Vietnamese universities, but the research is very limited. It's mostly all about application."

"I'm very proud of your efforts, my dear granddaughter. You're one determined young woman. Do you ask Paul for guidance?"

"Paul is always willing to help me, but of course he's also working hard. It's his last year and he has papers to write, as well as working on his practicum at TBAA. He gets credit for the work, but he also has to write reports on the cases he works on. I try not to take advantage of his good nature."

"I expect you'll also have to do reports on the practical work you do with TBAA. That starts in just two weeks. You'll be a very busy person all summer."

"Don't remind me, Grandfather. I'm feeling really stressed. Finals at U-Dub are just a week away and then I leave for San Diego for the summer. But I've talked to two of my professors and they've agreed to help me with an application to receive credit for the work experience with TBAA. That way, I'll enter my sophomore year here with an additional course under my belt."

"So you've given up on the idea of transferring to SDSU until you complete your undergrad degree?"

Lien laughed. "You, Catherine, my academic advisors, and Maria at TBAA have all talked me out of that fantasy. Even Paul, who'd love to see me move to San Diego for longer than just the summer, thinks staying at the University of Washington is sensible for now."

"I hope you'll humor your grandfather and promise me that, while you're working in San Diego this summer, you'll not get involved in any rescues. I know that you did so very successfully in Singapore and in China. But after visiting the Homeland Security Investigations agent in Mexico City, I'm convinced that these Mexican traffickers are sinister."

"I don't know this word 'sinister.'"

"Sinister means bad, dangerous, almost evil. They don't think twice about shooting anyone who gets in their way. Just thinking about that video I watched makes me cringe."

"I can make that promise. I'll be working in the office in San Diego, helping with girls who've been rescued, just what I want to do after I graduate. I see that as my strength. I'm hoping to counsel victims during their rehabilitation. I can relate to their emotional trauma from my own experience, and when I've added in the theoretical knowledge from my degree studies, I'll be even stronger in this role."

"You could do the same work here in Seattle. I know I've already given you my blessing to go down to California this summer, but without sounding too maudlin, you're my only granddaughter and I really worry about you." He choked a little.

"I don't know the word 'maudlin' either, but I can guess." She reached across to him, from where she sat on one of a pair of chintz chairs, and lightly stroked his forearm. "Don't worry, it's only a summer apprenticeship. But to tell you the truth, I'm finding winter here very harsh. I miss the sunshine and palm trees. San Diego would be more like home if I chose to live there after graduation. I always thought that I'd return to Vietnam to practice social work, but America has more support services … and very professional agencies. What is the term? Leading edge?"

Trutch had recovered from his moment of emotion. "Yes, although I think the more current phrase is *cutting* edge." His heart swelled anew as he recognized the growing maturity and wisdom of his granddaughter. "I admit too that I'm cautious about how you'll … umh … deal with your deepening relationship with Paul Pham."

As though on cue, the warbling tone of an incoming Skype call on Lien's laptop sounded from upstairs. "Oh. That would be Paul now. Let me go see what this is."

When Paul Pham's face appeared on her screen, he appeared to be crying. It stopped her breath. But then, she actually felt the force of his joy before she heard his words.

His elation came through a quavering voice. "They've got her. Juanita has been rescued. *Rescued*, Lien. She's safe." His hands trembled as he gesticulated.

Lien grinned and extended a hard toward Paul on the computer screen. "Wonderful. When? How?"

He spoke too rapidly and tripped over his words. "Just, just now. A little while now … ago. They got … Roger Upton, one of the SKIUS guys got her. Along with the police … the sheriff's office. She was in a labor camp near … east of Oceanside. They got her, Lien. And listen. They got two of her traffickers too. One of them is part of a big ring in Tenancingo."

Lien heard shuffling behind her and turned to see Pete and Catherine standing in the hall just outside her door, staring at her computer screen, huge smiles on their faces. Lien said, "Grandfather, Catherine. They got her. Juanita's been rescued."

"So we've just heard," said Pete. "That's fantastic."

"Fantastic," Catherine echoed.

"Hello, Colonel and Mrs. Trutch," Paul said from the screen, tears of joy glistening in his eyes.

Lien took control of the conversation. "Paul. I'll talk to my professors tomorrow. See if I can defer my finals and come right down to San Diego. I know I can be of help with Juanita. She's going to need a confidante … a friend while she's in Rehab."

"That may be a good idea, Lien. But at this point we don't even know if it's appropriate for her to go into counseling here in California. For that matter, I don't know if Customs and Immigration would *let* her stay in California for rehab. She didn't exactly enter as a documented alien. There are a lot of questions."

"Yes, and the questions will start as soon as TBAA and the others involved start assessing her wants and needs. That's where I can help. She's going to be interviewed by a lot of people — I assume the police and ICE will be among them. If it's anything like my experience in Vietnam, a lot of faces and voices will be coming at her. She needs a strong friend by her side. Someone to be with her throughout the process. I can do that."

"I know, Lien. It's our mission at TBAA to advocate for her."

"And what I'm telling you, Paul, is that I can be the face of that advocacy."

"Hmm. I'll talk to Maria. I'd love for you to get down here right away, rather than wait a couple of weeks."

***

An hour later, the same conversation happened at dinner. Lien explained to Trutch and Catherine that she would seek permission from her professors to go straight to San Diego, using the advocate scenario. "I know what Juanita is about to go through. She'll be confused, bewildered, frightened of the bureaucracy, alternately depressed and joyous. With my experience and the closeness of our ages, I can be the friend she'll need to get through this."

Pete pushed back in his chair, its legs scraping across the hardwood floor making a long chirping sound. He sat pensive for a moment, then said, "It's not that simple, Lien. I suspect the authorities will want Juanita to help them make a case against the Tenancingo person they arrested during the bust. If so, she — and you too if you're by her side — will be exposed to some very mean characters. This Tenancingo ring doesn't have a boundary around one family. This is an international gang of thugs with connections to the big cartels in Mexico. I saw that horrifying video of Tenancingo. I spoke to federal agents who are intimately familiar with how they operate. I've done a lot of research. And — oh damn it — I think this could be dangerous … if not to your physical safety, then to your mental well-being."

"Grandfather, I love you. And I understand your concerns. Paul doesn't think it's properly my role to be Juanita's advocate. You're worried about my safety. And I can tell from your expression, Catherine, that you also have reservations. But I know the fierce battle that Juanita has ahead of her. I can help her get through it."

Chapter Forty-Five

June, 2019
San Diego

Paul Pham turned onto Tooley street, the location of one of TBAA's transitional houses in North Encanto, where Juanita had been for the past 36 hours. He had spent the ride filling Lien in on some of the details. The densely packed neighborhood where Juanita stayed had a friendly, suburban feel, he'd said, in one of San Diego's most diverse areas, with many middle-class minority residents. The houses had been built in the 50s to meet the need for post-World War II housing. Most of them were at least 70 years old, but still reasonably well maintained. Juanita was likely to feel safe there. He'd met her the previous morning, just long enough for a welcome, but he hadn't really talked with her yet. She looked skinny and tired, but her appetite was good and she'd been sleeping a lot. She was emotional, exhibiting a mixture of joy and sadness. "You'd know something about that," he said.

Then, slowing, he said, "Here we are. Maria likes this street in particular because it has so many mature trees. Lots of broadleaves, like maple and black oak and box elders, to create shade." He slowed further and pointed to an older two-story hacienda-style house, with bright red Spanish tiles on the roof. "It's that big house on the corner. "

He drove by the front of it, and then turned left onto a large paved parking pad at the side of the house.

They sat in the car for a moment while Lien looked around. A wooden sign at the front of the parking pad read: *Private Parking, Vicki's House.*

"Who's Vicki?" Lien asked.

"Vicki McCarthy. She dropped out of high school in the 90s and spiralled downhill from there. Addictions, mental illness, homelessness — the unholy trinity. She died of liver failure at 36, three and a half years ago. Her father was devastated when she died. He bought this house, renovated it, and donated it to TBAA. He knew of the work that Maria and TBAA does. He wanted her to have it to help trafficked women."

Lien stared at the sign, its lettering blurring as she thought of her own father and Vicki's. Finally, she said, "*Troi Oi,* so young."

"Yes. At least she didn't die on a park bench somewhere. She was in a charity hospital for two weeks before she died. They kept her comfortable."

Another small tear of anguish slid from Lien's eye. "Let's go in and see Juanita. And what about her family?" She hadn't had a chance to ask. "Do they know Juanita's okay? Has she talked to them?"

"Not yet. Hopefully that will happen tomorrow or the next day. Her Dad's still in the hospital in Tijuana, unable to speak … at least for now. But I got to go with Alejandra, the TBAA rep in TJ, to tell Juanita's parents that she's been rescued and is safe. The old man understood perfectly. I've never seen happier, more relieved people."

"I hope they can see her soon."

"Me too. They've had a lot of bad news." He told Lien about the disappearance of Carlos, Juanita's 15-year-old brother. "He disappeared right after he went to the hospital, about six or seven days ago. The worry now is that he's somewhere out in the California desert wandering around with other illegal migrants."

"Oh no. How much more pain can Juanita's family bear?"

"I know." He grabbed Lien's suitcase and waited for her at the front of his car. "Let's go in the front door today. It's more formal for your introduction to your housemates."

He led the way around the corner and onto the front sidewalk, where a few succulents grew along the narrow concrete path. The front steps were also concrete and the portico a flimsy piece of corrugated plastic. But Lien's first impression of desolation changed as Paul opened the cipher lock and they entered the large, bright living room, furnished with long sofas and easy chairs of many styles and colors, afghans and Mexican rabozo shawls flung over the backs. Books, magazines and newspapers littered the low, wooden end tables and coffee tables. It looked comfortable and homey.

A short, buxom woman burst into the living room, her cheeks rosy with either temperature or exertion. "Welcome, welcome. You must be Lien. I'm Rita, the housemother here at Vicki's House. Most of the girls call me Mama. I just brought a batch of cookies out of the oven. We'll have some while we get acquainted. But first let me show you to your room." She shook hands with Paul and clasped Lien by the shoulders. "You'll stay here on the first floor in a bedroom close to mine and we'll share a bath. The other girls all stay upstairs. We have four bedrooms where we can sleep eight girls, but now we only have seven and this is a good thing because we know that Juanita, like all new residents, will do better in a room on her own, where she can grieve privately." Rita paused briefly for an audible intake of air. "Now you bring that suitcase Paul, and we'll show Lien her room. It is not the Hilton, but we're happy here and you, like all of our residents, will have the run of the house."

Lien and Paul shared a knowing smile as they followed Rita down a short hallway. "This here's the TV room." She pointed to a room on the right. "And this here's the Privacy Room. See that little sign? If it's turned to "Occupied" it means that someone needs to be alone in there, to use the phone, to meet with someone like a lawyer or the police, you know, or maybe a counselor. Our bedrooms and bathroom are at the end of the hall. We can access the bathroom from each of our rooms so we don't need to go into the hall in our jammies. Just lock my door on the inside of the bathroom if you're in there and I'll do the same. If it's urgent just bang on the door."

"Thank you." Lien smiled. Rita had obviously welcomed many girls and women over the years and had the patter down. But she was warm, energetic, and no doubt sensitive to the needs of the house residents.

"Now, Paul," Rita continued, "you come with me to help with the tea while Lien decides where she wants to put her stuff, and then I'll tell you how I think Juanita's doing. I'm not a certified professional or anything, but just like you, Lien, my experience in this house and before I got here make me qualified, if in a different way, to be a friend and mentor to these girls."

"Do we call the residents 'girls'?" enquired Lien quietly, remembering the professional guidelines she had read in a counseling textbook.

"Honey, when you're as old as I am, any female under 40 is a girl! And this place is home, not an office."

Shortly after their tea, Paul made motions to leave. He knew that Juanita and perhaps the other women as well, were still wary of males and he didn't want to be an unwanted or unexpected presence when they wandered into the living room. He said his good-byes and made arrangements to pick up Lien on his way to the office the following day.

"After you unpack a bit, I'll let Juanita know that you'll be in the Privacy Room to meet her," Rita said. "That OK with you? Maybe in about half an hour?"

"Perfect. Is she expecting me? And, does she know who I am?"

"She knows that you're a summer intern with TBAA, that you're studying sociology, and that you're a former victim, just like her, and want to offer friendship. That's all."

"Thanks. I'm anxious to meet Juanita. Ever since I heard about her abduction, and saw her picture, I felt a strong connection. I prayed for her rescue and now here she is. I expect she'll be as frightened, confused, and ashamed as I was. Having someone just to listen, without judgement or advice was very healing for me."

Later, as Lien sat in the tiny conference room, she questioned her ability to do the listening that she felt was so important. *Stay client focused,* her textbooks had advised. *Stay with their stories, do not be lured into telling your own story or give the wisdom learned in your practice.* What practice? All she had was her own experience and one year of sociology to rely on, Lien thought. But she would listen, listen, and listen. All she could offer was friendship.

She heard a tentative rap on the door, it opened slowly, and Juanita stood there. For a few seconds the two young women drank each other in. Juanita was taller than Lien, bowing her head slightly. The brassy blond hair had already been died black. Lien searched the dark eyes when they finally met her own. She almost gasped. She could have been staring into her own eyes, as she had seen them in a mirror shortly after her own rescue — lifeless, full of shame and fear.

"Hello, Juanita. I'm Lien. Please sit with me." Lien offered one of the two easy chairs. No desk separated them as Lien took the other chair. "Thank you for seeing me. It must be confusing to have met so many people in the last couple of days."

After a few moments of silence and no response from Juanita, Lien continued. "I hope that you'll begin to feel safe here at Vicki's House. Do you understand some English?"

"*Si,* I studied English in grades 7 and 8. But everything is confusing," whispered Juanita. "I'm in a foreign country, my father is ill, my brother is missing, and I am ruined. Nothing makes sense. I want only to be home with my father and mother, yet I am so filled with shame that I can't imagine seeing them."

THE ROAD FROM TENANCINGO

"Feeling shame is understandable. When all of our beliefs of right and wrong and our efforts to lead a virtuous life are stolen from us we have a hard time believing that we'll be forgiven."

Tears squeezed from Juanita's haunted eyes. "I was a good Catholic girl, but my God abandoned me. My parents will be ashamed that I've been violated, and now I question this God for not protecting me."

Lien thought of how tenaciously she had held the jade Buddha her grandmother had given her. The talisman had reminded her to hold onto hope. When it had been stripped from her neck by her captors, she believed that her spirituality had also been ripped away. She squelched the impulse to cry out, *me too, me too, I get it*. She resisted leaping from her chair to hug Juanita close and assure her that she was still one of God's children.

"Your healing will take a long time. We're all here to help you confront the terrible truths about the trauma you suffered. It will take all of the strength that you can muster. I suppose that the very first thing we can do is to help you recover that strength. You've had that strength in the past, you have survived. Together, we will recover it."

"I'm so tired right now. So tired. It's too much."

For the first time Lien could say, "I know, I know. You must sleep, get fresh air, walk on the beautiful earth, eat nourishing food, and meditate on the goodness that's possible in this troubled world. Let's go and have some dinner with the others. We can be together whenever you need someone to talk to. I won't intrude on the time you'll need to talk with people here at TBAA about your options, about what you'll do next, but I can promise to be your friend."

Chapter Forty-Six

June, 2019
Chula Vista, California

Officer Douglas DeWeese and Agent Don McBride stepped off an elevator on the third floor of the Sharp Chula Vista Medical Center and walked across the tiled floor to the nurse's station, located behind a gleaming white and black marble counter. Two women and a man, all of them in colourful pastel scrubs, worked behind computer screens. A female nurse and a white-coated physician, both on their feet, glanced at iPads and compared notes. One of the seated nurses looked up. Her eyes, surrounded by deep laugh lines, shone with compassion. "May I help you gentlemen?"

"I'm Officer DeWeese, with Immigration and Customs Enforcement," DeWeese said. He wore an armored vest over a blue polo-type shirt, and khaki trousers decked out with a holstered Glock 22 pistol. "This is Agent McBride, US Border Patrol. We're here about the Mexican kid pulled out of the desert yesterday. We understand he was moved from ICU this morning. Agent McBride is the one who apprehended him."

Don bristled, preferring to think of it as a rescue, rather than an apprehension.

"Oh yes." The nurse tapped a computer key. "Carlos Montero."

At the time of his rescue he had no ID. Now Don's eyebrows shot up when he heard the surname, the same as the 17-year-old who'd been rescued from traffickers a couple of days earlier. He still carried yesterday's edition of the San Diego Union Tribune, which featured the girl's rescue on the front page. Could they be related? Naw, probably not, he told himself. Just a coincidence. The surname Montero was as common as McBride.

"There's another ICE man sitting in his room. *Guarding* him I suppose." She frowned, making it clear that she didn't like his choice of words either. "Mr. Montero is our patient, but is he under arrest?"

DeWeese, a supervising detention and deportation officer, said, "He'll be detained when he's released from the hospital. Meanwhile we hafta have someone keeping an eye on him. What room is he in?"

"Actually, I think the attending hospitalist, Dr. Eggers, wishes to speak with you before you see Mr. Montero. Would you mind waiting in the little lounge just across the lobby there? There's coffee, tea, and juice in there. I'll page Dr. Eggers now. I don't think she'll be long."

Dr. Eggers wore sharply creased gray slacks and a mauve blouse, over which she wore a tailored white jacket, its main purpose seemingly to hold her cluster of name badges and magnetic access cards. She had a shock of salt and pepper hair coiffed into a big spongy Afro.

"Gentlemen, Mr. Montero is progressing nicely. He's out of danger, so we moved him here from the ICU this morning. He's pretty much rehydrated and his vitals are largely stable, except that he's still running a temp. That's related to his sunburn. Second degree over a large portion of his back and neck, as well as his nose. His biggest clinical issue is pain control. But he suffers headaches and nausea as well. There's also a risk of infection, so we have to keep him under close observation. He's not leaving this hospital for at least four days, if everything goes well. It will probably be more like a week, before I feel confident that I can release him."

DeWeese broke in. "That's all well and good, doctor. But we need to get him into Otay Mesa for processing. Unless he's got some notion of applying for asylum, he'll be deported as soon as possible."

"I understand officer. But I intend to keep him until I'm good and sure all danger has passed. I don't want him to go to a detention facility unless I'm one hundred percent sure he's healthy."

"We need to see him, Doctor."

"I'll take you down to Room 308 myself. But I'm remaining in the room while you talk to him."

The ICE officer who had been watching Carlos placed his iPhone in his pocket. He rose from his chair and nodded as DeWeese and McBride entered the room.

DeWeese walked directly to the bedside and stared down at Carlos. He spoke gruffly to him in Spanish. "Montero, how many people were in your party when you entered the United States?"

Carlos' gaze darted around the room, taking stock of the three people who'd just entered. He looked at Dr. Eggers as though he expected her to help him with the answer. She just nodded at him.

"Eleven counting the coyote. We left several people in the desert at the end of the first day. I think there were six of us when we found the highway and changed direction."

"We found five bodies, including that of your coyote. So, there'd be about five missing? What was your purpose in entering the United States?"

Dr. Eggers stood on the opposite side of the bed. She folded her arms across her chest and stared sternly at DeWeese.

"Let me try," said Don McBride to DeWeese. Without waiting for permission, he asked softly, in passable Spanish, "Carlos, why did you come into the United States?"

Carlos responded to the friendlier tone. "To rescue my sister. She was kidnapped in Guanajuato and taken to Tijuana to be a *puta* and then to the United States … to San Diego," his soulful, watery eyes staring at the officers.

"Carlos, is this her picture?" McBride unfurled the folded newspaper and held it so Carlos could see the front page.

Carlos' eyes lit up, but his face registered surprise. Two images of Juanita were printed side by side. The one on the left was the portrait he had seen many times. Taken eight months earlier, she had long dark hair cascading over a shoulder. Her teeth shone white, and her eyes sparkled, even in the newsprint picture. He barely recognized her in the photo on the right. Her face was gaunt, her hair the color of straw and shorn off short. There was no hint of her radiant smile. His eyes moved to the headline. He couldn't read much of the English but two words stood out like banners: *Juanita Montero*. He looked back up at Don. His eyes asked the question.

"*Si amigo,*" said Don. "She's been rescued. She's safe. She's here in San Diego with an agency that will take good care of her until she's ready to go home."

"I want to see her." He looked over to Dr. Eggers. "Where are my clothes?"

"There wasn't much left of them when they brought you in here, Carlos." She laughed. "But I'm afraid you need to stay here for a few days anyway. Maybe longer until we're sure you're really well. But I'm sure we can arrange for you to talk to your sister on the phone."

Don touched Carlos on the hand, careful to avoid any blistered skin. "I'll find a way to get *her* over here to see *you* in the next day or two, Carlos."

As they passed through the vestibule on their way out of the hospital, DeWeese said, "What are you? A law enforcement officer or a goddamned social worker, McBride?"

"Most of us are just human beings, DeWeese."

Chapter Forty-Seven

June, 2019
San Diego

Lien had barely finished breakfast with Juanita when Paul and Maria arrived at Vicki's House. "Good morning, ladies. *Buenos dias, mujeres,*" said Paul, beaming with pride at having used a Spanish phrase.

Lien and Juanita were the only residents in the small dining room, at a table laid with a white linen cloth. The smell of sausages lingered in the air. "May we join you at the table for a few minutes?" Maria scooted out a chair without waiting for an answer.

Lien smiled. "Of course. What's on the agenda for today?"

"Well, it'll be busy. But first, we have some big news for you, Juanita."

"Yes?" Her face reflected confusion, happiness, fear, trepidation, all rolled into one.

To ensure that her message was received with its intended clarity, Maria switched to Spanish. "Your brother Carlos was rescued from the desert a couple of days ago. He's in a nearby hospital recovering from heat exhaustion and severe sunburn. You can see him today, if you'd like."

For a moment it seemed as though Juanita had left the room. Finally, she smiled tentatively. "Rescued? He is okay?"

"He's in a hospital in Chula Vista, about 30 minutes from here. But he's okay. As soon as he's released, he'll probably be delivered back to Tijuana by ICE — the immigration enforcement police. In the meantime, a border patrol agent, the one who found and saved your brother, wants to drive you to Chula Vista to see Carlos. I'll go with you if you'd like."

"What about my parents? Are they still in Tijuana? Do they know about Carlos?"

"I called our representative in Tijuana as soon as I heard that Carlos was in Chula Vista. She and Paul — he was in Tijuana at the time," she gestured toward Paul, "drove to the Tijuana General Hospital right away to let your parents know."

Juanita looked at Paul and opened her mouth as if she wanted to ask him a question, but she remained silent. She lowered her eyes to her plate for a few seconds, and then she said, "I have too much to think about. My brother, my parents. I want to see them all, but I can't ... I can't see my parents. Not for a while."

"Whenever you're ready, we can arrange a phone call with your parents, Juanita. That might be an easier way for you to begin. Do you want to see Carlos today?"

"Yes, I think so."

"I'll call the border patrol man. His name is Don McBride. We'll see what time he can be here to drive us over."

Maria switched back to English and looked at Lien then at Paul. "Did you understand that?"

"Most of it," said Paul.

"Hardly any," said Lien, "But I think I get it. Her brother's in the hospital and wants to see her."

"Right. I'll go with her. Now, I suggest you two take some time off today and go do something together. It's a beautiful day. Or do you have classes today, Paul?"

"Uh no. It's Saturday, Maria." He blushed with pleasure at the thought of spending more time with Lien.

"So it is. So, take the whole day and do something fun. Juanita will be tied up most of the day, anyway. Some of the bureaucratic stuff starts happening this afternoon. She'll be interviewed by ICE."

Lien frowned, spoiling the radiant expression she'd been wearing all morning. "Oh my gosh. She won't have to go to a detention center, will she?"

"On no, no. Because of her situation, the team coming here this afternoon includes an ICE victim assistance specialist. Not too long ago victims of trafficking were sent to detention centers. Federal agencies didn't always see eye to eye. The FBI and the Justice Department needed the victims to provide evidence, so traffickers could be prosecuted, but ICE detained them and deported them. That policy was bad for both victims and law enforcement. The Trafficking Victims

Protection Act, which is enforced by the Feds, was developed to have both enforcement and humanitarian goals. ICE now takes a much softer approach to trafficking victims than other undocumented migrants."

***

Lien climbed into Paul's old Mustang. "Where shall we go?"

"I don't trust this old car to go far on a day like this. It's been overheating. I guess we could go to the San Diego Zoo. It's pretty famous."

"I've read about San Juan Capistrano, also famous. A mission. Isn't that near here?"

"About an hour north, up I-5. It's peaceful and spiritual. But I'm concerned about driving up there in this car."

"Let's rent a car then."

"Umh, well, this is embarrassing … but I don't think I can afford to rent a car."

"Maybe I'm feeling a little mischievous today. I have a credit card on my grandfather's Visa account. He told me to use it for expenses while I'm down here. I think we could justify 40 dollars or so." Her eyes sparkled. "Oh, come on, Paul. Let's go to the airport and pick up a rental car. San Juan Capistrano sounds wonderful."

Thirty minutes later, they were cruising up Interstate-5 in a new BMW M-3 convertible, top down, Lien's silken black hair waving behind her. "I have a feeling you're paying more than 40 dollars a day for this car," Paul said from the passenger's seat.

"I told you I was feeling mischievous."

Lien found street side parking on Ortega Highway, just a half block from the mission's new gatehouse. They paid the 20 dollar admission fee for two adults, again using Trutch's Visa card and entered the classic mission grounds to explore the quadrangle of historic adobe buildings, with their tile roofs and arched doorways.

After strolling through sculpted gardens and wandering through the old stone church ruins, Paul and Lien entered the Mission Basilica. The afternoon light sparkled through stained-glass windows and cast soaring gothic arches in a yellow light. Rows of dark wooden pews glimmered with the flickering lights of hundreds of candles. Lien had seen many opulent pagodas at home, but the ornate beauty of this place of worship left her speechless. She knew little of Catholic religion or of the history of the church in southern California, but the stunning yet tranquil edifice took her breath away.

Near the back of the nave, they sat in a pew in companionable silence. How long had it been, she wondered, since she had meditated? How long since she had truly relaxed and been at one with the universe?

Outside, she and Paul found a shaded bench in the garden and continued to sit silently for a long while. Paul then turned to her and said tentatively, "Lien, can we talk about us for a minute? This has been a wonderful first date, if you can call it that. You know that I adore you and I can sense that you like me too. I just don't know ..." his voice trailed off.

Lien turned to Paul and taking both of his hands in hers, she gazed into his eyes. "I think I know what you're trying to say and I've been struggling with the same thoughts."

"Well, I understand why you're so shy around men and I'd never hurt you ... but I need you to help me ... to let me know if it's OK to express my affection ... to touch you."

Lien glanced down with a little smile at her hands clutching Paul's. "I remember your kiss on my cheek at the airport as I left in December. I held that scalding spot for weeks. The wonder of that tender kiss has left me wanting more, but I'm unsure of myself. I know nothing of love between a man and a woman and I can't promise how I might react. I've been afraid of being a fool."

Paul laughed aloud. "Oh, sorry for laughing, Lien. You know what's funny? Here we are, two aspiring professionals in listening and counseling, and we've both been avoiding what we've wanted to say, fumbling around like teenagers."

"I know. I know ... but when it's your own heart and your own feelings, it's hard. I must remember this conversation. It's better than any textbook example."

Paul took his hand from Lien's and gently put his arm around her shoulders. She nuzzled comfortably, head on his chest. They both stared across the garden, quietly at ease with one another.

Chapter Forty-Eight

June, 2019
San Diego

On Sunday morning, Lien and Juanita went for a long walk on the leafy streets south of Tooley. The air was fresh, birds sang, children at play laughed, and church bells pealed in different sequences from several directions as they strolled. "How far are we from Saint Mary's Church in National City?" Juanita asked.

"I don't know San Diego very well. I only know of National City because the TBAA office is there. But I don't know where the church is."

"It's on Seventh Street. I went there twice with Tillie, but I don't know how far it is. They helped the detectives find me. I dropped a note asking for help in the offertory basket. I'd like to go there and meet the priest."

"That's a great idea. It would be good for you. Let's ask Paul or Maria about getting you over there."

They walked in silence for a few minutes. The neighborhood provided a sense of comfort, if only because of its certainty. Trees, older houses, children, dogs, picket fences. Lien asked, "How did it go yesterday with the Customs people?"

"They asked me if I wanted to go back to Mexico and told me they'd arrange it if I wanted. But when I told them I was unsure right now, one man seemed relieved. He asked if I was willing to help the authorities put Martina in jail."

"I think that means they want you to testify against her at a trial. What did you say?"

"I said I just didn't know about anything yet. I need to get my balance before making any decisions. I really need to know who I am. One man nodded like he understood. The other seemed impatient with that."

"I understand," said Lien.

"The man who asked if I was willing to help said I might be eligible for something called a T-Visa, and that I could stay in the US with that, even get a job or go to school here. I don't think I want to stay in the US. I want to go back to the Universidad de Guanajuato. It's just that I don't want to go back *now*. I can't face my parents and my family. I even felt guilty when my brother Carlos hugged me yesterday. I'm just not sure about who I am right now, Lien. I feel like I'm in … limbo? Is that a word in English too?"

"Believe me, I do know what you mean. Did they say anything like if you don't help with putting Martina in jail, they'll take you back to Mexico whether you're ready to go or not?"

"No. But I do wonder about that. I know what 'undocumented migrant' means. That's what I am."

***

Once back in the transitional house, Lien called Maria, who in turn called St. Mary's Catholic Church to ascertain the mass schedule. The last mass of the day was at 11 a.m. but once he heard the reason for the query, the Reverend Barella volunteered to visit with Juanita that evening. He clearly remembered receiving the note in the collection monies and had followed events on the news media. That evening, he and Father Ruiz visited with Juanita for an hour. Father Ruiz asked if she'd like him to hear her confession. Juanita declined. She wasn't ready.

***

On the Monday a week later, Lien attended an assessment review meeting in the TBAA conference room in National City. Around the table sat Maria, Paul, Dr. Peggy Jones, a clinical psychologist, two social workers, and Lien.

Maria opened the meeting. "Good morning everybody. We're here to review the assessment progress of Juanita Montero. As you know she's been with us for about nine days now and has been interviewed and observed by everyone in this room as well as by Homeland Security Investigations, ICE victim assistance persons, the San Diego County Sheriff's Department, the FBI, and prosecutors from the US Attorney's Office, District of Southern California. She's had a complete physical exam and was found healthy … in body, anyway. And there's no evidence of any addictions or chemical dependencies. So, two issues remaining are her emotional state and her status in terms of whether she stays in the US for a while or goes home to Mexico. Let's start with you, Peggy. What are your impressions or conclusions?"

"Sure. If everyone will open the blue folders I've provided, my written psych assessment is there. But I'll be glad to highlight it orally. The bottom line is that she does exhibit behaviors and patterns of emotional thought that are consistent with post-traumatic stress disorder. That's not in the least surprising, and I think at this point it's not acute to the extent of being dysfunctional. Her thoughts and speech patterns are both linear and clear. She reasons well, and, not surprisingly, scores high on the intelligence batteries I administered." Peggy looked up from her notes to gauge the reaction from the group.

"Is there a downside to any of this?" asked Maria.

"Well, she's pretty confused as to her identity right now. As we all know, she feels great shame at what she's been through, has a tendency to think it's her own fault, and doesn't think she can see her parents, for that reason. She tells me she has negative mood alterations, including sadness, depression, anxiety. And she suffers from sleep deprivation. But she denies any compulsion to hurt herself or any suicidal ideation. All told, she's stronger emotionally than many victims of trafficking we've seen here before."

Lien stared at her coffee cup and fiddled with her ballpoint pen as she flashed back to some of the same experiences now being described.

Maria said, "Assuming Juanita wants to stay on for a while and the immigration and customs people are on board with it, would you think she could benefit by spending more time with us, Peggy?"

"Absolutely. I think we can help her to find her feet again, through a combination of one-on-one counseling and the group therapy that occurs as an integral part of group living here. I would, of course, caveat this by saying that she must want to stay with us for a while."

"How do the rest of you feel about her situation and her chances? Lien, as our newest advocate, can we start with you?"

Lien blushed, "Well … I uh … actually, I'd feel a little fraudulent speaking out. I've only just finished my freshman year in social work. I'm hardly a qualified professional."

"That may be, Lien," Maria said gently. "But we're a team here. Everybody's impression counts, regardless of credentials. And you've had a great deal of practical experience in this field. You must have some thoughts about Juanita, based on the past week you've spent with her."

"Okay. Here's what I think. Juanita is strong, intelligent, and resilient. I think she's going to be just fine. But yes, she could benefit by staying here until she decides for herself that she should return to Mexico. Whether that means to her family or to the university, is up to her." Lien flushed with embarrassment. She suddenly felt stupid, thinking that she'd been expected to say something more clinically erudite.

"Well said, Lien," Maria observed. "Now, how about the rest of you? Paul? Carole? Gail?"

The discussion lasted for another 45 minutes and resulted in a consensus. After a short break, they all sat down again to review the second issue; the matter of Juanita's legal status related to her staying in the US for a while.

Maria had written these agencies on the whiteboard in the conference room:

DHS Department of Homeland Security
HSI Homeland Security Investigations
HSI VAP HS Investigations Victims Assistance Program
ICE Immigration & Customs Enforcement
USBP US Border Patrol
DOJ Department of Justice
FBI Federal Bureau of Investigation
US Attorney's Office
NGOs

"Here's the deal as far as officialdom is concerned," Maria said. "As you can see by the whiteboard, several federal agencies get involved in immigration status, law enforcement, and prosecutions where trafficking is concerned. I've written these up here because it's a real alphabet soup, and Lien, you may not have heard of all these."

"Some of them I have," said Lien. "So, would those abbreviations all be acronyms?"

"Essentially, yes. What's important is that they all get involved. HSI, the FBI, and the US Attorney's Office, all want Juanita to help put away the Rojas woman, Martina. When trafficking victims have been imported from another country, such as in Juanita's case, HSI is the coordinating agency. As I mentioned yesterday, they used to be strictly enforcement and investigation-minded and showed little sensitivity to the victims. Fortunately, that's changed and they now have a victim assistance arm staffed with people who actually show compassion." She paused to make sure everyone was following.

Lien and Paul both furiously took notes, Paul with pen and paper, Lien on an iPad.

"If Juanita agrees to cooperate, she'll see people from all of these agencies from time to time, but it's the VAP who will work most closely with us," Maria said. "The victim assistance officers do not actually deliver any social services to victims. Instead they arrange for NGOs to provide the services. In this case, they will coordinate with us to ensure a smooth transition for Juanita — they'll make sure she receives all the services she needs. And they'll maintain contact with her for the duration of the investigation and judicial process. I know that's a mouthful of bureaucratic gobbledygook, but that's the way the government works. This assumes Juanita decides to stay and help. If she chooses not to be involved with the criminal case, she'll probably be processed for deportation."

Lien said, "Excuse me. Yes, that is a lot of … I think you could call it *jargon*. Juanita told me last week that one of the customs and immigration men she talked with said something about a T-Visa that would allow her to stay and work here. Is that what you're talking about now?"

"Not necessarily. The T-Visa is a good deal for trafficking victims who think they'd like to stay long term in the US. But the problem is that it takes three years to obtain after the application process has started. During that time, the victim is in limbo — can't work, can't go to school and could be deported for any number of reasons."

"How could she stay then? What does this VAP group do to give her a legal leg to stay?" asked Paul.

"Well here comes some more gobbledygook. But since you asked, this is a good review for all of us. Since the passage of the TVPA — that's Trafficking Victims Protection Act — there are now temporary status measures that can be invoked for someone like Juanita to be legally in the US. In her case it will be what's called a 'stay of removal' or a 'public interest parole.' Sounds horrible I know but it's actually a compassionate thing for the victims."

Peggy said, "Obviously we can't influence Juanita to stay. She must make up her own mind. But I think it's important she know that seeing the perpetrators brought to justice can be extremely healing for the victim."

Maria's cell rang then, and she glanced down at the caller ID. "Excuse me. I'd better take this. It's from Alejandra in Tijuana." She asked them to continue discussing the choices among themselves and left the conference room.

Ten minutes later she returned, wearing a slight frown. "Well, there's good news from Tijuana. But there's also some worrisome news."

She had their full attention.

"Starting with the good news, Carlos, Juanita's brother, will be released from Smart Medical Center in Chula Vista tomorrow or the next day. He'll be driven back across the border by ICE and will then take his parents back to Oaxaca by bus. Señor Montero is also being released from the hospital within the next couple of days."

Everyone smiled. "That will be very good news for Juanita," said Lien. "May I have the honor of telling her when I get back to Vicki's House?"

"I think that would be fine. Don't you, Peggy?" She watched for a nod. "Now, here's the distressing news. The Monteros have no money and Carlos sold their herd of goats to raise the funds for his ill-fated rescue mission to San Diego County. They'll have to live at the subsistence level on their farm for a while. But Señor Montero will require speech therapy and occupational therapy several days a week, in order to recover a reasonable degree of functionality. He'll have to travel, three days each week, from their home in a place called San Agustín Etla to Oaxaca city. That's a distance of three hours in each direction. Or, the alternative, he would live in Oaxaca for up to a year or two. Either would be a crushing financial hardship."

"Oh no." Lien said. "If we tell Juanita all those details, I suspect she'll blame herself. It could be a real blow to her recovery."

"Well," said Maria, "Alejandra tells me the Catholic Diocese in Oaxaca is looking into a way to raise money to help. Until we know how that plays out, maybe we only tell Juanita the part about Carlos and her father both being released and heading for home."

All six faces were pensive.

Lien excused herself, stepped out of the conference room, and made a phone call to Everett, Washington.

Chapter Forty-Nine

July, 2019
San Diego

"Ready to come about?" Paul shouted.

"Ready," Lien and Juanita shouted in unison, looking gleeful as the wind whipped their hair and the sunlit bow wake rushed by on both sides.

"Helms alee," shouted Paul. He turned the wheel hard to port so that the bow slewed rapidly around through the westerly breeze, settling 90 degrees off the former tack, so they now pointed toward Point Loma.

Both women rapidly worked the sheets, Lien releasing the windward one with a rapid upward jerk of her hand, while at the same moment, Juanita hardened the leeward line, vigorously cranking the winch handle with both hands until the sail grew taut and filled with wind.

"Whoopee. In the groove," shouted Paul from his position at the helm. "You're both doing really well, considering this is your first time ever on a sailboat. Did you ever think eight miles an hour could be this exhilarating?"

Lien turned an ear-to-ear grin to him. "Why haven't we done this before?" Then she aimed her iPhone aft toward the downtown skyline and snapped off several photos.

"Seems like every time you're down here, we're always both too busy. Besides, it costs a lot of money to rent this boat for a day. Do you think we can use your grandfather's credit card again when we turn it in?" he joked.

Suddenly a series of pops sounded in the water near the bow. "*Madre de Dios*," shouted Juanita, with a look of terror. "Did something break?"

"No, no. Look forward, beside the bow on both sides. Quick. Look. Look," Paul said.

"*Troi Oi*," said Lien. "Dolphins. Dolphins. They're leaping in our bow wake. I've only seen them in an aquarium."

"It's called bow riding," Paul said. "They're surfing on our wake. Isn't it cool? Walk up to the bow. You can see them more closely. Take your cameras."

Both women scrambled to the bow, while Paul held their course steady to the southwest, riding the 12-knot wind. "There must be 15 or 20 of them," Lien said. "Look at them leap. So beautiful."

Juanita laughed exuberantly, for the first time in months. "*Oh, es tan hermosa!* It's so *fabuloso.* I don't have the words in English."

The afternoon passed joyously, with the stalwart crew making several broad reaches down the length of San Diego Bay and short-tacking their way back to the north. Fully sated with good picnic food, a couple of beers, perfect wind, and brilliant sunshine glinting off the cerulean waters, they moored the Catalina 35 at Cabrillo Isle Marina at four p.m. and headed back to Vicki's House, tired and happy.

"*Mis amigos,*" Juanita said from the back seat. "This afternoon I have found God again. Thank you."

***

The following day, Lien and Paul attended another team meeting, this one regarding a victim who had managed to free herself, and who would undergo an assessment in the next few days. When it finished, they stepped into the cantina adjacent to TBAA's office for a coffee. Seated at one of the three small stainless steel tables, Paul asked, "Do you have work at Vicki's House this afternoon, or are you free?"

"I should go back and spend a little time with Juanita. But I could be free later tonight. Why? Are you asking me for a date again?"

As expected, he colored slightly but swiftly created a distraction by dipping his biscotti in the latte and stirring it around. "Umh, well. Today's the Fourth of July. I just thought we could hang out. Maybe go to the fireworks tonight."

Before Lien could respond, Maria walked in. "May I join you two?"

"Sure," said Paul. He stood and dragged the other chair out from under the table.

"Lien," said Maria. "I don't suppose you know anything about a wire transfer for $50,000 from Everett, Washington. There's a stipulation that the money be transferred to Oaxaca to help the Montero family through their travails."

"Who me? Why should I know anything about that?"

Maria smiled and shook her index finger at Lien. "I don't know what to say. You're gutsy. Let me know how I can reach this Nakry to express our gratitude."

***

At six p.m. Lien and Paul rode the bus to Coronado and attended a soft rock concert in Spreckles Park. They found a spot to sit on the grass and listened to the music and revelry for an hour. Paul got up enough nerve to ask Lien if she'd like to dance just as the musicians, a five-piece combo and vocalist, struck up a slow tune from the 50s. Lien stood, took his hand, and led him to a spot next to the gazebo, where several other couples already swayed to the music and to the rustling of palm trees overhead. They danced so close that Lien could feel the warmth of his body, and she chuckled when lyrics from an ancient song popped into her head. She'd heard them several times on an oldies radio station in her grandfather's car — "Heaven. I'm in Heaven … together, dancing cheek to cheek."

Feeling mellow, and assertive, she said, "Let's dance to one more, Paul. Then we'll go find a romantic place for dinner."

Dinner was light but sumptuous at the Blue Water Grill on Glorietta Bay. The atmosphere was casual, the staff friendly and efficient, and the seafood specialties numerous and spectacular. Lien ate blackened halibut and drank a glass of crisp, dry white wine. Sitting on the patio, overlooking the marina and enjoying the breeze, but especially the company, she felt comfortably tender, almost numinous.

After they paid the bill, without using Trutch's credit card, they found a nearby grassy spot on Strand Way at the water's edge and sat to watch the fireworks. Lien got caught up in the exuberance, the patriotism, and the passion of the crowd as she watched aerial displays of starbursts, dahlias, crackles, and comets. She felt almost as if her own colors were bursting and flying across the sky.

The crowd rose for the grand finale, which came with a series of thunderous bursts and multiple bouquets of color blooming in the night sky. She leaned her head against Paul's shoulder and looped her arm through his as those around them belted out the lyrics of "The Star-Spangled Banner."

She had been in love with Paul for months. She could admit that to herself now. But how could this play out? She nestled closer. Perhaps that was the beauty of an ongoing story — she could always look forward to a new chapter.

Epilogue

Department of Justice
US Attorney's Office
Southern District of California
FOR IMMEDIATE RELEASE
Friday, December 20, 2019

Woman convicted of Sex Trafficking of a Minor

SAN DIEGO, Calif. — On Thursday, after a seven-day trial, a federal jury found Martina Guadalupe Rojas, of Tenancingo, Tlaxcala, Mexico, guilty of one count of sex trafficking of a minor, and multiple counts of conspiracy to engage in sex trafficking of minors, US Attorney Mark D. Logan announced.

According to court documents and evidence presented at trial, Rojas' older brother, Geraldo Eduardo Rojas, abducted a 17-year-old girl from her university campus in Guanajuato, Mexico, and transported her to the Rojas family home in Tenancingo, where she was held against her will, forced into prostitution, and later smuggled into San Diego County, where Geraldo Rojas was killed in a police shootout. Martina Rojas then entered California on a valid visitor's visa and took over the family business in California.

The trial further established that over a period of several years, the Rojas family, and Martina Guadalupe Rojas in particular, engaged in multiple schemes involving force, fraud, or coercion to transport minors into the United States and force them to engage in prostitution.

"Sex traffickers prey upon the vulnerabilities of their victims, luring them, or forcing them into a cycle of physical and psychological abuse that is often difficult to escape," said Fred Benson, Senior Agent in Charge of the San Diego Field Office of Homeland Security Investigations. "HSI, in partnership with the FBI and a host of other federal law enforcement agencies is committed to identifying and apprehending individuals who sexually exploit others for financial gain. HSI is the coordinating agency in all cases where sexual trafficking within the US has its roots internationally. We seek to provide victims with an opportunity to escape the violent existence they have endured and ensure their exploiters face justice."

This case is a product of investigative and enforcement work done by HSI, the US Border Patrol, the San Diego County Sheriff's Office, the National City and Oceanside Police Departments, and two non-governmental organizations, all working collaboratively.

Rojas faces a mandatory minimum term of ten years in prison, a maximum statutory penalty of life in prison, and a $250,000 fine. The actual sentence, however, will be determined at the discretion of the court after consideration of any applicable statutory factors and the Federal Sentencing Guidelines, which take into account a number of variables.

Presiding Judge Michele B. McNair, stating that the defendant's family possessed considerable resources and that there was a high flight risk, denied bond for the defendant. She set the penalty phase of the trial for January 16, 2020.

Acknowledgements

I owe a debt of gratitude to all of the following people who were instrumental in helping me bring this project to fruition.

My dear wife and life partner, **Elaine Head**, always my first reader and most vociferous critic.

My writing mentor and editor, **Pearl Luke**, who once again guided me through a number of structural and storyline improvements.

Murray Reiss, a detail-oriented and sharp-minded copy editor.

Seven beta readers, who all waded through the manuscript in installments and commented constructively on needed improvements:

Debby Bardavid
Christina Bruce
Linda DeWolf
Patti Lizkay
Wayne McFarland
Irene Frances Olson
Roger Upton

Dr. Karl Nicholas for helping me understand desert hyperthermia and ensuring that the symptoms I described and clinical language I used were accurate.

Marisa Ugarte shared insights into the realities of trafficking and NGO work in San Diego County.

The following friends and relatives whose names I borrowed for some of my characters:

My brother **Dave Logan** and his wife **Joanna.**

My brother **Mark Logan.**

My sister-in-law **Rosey Robertson.**

Fellow Vietnam veterans from 1966-67 **Simon Hobbs, Don McBride, Roger Upton, Andy Zorbis.**

My five-time fellow traveler with Tours of Peace Vietnam Veterans, **Michele B. McNair.**

I hope you all enjoyed your alter egos.

Thanks to one and all.

Author's Afterword

Tenancingo is real, and the events I described happening there are factual. I hasten to point out that there are two towns in Mexico that go by that name, one a shameful place and the other idyllic and quaint. Tenancingo the bad lies in Tlaxcala State, about two hours southeast of Mexico City. The other one, Tenancingo de Degollado is a picturesque hill town in the state of Mexico, about an hour and 45 minutes southwest of Mexico City.

An interested reader can find plenty of information about the shameful Tenancingo on the internet. The most revealing and informative sites are: (1) an article in *The Guardian*, dated April 5, 2015, and titled "Tenancingo: the small town at the heart of Mexico's sex-slave trade"; (2) a video entitled *Pimp City*, produced by The Fusion Group which can be found on Youtube; and (3) a series of articles by Elizabeth Aguilera, published in the *San Diego Union-Tribune* in 2012 and entitled "An Inhumane Trade: Human Trafficking." A Google Search for Tenancingo – sex – trafficking will produce many more references to the tawdry little town in Tlaxcala. Actual field research, or tourism, in Tenancingo, is not recommended to my readers. For those of you who read Spanish, you may be interested in a book entitled *Tierra de Padrotes: Tenancingo, Tlaxcala, un velo de impunidad*, by Evangelina Hernandez.

There are two NGOs (non-governmental organizations) featured in this story; Saving Kids in the US (SKIUS) and Trans-Border Anti-Trafficking Alliance (TBAA). Although both agencies are fictitious, they are modeled after two very real groups that are both doing fine work in the anti-trafficking realm. SKIUS attempts to mimic Saved in America, an Oceanside, California-based NGO comprised of volunteers, most of whom are retired military or law enforcement, who employ a combination of technology and old-fashioned detective work to locate victims and collect actionable intelligence in order that law enforcement can step in. TBAA is fashioned after the Bilateral Safety Corridor Coalition (BSCC). Headquartered in National City, California, BCAA is an alliance of over 60 nonprofit and government agencies arrayed along the US-Mexico border region to combat slavery and human trafficking.

There is a measure of solace in knowing that there are hundreds, if not thousands, of other NGOs in North America, working tirelessly through many dedicated people to combat human trafficking and assist its victims.

Growing awareness about the problem of modern slavery and human trafficking is also beginning to result in efforts on the part of corporations. A growing number of businesses are looking to address human trafficking through training, education, leadership initiatives, supply chain management, and financial analysis. One example is that of the western US burger chain In n Out, whose efforts at promoting awareness and helping locate victims is described in this story.

Many companies in the travel and tourism sector are also actively engaged in anti-trafficking efforts. Over 900 travel-related companies in 34 countries now subscribe to a common code for the protection of children from sexual exploitation in travel and tourism. Among those subscribing companies are Marriott International and its family of hotel brands. Following guidelines developed by the International Civil Aviation Organization (ICAO), airlines, including American Airlines, Air Canada, United Airlines, and Alaska Airlines, to name a few, are training cabin crews to recognize potential trafficking situations onboard and report accordingly. Out of curiosity, I Googled *airlines human trafficking* and got a long list of videotaped news spots reporting "hero" flight attendants who have successfully obtained help for trafficking victims on their flights.

While the forgoing indicates there is much support for anti-trafficking from civil society, it is ultimately government that bears the responsibility for the 3-Ps: prevention, protection, and prosecution. There is good news here. As of 2019, 174 nations have signed on to a UN Protocol on Trafficking, known as the Palermo Protocol of 2000. It must be noted, however that for many of these signers, particularly in the third world, implementing legislation is inadequate and actual enforcement is lax.

During my research for this novel, I was pleased to discover that in the United States there is a multitude of federal, state, and local law enforcement and social service agencies involved in fighting trafficking and assisting its victims. There is keen awareness among these levels of government of the scope and nature of the trafficking problem, and they all have dedicated men and women working hard to deal with the scourge.

One doesn't always think of the Department of Homeland Security (DHS), and Immigration and Customs Enforcement (ICE) in particular, as being compassionate entities. Their agents are seldom perceived to be warm and caring. So I was happy to learn that ICE and several other branches of the DHS, including the US Border Patrol, Customs and Border Protection, the US Coast Guard, and the Transportation Security Administration, all have programs aimed at countering human trafficking. In Fiscal Year 2019, ICE, also identified as HSI (Homeland Security Investigations), made 1,896 human trafficking arrests and (here's the heartwarming part) rendered assistance by their trained victims assistance specialists to 428 trafficking victims. At the Federal level, other agencies engaged in combating trafficking include:

Department of Justice: conducts investigations and prosecutions, funds victim services.

Department of State: engages with foreign governments, develops strategies to confront modern slavery.

Department of Education: raises awareness of human trafficking in school communities, encourages schools to embed the issue in emergency operations and management planning.

Department of Health & Human Services: funds victim assistance service programs, provides technical and training assistance to local communities.

Department of Transportation: partners with transportation industry leaders to train stakeholders, develop educational tools, disseminate awareness materials.

Department of Labor: assists law enforcement in identifying trafficking victims, engages internationally to implement models that reduce child labor and forced labor.

Department of Agriculture: works to raise awareness of human trafficking in agriculture and rural areas in the United States.

Department of the Interior: provides anti-trafficking training with federal, state, local, and tribal entities, provides victim services in American Indian and Alaskan Native communities.

Despite these efforts, the problem of human trafficking and modern slavery remains huge on a global scale. It is estimated that between 30 and 40 million people are currently in slavery, 5 million of this number are sex slaves. Average annual revenue from sex slavery is estimated at 90 billion dollars per year.

If this angers you, as it should, there are a few things you can do to add your voice to the outrage:

• Learn all you can about the scope of the problem, particularly in your locale
• If you can write, write — letters to the editor, op ed pieces, essays, articles, blogs, books
• If you are a public speaker, speak — to service and community groups, clubs, school groups, church groups, associations
• Buy more copies of this book, and my other books on the subject — give them as gifts to friends, relatives, community influencers (all proceeds go to anti-trafficking efforts)
• Write a check or donate online to an NGO in the business of combatting trafficking. There are hundreds. A few of my favorites are:
- Go Philanthropic Foundation, www.gophilanthropic.org
- Blue Dragon Childrens Foundation, www.bluedragon.org
- Childrens Education Foundation, www.childrenseducationfoundation.org
- Bilateral Safety Corridor Coalition, www.bsccoalition.org
- Unicef, www.unicef.ca, (Canada), www.unicefusa.org, (US)

Other Books by R. Bruce Logan

- *Back to Vietnam: Tours of the Heart* (with Elaine Head), 2013
- *Finding Lien*, 2016
- *As the Lotus Blooms*, 2018

www.rbrucelogan.com

ABOUT THE AUTHOR

R. Bruce Logan has retired from two satisfying careers — US Army officer and management consultant. He has devoted his retirement years to humanitarian work and philanthropy, largely in Southeast Asia. In 2012, he and his wife Elaine wrote the memoir, *Back to Vietnam: Tours of the Heart*. He has subsequently written three novels dealing with the abhorrent practice of child trafficking; *Finding Lien*, *As the Lotus Blooms*, and the one you are reading. When not traveling, Bruce and Elaine live on Salt Spring Island, in British Columbia.

NOTE FROM THE AUTHOR

Word-of-mouth is crucial for any author to succeed. If you enjoyed *The Road from Tenancingo*, please leave a review online—anywhere you are able. Even if it's just a sentence or two. It would make all the difference and would be very much appreciated.

Thanks!
R. Bruce Logan

Thank you so much for reading one of **R. Bruce Logan's** novels.
If you enjoyed the experience, please check out our recommended
title for your next great read!

Finding Lien by R. Bruce Logan

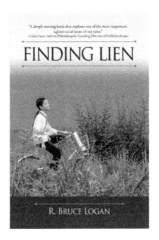

"A deeply moving book that explores one of the most
important, ugliest social issues of our time."
~Lydia Dean, author, philanthropist, Founding Director
of GoPhilanthropic

View other Black Rose Writing titles at
www.blackrosewriting.com/books and use promo code
PRINT to receive a **20% discount** when purchasing.

CPSIA information can be obtained
at www.ICGtesting.com
Printed in the USA
BVHW070213190720
583721BV00001B/4